MW01095100

DAUGHTER OF RAVENS BOOK 3

THE REBEL'S PRIZE

M.J. SCOTT

ABOUT THE REBEL'S PRIZE

Hunting traitors is easier than facing the man she never meant to love...

In the wake of treachery and broken bonds, Chloe de Roche has fled Illvya and a marriage that was never supposed to be real, to hunt the rebel mages trying to topple the empire. Bringing them to justice is the only way to clear her name and salvage something of the life she's been fighting for. But leaving Lucien behind might be even harder than finding the truth about the treachery buried in the heart of the empire...

Faced with Chloe's desertion, magic that undermines his ability to know the truth, and a threat to the emperor he is sworn to serve, Lucien de Roche is reeling. But even though his hopes that Chloe might grow to love him have been shattered, he can't turn his back on his wife. Bound by vows and honor, he has no choice but to follow her, even if she might break his heart...

Defeating those who seek to tear their world apart will not only take all their powers but an admission that they are stronger together than apart. But are they willing to risk their lives—and their hearts—to save an empire?

For everyone who loves kissing books with magic as much as I do.

Copyright © 2023 by M.J. Scott

Visit M.J. at www.mjscott.net

All rights reserved.

All characters and events in this book are fictitious. Any resemblance to real people, alive or dead, is entirely coincidental.

No part of this book may be reproduced in any form or by any electronic or mechanical means, including information storage and retrieval systems, without written permission from the author, except for the use of brief quotations in a book review.

Published by emscott enterprises.

ISBN eBook 978-0-6455567-2-8

ISBN paperback 978-0-6455567-7-3

❀ Created with Vellum

CHAPTER 1

When you run from your life for the second time, you expect things to go more smoothly than the first. But apparently that wasn't the case.

Chloe de Roche pulled the hood of her cloak farther over her head and eyed the inn across the street. *Everything will be fine.*

The knots in her stomach thought otherwise. Ten days of travel across Illvya, Kharenia, and now Miseneia had dented her convictions. The one thing that had gone right so far was that no one from Lumia had caught up with her. But her freedom had come at a cost. Ten days of traveling covertly, sleeping little, and looking over her shoulder for Imperial soldiers was exhausting. As was being set up as the scapegoat in a conspiracy against the emperor. And exhaustion would lead to mistakes.

If it hadn't been for the protection of Octarus, her sanctii, she might not have made it this far. She definitely wouldn't make it all the way to Partha traveling alone. Which was why she was watching an inn and steeling her nerves.

"He's definitely inside, right?" she muttered under her breath.

[Yes.]

Octarus's voice in her head sounded more certain than she

felt. The man she'd been seeking since she first left Illvya, hoping for his help to get her across the empire as fast as possible, had proven an elusive quarry.

She'd made her way to Orlee di Mer, where she'd first met Samuel Jensen, the ship's captain who had smuggled her to Anglion ten years ago. But when she'd gone in search of him in the *calle* on the edge of town he used as the base of his operations—or had when she'd last needed him—she'd discovered, after handing out quite a bit of gold, that he was on a run up to Jinkara in Miseneia.

It had cost her still more gold to find out when he was supposed to reach his destination. It was only because she'd been able to use portals for a few sections of the journey that she had managed to arrive a day ahead of him.

Earlier she had kept watch, gritty-eyed and longing for sleep, from behind a grimy window in a nameless dockside *kafia* as his ship, the *Salt Sprite*, had come into port not long after dawn. And then waited long hours drinking their bitter coffee as his cargo—what appeared to be legitimate trade goods—had been offloaded.

Finally, Samuel himself had stalked down the gangway and headed off into the depths of Jinkara's port district. The sight of him had made her smile for the first time in days. Not just from the relief that she was in the right place but also from seeing him after so many years. After all, he had saved her life in more than one way.

Octarus followed Samuel while she retreated to the cheap inn where she'd secured a room. Near sunset, the sanctii returned to report that Samuel and several of his crew had taken rooms at the Emperor's Pride—an ironic name for a distinctly seedy-looking inn—and appeared to be settling in for an evening of drinking.

The Emperor's Pride was on the opposite side of the docks to the inn she'd holed up in, closer to the edge of the respectable parts of the town. Samuel was doing well for himself, it seemed.

Which hopefully boded well for her.

She waited nearly two hours before heading out, trying to judge enough time for Samuel to at least eat and relax without allowing things to get too...unruly. She wasn't in any real danger with Octarus lurking invisible near her, but she didn't want to have to call for his help if she could possibly avoid it.

As a woman alone, her hair dyed a dreary dark brown to hide the colors of her magic, she didn't draw much attention. But a woman with a sanctii was notable, particularly the farther away from Illvya she got. Water mages strong enough to bond a sanctii usually became Imperial mages. For those to whom a life of service didn't appeal, finding employment was no issue. Which meant they most often lived in the empire's larger cities.

In a town the size of Jinkara, which thrived only due to its harbor, Octarus would stand out. And his gray face, with the paler strips of skin around his eyes, was distinctive. The last thing she needed was reports of a woman and a sanctii who fit his description getting back to Lumia and giving those who were probably looking for her a lead.

[All right,] she said in her mind to Octarus. [Stay close, but don't do anything unless I ask you to.]

She tugged at the hood of her cloak one more time, making sure it would stay in place. It was warmer in Miseneia than Illvya, but the harbor breezes were cool enough at night that her cotton cloak wasn't unusual. Satisfied the hood wasn't going to fall back, she crossed the street and pushed open the door of the inn before she could change her mind.

Inside, the babble of voices was loud and the air warm. Lanterns hung from the ceilings, giving enough light to have a clear view of the room and, she assumed, of her. But her entrance didn't draw much attention other than a few assessing looks from the men and women already eating and drinking at the tables. Her nerves eased back an inch. At least this wasn't the kind of inn where the only women to set foot inside were those who earned their living there.

A quick scan yielded no sight of Samuel's dark hair. But there was a second room beyond the first, so she made her way across the floor, ignoring the rumble in her stomach as the scent of the food being served rose around her. Miseneian cuisine was spicier than Illvyan but delicious. Jinkara's harbors meant fresh fish featured more often than other meat, served with rice or long, thick noodles and vegetables.

But she'd been too nervous to eat much all day as she'd waited for Samuel to disembark. Her hasty breakfast of two honey pastries and a pot of minted tea had only been supplemented by some herbed flatbread she'd bought on her way back to her inn. She ignored the rumbling. She would eat once she'd found Samuel and discovered whether he could—or would—help her.

The second room was less crowded, the tables farther apart, the lanterns dimmer. She hesitated at the threshold as her eyes adjusted. Heads started to turn in her direction, and she made herself step inside, not wanting to draw any more attention than necessary. It was harder to look around discreetly, but—thank the goddess—a familiar booming laugh rolled across the room before it became obvious that she was searching for someone.

She followed the sound, trying not to smile. Samuel was seated with several other men at a table in the farthest back corner, under a soot-encrusted lantern whose light was dim to the point of being nearly useless. She suspected it was left that way deliberately. Dark corners would be useful in dockside inns, and it didn't really surprise her to find Samuel lurking in one. If he conducted the shadier side of his business here, he would want as little scrutiny as possible.

The nerves came back with a vengeance, replacing hunger pangs with anxiety as she approached his table.

"Excuse me, are you Captain Jensen?" Better not to act as though she knew him until she knew who he was with.

Samuel's eyes widened briefly as she pulled back her hood, and he put his tankard of beer down with a startled thump that suggested she was the last person he'd been expecting to see. But he quickly schooled his face back to a determinedly unconcerned expression she recognized from the first time she'd gone looking for him more than ten years ago.

"Who's asking?" He tilted his head slightly as he studied her, the expression in his dark eyes giving nothing away. He looked so familiar that she lost all sense of where she was, and it took a moment to remember.

She straightened her shoulders. "I was told you might be able to provide me with some information on transporting some goods."

He raised an eyebrow and glanced quickly at the other men at the table. "Is that so? Well, Madame, if it's business you want to discuss, then perhaps you'd better follow me to my...office."

Chloe forced herself not to check her hand when he called her "Madame." The band of rubies Lucien had given her on their wedding day hung from a chain around her neck, well hidden by her clothes. It was worth far too much for the kind of woman she was pretending to be to own and would be a tempting target for thieves. Plus another key to her identity. So, to a casual observer, her marital status was anyone's guess. And it was more polite to call a woman on her own "madame" than "mamsille." Mamsille, in certain environments—like cheap dockside inns— might indicate a certain presumption of...availability.

Not that she really had much idea whether she was still married. She'd left Lucien behind and had no idea if she would be able to fix things between them should she get the chance. Or what that might mean if she did. She did know the absence of both the bond they'd shared and the man himself nagged at her like a missing limb.

Don't think about Lucien.

She had to deal with Samuel. Find Deandra. Without that, the state of her marriage would be something of a moot point because she likely wouldn't return to Lumia.

"Very well," she agreed.

Samuel slid out from behind the table and put his hand on her elbow. "This way." He hustled her across the room and out a side door before she had a chance to say much more. Then it was up a rickety-looking flight of wooden stairs and down a hallway.

"Where—" she started to ask, but he shook his head.

"Not until we're inside."

They reached a door at the end of the hallway, and he produced a brass key from his jacket pocket. After one last glance around the clearly deserted hall, he unlocked the door and then tugged her through it before locking it firmly behind them.

He leaned against it, arms folded. "All right," he said. "Care to explain exactly what in the salt-cursed depths of hell you're doing here, love?"

She took a breath, scanning the room carefully. A simple wooden desk, two equally plain chairs on either side of it. A fireplace, already lit, with a small rug pocked with scorch marks in front of it. A lantern hung above the desk, and two more bracketed the fireplace. Not much else, barring some loose sheets of paper, an ink bottle, and blotter on the table. The shutters were closed, so she couldn't get her bearings as to where exactly in the building they were. Perhaps it was, as he'd said, the room where he did business. So business she would do.

She squared her shoulders. "Looking for you."

His brown eyes narrowed. "That part I understand. The part I don't understand is *why*. Last I heard, you had departed...er, the place I saw you last. I assumed you'd be happily back home with your family where you belong."

It was her turn to narrow her eyes. "You were keeping track of me?" If so, how much did he know? Had he heard about her marriage?

"I keep track of the news from Anglion. Queen Sophia has made that particular line of my work dry up. Though it does make the legitimate side easier. But I'm guessing that's not what you're interested in. Not when you're supposed to be safely home in Lumia, not roaming through a dockside inn in Jinkara looking for me. So let me ask again, love. Why are you here?"

"I'm traveling up to Partha. I need to do so incognito. I can't go by sea. I thought perhaps you might have more connections than just your ship and could help me find passage in a caravan traveling that way."

His expression turned steely. "I remember you having a cast-iron stomach, so I can only think of one good reason why a water mage doesn't want to travel by water." He glanced over her shoulder. "Am I to take it that if I upset you, I might find myself addressing an angry sanctii?"

She stared at him a moment. There was more silver in his hair and beard now, and the lines beside his eyes, testament of his years of wind and weather at sea, were deeper than she remembered. But he was still handsome. Still the man who'd helped her get over some of the worst of her grief in Anglion. Still, she hoped, a friend. And still too clever for his own good. One didn't survive as long as he did smuggling people and other goods around the empire without being clever. She could lie to him, but if he found her out, he might refuse to help her.

"Yes."

"That's fast work. You can only have been home a few months."

"Nearly five," she said. "And I had time to make up for."

"Just as well that you're not asking to go back to Anglion, then. A sanctii would make that difficult."

"I'm aware," she said dryly. "Are you going to stand guard at the door the entire time, or can we sit down while we talk like civilized people?"

"I'm not that civilized, love," he said. But he stepped away from the door. "Your sanctii can guard the door as well as I can." He reached into his pocket again and pulled out an old gold coin on a chain. "And this will make sure no one can hear us."

"A scriptii?" She leaned closer, fascinated despite herself. "With an aural ward?"

He nodded and moved past her to the table, placing the scriptii on the wooden surface. A faint chime rang through the air. Presumably that meant it was active. He'd told her once that he had a small talent for illusion, though she'd never seen him use it. She imagined it had come in handy in his line of work.

But better not to think too much on illusioners. That would only make her think of the one she'd left behind in Lumia.

Samuel took one of the chairs and drew it back. "Have a seat."

She settled herself, loosening the buttons that held her cloak closed. "As I said, I'm looking to travel to Partha."

He made a circling motion with one finger. "I'm going to need you to go a little further back in the story to start with. Because I doubt you've been struck by a sudden urge to take in the Parthan vineyards or any of its other sights."

He knew her too well for a man who hadn't seen her for many years. "I'm trying to find someone. I have reason to believe they may be heading for Partha."

"That explains the destination. Not so much the incognito part."

"This person may not want to be found."

"Sounds like you." He blew out a breath. "Let's cut to the chase, love. If you're here, looking for me, then something has gone wrong in Lumia."

She shrugged noncommittally.

"Does it have something to do with what happened at the palace?"

"The palace?" she squeaked. She'd avoided seeking out the news from Illvya. For the first week because she was too worried that anyone in possession of a newssheet might just recognize her. After that, as she'd moved farther away from Illvya, because she didn't want to stand out by seeking out an Illvyan newssheet specifically. But she'd checked the local noticeboards in the towns she'd passed through. There had been no announcement of Aristides dying.

Which was something of a relief. The mail moved slowly, but when there was news as vital to the people as the death of their emperor, the Imperial mages made sure it reached every end of the empire with speed. Perhaps she'd been in time and Imogene and Lucien had quelled the plot against Aristides.

"You don't know?"

"I've been chasing a—um, moving fast. I haven't had much time to catch up on the news. Did something happen to the emperor?"

"Someone tried to make something happen. The news is they failed. I guess time will tell whether that's the truth. But it happened nearly two weeks ago. Just about long enough for you to make your way here, in fact." He leaned back in the chair, folding his arms. "I'm not an idiot, love. Never have been."

She sighed. "Fine. Yes, something happened at the palace. The person I want to find may have had something to do with that."

"And the reason it's you rather than the Imperial army chasing after them is...?"

"It's in my best interests to do so." She lifted her chin. "And it's in your best interests for me to not tell you any more than that."

"Does that mean you think the Imperial army is also looking for them? Or you?"

"You're not an idiot, so don't ask questions that may just cause you trouble. I said I needed to be incognito. Make of that what you will. Now, I have gold. I need a merchant caravan or something like it that's traveling to Partha. Is that something you can arrange for me, or do I need to look elsewhere?"

He scowled, shaking his head. "I can do it. It'll take a day or two for me to find out who's around and where they're headed. Partha is not the most common destination from Miseneia, though there are some caravans that travel that far."

If anyone should know the trade routes of any given place in the empire, it was him. "Good. I can wait. But not for too long."

He studied her a moment. "Are you sure this is what you want?"

"I'm sure. It's something I have to do."

"Very well." His expression suggested he thought she was being foolish. Based on what?

She resisted the urge to look away. He knew about the palace. How much more did he know? He hadn't said anything about her marriage, but that didn't mean he hadn't heard the news.

The weight of Lucien's ring on the chain around her neck was suddenly heavy. How closely was Samuel still watching the news and gossip from Lumia?

As he'd said, he was not an idiot. Indeed, he was a smuggler who'd run a dangerous line of work successfully for many years. You didn't survive so long in that game by being ill-informed. She knew that previously he'd followed the happenings of the Illvyan court, given that it was often those who fell afoul of politics who might need his services to leave the empire. But Illvya and Anglion were no longer staunch enemies. People could move freely between the two countries, so perhaps refugees weren't part of his business anymore. If he'd turned legitimate businessman—and the cargo he carried into port suggested he had—maybe he had no need to follow the court gossip and may not have heard the news that she had married again. To another aristo. Or maybe old habits died hard.

"I hope your family were glad to see you when you came home. They must have missed you." His expression softened slightly.

She nodded, suppressing a guilty wince. They wouldn't be so happy now that she'd fled again. She was bringing up all the old trauma she'd caused in the past just when they thought they had her safely home. It had been a cruel thing to do, but she figured it was better for them to have an alive daughter whom they didn't see than a grave to visit.

"They were well," she said. "And glad to see me, as you say.

I'm looking forward to being home with them again once my travels are done."

"You're an easy woman to miss, love. I know I did." He flashed her a smile.

She lifted an eyebrow. It hadn't been so long that she couldn't spot him being deliberately charming. "That was your choice. And a long time ago."

"Doesn't mean a man can't have regrets. Especially when you stand here looking as beautiful as the day I left you. Except perhaps for the choice of hair dye?" He grinned suddenly, the smile full of his not inconsiderable charm. "I like the red and black better."

So did she. "I'm trying to avoid attention."

"Difficult for a woman like you," he retorted, grin widening.

Was it a test? To see if she would flirt back? Did he truly regret breaking off the...arrangement they'd shared in her early years in Anglion? Well, if he did, she did not. And she was married now.

"Well, I'm sure you've found other company to console you," she said gently. "And we were talking of caravans, not old memories."

He smiled ruefully. "No second chances?"

"You will always have a place in my affections for what you did for me. And my friendship. But what's past is past."

"You always were a wise woman." He straightened. "The caravan master might want to speak to you first. Most of them don't take many passengers. They'll prefer those who have some skills to contribute to the journey."

She shrugged. "That seems reasonable. And I have skills to offer." She knew enough about healing to be useful on a journey, and she wasn't afraid of hard work. And she was sure she'd be able to convince a caravan master to give her a chance. After all, she'd faced down the emperor of Illvya and the king of Andalyssia, not to mention the queen of Anglion. If she couldn't convince a Miseneian caravan master that she could be helpful

on a journey, then she deserved to be kicked out of the diplomatic corps should she ever return to it.

"They may also want a deposit to secure your place."

She nodded. "That's not a problem. Though I didn't bring
much coin with me tonight."

"I can make the payment for you, and you can pay me."

"That is kind of you, thank you. You always were a good man,
Samuel." She didn't know if that was a sensible thing to say, but
after all, once upon a time during those early months in Anglion
when she hadn't been sure that she might survive the grief and
homesickness, Samuel had been the one who'd come to check on
her and the one who she'd finally let into her bed. He hadn't
stayed there long, not wanting, he'd said, to cause her trouble.
Though she imagined that that worked both ways and he had
plenty of women willing to share his nights. One in every port—
wasn't that what they said about sailors?

Though if that was the life he chose to lead, who was she to
argue? It wasn't as though she had been chaste her entire life,
and she'd currently abandoned her husband. Some members of
the court would consider that a graver offense than a discreet
affair. But she didn't want to give him the wrong idea, so she
pushed back the chair and stood.

He did, too, shaking his head as he scooped up the scriptii
from the table. "No I wasn't. But I'm a respectable man of business now. More's the pity. Young Sophia making up with Aristides has taken half the fun out of life."

"Oh, I'm sure you still find some mischief. You can't tell me
you don't still hide part of your cargoes from the tax collectors."

He barked a laugh. "Now that would be telling, love. But,
speaking of business, I have more of it to attend to tonight. We
need to get on. Where are you staying?"

She considered a moment. Should she trust him? The hard
truth was she didn't have another good option without Lucien's
magic, so perhaps it didn't matter whether she could or not.

"Chloe, love, if you think I can't find out where the pretty

Illvyan woman who's new in town is staying in less than an hour, you're insulting my intelligence again."

"The Copper Fish," she said with a sigh.

His mouth quirked, the dimple in his tanned cheek popping into view. Just as well she was married. He may have grown older, but he was still handsome.

"Good. Let me see you back there, and then I'll be in touch in a few days."

"You don't need to walk me home, Samuel. I have a sanctii."

"I'm sure you do, love, and you can tell me more about that one day. But if you're trying not to catch anyone's eye, then it'll be easier if you have a man escorting you through this part of town. Your sanctii committing violence on some poor sailor who asks you how much for a tumble would be remarked on."

She snorted and swept a hand down over her shabby gray dress. "I doubt anyone wants to tumble this."

Samuel raised an eyebrow. "You may have dyed your hair a hideous color, love, but there's no hiding your face. You've always been beautiful. And most of the ladies working the docks are not. At least not after a few years. You'd be marked as fresh meat before you'd taken twenty steps. Especially now that the sun has gone down. Unless you can do something to hide that lovely face of yours, you'll take my arm, keep your head down, and let me walk you home."

Chloe hid her wince. If she could have disguised her face, she would have, but she'd severed her bond with Lucien and given up her access to his skills as an illusioner in the process. She'd never had much talent in that direction, and she definitely couldn't pull off one of the complex facial illusions that were part of the reason she was headed to Partha. If Lucien was with her, he could have done it easily enough. Of course, if Lucien was with her, she wouldn't need Samuel in the first place.

"Fine," she managed as she mentally cursed Deandra and her ash-burned fellow conspirators. "You can walk me home."

CHAPTER 2

Time crawled for the next two days. Samuel had issued strict instructions about which parts of town to avoid during the daytime and even stricter instructions about staying inside at night, then left with a promise to be back in touch when he found a caravan that would suit her needs.

She spent the first day worrying that she'd been foolish to trust him and that he would decide to turn her over to the authorities in return for whatever reward might have been placed on her head. But no Imperial guards had arrived at the inn to pound on her door in the middle of the night, and she reluctantly decided her fears were unfounded. After all, a smuggler who turned people over to the authorities wouldn't stay in business very long. Samuel might be partly a legitimate trader now, but she doubted he had fully embraced respectability. If he still did anything connected with the shadier side of life in the empire, he probably wouldn't betray her. His reputation would matter.

The second day, she began to worry it was taking too long and that something had happened to make him leave town before he could find someone to help her. She'd sent Octarus down to the docks to check that the *Salt Sprite* was still in the harbor. He'd reported back that it was and that everything seemed normal. No Imperial guards in sight—there was no garrison in Jinkara—nor any sign of the town guards in their distinctive bright green jackets paying any particular attention to the ship.

She stuck close to the Copper Fish, venturing out occasionally to see the few sights the town offered and make sure the innkeeper didn't start to think there was a nefarious reason for her lurking in her room, but not wanting to miss Samuel should he call or send a message.

Jinkara wasn't large, and its opportunities to entertain herself in ways that wouldn't deplete her funds were limited. She didn't want to visit the temple or anywhere else where news from Lumia—such as descriptions of people the Imperial Guard might be seeking—might be posted. There had been nothing on any of the public noticeboards anywhere she'd stopped on the journey from Lumia, and nothing had caught her attention here. If the emperor was hunting for her, he was doing so with discretion, perhaps not wanting to tip her off.

In the end, she'd resorted to buying a small stack of novels from a secondhand store a few streets back from the town square and carrying them back to the Copper Fish. She'd missed ten years of Illvyan literature, so it hadn't been hard to find stories she hadn't read.

She was finishing her dinner in the small dining area of her inn late on her fourth day in Jinkara when Samuel slid into the empty chair opposite her.

"Evening, love," he said easily. "Enjoying your meal?"

She slurped up the last forkful of noodles. She'd grown used to the spiciness of the sauce over the last few days, but her mouth still felt somewhat like she breathed fire. "Yes. The food here is surprisingly good, considering."

"Considering what?" Samuel asked with a smile. "The fact that the Miseneians have never met a pepper or spice they dislike?"

She laughed. "Something like that. But I don't mind. It's part of the fun of traveling, isn't it? Trying new things."

"Indeed it is, love, though not everyone shares that view." His smile widened. "But it seems you do, and I'm glad for it. If only because your travels to Partha are going to take you to many new places."

She put down the fork, then sipped the last of her honey beer—the inn's specialty—to cool her tongue. The beer was a far safer choice than the wine she'd tried her first night. At least, they'd called it wine. It tasted more like vinegar that a rat had died in. The beer, however, was unobjectionable and not strong enough to steal her senses. She'd need her wits about her to sweet-talk a caravan master.

She wiped her mouth with her napkin, trying not to appear too eager. "Does this mean you've found someone who can help me?"

He wiggled his fingers back and forth. "A potential partner for your journey, yes. But they would like to meet you first. They did seem enthusiastic when I told them of your magic, but still, they're trying to make the right choice."

A way to get safely back on the road. She tamped down a smile of satisfaction. "And you trust this person?"

Samuel nodded. "I know them by reputation. I've never heard that they take advantage of people. Quite the opposite, rather. Though the price may be a little higher than you were wanting to pay."

She shrugged. She could figure the money part out if she had to. "I'd rather pay for someone trustworthy than spend a month wondering if someone's going to put a knife to my throat in the dead of night."

His mouth quirked. "Glad to hear it. Well, if you've finished with your dinner, I suggested a meeting at the Emperor's Pride at the eighth hour."

She nodded. It had to be getting close to that now. She'd fallen asleep earlier, dreaming away half the afternoon. Too many restless nights catching up with her. And then she'd been later down to dinner than she'd wanted to be. She tried to dine early, before the rowdier customers started to filter into the inn. "Very well. I'll go upstairs and fetch my cloak."

"And your purse," Samuel suggested. "I imagine some sort of payment will be wanted to secure your passage."

She nodded. "And my purse." She hesitated, wishing she still had access to Lucien's power, but she'd given that up when she'd broken the bond. There was no way of knowing whether Samuel was telling her the truth. Only her instincts, honed by her years in Anglion. So far, there was nothing in his manner that suggested she was in any danger.

She could ask him to bring the caravan master to her, of course. But she didn't necessarily want strangers knowing where she was staying. Samuel might be wily enough to hunt her down, but she didn't need to advertise her whereabouts. "I'll meet you out front. I won't be long."

The stairs creaked as she hurried up to her room, the sound familiar now. "Octarus?" she whispered as she scooped her cloak off the bed. She hadn't bothered to light the candle. The window let in enough light from the street for her to see.

The sanctii appeared, blending well with the shadows. "Go out?"

"Yes. Has anyone been in the room?" So far she'd had no trouble at the inn, but it didn't pay to relax. She was under no illusion that the place was entirely safe. If she'd wanted security, she would have paid for one of the respectable inns around the square. But she couldn't risk being recognized. Nor, quite frankly, did she want to waste her money.

"No." Octarus had been watching over her and the inn, except for the times she sent him down to the docks. He didn't seem overly interested in the goings-on of Jinkara. And he hadn't mentioned encountering any other sanctii. Just as well. Word of her whereabouts would travel quickly back to the palace if they encountered the wrong person.

"We're going back to the Emperor's Pride," she said. "Samuel may have found us a caravan."

He nodded, seemingly unperturbed by this news. "I will be close," he said, then vanished again without giving her any chance for further instructions or plans.

Not that she really needed it. She could call for him at any time, and he would hear.

And they'd already agreed that he would intervene if she was at risk.

Though *only* if she thought she was at risk.

He understood that currently it was more important that he stay unseen than interfere in any minor difficulties.

Still, as she fastened the cloak around her shoulders and descended the stairs to the front door, it was comforting to know that he was there. Company of a kind. She remembered the aching loneliness of her flight to Anglion.

And yes, this time she hadn't left a dead husband behind her. But she had left Lucien.

And as much as she told herself that she shouldn't miss him, she did. The ache of it burned in her chest. Alongside the guilt every time she stopped to think about how angry he must be that she'd fled.

Or perhaps he'd been too busy with the aftermath of whatever had happened in the palace to worry overly much.

But she'd told him she would stay. She'd broken her word. Lucien wasn't a man to take broken promises lightly.

Perhaps she might earn herself some grace if she *had* actually managed to save Aristides. Though she had no way to prove her own innocence from those who'd set her up to take the fall for the attempt, not until she found Deandra and the illusioner who'd invented the spells that could disguise a person's face so well. And remove their memories. A neat trick that circumvented the truth-seeking magic that was one of the main weapons of the Imperial judiciary's powers against criminals.

If a person couldn't remember doing wrong, a Truth Seeker like Lucien had no way of telling if they had.

And she had no way to prove that her memory hadn't been tampered with, so she couldn't prove her innocence either. Not with words. She was going to have to do it in a more direct fashion—by wringing the truth out of Deandra.

She'd put up with any amount of uncomfortable travel across the worst roads of the empire for the satisfaction of doing just that.

✧ ✧ ✧

The night air was cooling, though it still smelled of the docks, as it always did in this part of town. Samuel didn't seem inclined to talk as he escorted her in the direction of the Emperor's Pride, though he nodded and said hello to a few people they passed.

Chloe was disinclined to conversation herself, trying to rehearse the points she'd been coming up with over the past few days that would make her seem useful to a caravan master. She'd practiced the speech she wanted to give a few times in her room, and it had sounded convincing enough. She only hoped it all wouldn't fly out of her head from nerves.

The lanterns in front of the inn burned brightly, and Samuel held the door for her, ushering her in with a cheery "Evening, boys" to the two guards on the door.

The shorter of the two gave her an appreciative look, dark eyes bright under dark brows. The lantern light gleamed off his bald head as she smiled tightly back.

The other guard's attention stayed on Samuel. "Evening, Captain. Looks like a good night." His Illvyan was tinged with a Miseneian burr.

"Indeed, but mostly a good night for business, I think," Samuel said, smiling affably.

"Eager to be leaving us, then?" the guard countered.

Samuel laughed. "Never. But then again, a man needs to earn the coin to enjoy the hospitality of this fine establishment. And on that note, gentlemen, the lady and I have business."

That earned him smirks.

Samuel ushered Chloe through the door and then through to the second room, steering her toward the staircase they'd used the night she'd found him.

Made sense if that was the room he used for his business. He knew she wanted discretion. Still, underneath the cloak, she slid her hand through the pocket in her dress to the place where she had her dagger secured. A gun might have been better, but she hadn't brought one when she fled. She didn't even know if Lucien kept any in the townhouse. And it was the sort of thing that would have caused questions if she'd tried to buy one in any of the towns she'd passed through so fleetingly.

Perhaps the caravan would pass a larger city where she might secure such a weapon, or perhaps after tonight, that was a final task she could ask Samuel to perform for her before they parted ways again.

She tucked the thought away. Better to concentrate on the more immediate problem of securing her passage.

She followed Samuel up the stairs, hoping everything would go smoothly and she might be leaving soon. She was only guessing at Deandra's destination, aiming for Partha, and every day she stayed still, the other woman got farther ahead of her.

But there was nothing to be done about that. She couldn't travel the whole distance on her own without risking some mishap on the way. Taking the public coaches put her at risk of discovery. One stray temple prior or Imperial mage primed to be on the lookout for her and chancing to take the same coach would ruin any chance of finding Deandra. A caravan was the best option.

Samuel paused at the door and glanced back at her. "Ready to put your best foot forward, love?" he asked softly.

She lifted her chin. "Always."

"Glad to hear it."

He pushed open the door, waving her through. She smiled at him as she passed, and she was several steps into the room before she registered who was sitting at the table.

Not an unknown caravan master but a man she knew all too well.

One who knew *her* all too well. And had no reason to be glad of that fact.

Indeed, his green eyes were cold as she met his gaze, turning the fizz of anticipation in her stomach to ice. As cold as the expression on the face of the woman sitting beside him.

For a moment, she wondered if she'd fainted and might be dreaming. Because the woman beside her husband was Sejerin Silya. An Andalyssian seer. Who should have been in Deephilm where she belonged.

"Hello, wife," Lucien drawled, and she was suddenly icily certain that this was real.

A wave of anger filled her, and she whirled to face Samuel. "You bast—"

He cut her off with a wave of his hand. "Sorry, love. But your *husband* outranks me by quite some way, and he's a goddess-damned *Truth Seeker.* I've no mind to fall afoul of the Imperial judiciary."

"You could have warned—"

He glanced over her shoulder, expression wary. Looking at Lucien, no doubt. He was very carefully avoiding touching her, his hands braced on his hips. "You need to hear him out. He's come looking a long way for you. Don't be so quick to dismiss."

"You don't know what you're talking about," she hissed.

He smiled lopsidedly. "Maybe, but maybe neither do you. Talk to your husband. I'll be outside."

He pushed her a little then, a gentle shove toward the table, and before she could register any further outrage, he vanished back through the door and the lock clicked firmly shut.

Perfect. Trapped in a room with her outraged husband and an Andalyssian.

She closed her eyes a moment, hand tightening on her dagger. If Samuel was wise, he wouldn't be waiting outdoors for her when she emerged from this room, because she might just succumb to the urge to bury the blade in his gut.

Reluctantly she turned. Sejerin Silya wore her usual unimpressed expression, her ice-colored eyes steady on Chloe, the faint lines at their corners deepened slightly. She wore a plain gray dress without her usual red cloak, and her pale red-gold hair was braided for travel around her head, but she was no less intimidating for not being cloaked in the trappings of her office.

Lucien sat beside her, all his attention focused on Chloe. Perhaps someone who didn't know him would have assumed his stony expression meant he was also unimpressed, but Chloe knew better. He was furious. The emotion practically stained the air black around him. No bond required.

She could see him willing himself to stay seated and appear calm. She stayed where she was, not sure that approaching the table would be wise. And for possibly what would be the first time since she'd met the woman, she was somewhat glad that Silya was there. Surely Lucien couldn't strangle her to death in outrage with an Andalyssian seer to witness his actions?

"Would you care to sit?" Lucien asked, his voice cold. The muscles in his jaw tensed as he nodded toward the chair opposite him.

Chloe ignored the chair, keeping her eyes on him. If they'd been traveling fast trying to catch up with her, neither of them showed any signs of it. Lucien's deep green jacket was as immaculate as always, his blond hair neat. His stony expression only highlighted the chiseled lines of his face. Perhaps slightly too chiseled. Had he lost some of the weight he'd gained after his illness? She wanted not to care, but she couldn't stop herself from studying his face, even as she fought to keep any trace of concern off her own. It was probably only the impact of hard travel.

But regardless of how arduous the journey had been, it had clearly given Lucien time to work up quite the temper. She didn't want to be too close if he exploded. "I think I'm fine here," she said carefully.

"Sit," he said. "After all, you must be tired from your travels." His eyes scanned her briefly, and she saw his mouth tighten as his gaze lowered to her hands. Bare of his rings.

For the briefest moment, she had the urge to hide them behind her back and stay where she was. But everything about Lucien suggested it wouldn't be wise to push him. Still, she didn't rush toward the table to take her seat. Instead, she moved slowly and deliberately pulled out the chair with exaggerated care before she smoothed her skirts and sat. "I will admit that the journey has been tiring."

Lucien's eyes narrowed. "Do you think this is a time to be flippant, wife?"

"I thought, perhaps, that it might lighten the mood you seem so clearly to be in."

His head tilted slowly as though she was a specimen he was studying. "I fear you were mistaken. I do not find myself in the mood for merriment."

Chloe clasped her hands in her lap, feeling that it was safer to keep them there rather than betray the fact that they were trembling. She had seen Lucien in many moods over the years. Happy. Sad. Bored. Even angry. Rarely had that anger been aimed at her. And never, even at his most irritated, had she felt as though she'd pushed him beyond his limits.

Though whether her quivering fingers were from concern over just how angry Lucien might be or from resisting the sudden overwhelming urge to crawl across the table, climb into his lap, and let him hold her until she felt safe again was not entirely clear. So she stayed silent. All three did, until the room fairly rang with the lack of sound.

Under the weight of Lucien's frosty green gaze, Chloe broke first, seeking to steer the conversation into polite and safe waters if she could. "Sejerin Silya," she said. "This is an unexpected pleasure."

Silya raised one eyebrow. "Indeed, Lady Castaigne. This is not particularly where I had envisioned myself when I accepted the emperor's invitation to Lumia."

Chloe nodded. It hadn't exactly been an invitation, more like an order. Aristides was determined to get to the bottom of whoever was plotting in Illvya, and when he'd once more found evidence of Andalyssian involvement, he had extended the very long arm of his Imperial authority and summoned several of the most senior ranking members of King Mikvel's court to Lumia. Of course, Chloe had left before any of them had arrived, and even though she was curious to know what had happened, for now it was possibly better not to ask.

She turned her attention back to Lucien. "Well, my lord, are you going to tell me how you found me?"

Lucien shrugged. "It wasn't so difficult. After all, at least two of the sanctii in Lumia are bonded to people who had quite a keen interest in determining that you were safe. They were...helpful."

They had tracked her via Octarus? *Goddess* damn *it*.

She hadn't considered that possibility. Didn't even know it *was* a possibility.

Of course, what happened in the sanctii's realm was a subject humans knew little about. But Octarus hadn't reported seeing either Ikarus, Imogene's sanctii, or Martius, who was bonded to her father.

Had they concealed themselves from him? He was, after all, bound to her and should have reported any threat. Sanctii guarded their mages, and Octarus's protective instincts were still on high alert after the murder of his former mage. The bond Chloe had formed with him in desperation, trying to control his grief-stricken rampage, was still only a few weeks old, and he had, so far, been very insistent whenever it came to matters of her safety. It was possible, perhaps, that Ikarus or Martius had told him that helping them find Chloe would help solve Rianne's murder. That could very well have swayed him.

Still, if Ikarus and Martius had ratted her and Octarus out, then that explained how Lucien had found her so fast.

"I see," she said, resisting the urge to scowl. "How fortunate for you that they're fond of me."

Lucien raised one eyebrow. "Ikarus and Martius aren't the only people motivated to find you, wife," he said. "Though you didn't make it easy. I suppose I should be grateful that you merely broke my portal rather than burning the whole house down."

"I'm not the one with the penchant for starting fires." No. That had been whoever had set off an explosion at the parliament. Or, going further back, those responsible for the explosive spells that had half destroyed the palace in Kingswell. "Or perhaps you think I am, indeed, party to treason? Have you come to arrest me? Is that why you've worked so hard to find me? Aristides sent you?"

"You think Aristides would send me to arrest my own wife?"

She didn't doubt for one second that the emperor was ruthless enough to do exactly that. "Why not? You are, after all, one of his Truth Seekers. Honor and duty above all, is it not?"

"I used to think so," he said.

What did he mean by that? The desire to ask burned at the tip of her tongue. Did he mean he no longer could hold to his honor or his duty? Or that he now held something else as equally important?

She didn't know.

And she couldn't ask. There may not be an answer he could give that wouldn't break her. She was trying to stand strong. To keep him out of this. The fact that he'd come after her was still a shock. Half of her had expected that he might take the chance to wash his hands of her and their unfortunate entanglement and divorce her in her absence. She couldn't imagine that his mother would have suggested he do anything else.

She had run from the ashes of her first marriage, and to flee her second was...well, she didn't want to think too hard about what Lumia's aristos might say about that choice. She knew her reasons. She also knew that many other people wouldn't understand—or believe them. Or forgive her.

Lucien being one of them.

But with the anger he was struggling to contain, this was probably not the time to prosecute the current state of their marriage or the topic of forgiveness. Perhaps it would be wiser to stick to safer conversational waters.

She shifted her focus back to Sejerin Silya. "I understand why Lucien came after me, Sejerin, but I confess I am surprised that you decided to join him."

Silya regarded her for a long moment, and Chloe resisted the urge to shrink back. The Andalyssian seer was something of an imposing figure even when she was...well, not in a *good* mood, because Chloe wasn't sure she had ever seen Sejerin Silya in a good mood. Mostly she'd seemed actively disapproving. Particularly on the morning she'd found Chloe and Lucien in a cave, where they'd spent the night together sheltering from a storm. Her outrage at that breach of Andalyssian propriety had resulted in Chloe and Lucien's first marriage. Silya was not a woman afraid to wield some righteous indignation to achieve her goals.

Right now, though, she appeared calm. At least in comparison to Lucien.

"I follow the will of the goddess," Silya said, her pale eyes giving nothing away.

"The goddess asked you to go with Lucien to find me?" A shiver crawled down Chloe's spine. It had been a moment of goddess-sent warning that had convinced her to run in the first place. A vision of her own death if she didn't. Had Silya seen something like that?

"All the way down as I was flying in that creation of your

emperor's, I dreamed of flying north with ravens," Sejerin Silya said simply. "At first I thought it was merely reassurance from the goddess that we would return safely from Lumia, but then when we arrived and learned that you had vanished, then it made more sense, daughter of ravens. The dreams did not abate, so when your husband, Lord Castaigne, indicated that he wished to seek you out, I knew that I was supposed to accompany him."

Daughter of ravens. Silya had called her that once before. Chloe still had no idea if it meant anything more than her just being Henri's daughter, raised with the ravens of the Academe di Sages. Whether Silya's visions showed her anything about Chloe was actually something to worry about.

Still, true or not, the presence of the seer was hardly welcome. "I see," she said cautiously. "And will we be returning to Lumia?" Hopefully not. If they immediately dragged her back to the capital, then it was likely nothing good awaited her there.

"Don't you wish to know how Aristides is?" Lucien said unexpectedly.

Chloe's focus snapped back to him. "I've heard no word that he died. I hope that means my warning was successful."

"It was, to a degree. There was still some damage to the palace and others. But in answer to your question, no, we are not returning to the capital. We are to continue on in this journey, looking for Deandra." His gaze narrowed, the green of his eyes, if anything, frostier still. "I assume that's where you were trying to go in your addlepated scheme."

She stiffened in the chair. "*Addlepated?*"

Lucien's mouth thinned. He turned to Sejerin Silya and inclined his head politely. "Sejerin, perhaps you would give me a few moments alone with my wife?"

Damn.

If she thought it would do any good, Chloe would have asked Sejerin Silya to stay. But she doubted the seer would side with her. After all, she was the one who'd married them the first time. And in Andalyssia, husbands had more authority over their wives than in Illvya. Silya would think it quite within Lucien's right to chastise her as he saw fit.

Eventually the seer nodded. "Of course, Lord Castaigne. I will wait outside."

"I'm sure Captain Jensen can find you something to eat and drink should you wish it," Chloe said. "He is a good man."

Lucien snorted softly, but he didn't argue with her.

Sejerin Silya rose from the chair and made her way out the door, closing it behind her. Lucien's hand clenched, then his fingers flicked wide, and she felt the wards flare around her.

Perfect. Now she was locked in a room with her husband.

Lucien didn't speak, just sat there, leaning back in his chair, arms folded across his chest, head tilted at an arrogant angle, and his eyes fixed on her as though he half expected her to make another run for it. She wondered how long it would take before he broke and started yelling at her. In some ways that might be easier to take than the frosty disdain she was currently receiving.

"Samuel has done no wrong in this," she said. "I trust you won't do anything vindictive."

One eyebrow lifted. "Samuel?"

"Captain Jensen. You know very well who I mean."

"You seem overly familiar with the man. Am I mistaken, wife, and you have established a trading business since you left Lumia?"

"You also know how I know him," she said tightly. "He was the captain who took me to Anglion."

"That makes him a smuggler," Lucien replied, "and I would be well within my rights to see him face punishment for those crimes."

"Is it a crime to save my life?" Chloe retorted. "Would you prefer that whoever Charl was working with saw that I had an unfortunate accident and died? After all, it didn't take them long after my return to try to set me up to take the blame for an attempt on the emperor's life. Samuel may not have led a blameless life, but he's never tried to kill me."

"Your captain can go to hell as far as I'm concerned," Lucien said. "I am interested in you."

"Well, you found me. I'm here. What more do you need to know?"

His hand thumped down on the table. "You *ran*," he snarled. "Worse, you broke the bond."

"I thought it was for the best." Her choices had been limited. Or really, there'd been no choice at all if her vision was true. But she couldn't tell him that. She'd sound crazy. Even though she had been trying to keep him out of it. Not taint him with the accusations against her.

"I thought you had died," he roared. His hand thumped the table again. "When I felt that bond break, I thought you were *dead*, Chloe. Do you know what that felt like? To think that I may have lost you. Can you imagine that? I was trying to save the emperor, and Imogene was panicked because she didn't know where you'd gone, and I felt the bond just...end." For a moment, the anger in his face was replaced by something closer to anguish before he got control of himself.

She stared at him, horrified. She hadn't thought that he might interpret the sudden snap of their bond in that fashion. She hadn't meant to be that cruel. "I...I didn't think."

"No," he said. "You just ran. Did you think I would not protect you? Do you not trust me that far, at least?" His voice was a snarl again. Vicious and deadly. But it was the snarl of a wounded animal, she thought, fueled by hurt as much as rage.

"I trusted you," she said, "but you couldn't protect me."

"Why the hell not?"

"Because your magic doesn't work against this magic. You can't prove that my memories haven't been altered, so you can't tell if I'm speaking the truth. It would be only your word." Which was why they needed Deandra. She was the only person, so far, who they had reason to believe knew how to cast the memory charms involved.

"There are those who think my word is beyond price," he bit out.

"I know. But if the emperor had died, do you think the judiciary truly would have taken your word over the potential guilt of your wife? The wife of a known traitor?"

"You are *my* wife," he said. "Not Charl's. *Mine*."

He stood abruptly, his chair toppling over with a crack that made her glad the room was warded. Before she knew what was happening, he was at her side of the table and pulling her out of her own chair.

"Mine," he repeated, then crushed his mouth down on hers.

CHAPTER 3

She'd never been kissed by a thunderstorm, but she imagined it might feel something like this. Wild. Unconstrained. Spectacular. Terrifying. Possibly able to destroy your entire life. At the very least, breath stealing. She leaned into the kiss, still not entirely sure she wasn't dreaming. Lucien pressed against her. Her back against the wall, the frantic thump of her heartbeat in her ears, the sudden aching want consuming her. All these felt like things conjured up in a fever dream. Her fingers gripped his hair, pulling him closer. He seemed glad to oblige. Seemed as though he might be happy to never stop kissing her, even though she wasn't sure what part of the kiss was passion and what was anger.

And that was the disorienting thing. She couldn't feel *him*. Couldn't feel the swirl of his emotions and magic that she was used to sharing through their bond. Leaving her with no idea what he was trying to do by kissing her. She didn't know what he wanted from her. Or what she wanted from him.

She had to make him stop or she would never be able to walk away. She forced her hands out of his hair down to the broad planes of his chest and shoved.

He let her. Stepping back, breathing hard, eyes wide as he

stared down at her, the twist of his mouth half amusement, half frustration.

Not that she'd expected any other reaction. Even pushed to the limit, she didn't think him capable of pressing where he wasn't wanted. Not when it came to physical intimacy, at least. But as heart pounding and mind melting as that kiss had been, the physical intimacy was not her immediate concern. No, right now she had to work out how to make him leave.

So she could leave, too, and get back on Deandra's trail.

Pulling the frayed edges of her wits back together while ignoring the traitorous parts of her body that thought she was being an idiot and just wanted her to fling herself back into his arms was difficult. Her hands trembled, and she folded her arms as she slid a half step to the side, increasing the distance between them. Increasing her margin of safety.

Her ability to think.

"You should return to Lumia," she said, ignoring the breathy fogged tone of her voice. "I am perfectly capable of finding Deandra on my own."

His eyebrows rose. Which only focused her attention on the fact that his green eyes were now mostly black, his pupils wide with lust. "You haven't gotten very far." His voice wasn't entirely steady either.

She moved away another step. "Far enough. And I have encountered no difficulties." Not strictly true, but it had been nothing she couldn't handle. "Until today."

"I am a difficulty?"

"Yes," she said bluntly. "Why are you here?" Before he could reply, she added, "If you say, 'Because you're my wife,' I may hit you. I am not your possession, Lucien."

"Well, firstly because I wanted to know if you were alive."

Firstly? Her shoulders tensed. "Given you had the sanctii to track me down, that issue could have been settled relatively quickly."

"Secondly, because I wish for you to *remain* alive."

The bluntness of those words cleared her mind a little. "And I cannot do that without you?"

"It's clear that you have enemies. Powerful ones. Who seem to be growing reckless."

He was right about that. But wrong if he thought she would let him ruin his life trying to solve her problems.

As though he could read her mind, he said, "Before you say something ridiculous like your enemies are not my problem, I will remind you again of the fact that we are *married*."

"A marriage with an expiration date."

He took a half step forward, as though he wanted to deny that fact. But he stopped himself. "We will leave that discussion for another time. But that expiration date has not been reached. You promised me a year, Chloe. You have not given it to me."

"Other matters seemed more pressing."

"Than wedding vows? Vows, if I need to remind you, that you have made twice now."

"If you truly are concerned about helping me stay alive, then yes, they were more pressing than my vows."

Now it was his turn to fold his arms, distracting her momentarily with the flex of muscle under fabric. He still hadn't entirely regained the weight he'd lost when he'd been poisoned. But whatever he'd been doing for the last few weeks, it seemed to only sculpt the somewhat leaner planes of his body more sharply. "Be that as it may, the fact remains that I made vows, too. And I do not forsake them."

Goddess-damned stubborn man and his stupid honor. He was going to wreck himself.

"And even if I was minded to forsake them," he added, "you have forgotten the other part of the equation we need to consider."

"Which is?" she asked blankly.

"That if you are innocent as you claim, then your enemies are my enemies. Enemies of the crown, in fact. And you cannot argue that protecting the crown is not my concern." One brow arched arrogantly, as though daring her to try.

She clenched her teeth and swore in her head. He'd trapped her neatly. He was a marq and an Imperial Truth Seeker. Bound by a double set of oaths to serve Aristides. Damn it.

A grin flashed across his face as though he knew exactly what she was thinking. But the amusement disappeared as quickly as summer lightning.

"Well? I'm waiting."

She relaxed her jaw with an effort. "I am beginning to see why some people find Truth Seekers annoying. It's the self-satisfaction."

"You think I am *satisfied* with the current situation? With my wife fleeing from me without so much as a word? With my emperor attacked and my magic thwarted?"

She could only stare at him again.

"And," Lucien continued, "not to put too fine a point on it, but I am not the only one with a vow to protect the crown."

Chloe flinched. The fact that she was technically a deserter from the diplomatic corps, a branch of the Imperial army, was something she had only considered after she'd fled the capital. The Illvyan army didn't execute deserters outside wartime, but she, over the past week of her travels, had resigned herself to the fact that perhaps she'd blown up her fledgling career—the one she had always dreamed of—before she'd even gotten started.

"That's why I'm following Deandra," she said defensively. "To find her and bring her to justice."

Lucien's eyebrow arched again. "Some would argue that that is not the role of a diplomat."

"I'm still part of the army," she said. "Someone had to follow."

Lucien looked around the room. "And am I to assume that you have Deandra stowed away somewhere in the inn?"

"I have a plan," she said, scowling.

"You have a vague idea at best," he countered. "Which is why you were looking for a caravan headed for Partha."

"How do you know that?" Chloe asked. She was going to have words with Samuel once this very awkward conversation was over—if it was ever over. When he'd been a smuggler of people and goods, he'd known how to keep his mouth shut. "Did Samuel tell you?"

"As luck would have it, I have a caravan heading north. And a caravan master who keeps me informed. She told me there had been an inquiry from a woman seeking passage north."

"And you assumed it was me?"

"I assumed it was worth investigating. Turns out I was right."

There was the satisfaction again. Infuriating man. "Why do you have a caravan traveling north? Truth Seekers don't sell their services."

Lucien snorted. "You always were more focused on that part of my life rather than the part where I was the heir to my father's title."

"Because back then I knew your father had the estate well in hand and being a Truth Seeker seemed to take all your time." She and Charl and Lucien's lives had firmly revolved around the capital and their circle of friends. Yes, Lucien's work had taken him away at times, and yes, there were occasions when he had returned to his family's estate to see them and do whatever heirs did. But neither of those things had ever seemed to make much of an impact on him.

Of course, now Lucien's father was dead, and Lucien was the marq. Responsible for Terre d'Etoi. He hadn't pushed for them to visit the estate in the time since they'd wed. In fact, the last time they discussed her role as marquesse, he'd appeared to perhaps prefer that she didn't get too involved if she wasn't sure she would stay.

Likely his mother, had she had the chance, would have taken it upon herself to start ensuring Chloe could perform her duties as marquesse, but there'd been no time for that yet.

All she really knew of Terre d'Etoi were her memories of the two times she and Charl had visited with Lucien, once for Fete de Froi and once for Mignon's betrothal ball. But she'd gone no farther than the immediate grounds around the house. Both the garden and house were beautiful, but she knew nothing of the land that made up the estate. Or even whether Lucien had holdings elsewhere.

"Tell me, Chloe," Lucien said, "what are the major exports of our family?"

Chloe lifted her chin. "Why would I know that?

He shrugged. "You married me."

"Married you temporarily," she hissed. "I never expected to be involved in the trade affairs of your estate."

"Well, fortunately for you, I *am* involved in the trade affairs of my estate, which include, amongst other things, some very fine vineyards and quite the prized flock of serineau sheep. Do you know what those are?"

She blinked. Serineau sheep produced some of the finest and warmest wool in the empire and were highly sought after. They were, however, finicky to breed, and those who were successful guarded the secrets of their flocks closely. Imogene and Jean-Paul had sheep but of the more regular kind, though Imogene had given her a shawl made of serineau wool for her Ascension. She hadn't taken it to Anglion, and she had no idea where it might be now.

Even in Anglion, she'd occasionally encountered serineau wool, though the Anglions had their own breeds of fine wool sheep, particularly in the northern regions where Queen Sophia's husband, Cameron, was from.

"Yes, not being an idiot, I am aware of serineau wool." Though, if she was honest, her mind was spinning. She'd always thought about the political and social obligations of having a title. And yes, while she'd stayed at Sanct de Sangre with Imogene, she'd learned a little of how busy it kept both Jean-Paul and her friend to run their estate. But she'd still never thought of the business of it and all the details that might entail.

She'd worked herself to the bone merely running a small store in Kingswell during her exile. She couldn't imagine running an estate the size of Lucien's. And she hadn't thought of him as a farmer. Her mouth quirked slightly, picturing him in breeches and a rough linen shirt, chasing after a recalcitrant sheep. But then again, he had servants and staff and tenants to do that kind of thing. Though maybe that was unfair. She knew he cared for his estate, though his twin duties as marq and Truth Seeker due to his magic stretched his obligations somewhat.

"Then you will know that it's a lucrative commodity. Though not the only one we trade."

"And you just happened to have a caravan heading north at this very moment?"

"Yes," he agreed. "It's difficult to get caravans up to that part of the empire safely during the peak of winter, so trade slows over winter and resumes in early spring. The Andalyssians and the Parthians are quite fond of our wool, it turns out." He smiled. "Actually, they don't mind my wine either—or the brandy, rather. They take more of that than the wine."

She didn't remember drinking brandy in Andalyssia. There'd been wine, yes, but the liqueurs served in the palace at Deephilm had mainly been kafiet, a mountain herb distilled into something that had the kick of one of the ice giants of their legends. But kafiet was rare and expensive, so she assumed those who didn't live in the palace with the budget of a king at their disposal might appreciate other liqueurs and alcohol to keep them warm during the worst of Andalyssia's winter. And Andalyssia was primarily snow and ice and mountains. What little fertile ground they had was given to growing grains and vegetables and feeding livestock. The important things. Luxuries they didn't produce could be bought with the wealth of the gold and jewels found beneath the mountain.

Like Lucien's brandy, it seemed. Just her luck. Or his.

"So, you were just going to travel with the caravan up to Partha and hope you found me along the way?"

Looking somewhat bemused, he shook his head. "We caught up to the caravan. It had left Terre d'Etoi before...well, before any of this happened. It's faster to travel via portal than caravan, after all."

And he and Silya hadn't necessarily been trying to avoid detection like she had.

"We had a vague idea which way you were headed, but it seems the goddess wanted us to be reunited." He glanced at the door. "Or at least, that's what Sejerin Silya said when Captain Jennings led us to you."

Silya, who had dreamed of ravens flying north. "Did Silya tell you to head north?"

Lucien shook his head. "We knew what Violette told us about the man who was teaching the facial illusions. It didn't take such a stretch to figure out which direction you may have been headed. And you couldn't travel by sea with Octarus, so it seemed likely that you would head for one of the caravan hubs. Silya didn't object to the direction I proposed." He paused. "Which I guess is an endorsement of a kind. If she did see something, then it didn't conflict with my proposed route."

"How fortunate."

"Yes. It was. We found you before anyone less friendly could," he said, his expression cooling again. "So, on behalf of my caravan master, I am conveying an offer to travel north if you desire."

"Maybe I can't afford the prices a Castaigne caravan wants to charge."

"I think you may find that you can't afford the price of refusing the offer. So say yes."

Her breath hitched a little, though whether in annoyance or relief she couldn't have said. Relief, yes, that he wasn't dragging her back to the capital to face the consequences of her hasty departure, which hopefully meant she hadn't been judged guilty in her absence.

"And Aristides is happy for you to go on a jaunt north?"

"The emperor was keen for me to find you," Lucien said. "He is equally keen to find those who attempted to kill him."

That was a sentiment she appreciated. Though she would have preferred if she had no involvement in schemes imperiling the emperor. But she had come to the limits of the ways in which she could delay giving Lucien an answer. He had found her. She doubted he was going to leave.

She sighed. "I think I never want to attend another wedding ball in my life. So far, they have only ended in disaster."

His face was even more unreadable. "Are you intending on having another wedding?"

"No," she said flatly. Regardless of what happened between her and Lucien, eventually when this all played out, she couldn't imagine letting her heart be taken yet again. So far, her record when it came to love and relationships was one of unmitigated disaster, it seemed. One treacherous husband dead at the hands of the Imperial executioner. One affair with a sea captain who left her for her own good. And now Lucien, who seemed to have lodged himself in her heart but didn't deserve the trouble she was bringing to his life. Perhaps if the army did end up dismissing her, she might just be better off joining Valentin and Irina as a temple healer and leaving annoying things like romance behind.

"What about the crown prince?" she asked, not wanting to think too hard about the people she'd left behind in Lumia.

Lucien's mouth thinned. "He was conveniently still asleep in the temple during the attack, and he's currently recovering in the palace."

"The emperor let him return?"

"He's being watched," Lucien admitted, "and is not allowed to leave the palace grounds, but by the time I left, we had found no proof that he knew anything about the attack. He maintains his innocence." His expression soured.

"The men I overheard said he was involved."

"They are dead. Dead men can't bear witness." He was clearly as frustrated as she was by that fact. "But the emperor at least heeded our advice that Alain should not be allowed to leave the palace."

"Does that mean Aristides doesn't trust him?" Her stomach curled with sympathy. A father having to face the possibility of his son's betrayal. That couldn't be easy.

"I'm not sure what the emperor feels. But he has been emperor a long time. And is no one's fool. He won't let Alain flee."

"Good."

"You haven't answered my question."

"What question was that?" she asked.

"The one about whether you want to join my caravan."

"Do I have a choice?"

"You don't have a choice about me going with you, or rather you coming with me," he said. "You may have some choice as to the destination of that trip."

"So, if I don't want to go with the caravan, you'll what, take me back to Lumia? Put me under house arrest, like the prince?"

"It would probably be what the emperor would be advised to do," Lucien said bluntly, "until all of this is cleared up."

It wasn't much of a choice. Return to the city and ignite what could only be a whole new scandal centered on her. No doubt she was already the center of a new scandal, and the gossip mills were swirling and chatting like a flock of crows disturbed. Or else accept that Lucien wasn't going anywhere and do what she'd set out to do. Locate Deandra, find a way to prove her own innocence and the crown prince's guilt, if he was truly guilty, and solve this matter once and for all.

There was no third option. Possibly she could convince Octarus to do something to spirit her away, but if the other sanctii were working against her, not to mention Lucien having the Imperial intelligence network at his disposal, she doubted she would get very far. Letting him take her to Partha seemed the lesser of two evils.

"And Silya?" she asked.

Lucien hitched a shoulder. "She will come with us."

"Doesn't Aristides want her in the capital?"

"She isn't the only seer who accompanied the Andalyssians, and I think he's actually more interested in the actions of the Great Houses and whether they have any connection to this matter. I think he took it as a gesture of good faith that Silya was willing to assist me."

That was one way of viewing it. Silya seeing a chance to meddle might be another.

"And," Lucien added with a shrug, "it didn't hurt her case that Domina Francis supported her."

Well, damn it. Clearly there was no chance of Silya returning to the capital if Domina Francis had endorsed her plan. But then perhaps she was relieved not to have to deal with Silya or navigating the delicacies of the differences between the temple's views of the goddess and the Four Arts and those held by the Andalyssians. Though it was likely that other seers and perhaps even a few patrarchs were amongst the Andalyssians summoned, Silya was, based on the time Chloe and Lucien had spent in Andalyssia, the most influential. Or maybe the most willing to interfere.

And even if Domina Francis had been minded to put up with Silya politicking in Lumia, Chloe couldn't imagine that she would ignore the foretelling of a seer. It was a more common form of magic amongst the Andalyssians, it seemed. Or perhaps a more cultivated one. The talent was rarer and unreliable in Illvyan water mages, but the Andalyssians had incorporated it into their version of the religion. The materials Chloe had studied before her assignment to Andalyssia suggested that there was at least a reasonable degree of reliability to the seers' talents. Why else would they have gained the power they had?

Perhaps Silya's powers would prove useful. She was, at least, one more mage in the party.

Chloe sighed. "Well, then. I guess we're traveling north."

Lucien nodded. "I want your word that you're not going to try anything else stupid."

She bristled. "Stupid?"

He waved a hand at the door. "Like trying to sneak out the window in the middle of the night with your sanctii. Believe me, none of the other traders are going to give you the assistance you're looking for."

"You bribed the other caravan masters not to give me passage?" Her voice rose in outrage. "How?"

"In the usual fashion: money. I don't only run goods through my own caravans," Lucien said. "I utilize other traders from time to time. The caravan masters don't want to lose the business of the Marq of Castaigne. Unless you can offer them a trade deal better than I can, I don't think you will be able to sway them."

"I am the Marquesse of Castaigne. Perhaps I could."

"Nice try, but they would probably need you to have actual goods to transport. And given you don't really know what the estate produces, let alone how to get your hands on any of it, that seems unlikely."

She glared at him. "There are times, my lord, when I remember why I disliked you."

"You didn't dislike me kissing you."

"You surprised me."

"Yes, that's clearly why you kissed me for several minutes before you pushed me away. Ladylike shock."

Her cheeks heated. "Exactly."

He barked a laugh. "If that's what you wish to tell yourself. Maybe I should kiss you again. Get you reaccustomed to me. I don't think it would take too long."

She held out a hand to ward him off. Another of his kisses

melting her resolve was the last thing she needed. Which meant it might be wise to change the subject.

"You'd really drag me back to Lumia?" she asked. "If I tried to go on without you?"

Lucien's expression was resolute. "I will keep you safe by whatever means necessary. Including protecting you from your own foolishness if I must."

"If you keep calling me stupid, my lord, then I do not like your chances of kissing me again."

"Reckless is not the same as stupid," Lucien countered. "What you did was brave, but you must admit it's a difficult task to attempt alone."

"Harder still to do from one of the emperor's prison cells."

"I would not have allowed them to arrest you."

"You may not have been able to stop them. You may, in fact, have ended up in one alongside me."

"Be that as it may, I would request that you consider matters a little longer before acting next time. And tell me if you are in trouble."

"I was more concerned with saving lives. And Imogene was closer. Besides, I have survived quite well so far. I have a sanctii," she pointed out.

"It's entirely possible that they do as well."

She had considered that possibility. But if Deandra controlled a sanctii, she hadn't used them at the parliament. And none had tried to interfere with Chloe or Octarus at the palace.

But Lucien was right. Capturing Deandra alone was unlikely. Chloe knew that once she found Deandra, she'd have to summon help. She could live with that, but she couldn't have lived with giving up the hunt. Couldn't give it up now even though part of her thought perhaps letting him take her back to the city where she could be guarded, disgraced or not, might be wiser. But no. Deandra had tried to set her up for a crime she hadn't committed. She'd been tainted once by Charl's treachery, and now she was being directly tainted once more by someone else's actions.

She wanted to clear her name herself, not just sit and wait for others to save her.

She lifted her chin. "I won't do anything stupid."

"Good," Lucien said. "Then we can depart in the morning." He tilted his head. "Unless you wish to delay."

"Why would I want to do that?"

"Perhaps you have unfinished business with Captain Jensen."

She scowled. "I came to him to find a caravan. And while I may not approve of the methods by which he found one for me, it seems he did, in fact, succeed. So that concludes our business."

"Are you sure?"

She didn't need the bond to interpret his tone. Male jealousy wasn't difficult to identify. "As you pointed out, I am your wife. I made vows." He had no reason to trust her, but the fact that he thought she might stray was irritating.

"In the morning, then," he said.

She nodded.

"Where are you staying?"

There wasn't much point trying not to tell him. After all, Samuel had told him she was in town and looking for a caravan. She had no doubt that Lucien could get the name of the inn from him as well. "At the Copper Fish."

"Is it nearby?"

"Yes. A few blocks back toward the town square."

"Not the most salubrious part of Jinkara."

"It's a seaport. The salubrious parts are limited and expensive."

"We are staying at the Crown and Tree."

Unsurprising that he would choose the most expensive inn in town. When she'd arrived, she'd inquired about the available accommodations. It hadn't taken long to discover that not only was the Crown and Tree unsuited to her budget, but it was also a likely stopping point for rich travelers moving through Jinkara. In other words, Illvyans who might recognize her. She'd avoided it ever since.

Perhaps she should have had Octarus watching it. She might have had advance warning that Lucien had arrived and been able to leave ahead of him.

Though now that she was back in the same room as him, at least some of the ache of missing him alleviated, she couldn't be entirely sorry that she hadn't. Not that she was going to tell him that. She didn't know what he wanted from her. Or what she wanted from him. Kiss or no kiss.

"I have secured you a room there as well," Lucien continued.

"Feeling confident, weren't you?"

"Confident that you would either be accompanying me north or returning to Lumia. And that either way, it would be sensible to have you stay somewhere I can keep an eye on you."

Her back stiffened. Was she a child in need of supervision? "I've already paid for my room at the Copper Fish. I may as well stay there one more night."

"I'm sure the innkeeper will be happy enough to be able to rent your room out a second time. You have no need to request a refund of whatever you've paid."

Meaning he would be footing the bill from now on.

Which she should be grateful for. And really, she could spare the few coins she'd paid for the night if Lucien was funding the rest of the journey. But he was in full arrogant aristo mood right now, expecting the world and everyone in it to comply with his wishes. And the situation was complicated enough without allowing him to get away with thinking she was going to jump if he snapped his fingers.

"You and Silya could always move to the Copper Fish," she said, mostly to be contrary. "The innkeeper there would benefit more from your patronage than whoever owns the Crown and Tree."

"Perhaps. But I imagine the security at the Crown and Tree is better," Lucien said, his jaw tightening. "And King Mikvel will not thank me if any harm comes to his seer."

Damn. She hadn't thought of that. Lucien had more than her safety to worry about, and he was right about the Crown and Tree being more secure. Though she was certain Silya could defend herself if necessary.

She suddenly lacked the energy to keep arguing with him.

"Very well, my lord," she agreed. "Then we may as well get to it so we can be well rested for the morning."

CHAPTER 4

Chloe was glad of the sounds of Jinkara at night as they walked to the Copper Fish. Without those, the complete silence between the three of them would have felt even more awkward. Silya made no effort to start any kind of conversation, and Lucien walked behind them. From the wary glances of the people passing from the opposite direction, she could only imagine his expression was grim.

Sa Ghislani, the innkeeper, looked up from behind the wooden table in the entryway as they entered. Dressed in leafy green linen, her eyes painted in gold that made them stand out against her light brown skin, she looked imposing.

"Sa Castaigne," she said, lifting an eyebrow. "No *guests* in your room." She inclined her head ever so slightly toward Lucien, making the copper beads that decorated her braided gray hair clink softly.

Chloe's cheek went hot. Sa Ghislani had been very clear about her rules when Chloe had first inquired about a room, clearly suspicious about a woman traveling alone. In the end, she had managed to convince the innkeeper that she was respectable. But Sa Ghislani's expression suggested she was reconsidering her opinion.

"My wife is merely here to collect her things," Lucien said, stepping forward before Chloe could offer any reassurance herself. "She will be leaving your fine establishment this evening."

"Your wife? She wears no ring." Sa Ghislani folded her arms across her chest, eyes stern.

Lucien's eyes dropped to Chloe's hands, and his expression turned grimmer. Chloe resisted the urge to pull the chain bearing her wedding ring from beneath her dress to show him she still had it.

"No refunds," the innkeeper added quickly.

"None required," Lucien said, apparently collecting himself enough to manage to keep his voice polite.

Sa Ghislani looked momentarily relieved, but then she turned her attention back to Chloe, concern drawing her brows down. "Is this man truly your husband? I can call for Ferain."

Ferain guarded the inn's doors at night and dealt with anyone who grew too unruly in the taprooms. He was taller than Lucien, bald as an egg, and had a scowl that seemed to work wonders on anyone thinking of causing trouble. Just for a second, Chloe was tempted to see what would happen if she claimed Lucien was forcing her and Ferain waded into the situation, but in Lucien's current mood, she doubted he would find it amusing, and Sa Ghislani didn't need the trouble.

"No need, Sa," she said. "He is my husband. You can ask Sejerin Silya to confirm it. She is a—" She hesitated, trying to remember the Miseneian term for domina. "—*hidadra*. I will just go upstairs and get my things."

"Very good." The innkeeper turned to Silya, bobbing her head respectfully. "Lady, I can have refreshments set out for you in the parlor."

"Thank you, but do not trouble yourself. We will not be long," Silya said.

And she, like Chloe, probably knew Lucien was unlikely to agree to moving away from where he was standing. He'd positioned himself neatly in the center of the room, where he had a good view of the stairs, the front door, and the second door that led to the dining room and the taproom beyond, not to mention the working areas of the inn like the kitchen. In other words, all the places where Chloe might try to sneak out. She'd have to climb out the window and scale down the roof at the back of the inn to avoid him. Even if she could manage that, she doubted she'd get far. Particularly if Octarus was talking to Martius and Ikarus.

"Very good. But please ask if there is anything we can do for you, Hidadra." Sa Ghislani pointed to the quartered circle hanging on the wall above a tray where salt grass and incense smoldered slowly. "We respect the goddess here."

Chloe headed for the stairs. When she stepped inside her room, Octarus was waiting for her, standing in the middle of the room with his arms folded. She still hadn't learned the nuances of his body language, but he seemed tense.

"Mate," he said.

"Yes," Chloe agreed. "It seems so. You didn't tell me you had spoken to Ikarus. Or was it Martius?"

He shrugged as though to say it didn't matter. "Did not ask about other sanctii. And mate safe."

"Mate annoying," she muttered as she tugged her bag from under the bed. She straightened and faced the sanctii again. "You should have told me he was coming."

"Safe," Octarus repeated, expression implacable. Then he added, "Solve."

Chloe blinked. *Solve?* Was that why he'd helped Lucien find her?

Had he decided that there was a better chance of catching the people who'd killed Rianne, his former mage, if she was with Lucien? She could see how that could maybe take precedence over the bond they shared, given that she hadn't directly ordered him not to tell other sanctii where they were.

Which was her fault. She had grown up with a sanctii. She

knew the ways in which they could work to achieve their own motives when they wanted. Technically, yes, a mage could treat a sanctii like a slave and force it to do only what they willed via the bond. Certainly that was what Anglions thought Illvyan mages did—deploy the sanctii as mindless controlled weapons.

And certainly not all Illvyan mages had treated their sanctii well. But an adversarial relationship was hardly the most pleasant way to spend your life with another being. Particularly one as powerful as a sanctii. There had been instances of water mages mysteriously vanishing over Illvya's history. A reminder that the bond was an agreement. Sanctii would have stopped agreeing centuries ago if they didn't like how they were treated.

Her father treated his connection with Martius as a partnership. Which meant that yes, from time to time, the sanctii might do unexpected things, just as Octarus had.

And it wasn't as though she and Octarus had formed their bond in the usual fashion. She'd offered him a bargain in the heat of the moment, desperate to think of something that might stop his grief-fueled rampage. A chance to catch Rianne's killers in exchange for his bond.

Apparently, he, like Lucien, had decided that she had a better chance of doing so with more people helping her.

"Mate. Safe," Octarus said again. "Apart sad."

"I'm fine," she said, shaking her head.

The sanctii mirrored her action. "No, were sad. Now, mate."

If only it was that simple. But she could hardly explain what lay between her and Lucien to Octarus when she didn't know herself.

"Lucien and I...it's complicated. I don't think we'll stay married. Mated, that is." She heard the wistful note in her own voice and straightened. Time enough to worry about her marriage and Lucien later when Deandra and the others were safely dealt with.

"Mate," Octarus repeated firmly and then vanished.

Clearly the conversation was over.

"I'll be at the Crown and Tree," she said to the empty room, despite the fact that he was more than capable of finding her wherever she might go, and then turned her attention to packing.

✦ ✦ ✦

After Chloe handed her key back to Sa Ghislani, Lucien held his hand out for her bag, and she passed it over without arguing. He then wasted no time in hustling them out the front door and across town to the Crown and Tree, keeping the pace brisk enough that Chloe was quite warm by the time they reached the inn. Too warm to raise the hood of her cloak to hide her reddened cheeks and what her reflection in the glass of the front doors revealed to be somewhat windswept hair, the humid air of the port freeing curls from the tendrils that had escaped her crown of braids.

The man who opened the door for them wore a long embroidered coat and a far friendlier expression than Ferain's.

The innkeeper—or concierge, maybe—was dressed in an even finer red velvet coat over a snowy white linen tunic and came out from behind his post at the front desk to greet them, a broad smile on his face.

"Ah, Lord Castaigne. You have returned. I trust you had a pleasant evening." He followed this with a respectful bow in Silya's direction. "Hidadra."

"I did, thank you," Lucien said as the man straightened. "This is Lady Castaigne. I trust the third room is ready for her?"

"Of course, my lord," the man said. "All is in order. Welcome to the Crown and Tree, Lady Castaigne. How happy you must be to be reunited with your husband."

"Indeed," Chloe murmured. "My delight cannot be truly expressed in words."

Silya snorted softly. Lucien's eyes narrowed, but he didn't comment.

"Perhaps the key?" Chloe suggested. "We will be leaving early, and I'd like to retire."

"Of course."

Sa Ghislani produced the key with a flourish, and another servant was summoned to escort them up to three flights of stairs and along a long corridor whose wooden floors were softened with layers of rugs. He stopped at one of the doors and gestured toward it.

"Your room, Lady Castaigne," he said. "Please let us know if you need anything. I'm sure your husband can explain the dining arrangements with you."

"I'm sure he can," she agreed with a tight smile. She wasn't hungry but was starting to think a stiff drink would be welcome.

The servant nodded, bowed again, and left.

Chloe fitted the key into the lock, and it turned with little resistance. She started to open the door.

"May I have a word, Lady Castaigne?" Silya asked.

Chloe turned back, startled. "With me?"

Silya smiled. "Is there another Lady Castaigne here?"

"No," Chloe said, then paused. She didn't particularly want an intimate discussion with Silya, but she couldn't think of a decent argument for refusing. And really, the evening had already been very strange, so why not finish it with a conversation with an Andalyssian seer? She pushed open the door. "After you, Sejerin."

Silya walked through, and Chloe followed her, shutting the door firmly before Lucien could join them. She turned the key in the lock and then faced the seer. The room was at least three times as large as the one she'd had in the Copper Fish and far more lavish. The bed was draped in filmy silk curtains, held back with gold cords, and covered with a green velvet spread embroidered with golden leaves. It, too, was at least three times larger than the one at the Copper Fish, and she suddenly longed for nothing more than sleep.

She suspected that caravan travel wasn't going to be conducive to restful nights, let alone luxurious places to spend them.

"That was not exactly polite," Silya said. "Your husband misses you."

Chloe crossed over to the bed and placed her bag on the low padded bench at its foot before she turned back to Silya. "With all due respect, Sejerin, if you are here to deliver a lecture about the state of my marriage, hold your breath."

"Do not underestimate that man," Silya said, frowning. "He was fierce in his pursuit of you. He cares."

"He thinks I might get myself killed," Chloe said. "He doesn't trust me."

Silya tilted her head. "I think that he does not trust those who are trying to kill you, Lady Castaigne. I think you would be wise not to trust them yourself."

Chloe shrugged. "I don't trust them, but that doesn't mean I had any choice in following them." She hesitated. "How much has Lucien told you about what happened?" The Andalyssians hadn't arrived in time for their wedding ball, so she didn't know exactly how much Silya knew about everything that had happened. Given that Aristides held suspicions about Andalyssia's involvement, it seemed likely that some things had been kept from her.

"I know about the magic that alters one's memories," Silya said with a scowl. "Such things are not balance. On that matter, your Domina Francis and I agree. It is a dangerous magic and should not be allowed to proliferate."

"I agree," Chloe said. "The Truth Seekers are one of the ways our legal system works well. If people can fool that...." Of course, in many countries, the courts operated without Truth Seekers. But when it came to crimes like treason and murder, they had always played a vital role in settling cases.

"Which begs the question of why you have weakened your husband by breaking the bond between you," Silya said.

Chloe frowned. "You didn't approve of the bond."

"Such things are not normal in Andalyssia, no. But Domina Francis explained a little of what happened to your husband, how ill he was when you returned and how the bond helped sustain him." She lifted an eyebrow. "Which made me surprised that you had broken it so cavalierly."

"I didn't want him in danger," she said. "And he is recovered now."

She thought back to the anger and the kiss. Her husband might be physically well, but she couldn't say much about his current emotional state.

Silya opened her mouth as though she wanted to argue, then snapped it shut again. "Very well. I am sure you will work things out between you without my interference. He is angry right now, but he will calm down now that you are together again."

"I'm not so sure about that," Chloe admitted. "And perhaps I deserve his anger."

"Well, you cannot change your past actions, Lady Castaigne. Which, if I may remind you, include twice making vows to this man under the eyes of the goddess. Some would think it foolish to try to deny those vows."

Her among them? Chloe's irritation spiked again. The temple in Lumia had no issue with divorce.

"After all," Silya continued before Chloe could argue, "we are headed north, and you will need the luck of the goddess to find your quarry. In the south, your lands are easy, and perhaps that weakens your faith. But in the north, we live dangerous lives. We do not tempt fate."

"Partha isn't Andalyssia."

"No, but it is not Lumia either. My grandmother came from Partha. She had the sight, too. Magic runs deep there. You will need your wits about you and all the resources you can muster. Do not weaken yourself or him."

Lucien waited in the hallway for Silya to emerge from Chloe's room, trying, as he had been for nearly two weeks now, to stay calm.

Chloe was alive and unharmed. That was what was important.

The fact that he was half tempted to wring her neck for scaring him badly enough that he was sure he'd lost ten years of his life was another matter entirely. As was the fact that he didn't entirely trust that she wouldn't run again.

In fact, the urge to make her unlock the door, shoo Sejerin Silya out of the room, and then haul Chloe into bed pounded through him like a beating heart. He'd keep her there until they both forgot everything that had happened in the last two weeks.

But along with the relief that she was alive, and the desperate need to touch her, there was still the anger. She had run. She hadn't trusted him.

She wasn't wearing his ring. That realisation had felt like a blade to his heart.

It had taken almost every ounce of will he possessed not to ask her where it was.

To demand she put it back on.

He'd only stopped himself because he wasn't sure she was still his wife. Not when everything between them felt so broken.

He still didn't know what he felt. What was true. Other than knowing, bone-deep, that if he told her any part of what he felt, he suspected she might just run again.

It would be easier to take her back to the capital. But no, Aristides had tasked him with finding Deandra Noirene and whoever she was working with. Chloe hadn't found her, so that meant the hunt had to continue.

Even if his instincts wanted Chloe safe, if he took her back to Lumia, some people would interpret that as him believing she'd played some role in the attack on the palace. The rumor mill amongst the court was alive and well. It hadn't taken long for news to spread that she had left the city, and speculation had followed about why. He was a Truth Seeker, one who had famously condemned his best friend to death. If he dragged Chloe back to the city without the true perpetrators in custody, that speculation would grow. That was the last thing either of them needed.

Nor could he ignore the fact that if he took her back to Lumia, there was no guarantee she would be safe.

Not with traitors armed with memory-altering, face-shifting magic who seemed intent on disrupting the empire. Who were willing to sacrifice her to achieve their aims. Particularly if there was also a crown prince willing to sacrifice his own father at the heart of the plot.

He pressed his lips together as he considered Alain. Aristides had confined him to the palace, yes, but the emperor had made no more definitive move against his son. And the palace was practically a small city. Impossible to entirely lock down, which left Alain free to scheme if he wanted. If he was involved with the attack, then clearly he had methods of communicating with the emperor's enemies without being discovered.

Which left them with little progress in the investigation so far. Imogene had conveyed Chloe's message, and they'd found the dead bodies in the garden, but to him, that night was mostly a blur, first of anticipation, dancing with Chloe, and then of fear and grief after the heart-stopping snap of their bond dissolving.

A sensation so fierce and clear that it stopped him amidst the chaos of evacuating the palace. And it somehow carried him through the aftermath of the explosion that had followed. He knew he had continued to function that night, had made sure the emperor was safe with Imogene, had worked with the others to search for any injured people once the fire had been taken care of by the water mages, had sat through a briefing with Aristides, who'd gotten out with only a grazed arm but whose rage had been palpable.

And then felt a degree of something when Imogene repeated what Chloe had told her, that the prince had been involved. Even through his own storm of emotions, Lucien had been able to see the blow hit Aristides when he heard that his own son might have plotted against him, followed by the realization that he had no way of knowing truly. Not when Alain was in the temple, conveniently afflicted with the loss of memory about anything that had happened at the parliament.

But Aristides had snapped into action like the emperor he was, pushing aside his personal feelings to safeguard his empire. He'd summoned the parliament's ministers, his generals, and his chief advisers among the court to work out how they were going to handle the chaos that might result in the city from an attack on both the palace and the parliament in such a short span of time.

Lucien had stayed, ready to help, but then at some point, Aristides had looked at him and said, "I will speak to you in the morning, Lord Castaigne. I suggest you go to bed."

After that, Imogene had bundled him off to his townhouse and handed him over to the care of his staff after a brief explanation of what had happened. He'd shaken off their concern, insisting he was unhurt. It didn't take long to check the wards and learn Chloe had been there, and even less time to think to check the portal and discover the thorough job she'd done of breaking it. The rage had swept up over him to join the grief.

Just as well he had no talent for blood magic and couldn't pull the whole thing down around his ears. Instead, he'd spent what was left of the night lying sleepless in the bed that was decidedly empty without Chloe, wondering whether she was still alive. Even if she'd made it through the portal, that didn't mean she was safe. Not with the bond breaking.

But even though he'd wanted to try to follow her, he'd also been hamstrung by his oaths. He was a Truth Seeker, and his emperor needed him. Plus, he realized quickly that Chloe also needed someone to assert her likely innocence to the court.

Therefore, he waited over those first few days of chaos, until the Andalyssians had arrived and Aristides had finally decided to send Lucien and Silya to hunt for Chloe and Deandra. Waited and worried and raged, hating the fact that his magic was useless against the memory charms, that he couldn't fix the situation.

Much like he was waiting now.

The door opened, and Silya slipped out. She stopped after she closed the door and looked him up and down.

"Go to bed, Lord Castaigne," she advised. "There is still a long journey ahead of you."

CHAPTER 5

Lucien barely spoke during breakfast the following morning. Chloe ate fast and attempted to maintain a polite conversation with Silya, but she was relieved when the meal was over. Though less so when she walked out of the hotel and saw the covered wagon waiting to take them to the kharaevenia, the trading post on the outskirts of Jinkara where the caravans gathered and conducted business.

The wagon appeared sturdy and serviceable but not necessarily comfortable. The driver perched up front looked up and smiled as the doorman said, "Good morning, Lord Castaigne." He wrapped the reins around a metal hook beside him, clucked his teeth at the four dusty brown horses, and climbed down from his seat, nodding at Lucien. "Good morning, my lord. My ladies," he added as he caught Chloe's eye. He looked young and fit, clearly Illvyan, though he wore a linen tunic in the Kharenian style over his breeches and boots.

"Daviel, this is Lady Castaigne," Lucien said, nodding at her. "And this is Sejerin Silya. You can address her as Sejerin."

The driver nodded. "Yes, my lord." He walked to the side of the wagon, unlatched something, and lowered a set of steps. "If you care to alight, I'll put your bags in the back."

Chloe looked at Lucien curiously. "He's one of yours, I assume?"

"One of ours, to be precise about it," Lucien said, offering his hand.

It took her a moment to lift hers. *One of ours?* Did that mean he still wanted to remain married? Or had he spoken without thinking?

He frowned slightly as she hesitated, and she hurriedly climbed in, not sure he wouldn't pick her up and just put her inside if he thought she might be having second thoughts.

The interior of the wagon was dim but not as dark as she had expected. Two low-backed benches, padded with leather, though far more utilitarian than any of Lucien's carriages, faced each other in the first third of the space. They looked as though they might seat three people each if no one was overly worried about bumping elbows. Not too crowded, perhaps, with just three of them.

She slid across the bench facing forward, taking the seat at the end. Part of the heavy canvas covering the wagon's frame was rolled up, and instead of watching Silya and Lucien taking their places, she stared out the window, wanting a last glimpse of Jinkara. To her surprise, she saw a familiar face standing across the street under the shelter of an awning of one of the stores not yet open.

Samuel.

Their eyes met and he tipped his head and offered her a quick salute before stepping back into the shadows.

She nodded back, unsure whether he could still see her. Lucien had taken their leave of the Emperor's Pride too fast for her to have a chance to say farewell to Samuel. She wasn't sure she would have kept her temper anyway, given that he had revealed her location to Lucien. It would have to be enough, perhaps, that they both knew that the other was well. Who knew? Their paths might cross again someday. A legitimate trader could have reason to come to Lumia.

The wagon lurched into action, and Chloe gratefully clutched the leather strap attached to the strut that supported the canvas. If this was going to be how the journey went, then she would be able to tell Imogene she'd found a mode of transport as uncomfortable as the charguerres that the army sometimes used. Those were fast but notorious for being hard on the spines and seats of those carried within them.

After they'd gone a hundred feet or so, she realized the wagon was going to be much slower but likely equally uncomfortable. But she found some kind of rhythm to the jolting motion as they navigated their way out of the center of town and toward the northern edge to the kharaevenia. It was easy enough to tell they were getting close when they began to pass large pens of cattle, sheep, and goats that turned the air coming through the canvas to a fug of dust and hay and manure.

The wagon circled the outskirts of the yards and made its way across to where there seemed to be at least fifty or sixty similar vehicles waiting. Beyond them, a forest of tents of various sizes spread out amongst small wooden huts, which were apparently the domains of the caravan masters.

The wagon eventually halted beside one of the others, and Lucien wasted no time, lowering the steps and helping them down from the wagon. "This way," he said and led them through the throng of tents to one of the small wooden buildings.

"Have you been here before?" Chloe asked.

He nodded. "We were here yesterday talking to the caravan master. Besides which, I can spot my own standard easily enough." He pointed to the flag that flew from the top of the hut, the breeze just strong enough to keep the de Roche tower and stars in dark green and silver billowing. "That is the secret to navigating this place—learning everyone's crests." He gestured at the other huts, each sporting one or more flags. There must have been close to fifty, a riot of brightly colored fabrics dancing in the air, the sound of them adding to the general noise of the kharaevenia. She recognized a few of the crests as Illvyan, but most were unfamiliar.

The building had two steps up to a deep porch. Lanterns lit the inside of the small room, but the air was cool. She caught the shimmer of wards on the walls. A cooling charm most likely, along with whatever other protections had been added. Unexpected but welcome.

The woman sitting behind the large desk that took up half the space was also unexpected—because she wasn't a man. Her robes were a vivid blue that set off her gleaming dark skin and eyes. Her black hair was braided away off her face, rings of gold and blue stone dancing in her ears. Kharenian, perhaps, rather than Miseneian.

"Good morning, my lord," the woman said, smiling with a flash of white teeth as they entered. "I see you have been successful in your venture." Her gaze moved from Lucien to Chloe, curiosity lighting her eyes.

Lucien nodded. "Yes, this is my wife, Lady Castaigne. Chloe, this is Mali inFalusi. She's in charge of the caravan that will be taking us to Partha."

Mali bobbed in a brief curtsy. "Good morning, Lady Castaigne. Welcome to Jinkara."

"Good morning, Madame," Chloe said politely. "Or is it Mamsille?"

"It's Madame." Mali laughed and waved her hand out toward the sea of tents. "My husband is out there somewhere, organizing the last of the wagons, I hope. He is good with the animals. I handle the rest." She smiled as she said it, but looking at the stack of papers and ledgers piled on the desk, it seemed her words were no exaggeration.

Chloe nodded. "And what is our cargo?"

Mali smiled approvingly. "What's left of last year's cloth from your serineau flocks, my lady," she said. "And casks of brandy and a few other things. No livestock, you'll be happy to hear."

"You don't like driving beasts?" Chloe asked. That seemed strange for someone who had chosen the life of a trader.

"I do not mind them so much," Mali admitted. "But they do slow the caravan things down. This way we will only be limited by the speed of the horses and the oxen rather than the need for goats and sheep and cattle to be fed and watered so often along the way. It makes us slightly nimbler. I understand you may need some diversions from the route, which is another reason to choose goods that do not grow road weary."

Chloe glanced at Lucien, wondering if Mali knew the true reason behind their travels. "Let us hope things are not too exciting."

"Yes, my lady. I far prefer trips where it all goes smoothly."

Regardless of how much Mali knew, the fact that Lucien was accompanying the caravan had to be cause for a good deal of speculation. How long had it been since one of the de Roche family had traveled with one? She couldn't picture any of Lucien's sisters amongst the dust and noise. No one rose to be a caravan master through being a fool. And an intelligent woman would know that it was unusual for her lord to accompany a caravan north. Serineau cloth was valuable but hardly enough to warrant the personal attention of a marq whose occupation kept him in the capital or traveling as the emperor demanded rather than the needs of his estate. Mali and the other workers making the journey must rightly suspect that perhaps it was his other duties that had caused him to join them.

Lucien nodded. "We've taken enough of your time, Mali. What time do you expect to depart?"

She pointed at the clock sitting on a shelf on the rear wall. "Perhaps another hour or two. We are aiming to leave before the midday traders begin to arrive. That will give us time to get to the next decent campsite with light to spare." She focused back on Chloe. "We will review the day's travel and make sure everything is in order before we settle in for the night. Which in turn will make the next morning run more smoothly. Sometimes after the first day's travel, we redistribute the loads slightly, see which beasts are reacting well or which may need to be changed in their pairings."

Chloe tried to look as though she knew what Mali was talking about. "Does that happen often?" She didn't know a lot about horses and even less about oxen, but she had a vague idea that they tended to work in established teams.

Mali waved a hand. "Beasts can be contrary, just like people. They have their moods and tempers. Most of our teams are well established, but we have a few new horses and two new oxen this journey. It may take some time to bed down the best teams. But it is nothing that should delay our journey, Lady Castaigne."

"Well, I look forward to learning more," Chloe said. "Lucien's trading concerns are broad, and it will be good for me to gain some experience of them firsthand."

Mali lifted an eyebrow. "That is not a sentiment that many women share. Wagons and tents are not to everyone's taste. This can be tiring work but interesting." She laughed, the sound rich and deep. "Which is just as well, or else I would be entirely in the wrong line of business."

Chloe smiled back. "As it happens, I quite enjoy travel myself." She didn't know whether Lucien had told Mali about her being in the diplomatic corps. And given the fact that she didn't know her current status within the corps, perhaps she should refrain from mentioning it herself. But the thought that she was going to see some new parts of the empire, even under the current circumstances, was something she had to admit was cheering. And as much as Lucien was annoying, it was good not having to navigate all the unforeseen and unknown places she was about to experience by herself.

"If you wish to rest, my lady, before we set off, there is a tent behind the store which has been set aside for yourself and the Sejerin. It will be more comfortable than a wagon. And we have some horses along, so you can spend some time riding during the day, if you prefer." She turned her attention to Lucien. "I assume you will ride some of the way, my lord?"

He pulled a face, nodding. "Yes, better than spending all day in a wagon. I remember the first time I traveled with a caravan with my father. The weather was terrible, and he wouldn't let me ride. Those wet days inside the wagon seemed to last forever."

Mali laughed again. "Well, we do not need to fear the weather much. At least for the next few days while we are still within Miseneia. We may hit some rain as we go farther north where spring will be lingering, but nothing that should keep you cooped up in the wagon all day." She tapped a scroll that lay on top of one of her ledgers. "Would you care to see the route we are taking, Lady Castaigne?"

Chloe nodded. "I would, but I'm sure you must have much to do to organize before we leave. I would not like to get in your way. Perhaps you can show me tonight?"

Mali nodded. "Very well, my lady. I look forward to it."

✧ ✧ ✧

"Didn't Mali say something about a tent?" Chloe asked as they left Mali's office and Lucien started to walk back down the row of similar buildings.

"I'd rather we stayed together," he said. "And I have things to see to."

He didn't offer any more explanation than that, and stretching her legs seemed a better option than sitting in a tent before spending the rest of the day sitting in a wagon, so she followed him.

The three of them didn't attract too much attention, though a few people glanced at Silya curiously. With her red-gold hair and ice green eyes, she stood out. The fact that she carried herself like someone used to having a path clear before her probably also helped. At least she wasn't carrying the staff of office she did in Andalyssia. That definitely would have attracted notice.

But curious looks didn't translate into any attempts to speak to them. Perhaps at a trading post, even Andalyssians weren't an unknown quantity. The conversations taking place around them were using quite a few languages. Illvyan still seemed to be the predominant one, but she caught snatches of Miseneian and Kharenian, and others she didn't recognize. No Anglion, which was hardly surprising. Sophie was opening her country's borders, but it would likely be a while before Anglions embraced the empire's trading routes.

Probably just as well. Aristides currently had enough on his hands with old enemies and plots without trying to shepherd his new alliance through the niceties of establishing diplomatic relations across the entire empire. That would require more than just a delegation of—

"Lady Margaretta," she blurted, coming to a stop.

Lucien twisted to look back, saw she'd stopped, and then turned on his heel to rejoin them. "What about her?"

"Were any of the Anglions hurt?" she asked, trying to pitch her voice as low as she could and still have him hear her. "Did they leave?"

"No," Lucien said. "Though when we left, how long they might stay was under discussion."

"I see," she said and fell back into silence, the enjoyment she'd been taking in the warmth of the sunshine and the prospect of travel fading as her brain started to chew on the likely ramifications if Margaretta decided she and her people should return to Anglion. Chloe wouldn't have blamed her. There had been two attacks in the capital since the Anglions had arrived. Anyone with half a brain might decide they would be safer at home.

Of course, the court in Kingswell had its own experience with the impact of political violence.

Hopefully Sophie wouldn't recall the delegation. The new queen was pushing the Anglions out of their temple-imposed exile as hard as she could. Admitting her first diplomatic attempts had been thwarted didn't seem like a path she'd choose. It would only make those resisting her change more entrenched. Yet another reason to find Deandra and her friends and bring them down. Chloe bit her lip, thinking as Lucien set off again.

The wagon he led them to wasn't the same one that had brought them to the kharaevenia. It was perhaps half as large again. She hoped that didn't mean the three of them were expected to sleep inside it. It was large but hardly spacious. Especially when she would be sharing it with both her currently annoyed husband and an Andalyssian seer.

Though maybe sticking close to Silya wasn't such a bad idea. She wasn't yet ready to contemplate time alone with Lucien.

A young man dressed in dark breeches and boots, a long loose white linen shirt, and a broad-brimmed hat like most of the men they'd passed so far was standing in the shade cast by the wagon, next to a pile of familiar-looking luggage. His face was hidden by the hat, but something about his bearing was a shade too upright for her to believe he was one of the local caravan workers.

As they approached, he lifted his head, and she saw he was Illvyan. Or most likely so with his pale gold skin and green eyes.

And, Chloe realized, a member of the small troupe of Imperial guards who normally watched over Lucien's townhouse.

She forced herself to keep moving forward, stilling the instinctive flinch that passed through her, the desire to disappear back into the crowd just in case they were coming for her, despite Lucien's reassurances. She racked her brain for the young man's name. She didn't encounter the house guards that often, much as Lucien had promised the very first night she'd spent in the townhouse. They tended to stay outside, guarding the perimeter, when she and Lucien were home, and they did a very good job at being unobtrusive the rest of the time. Fortunately, her brain coughed up the name just as they reached the man.

"Corporal Chartres," she said briskly. "How nice to see you."

"My lady," he said, nodding politely.

Not a salute, she noticed, which technically, given that she was a lieutenant and outranked him, she was owed.

But then he didn't salute her at the house either, so maybe he was sticking to those protocols, treating her as Lady Castaigne rather than a lieutenant in the Imperial mages.

If indeed she *was* still a lieutenant in the mages.

Lucien greeted him with a brisk nod. "Corporal. I see our luggage was delivered safely."

"Yes, my lord. Not long ago. We'll load it up and get everything settled once the horses are harnessed and the rest of the load finalized. We weren't sure if there was anything breakable inside that might get damaged during the loading."

"We have all packed to travel, Corporal," Lucien said. "I don't think there's anything that is likely to be harmed. At least not any more than it would be from the journey itself." He cast a glance over his shoulder at Chloe and Silya. "Unless either of you are carrying something you're concerned about?"

"I have some medicines," Silya said. "But they are in a case designed for travel and should be safe enough."

Chloe stiffened slightly. What kind of medicines? The Andalyssians had something of a history when it came to herbs —both the healing and deadly kinds. Andalyssian firewort had nearly killed Lucien.

"Chloe?" Lucien prompted.

"No." She shook her head. "Nothing fragile."

He turned back to the corporal. "There. Nothing to be concerned with."

The corporal nodded. "Very good, my lord. That will speed matters once the horses arrive. It shouldn't be long." He gestured at the side of the wagon, where the steps had already been lowered. "If the three of you wish to wait inside, I already activated the cooling charm, so it should be comfortable. Better than staying out in this heat for the ladies."

Chloe didn't mind the warmth of the sun, but Silya did look hot despite the fact that she wore light cotton and had braided her hair up like Chloe's. Two spots of pink warmed the cheeks of her pale Andalyssian skin, and her icy green eyes were squinted against the sun. The tip of her nose was starting to look pink, too. Perhaps someone in the kharaevenia could sell them a few of the wide-brimmed hats everyone else seemed to wear.

She doubted Silya had ever encountered temperatures like the climate in Miseneia, and it might be wise to get her under shelter. Whether or not she approved of cooling charms, it wouldn't do to have one of King Mikvel's advisers becoming ill from sunstroke.

"Inside sounds lovely," she said, smiling gratefully at the corporal. "Sejerin, after you."

Lucien remained outside, speaking in a soft tone to the corporal so that Chloe couldn't make it out, but eventually he climbed in with them.

The wagon was laid out in similar fashion to the one they had traveled in early. Two bench seats, facing each other, the padding looking a little more robust and the backs higher. Toward the rear, separated by a low frame across the breadth of the space, there were shelves loaded with paper-wrapped packages and small crates lashed into place. In front of the shelves lay piles of rolled fabric she suspected might be their bedding.

A reminder that even if someone had thought to make this wagon slightly more comfortable, there would be tents and sleeping on the ground in her future.

Well, she wasn't a fragile flower. She had camped with her family a time or two, and there were worse things than a few weeks sleeping in tents.

Lucien settled into the position opposite Chloe's, his long legs stretching toward hers. The distance between the seats was sufficient that there was no chance of them touching, but she still had to resist the urge to tuck her feet back, safely out of the way.

No need to let him see she was nervous.

He pointed out the cupboards under the seats that held blankets, a large leather flask that came with a set of tin cups, and a covered basket that contained their lunch apparently. "Do either of you want tea? I could ask the corporal to fetch some."

"I could make tea," Silya said.

Chloe shot her a wary glance. "Normal tea or one of your medicines?"

The seer smiled tightly. "Do not look so concerned, Lady Castaigne. I am not here to finish off you or your husband. My kit contains no firewort or anything vaguely lethal. Well, I suppose one could take too much of the Armesia syrup, but that seems unlikely. It tastes bad enough that it is difficult to sneak into anyone's food or drink."

The fact that Silya knew about Armesia didn't ease Chloe's nerves. Clearly she knew something of healing to be carrying such a thing. Which meant she was probably well versed in Andalyssian poisons as well.

"I assure you, it is nothing but a basic kit to treat minor ailments and inconveniences. The same as anyone might take with them traveling." The seer's gaze flicked to Lucien. "After all, I have had ample time to poison your husband already. I doubt he or his guards know enough about healing to detect anything I might have tried on our journey to Jinkara. Yet here he is safe and well. If we are to travel well together, you will have to trust me."

"So it seems."

Silya chuckled. "Given our task, I will not tell you not to be so suspicious. It may stand you in good stead."

Chloe wasn't entirely sure how to take that statement, so instead she turned her attention to Lucien. "Just how many guards did you bring with you?"

He had forgotten to mention anything about that the

previous evening or even over breakfast, but now that she thought about it, it made sense that he hadn't come entirely alone.

"A few," Lucien admitted. "They'll take turns driving the wagon and mingling with the others."

A few. That probably meant at least five. Maybe more.

"And you just forgot to mention that you were traveling with Imperial guards? What, in case I was recalcitrant?" If he'd brought some of his household guard, she would have felt more comfortable. They were sworn to his service. To *her* service, in a way, though it was Lucien they would obey. But household guards wouldn't be used to arrest her.

Lucien shook his head. "They are not intended for you."

She wasn't entirely sure she believed him. If they had been coming to arrest her, knowing she had a sanctii to protect her, a few guards would not be overrated. Though she would have expected at least one of them to be a water mage with a sanctii of their own, and Octarus had said nothing about another sanctii in the camp. Though, given he'd stayed silent about his communication with Martius and Ikarus, perhaps she should ask him outright.

"They are here because Aristides insisted that Sejerin Silya required more of an escort than I could provide on my own to ensure her safety," Lucien continued before she could. "And I imagine he was concerned for my safety as well." He shrugged. "And it may prove useful to have some extra help on hand for when we find Deandra and her friends somewhere not handy to an Imperial garrison. Corporal Chartres is a good, strong blood mage, and several of the others have useful skills." He glanced at Silya, his expression somewhat apologetic.

She merely shrugged and said, "I am not in my own country. I do not expect you heathens to practice magic as I approve of it."

Lucien laughed, and Chloe realized that somewhere along their journey to Jinkara, he and Silya had grown comfortable together. "Well, this heathen is glad to hear it, Sejerin. It may become necessary given our quarry."

The seer's eyes sharpened at that. "To bring those who are trying to promulgate this wickedness to justice, I will gladly put up with a little unorthodox magic."

"I'm glad to hear it. And may we succeed in bringing our enemies down, by heathen means or otherwise. The goddess will approve either way."

Silya nodded. "It will be balance."

She looked, Chloe thought, a little more comfortable inside, the color in her face having faded back from overheated-looking to merely warm. The interior of the wagon was pleasantly cool, though she could feel the heat on the canvas walls. Whoever had set the cooling charm did good work.

"So, what exactly is the plan?" Chloe asked, settling back against the bench.

Lucien shrugged. "The caravans communicate as they travel, so our plan is to proceed forward on the route and send out feelers to see if there is any mention of a woman fitting Deandra's description. At the same time, we have other feelers out to look for this theater troupe."

"And if we receive word that someone has found either her or the troupe?"

"That depends somewhat where they are. If they're on a route and we'll get there in a reasonable time, I guess we'll continue with the caravan. But if not, then we can proceed through portals or, if greater speed is needed, through other methods."

"A navire would hardly be discreet, if that's what you mean."

Lucien shrugged. "I agree. I'm sure they'll be wary of Imperial troops, but then again, perhaps they think they have carried out their attack without being identified and are retreating somewhere to form their next plan. They must have learned by now that their efforts in Lumia were not successful." He frowned at her. "Another reason for them to dislike you. I hope

I don't need to tell you that you need to be careful if we do find them."

"I wasn't planning on challenging Deandra to a duel or storming their lair, if that's what you mean."

"Good. Though I expect we will need to be patient. If they have any brains between them—and given the nature of their plots, we have to assume they do—then they'll be lying low."

Yes, lying low made sense. And seemed to be something Deandra was good at. "That seems reasonable."

Lucien's mouth quirked slightly. "I'm glad you approve, my lady," he said. "Of course, you should feel free to share your own plans if you think they could improve on ours."

She was hardly going to admit to him that she hadn't entirely formed a plan. "Yours sounds similar. Find Deandra or the theater troupe, then decide the next course of action. But she— or they—are our best chance." She turned back to Silya. "Unless something has come of the poison, of course. The asphenyet that Irina thought came from Andalyssia." Poison carried by the man who'd stabbed Rianne after trying to kill Lady Margaretta. He was the reason they had learned about facial illusions, but he'd died before he could provide them with any actual answers. "Did you have time to look at it before my husband dragged you from the capital?"

Silya nodded slowly. "Yes. Irina...no, forgive me, *Her Grace* was correct in her assessment. It was asphenyet. I have sent word back to Deephilm to check on everyone who has ever grown, sold, or prepared this herb. Those we know of. Asphenyet is closely controlled. If someone has been selling to outlanders, then that is something that must be stopped."

She looked genuinely indignant at the thought. Did she truly think that no Andalyssian had ever sold poisons beyond Andalyssia before? Or was she annoyed that she didn't know about it already if they did? Hardly a question Chloe could ask her outright.

"I think we all agree on that," Chloe said. "And if we have no new information on that topic, then our current course seems best."

Lucien's mouth quirked, but he didn't argue. Silence descended over the carriage again. Apparently, he was done with the discussion. And as much as Chloe was interested in learning more about Andalyssian purchases, pursuing that subject right now didn't seem like the best way to build trust with Silya. She might view it as interrogation rather than curiosity.

Which left her wondering what she *could* say to Silya.

"Irina must have been pleased to see some faces from home," she said, trying to be diplomatic. The last thing Irina wanted was to return to Andalyssia. She'd made that clear when she'd chosen to marry Valentin to secure her position in Lumia.

Silya lifted a brow, as though surprised that Irina would be Chloe's choice of topic. "One of her uncles was in the contingent. I believe he brought her messages from her sister and her father, but of course, the news of her marriage may have altered any plans those contained." Her icy eyes pinned Chloe. "That was neatly done, my lady."

Chloe shook her head, holding up her hands. "Believe me, Sejerin, I had nothing to do with that one. That was all the duq. Did you meet him?"

Aristides would not have let Valentin and Irina avoid the Andalyssians. Valentin had married her to grant her the protection of his title. As a duquesse of Illvya, she no longer had to fear being dragged home against her will. The emperor would have expected them to act as though they were secure in their positions and tell her family the news themselves.

"Yes, at the temple," Sejerin said. "Domina Francis explained he is quite the healer."

"Yes," Chloe agreed, "which I think was why he was happy to help Irina. It seems she has the potential to be quite the healer as well."

"She could be a healer in Andalyssia," Silya said.

Chloe shrugged. "Yes, but not in the same way as she can in

Illvya. And if she feels that the goddess has called her to use her magic in this way, then really, who are either of us to gainsay that?"

Silya's mouth flattened briefly. "It is a difficult choice she has made to cut herself off from family and House."

"Will they disown her, then?" Chloe asked. "After all, a duq is not such a bad husband for a younger daughter of a Great House."

"Not just any daughter but the queen's sister," Silya pointed out. "I am sure her father was hoping to make an advantageous marriage for her."

"Well, Lord Arbronet is quite the advantage," Chloe said. "The man is richer than just about anyone bar the emperor." Which might not be enough to redeem him in the eyes of the Andalyssians, depending on how much they knew about him. Though even if they disapproved, there was little they could do. Thanks to his title, Valentin was one of the most powerful men in the empire. And that was without considering the fact that his talent for healing meant he also had the firm support of the temple. Mikvel would be a fool to protest the marriage, even if Irina's family were less than thrilled. His queen, Katiya, would most likely only be happy that her sister had found a way to be happy. Another reason for Mikvel not to complain. He adored his wife.

"The man is also a scandal and a rogue," Silya said bluntly. "Or so I have been told."

"Well, Irina already knew that when she agreed to wed him," Chloe said. "And how things work between them is a matter for them both to decide. Hopefully her family will warm to him over time. After all, it cannot hurt King Mikvel to have closer ties to the Illvyan court if he wishes to deal with those back in your country who are minded to cause trouble." She stared at the seer for a moment. "Unless, my lady, *you* think such trouble is justi-fied. I hope the fact that you are here means perhaps you do not."

"I do not support chaos and mayhem. Such things are not in accordance with balance."

Not exactly a resounding declaration of her support for the emperor or the empire. Or Irina's marriage, for that matter.

"Sejerin Silya has agreed to help us," Lucien interjected gently. "I have no cause to doubt her sincerity."

It would be rude to ask him exactly what he meant by that. Had he used his power on the seer? Confirmed whatever she had agreed to do as truth before they left for Lumia?

It wasn't outside the realm of possibility. This was, no matter what personal stakes Lucien had in the matter, an investigation of a crime committed against the emperor. Even with the uncertainty surrounding whether there were ways to circumvent a Truth Seeker's magic, it was difficult to imagine Aristides hadn't wanted some sort of surety.

Once she wouldn't have had to ask, of course. When they'd shared a bond, she'd been able to use a little of Lucien's power herself. She might have been able to see for herself that Silya was being truthful. But she had destroyed the bond and forfeited any ability to share magic with Lucien. Whether or not she'd forfeited everything else they had once shared...or had been beginning to share, perhaps, remained to be seen.

CHAPTER 6

By the time the caravan got underway, rolling away from the kharaevenia at a speed scarcely above walking pace, Chloe was thankful for the cooling charm inside the wagon.

The canvas flap between the front of the wagon and the driver's seat was closed, but it was hardly impregnable. Wafts of warm air and dust found their way through the fabric as the wagon rumbled along. The charm mitigated the impact, keeping the interior comfortable if slightly dusty. Without it, they would have been sweaty and coated in road dirt before they had gone two miles.

The charm, however, couldn't soften the ride. The driver—Corporal Chartres, to her surprise—seemed to know what he was doing, but no amount of skill could turn an uneven road to a smooth one. She would have to ask Imogene why no mage ingenier had yet managed to invent a charm for that. Generations of them must have contemplated the problem. Which must mean there was some reason it couldn't be done.

In the meantime, she tried to find a comfortable position, telling herself that it would be like riding a horse once she found a rhythm to it. Until then, she could distract herself from the discomfort by tackling another uncomfortable task and making small talk to fill the time.

"How many wagons are there in the caravan?" she asked Lucien.

"Around twenty," he said. "Mali was negotiating for some goods this morning, so that may have added to the final tally."

Twenty. Enough to mean they wouldn't travel fast. But for the moment, their aim was to move undetected toward their quarry, not to rush and scare them away.

"If you have any real interest in the details, Mali will be happy to talk to you," Lucien continued. He tipped his head toward the front of the wagon. "Her wagon is the one in front of ours."

"She doesn't take the lead?"

"No, that's Guat, her husband. He has the lead oxen team, so he sets the pace. The outriders go ahead of him, and his wagon carries some of the caravan guards. Mali likes to be farther back, as I understand it. Every caravan leader has their own style."

He sounded as though he knew what he was talking about.

"And how far will we travel each day?"

"That varies with the terrain and the distance between camps and towns. The oxen are slower than horses, but they have their advantages. Today is a shorter leg. The camp we're aiming for isn't as far as some of the others. We'll be there a few hours before sunset."

Sunset felt a long way away.

She settled back against the leather, searching for some semblance of patience. Until there was any definite news about either Deandra or the theater troupe, this was the pace they had decided upon, and chafing against it would just drive her mad. Though sitting across from Lucien and finding his steady green gaze waiting for her every time she looked up might do a better job of driving her crazy than the speed of their journey.

The first few hours travel, before they halted for lunch, seemed to last three times longer than that. They'd pulled off the road into a cleared area at the edge of a patch of scrubby woods. It was obviously intended for caravans and other travelers. There were a few trees left standing for shade around the edges of the flattened earth and a well to draw water, as well as several small firepits and a row of wooden huts she assumed were some sort of basic toilet. Necessities only. She hoped the camp they were headed for wouldn't be quite so spartan.

She walked around the wagon a few times, stopping to pat the horses when Corporal Chartres invited her to. He was checking their feet and fastening feedbags. She made him show her how to attach the bags, insisting she intended to be useful when he tried to wave her off.

The wind was warm and dusty outside the wagon, but it was still nice to be in fresh air for a time. She was scratching one of the lead pair's ears and laughing as they munched placidly when Lucien came to escort her over to the trees to eat bread, cheese, cold roast meat, and vegetables, washed down with water, then cold tea. She ate fast and then circled the clearing a few more times to stretch her legs while trying to stay out of the way.

It didn't take long under the heat of the midday sun to realize that even her light woolen dress was too warm for this journey. She had planned to buy a few cooler dresses for her wardrobe in Jinkara once she'd found passage north, but Lucien hadn't given her any time this morning. The weather would cool again as they moved north, Miseneian spring being warmer than even summer in that part of the empire. But she needed something that would be comfortable to move around in until they got that far or she would be forced to spend most of her time in the wagon.

Hopefully their first stop in a town large enough to buy dresses wasn't too many days away. Until then, she was just going to have to make do.

She waited under a shady tree, fanning herself idly with a piece of fallen bark, when Lucien loomed up by her side.

"Did you eat enough?" He'd headed off to speak to Mali after finishing his own meal, and Silya had returned to their wagon, clearly preferring the cool but insisting that she didn't need Chloe's company to finish the glass of cold tea she'd taken with her.

"Yes," she said firmly. "I'm fine."

He nodded. "Good. Mali wanted to know if perhaps you'd want to ride for a while this afternoon? We won't stop again before tonight's camp, barring anything unexpected delaying us."

"How far is that?"

He peered skyward as though assessing the position of the sun. "A few hours. Three at most."

Three hours in the sun sounded like a lot. She had gotten somewhat back into the habit of riding at Sanct de Sangre, but not for hours at a time, let alone in summer.

"Are you going to ride?" The thought was a daunting prospect, but so was three hours in the wagon alone with Silya. That was all too likely to turn into a three-hour lecture about why Chloe should repair her relationship with Lucien.

He nodded. "Might as well enjoy the fresh air. It gets monotonous, sitting in the wagon all day. I don't want to do that for weeks on end."

No, she couldn't blame him for that. He was used to being busy. He worked, if anything, too hard. Hours of inaction each day with only small amounts of estate business to think about when they received messages or mail wasn't going to keep him occupied.

When he'd been convalescing, he hadn't had the energy to protest the fact that she'd stopped him doing any work, but she couldn't imagine it was going to sit well with him over weeks of a journey. It wasn't something she was looking forward to either.

But maybe they would find Deandra and the troupe and be able to leave the wagons to their journey sooner than that.

But if they didn't, well, riding at least part of the day had to be preferable to being cooped up in the wagons.

Lucien was waiting for a reply.

"I haven't ridden that far in quite some time," she admitted.

"We won't be moving at a fast pace. It's a good way to build up your stamina," he suggested after a pause. "After all, whether you choose the wagon or a horse, you're going to be sore for the first few days until you get used to it."

She grimaced. "So it seems. At least the wagon doesn't bounce as much as a charguerre."

That earned her a quick smile.

"No," Lucien agreed. "They don't move fast enough for that. The charguerres move so quickly, they would rattle no matter how well designed. Not that knowing that makes it any more pleasant to experience."

No. She'd only ridden in a charguerre on the journey to Deephilm. It had been uncomfortable even at the slower pace caused by the mountainous terrain. It was a case of choosing the least bad option, perhaps. At least on a horse, she could probably avoid awkward conversations.

"Very well. Let's ride."

✧ ✧ ✧

Riding turned out to be more pleasant than she'd anticipated. As Lucien promised, the pace was slow, and the chestnut mare chosen for her had a comfortable stride. And even if a horse was no faster than the wagon, the scenery was better.

Somehow the air didn't feel as hot from the back of a horse. Lucien had produced a broad-brimmed hat that kept the sun off her face, and she had managed to arrange her dress around the mare's side saddle. It wasn't her favorite way to ride, and she added a split habit to her mental list of clothing to buy.

After the first hour, a cooler breeze arrived, easing the worst of the heat. The landscape wasn't the most exciting she had ever traveled through—being mostly farmland full of sheep and huge black Miseneian cattle—but it was new. Lucien stayed close to her, riding a big bay gelding and offering comments about their route at odd intervals. The rest of the time, he was silent, seemingly lost in his thoughts.

The last time they'd ridden together was at Sanct de Sangre. Back then, they hadn't really spoken much either, Lucien still recovering and both of them avoiding discussing exactly what they should do about the marriage neither of them had planned on once it became clear that the quick divorce they had intended was no longer going to be possible.

It seemed like everything and nothing had changed since then.

She would have to talk to him sooner or later. But it seemed wise to let him have a few more days to get over the worst of his temper before she tried. Until then, she would keep some distance and distract herself with the travel.

By the time they reached the campsite where they were staying the night, she was glad to dismount and only half succeeded in not groaning as she did so, her legs and back and other more delicate parts protesting the time in the saddle.

She noticed Lucien grimacing slightly as he dismounted, so she possibly wasn't the only one feeling their journey.

But the wince had vanished from his face by the time he held out a hand to take the reins of her horse. She handed them over, and he led the horses off, leaving her in the company of one of the guards, who offered to take her back to the wagon and then show her where she could wash.

Sadly, the long hot bath that may have helped ease her muscles was something the camp didn't offer. It was a permanent site, complete with some wooden huts equipped with basic washing facilities. There were basins for washing hands and faucets set high on the wall to sluice under, but no bathtubs.

But the water was sun warmed, and the lingering heat of the day made it comfortable to rinse the sweat from her skin and dry off. If they ended up reaching the far north, she'd have to hope there would be ways to warm the water at the sites or get used to using warming charms to finish her toilette.

She didn't bother trying to wash her hair. Wearing it braided out of the way in between towns seemed the easiest option. If they hit a longer stretch of travel, she would have to wash it on the road eventually, but for now, it was fine. They were supposed to reach Fallea, the next large town, in a few more days. Her hair could wait until then.

By the time she emerged from her hut, the camp was well on its way to being settled for the night. Tents had sprung up in organized rows, and the horses and oxen were penned into the yards bordering the site. As she waited for Silya to appear from the hut next to hers, she watched the bustle, feeling somewhat guilty that she wasn't helping. It might be Lucien's caravan, but she didn't want to behave like a useless aristo.

She knew well enough how to light a fire, and it couldn't be that difficult to groom a horse or help raise a tent or chop vegetables or find wood or do whatever else would be useful, even if she wasn't as fast as the caravan workers to begin with.

The smoky scent of grilling meats began to tease her nose, and her stomach rumbled in response just as Silya stepped out of the bathing hut next to hers.

Corporal Chartres had clearly been keeping an eye out for them, because he appeared from behind the huts almost before Silya had finished closing the door on hers and escorted them to the dining area. Another dirt clearing, this time square rather than a circle. The far side was bordered by a row of firepits, and the rest of the space was taken up with rough-hewn wooden benches. There were a few tables, but they were given over to the food being cooked rather than having room for people to sit at them.

She sat on a log bench with Silya and ate grilled chicken with more of the ubiquitous flatbreads, and vegetables, followed by sliced apples drizzled with spiced honey. And hot tea this time.

Lucien was nowhere to be seen. Neither was Mali. Perhaps

discussing caravan business elsewhere. Well, no one would let either of them go hungry, and if he didn't choose to join them for dinner, that made things easier.

The caravan workers wasted no more time eating than they had setting up camp. All bar one of the fires were extinguished as soon as everyone had been served. That one was banked carefully and kettles of water placed nearby, ready for fast tea to fortify those on night watch and to assist in cooking whatever breakfast was going to be.

But the night was hardly cold, so the fires weren't needed for warmth. Miseneia, being dryer than Illvya, had fewer forests. She'd learned that they were careful with wood. Some parts of the country were desert, and she understood the nights there grew cold quickly, but here on the plains, it was comfortable enough even once the sun had set.

By the time she was starting to wonder where they would be sleeping, Corporal Chartres, who had positioned himself on the bench next to theirs, put down his mug. "I can show you to your tents, my ladies," he offered.

They walked toward the center of the rows of tents, and the corporal stopped in front of the biggest one. Lucien's standard hung from the canvas beside the flap. A second more modestly sized tent stood beside it.

"That is your tent, Sejerin," he said somewhat unnecessarily, indicating the smaller one. "And yours, my lady." He nodded toward the larger. "Lord Castaigne is already inside."

Damn it, she hadn't thought about sleeping arrangements. Of course she and Lucien would be expected to share the larger tent. Her jaw tightened, but she managed not to frown. The corporal wasn't to blame for the fact that she didn't want to sleep with Lucien, nor were the sleeping arrangements his decision.

"Thank you, Corporal." She didn't move toward the tent, turning back to Silya, who looked somewhat amused.

The corporal took a step closer to the seer, gesturing toward her tent. "The tent has a cooling charm, Sejerin. And there are blankets if you get too cold in the night. We'll be keeping watch, so you can ask someone if you need anything else."

"I am sure I will manage," Silya said. She nodded at the corporal and then at Chloe. "Sleep well, Lady Castaigne." She disappeared into the tent, pulling the flap down firmly behind her.

Chloe turned to face her own tent, studying the sturdy sand-colored canvas. Light flickered within, the glimpses of it through the half-open flap warm and golden. Lanterns or earth lights, perhaps. Cozy. Intimate. Precisely what she didn't want, knowing Lucien was inside.

What would happen when they were alone? They hadn't spoken anymore about the kiss, but she wasn't sure she trusted herself alone with the man.

She needed to keep her wits about her, not let him steal her senses with his stupidly handsome face.

She had a sudden wild impulse to declare that she'd sleep in the wagon, but the corporal would probably just think she'd lost her mind.

He smiled at her and gestured at the open flap. "Good night, Lady Castaigne."

Right. She was keeping him from whatever else he was supposed to be doing. Like getting some sleep if he was going to spend part of the night standing guard.

She sighed and ducked her head to step through the flap, pausing just inside to let her eyes adjust to the light.

The flap dropped shut behind her, and she heard the chime of a ward, but she couldn't focus on what Corporal Chartres was doing when she had to focus on her husband.

Lucien sat behind some sort of small portable table set near the right-hand wall of the tent, writing in a ledger under the light of a lantern. He looked up as she hovered by the door.

"Good evening," he said carefully, as though not sure of her mood.

"Hello," she said. Then, as nothing else intelligent occurred to her as a conversational gambit, she turned her attention to the tent itself. It probably could have slept eight or ten people had it been set up with the same rows of pallets she'd glimpsed inside some of the caravan's smaller tents. Instead, it felt like a small room.

In fact, she wasn't sure it wasn't larger than the first room she'd ever rented in Anglion. Certainly it was better furnished. Layers of Miseneian carpets had been rolled out to cover the dirt floor, and earth lights dotted around to supplement the light from the lanterns. There were two other small tables not far from Lucien's. One held a tin washbasin and jug and the other a flask, water glasses, and a bowl of fruit. Her luggage and his trunks were nearly stacked against the left wall, half hidden by a green cloth.

Despite the relative luxury, there was, to her dismay, only one bed, covered in layers of blankets and pillows in more shades of green. Large, yes, but clearly intended for them to share.

As she stared at it, Lucien must have noticed. "We can divide those if you prefer."

She glanced at him questioningly, and he shrugged. "I didn't think there was an easy explanation for us wanting to sleep apart. After all, we are supposed to be the happily newly married marq and marquesse."

And the caravan was full of his people. People who deserved to think their lord was settled and that his marriage was harmonious.

"I'm sure we can manage. It's large enough for us to share," she said eventually.

He lifted an eyebrow. "As you wish. I must finish some work here. Did you want to sleep?"

There wasn't much else to do. She could summon Octarus, but there was little to discuss with him. But it was early, and despite the long day, she wasn't sure she was ready to sleep. She had the last of the books she'd purchased in Jinkara, but with

Lucien's presence looming large, she doubted she'd be able to concentrate on reading.

"What are you working on?" she asked.

"Just checking some of Mali's notes on the route and the trades she has planned," he said. "I won't be much longer. You should go ahead and go to bed if you wish." He dropped his gaze to the ledger and picked up the pen again.

Was he trying to give her privacy? Or ignoring her because he was still angry with her?

There was no way of knowing, and standing in the middle of the tent like a statue wouldn't help matters. Suppressing a sigh, she began to rummage through her bags to find her nightgown. Fortunately, her dress was one that she needed no assistance to remove. She snuck a look at Lucien before she started to unfasten it, but his eyes were fixed on the ledger, his expression giving no hint that he was even aware of her.

Of course, the somewhat tense line of his shoulders suggested otherwise. But she had no desire to draw his attention, so she turned her back, removed her dress, dropped the loose cotton nightgown over her head, then wriggled out of her undergarments. She folded everything and put it back in the bag, slipping off the chain with Lucien's ring as she did so. Her hair was already braided, so there was little else to do. She blew out a quick breath and considered the bed.

It had looked large before, but now it seemed small. Especially when she imagined Lucien lying in it.

Another glance over her shoulder revealed his attention still fixed on the ledger. Somewhat annoyed, she crossed to the table and grabbed a handful of the small black grapes to give her something to do before Lucien finished his work.

Returning to the bed, she slid under the covers, though the tent was pleasantly warm. Then, realizing she couldn't sit up against a tent wall as she could one in a house, piled several of the pillows behind her back and ate grapes with the same degree of focused attention that Lucien was giving to his figures.

They were delicious, sweet and juicy. In another life, she might have offered to share, but if he was going to ignore her, then she would ignore him.

Or pretend to.

But try as she might, her eyes kept straying toward Lucien, who didn't so much as look up until he finally put his pen down and closed the ledger, piling up the small stack of letters and paper and ledgers neatly in the center of the table before he pushed back his chair. But he still didn't look directly at her. She curled her arms around her knees and watched as he circled the tent, checking the wards and adding...well, she wasn't entirely sure what to them.

Irritation bubbled up.

"If you're spending all this time making wards to keep me in, you're wasting your energy."

He glanced back over his shoulder. "What makes you think these are to keep you in?"

"Oh, I don't know, maybe because you keep looking at me as though I might vanish at any second."

It was his turn to frown. "Do you blame me? You *did* vanish."

"Yes, but I told you I wasn't going to leave again." Something flashed across his face, an emotion she wasn't sure she had seen but rather felt in her gut. Her spine stiffened. "You don't believe me."

Lucien went still and his gaze dropped for a second before he looked back up.

"It's true," she insisted. "You don't believe me."

"Do you blame me? You ran rather than coming to me for help. That tells me you don't trust me, and if you don't trust me or the vows that I made to you, why would you stay with me? How can I know that you won't just run again if things get difficult?"

Her jaw clenched. "I didn't lie to you. I left."

"You left because you didn't trust me," he said flatly, and she didn't need the bond to read the anger that lay beneath those words.

Her gut twisted. She'd never had Lucien doubt her before— or at least not doubt her honesty—but he was a man who lived by the truth, and perhaps she had finally pushed him beyond his limits of tolerance. "What will it take for you to believe me?"

He shook his head, mouth a thin line. "I don't know."

"And where does that leave us?"

This time his gaze didn't shift. "I don't know that either."

"You could use your magic," she said. "Know that I'm telling the truth."

The flinch was almost imperceptible, but she saw it. "I promised you I would never use my magic on you."

"I'm asking you to."

"Is there any point? With these memory magics, I can't be certain of the truth from anyone."

"I'm not asking you to read a memory," she said. "I'm asking you to see the truth of a statement that I'm making now."

He shrugged. "You can believe it now and then make a different choice in the future."

"That's always been true. Why is it bothering you now?"

His mouth flattened again, and he shook his head. "That's not something I'm willing to discuss."

Her throat tightened. Lucien didn't *trust* her. It felt like the ground shifted beneath her. She'd always been able to rely on him, knowing his honor was the bedrock of everything he did, even when it had come to Charl. Honor and duty that he had clung to, regardless of what it had cost him. But maybe she had finally pushed him too far.

She let her arms go, throat tightening with regret, and slid under the covers. "Well, then," she said, "I guess we may as well go to sleep. This is not something we can solve tonight, it seems."

"No," Lucien agreed. And something in his voice made her wish for another blanket, despite the warm air.

CHAPTER 7

Chloe looked tense, even asleep. Curled up on the far side of the pallet, her back to him, clearly determined that they shouldn't touch. Probably just as well. Lucien wasn't sure he trusted himself if she touched him.

Even in the faint light in the tent, she was beautiful. And heartbreaking.

He couldn't let himself touch her if she was going to leave again. He'd learned that when the bond broke, when he thought she was dead, and it had felt like the world was shattering around him. If he was going to lose her for real, then he needed to ward his heart away. Prepare himself.

Not possible if he took her to bed again.

No matter how much he wanted to.

Which made lying next to her, the soft, steady breaths she took seemingly setting the rhythm of his own heartbeat, a peculiar kind of torture.

Even the other sounds of the camp couldn't distract him. The rustle of the tents, the occasional far-off nicker of a horse, and the soft footfalls of the night guards passing by at regular intervals all registered but didn't shift his focus from her.

So close. Close enough to touch the smooth skin he remembered so well. Close enough that the faint floral scent of her perfume floated in the air, taunting him. He gritted his teeth, staring up at the canvas roof.

It had been a long time since he'd traveled with one of the family's caravans—not since he was a youngster, still at the Academe, sharing a tent with his father. No thought of the magic that would change his life.

Then he'd been excited, eager to travel and learn. Now it felt as though the weight of the empire rode his shoulders. He couldn't trust his magic. He couldn't trust his wife. Someone was trying to kill his emperor.

It made him want to...well, he didn't know exactly what, but one of the things was probably to touch Chloe in all the ways he shouldn't. If only to make himself forget for a while. But no, that wasn't fair on either of them.

She shifted, burrowing deeper into her pillow. His breath caught, wondering if she would wake, perhaps, and they could talk some more, see if they could manage not to be so angry with each other. But she didn't rouse.

She'd been angry with him before, of course.

When she'd first returned from Anglion, she had hated him, or at least thought she did. He deserved it at that time, after a fashion. Or at least he'd understood that she was taking the anger that really should lay on Charl's shoulders out on him because he was still there and Charl was not. But now he was angry, too, and she was...well, he wasn't entirely sure how she felt. Guilty, if he had to guess. Annoyed that he had found her so fast. Determined to find Deandra and worried about the fate that awaited her back in the capital.

He wasn't sure on that part either. If they found Deandra and proved Chloe's innocence, that was one thing. But she had still left a mess by running, one that wouldn't be easy to solve. And the worst thing he could do in terms of reducing any scandal that might result would be to remove his protection, which left him in a marriage that he didn't know if he could live with.

Not if she truly had so little faith in him.

He could stomach her not being in love with him, given enough time, but if deep down she didn't believe he would be on her side, that was another matter.

She shifted again, a piece of hair falling over her face. His fingers curled against the urge to brush it back, and he stifled a groan.

This was going to kill him.

Perhaps he should have let her share a tent with Silya.

Though he doubted either woman would have been happy with that choice, and he couldn't afford to annoy Silya. They might need her knowledge of Andalyssian magic before this was over, and she was a witness whom no one could argue was biased in Chloe's favor.

He was just going to have to resign himself to uncomfortable nights. Finding Deandra and getting to the bottom of how the memory charms worked would be worth that price.

If only to restore some sense of sanity to his world.

After three nights on the road with the caravan, it seemed impossibly luxurious to have hot water and an entire bath to herself. The inn where Lucien had secured rooms for the night was nowhere near as well appointed as the Crown and Tree, but that was only to be expected when Fallea was half the size of Jinkara. But the room was clean and pleasant, the bath spacious, and the water hot. That was all she really cared about.

She lathered her hands, stroking the soap over her arms just to enjoy the sensation. It smelled like lemons and mint, a nice change from the constant aromas of horse, oxen, dust, leather, woodsmoke, and sweat that seemed to surround the caravan. She washed and rinsed her hair twice, the water darkening slightly as the soap removed some of the dye. A few more washes and it would be back to normal, unless she decided to dye it again. It shouldn't be necessary. Lucien could use illusions to disguise her if needed.

As the water began to cool, she contemplated warming it again. The heat had eased some of the aches and pains from the long hours of travel, but she suspected that nothing short of a healer or time would erase them completely.

Nor would it erase the tension between her and Lucien that she was trying to avoid by hiding in the bath too long. After three days, she wasn't sure it would ever dissipate.

Her stomach rumbled, and she smiled ruefully. Apparently, her body wanted food more than a longer bath. Something not cooked over an open campfire. The meals provided for the caravan were good but, out of necessity, somewhat repetitive. The inn might not be particularly fancy, but hopefully dinner would at least be different. And it would be nice to not finish a meal smelling of smoke.

Hunger won over the faint hope that she might soak all her worries away. She climbed out of the bath, toweled herself off, combed out her hair, and then took the worst of the water out of it with a charm, knowing the warm night air would take care of the rest.

She contemplated the three cotton dresses she'd bought earlier. Looser styles than Illvyan dresses, which would hopefully make them cooler, too. She hadn't found a habit but had secured sturdy breeches and a few loose tunics that would serve well enough. Some of the women traveling with the caravan wore trousers, and she had no issue with that, but the dresses were more appropriate for dinner. Two were sensible colors, one dark blue and the other a tawny brown, but the third she'd bought not for traveling in the caravan but for evenings like these, when she might need something more elegant for a night staying in a town.

It was a pale green, still simple in style but with deep borders of embroidery around the modest neckline, the cuffs of the sleeves, and the hem that reminded her a little of Andalyssian embroidery, though it was done in only one deeper shade of green rather than House colors like the Andalyssians would use. The pattern was a swirl of curls and flourishes that resembled ocean waves. An interesting choice in a hot country.

Perhaps it was a trick to bring a sense of cool in the heat of the day. She just hoped it was cooler than her woolen gowns.

She crossed to the wall and used the bellpull to summon the maid the innkeeper had mentioned was available. The dress, though simple, wasn't one she could fasten herself, and Lucien— possibly reacting to the awkwardness of the last few nights, when they'd both stuck to the edges of their shared blankets as though the middle of the bed was live coals—had gotten them separate rooms. She wasn't sure if she was relieved or annoyed about that.

Despite the awkwardness, she'd slept better knowing he was close. She wasn't sure he would have said the same. There were shadows under his eyes each morning, but he'd waved her off any time she'd asked if he was well, and she didn't know how to break through the barrier yawning between them.

He was polite and courteous, but there was none of the easy closeness they'd begun to share back in Lumia. He was treating her the way she'd seen him treat ladies of the court he had no interest in. Kind but distant. Holding them at arm's length.

As much as she didn't want to admit it, it stung.

They'd been friends since they'd first met. Happy to spend time with each other. But she didn't know how to return to that friendship without making a decision she wasn't ready to make and telling him she wanted their marriage to be real. Not that she knew whether he would forgive her even if she did. Which left "strained and polite" as the default mode between them.

She steeled herself for another evening of it as the maid helped her dress and pinned her hair up. The girl was just sliding a final pin into the arrangement of braids and curls when there was another knock on the door. One Chloe recognized.

Lucien.

"Come in," she called, trying to sound cheerful. She didn't know what the customs were for married people in this area, but the innkeeper hadn't blinked when Lucien had requested separate rooms.

The maid made one of the neat little bows with one hand over her heart that the Kharenians and Miseneians used in place of curtseys, then slipped past Lucien as he stepped into the room.

His hair was slightly damp, and he'd changed into a clean white shirt paired with a black jacket and trousers. Despite the faint hint of fatigue on his face, the few days in the sun had deepened the golden tones of his skin, making his eyes even greener.

"Good evening," she said. "Am I late for dinner?" They'd settled on meeting at the seventh hour, and she hadn't heard any chimes through the window yet.

"No," Lucien said. "I have an offer for you."

"An offer?" she asked, confused. Was she about to be traded for a herd of goats that might prove less troublesome than a wife like her?

He nodded. "Apparently the theater in town has a performance tonight. I thought perhaps we could go."

"They have a theater here?"

"Well, a building that serves for such things," he said. "I make no guarantees as to its standards, but my understanding from the innkeeper is that they get troupes through here fairly regularly, as well as local performers."

That gained her attention. "And is it a troupe playing tonight?"

He smiled, the expression somewhat feral. "Yes. I thought perhaps it would be worth looking."

"Of course," she agreed quickly, then hesitated, glancing down at her dress.

"I'm sure that will be suitable," he said. He cocked his head, studying her. "Though perhaps you should return to that store in the morning to see if they have an evening gown. This may not be the first such stop, and some of the towns will be larger than this."

Larger meaning the theaters would be more expensive and their patrons better dressed. "That's a good idea. If we have the space." She should have thought of it earlier. Hunting for Deandra's troupe could well mean this wouldn't be the only night they would spend watching whatever passed for entertainment in whatever parts of the empire they ended up traveling to. She had pearl earrings and a necklace Sophie had given her in her bag. They would add some elegance to her outfit. She wasn't yet ready to put Lucien's ring back on her finger, even though she caught the tightening of his jaw at times when he looked at her bare hands.

"I'm sure the wagons will cope with the weight of a few more frocks," Lucien said.

"I'll look in the morning, then."

He smiled and gestured toward the door. "We should go down to dinner if we're to make it to the theater in time."

She took half a step and then froze as a thought struck her. "If it is the troupe Deandra is connected with, she might spot us before we can see her and flee."

Lucien nodded. "Yes, that crossed my mind. As did the fact that I am able to alter our appearances."

He gestured to his face, and she blinked. "The facial illusions? You can do them on both of us?" Without the bond giving her access to Lucien's magic, she had no hope of using it on herself.

"I should be able to. The innkeeper told me the show should only be two hours at most. Not as long as an opera."

She frowned. "Are you sure? We could always send Octarus to check."

"I would rather see for myself," he said. "After all, I can sense the illusions if they're being used as well. And we don't know if there's a water mage working with them. If there is, they may have a sanctii who would notice Octarus."

That made sense, at least. Octarus had been keeping himself out of sight so far. He hadn't offered any complaints about the journey, so she had to assume he was happy. He would have traveled with Rianne. Perhaps he enjoyed it.

She turned to the armoire where her luggage had been stowed, intending to find her jewelry.

"There is one more thing," Lucien said.

"Yes?" Chloe asked, trying to sound calm.

He pulled an envelope from his pocket. "A message."

"Who is that from?" Her stomach tightened again. The emperor? The diplomatic corps? It took her a moment to recognize the crest as Lucien passed it to her.

"Imogene," she said eagerly. "Should I read it now? Do we have time?" Her hands were already opening the envelope.

"As though I could stop you," Lucien said with something approaching a laugh.

That made her stomach relax slightly. "I'll read fast," she promised, unfolding the paper.

There were only two sheets. And it wasn't until she noticed how short the letter was that she stopped to think how Imogene had known where to find her.

She looked up at Lucien. "You sent word that you had found me." She didn't ask how. He may have used a sanctii or the Imperial mail. Jinkara was large enough to have a mail stop, and if he'd marked it "urgent," it would have been hurried to the nearest portal. And then on to Lumia, forthwith.

"I wasn't the only one concerned for your well-being. Of course I sent word," Lucien said. "I'm sure your family will be writing in due course, too."

She went slightly red at that, hoping she hadn't worried them too much. Though if it had been Martius who'd helped find her, then her father would have been able to reassure her mother fairly quickly. But it was too late to change what she'd done.

She turned her attention to Imogene's letter, scanning the contents quickly.

Though the phrasing was circumspect, it was obvious Imogene was delighted that Chloe was safe. She reported that the emperor continued to be well, and that the capital had been relatively peaceful. The last two paragraphs, however, were something of a scolding, a sternly worded suggestion that she accept Lucien's help and not to be stubborn. Which made her smile.

Imogene was one to talk about being stubborn. But then, Chloe wasn't sure Imogene had ever done to Jean-Paul what Chloe had done to Lucien. For one thing, Jean-Paul and Imogene were a love match, not the odd pairing she and Lucien were. No doubt they had butted heads over the years of their marriage, but Imogene had never had cause to flee her husband. Nor had they ever shared a magical bond.

The final postscript was two lines adding that Irina and Valentin seemed to be settling into married life, and Irina was continuing her studies at the temple.

The mention of the temple made Chloe's stomach tighten again. The healers must have been busy in the wake of the attack on the palace. And Valentin, most likely, would also have been working with the Andalyssians to identify the asphenyet. But clearly if there had been any further developments in relation to that, Imogene hadn't seen fit to include them.

Chloe scanned the short letter again. No hint of anything more, no sign of any of the ciphers the diplomatic corps used. She folded the paper up, vaguely frustrated, and slipped it back into the envelope.

"What does she have to say?" Lucien asked. He'd taken a seat in one of the armchairs closest to the fireplace while she read.

"Nothing too important," she replied. "She's happy that you have found me and suggests I—"

"Behave yourself?" Lucien interjected, mouth quirking slightly.

"Very funny. No, she said I should tell you that the emperor is well."

Lucien nodded. "Yes, the dispatch I received said much the same."

"She doesn't, however, say anything about any progress with the Andalyssians or otherwise." She looked at Lucien. "Did yours tell you anything?"

His mouth flattened for a moment. "No," he said. "So, it seems our journey will continue." Outside, the temple bell started to toll, and he glanced toward the window. "Which means, wife, we must eat quickly so I have time to build our disguises before we have to be at the theater."

✦ ✦ ✦

The illusion Lucien had cast on Chloe was beautiful, but he preferred her true face. With her eyes charmed to bright blue and the brown she'd dyed her hair warmed to a honey shade, she looked like a stranger. He had known her face so well for so long that he was somewhat startled every time he glanced at her. Which didn't help the distance between them. His fingers itched with the urge to dissolve the illusion, just so he could reassure himself that it was really her.

At the same time, part of him felt oddly guilty, almost as though he were being unfaithful.

Not that he'd touched her any more than necessary with the illusion or without. Without the bond, he had no way of knowing how she truly felt about their situation.

Perhaps she felt just as strange looking at him. Seeing his

own reflection in one of the mirrors in the foyer of Fallea's theater was also startling. Brown eyes and hair and deeper skin made him blend into the crowd.

Though if Chloe found the effect unsettling, she was good at hiding her discomposure.

But if he couldn't see any traces of her beneath the illusion, no one else would be able to either. That was one thing to cling to—that he was keeping her safe, at least, even though holding both illusions made him feel like he was trying to juggle mist and fog, sorting and sustaining the dual strands of magic.

The strain of it was building but so far still mild. They would be safely back at the inn in a few hours, well before it should grow too difficult to maintain.

At least Silya had decided against accompanying them. He doubted he could hold three illusions at once—not that he'd told the seer they were planning to use the disguises after she declined the invitation—and even if Deandra had no idea who Silya was, she was clearly Andalyssian. Enough of an anomaly here in Miseneia to perhaps make Deandra wary.

Silya had told him to send for her if he found trouble, and he'd left it at that. The heat and the journey seemed to be taking a toll on her. It would be easier on her as they moved farther north and the weather cooled. Better that she rest and be ready to intervene when she was truly needed. Chloe had Octarus, and with a sanctii at their back, they should be able to handle whatever troubles they might encounter for one evening. Not that he expected there to *be* trouble. The likelihood of stumbling over Deandra in Fallea was vanishingly small.

Chloe smiled up at him as they took their seats in the lower stalls. He couldn't remember how long it had been since he'd attended a theater without sitting in a box. Perhaps back to his Academe days, when he and his friends would take cheap seats in venues featuring plays or shows that aristo society wouldn't entirely approve of. But since he had come of age and then discovered he was a Truth Seeker, he'd had to play by the rules.

These days he watched operas and plays seated in one of his family's boxes or those of his friends' equally aristocratic families.

This theater was possibly one of the smallest he had ever been in, but it was well kept. The velvet curtain hanging across the stage looked relatively new, the woodwork gleamed with polish, and the seats were padded cloth, not mere wooden benches.

Chloe looked around curiously and then glanced down at the program. "This would be more useful if either of us read Miseneian." She cocked her head, blue eyes curious. "Or do you?"

He shook his head. "No. I can speak a little, but it's not a language I've had need to learn to read."

Her lips curved. "I guess tonight will just have to be a surprise, then." She kept her voice low, as though she didn't want to draw attention.

They weren't the only ones speaking Illvyan. Towns on the trade routes attracted travelers as well as traders, and Illvyan was the common tongue of the empire.

She fanned herself with the program.

He almost wished he had one, too. The air was thick inside the theater, warmed by the lanterns and the number of people in the audience. Tonight's performance was popular. Fallea was close to the border of Miseneia and Sasskine, and the innkeeper had mentioned part of the performance would be Sasskinian music. Maybe that was the attraction. Which lowered the likelihood of it being Deandra's troupe, but it was still an opportunity he couldn't afford to miss. Stumbling over Deandra accidentally would be the best outcome they could hope for.

The crowd began to hush, the curtains rose, and the play began. It was a Miseneian form—not quite an opera, not quite a play—with some songs between the scenes. He could follow the plot, such as it was, easily enough, it being a typical tale of ill-fated lovers.

He kept his attention on the stage, trying to ignore the fact that if he moved his arm just slightly, he would be touching Chloe's. But there were no signs of magic being used onstage. The effects were well done, but they were nothing he hadn't seen a hundred times before. Eventually he gave up trying to detect magic and settled back to watch. The music was pretty, though he didn't understand the words of the songs. And the short play—fortunately in Illvyan—that followed was even funny in parts.

Chloe's laughter, even disguised by the illusion, did something to ease the pit of tension that seemed to constantly fill his stomach. But by the time the final curtain fell, the weight of the illusions had grown heavier, requiring more of his focus to hold them steady. Not much longer, at least. He could remove them once they were safely back at the inn.

It seemed, though, that the audience was in no hurry to leave. The applause went on and on, and then the crowds lingered, chatting and laughing rather than clearing the aisles. He bit back his rising frustration.

Chloe leaned a little closer. "I didn't notice anything, did you?"

"No. There was no magic being used that I could detect."

She sighed. "I guess we try again in the next town."

"Agreed. I'd still like to try to find out a little more about the troupe. It shouldn't take long to go backstage."

One of her eyebrows lifted. "You're not—" She hesitated, then continued, voice barely audible. "—a marq here. Are you sure they'll let you backstage?"

"Technically, I'm a marq everywhere," he whispered back. "But I don't need to throw the weight of a title around. I've never met actors who don't want to meet their admiring audience. I'm sure we'll manage."

He stood and offered her a hand. She took it but then pulled free again once she was out of her seat, smoothing her skirts, the gesture a handy excuse.

The loss of the brief touch made his stomach twist again, and his jaw tightened.

Chloe walked ahead of him into the foyer. He kept a close watch on the people moving around them, just in case, letting his eyes roam across the entire room, making sure he hadn't missed anything. A notice board next to the box office caught his eye, the colorful papers pinned to it drawing attention. He was too far away to read what they said, but likely they were the flyers used to tell patrons about forthcoming performances. The opera houses and theaters in Lumia used the same methods, even if the posters were more elaborately illustrated and displayed in extravagant gilt frames.

"Wait here. I just want to check something," he said to Chloe.

He wove through the dwindling crowd and was pleased to see his suspicions proved correct. Better still, the lists were written in both Miseneian and Illvyan, so he could make sense of it. It was indeed a list of dates with names of various performers and troupes listed beside them. A few of them he recognized as Miseneian and Kharenian, but many of the theater troupe names were Illvyan, offering no hint of their origins. The box office itself was closed, the curtain across the front of the small booth pulled shut, with no sign of any of the young boys who had been selling tickets earlier.

His mouth twisted. Eager as he was to return to the inn and release the illusions, they were leaving too early in the morning to have a chance to return and ask then. He would have to try backstage after all.

He turned back to the list, committing it to memory. Perhaps one of them might mean something more to Chloe. One thing he'd learned in his years in the judiciary was that most people were not as clever as they thought they were, and it was often small details that revealed their guilt or innocence. Things they would never have dreamed might expose the truth about them.

He turned to beckon her over, but she was talking to a short redheaded woman who he recognized as one of the singers from the performance.

The two of them were laughing, the redhead looking pleased. And if Chloe had charmed her, she might be the easiest way for them to learn more about the troupe and get backstage if they needed to. He hurried back.

Chloe smiled as he joined them. "Luc, this is Sa Maibe. She sang that beautiful song in the middle of tonight's performance, the one we liked so much."

Sa Maibe's smile widened, and her gray-blue eyes looked pleased with the compliment. "Your wife is too kind, but I am glad you enjoyed the performance."

"We did indeed," Lucien agreed. He shot a look at Chloe, but she gave no indication that she needed his assistance in whatever her plan was, so he decided to wait and play along. After all, she was the diplomat, not him.

"I told Sa Maibe about the plan in our town to build a theater," Chloe continued with a smile. "I was asking her if she knows about the business side of how the troupes arrange where they are to perform."

Clever. He smiled encouragingly at Sa Maibe. "That would be useful indeed. Please, Sa Maibe, don't let me interrupt." He broadened his smile. He wasn't a natural charmer like Valentin or Charl, but he knew well enough that women found him attractive and how to use that when he had to. Even with his face disguised, he hoped his smile would still have the desired impact.

Sa Maibe blinked up at him once, dimples flashing in her cheeks, then turned her attention back to Chloe, which he appreciated.

"I was telling your wife that my husband runs our troupe, but unfortunately we only work in Miseneia and Sasskine," she said. "That circuit is large enough to keep us occupied, and as you can see, our particular art form involves the traditions of those two countries, and there is less of an appetite for it elsewhere. From time to time, we have been invited to festivals that are celebrating the width of culture in the empire elsewhere, but those trips are long and can be disruptive to our usual schedules. But there are troupes, of course, that travel far and wide. Some go as far north as Elenia and Partha.

"In fact, I believe Si Hanaan, who owns the theater, had such a group here last year. I was out of town performing in Jinkara, so I did not manage to see them myself, but they had a very good reception. My friends were talking about it for weeks. Apparently, they had an illusioner amongst their number, and the effects they used were second to none." Her smile turned a little lopsided. "We do not use illusions as it is not our tradition, but I have seen performances where they can do amazing things. But of course, the two of you are Illvyan, and surely you have seen performances in the capital and would know all too well what such things are."

"We have been fortunate to see performances in Lumia a time or two," Chloe agreed. "Some of them are simply astonishing. My husband has a preference for opera, and illusions are quite common in those."

Lucien tried to look as though opera was his life. "Yes. It's startling what they can achieve. That kind of troupe sounds like it would be quite the coup for us to obtain for our theater's opening season. Do you recall the name?"

The redhead's forehead wrinkled. "It was something unusual. But I am sorry, no, I do not recall. My brain turns to mush after a performance."

"It must take a lot of energy," Chloe said, sounding sympathetic. "We should not keep you much longer. Perhaps we can ask Si Hanaan. Is he likely to still be here?"

"Oh, yes. He always stays and closes up himself. He will probably be in his office downstairs. I can show you where that is."

He saw a flash of triumph in Chloe's eyes before she offered a demure smile of thanks. "That would be wonderful. If it's permitted for us to be there?"

Sa Maibe nodded. "You are with me. We are performing for a few more nights, so at the moment, the backstage belongs to us, and no one will question me having some guests. Come, it will only take a minute for me to show you where Si Hanaan's office is. It is hardly an inconvenience."

"Well, we are grateful for your kindness," Chloe said.

Sa Maibe nodded. "Come then, I will show you now."

✦ ✦ ✦

"Well, that was informative," Chloe said as they headed back to the inn. It hadn't taken long for Si Hanaan to supply them with the name of the troupe that had made such a splash with its illusions once Chloe and Lucien had repeated their story about friends opening a theater in Illvya.

Her heart had started pounding when Si Hanaan had immediately known the troupe Sa Maibe was referring to. Chloe had been hard-pressed not to leave immediately and hurry to the inn so Lucien could send a message to Lumia.

The Silver Crown Players. She kept turning the name around in her head, wondering if it held any particular significance. Any time she'd seen Aristides in a crown, it had been gold. But regardless of whether the name was meaningful, it was a lead. Something the emperor could focus his resources on finding.

Lucien made a noise of agreement, and she glanced up at him. He was focused on the street ahead of them, eyes scanning the crowd. He'd taken her arm again as soon as they'd set foot outside the theater, and the muscles in his forearm were tense under her hand. Perhaps he thought it safer to wait until they could talk back in the privacy of the inn.

She turned her mind back to the conversation with Si Hanaan. He'd had no news of the troupe for a few months but was still expecting them back later in the year. According to him, they spent most of the summer in the north, retreating south as the weather grew inhospitable. Maybe their silver crown was the snowcapped mountains of the north. Partha wasn't as mountainous as Andalyssia, but its ranges were still known for being dangerous in winter.

There were still enough people moving through the streets in the warm night air to make their progress toward the inn slow. She wanted to tug Lucien forward, but he seemed content with the leisurely pace.

She bit her tongue, trying not to let her excitement override good sense. The journey back to the inn probably only took ten minutes, but it felt like an age.

As they climbed the stairs in the inn, Lucien tugged at his cravat, blowing out a breath.

"Something bothering you?" she asked.

"Just the weather in this country."

The warmth of the day didn't seem to have lessened much at all. The air was heavy and damp feeling despite the heat. Even with the lighter dress, she was close to too hot. Within the confines of the town, there seemed to be less of the breezes that had made the last few nights in the caravan bearable. And Lucien was wearing warmer clothes than her.

"It will be better in the rooms. As long as the cooling charms hold up." She passed through the door he held for her and breathed out a sigh of relief as the cooler air in the inn's foyer registered. She glanced back at Lucien. "Do you want to talk in your room or mine?"

"Mine," he said firmly. "I need to make some notes, and then we can perhaps discuss what needs to happen next."

He was the Truth Seeker, more versed in this kind of thing than she was, so there was no reason she could think of to object. "Your room it is," she said.

She climbed the stairs ahead of him, refusing to look back, wishing she wasn't just that bit too aware of his closeness, the knowledge that they would soon be alone sitting warm and dangerous in the pit of her stomach. Sitting next to him in the dark of the theater had brought back memories of the opera and other nights they'd shared. Part of her had wanted him to shift his hand to take hers, to whisper in her ear about what he'd like to do to her in the dark—not that they could have done anything in the stalls—and she'd devoutly wished for a fan to cool herself at several points until she'd been able to rein in her wayward thoughts.

It took him a few seconds to open the door, the key rattling in the lock. "After you."

She walked into the room and turned to watch him lock the door and lay a hand on the wards to stir them to life.

"I will admit," she said, "it will be nice to see your real face. It's too peculiar to watch you that way."

"Yes," he agreed. "It is odd."

He began to gesture as though to drop the illusion, but as Chloe felt his magic chime around her, he stumbled and then sank to his knees.

CHAPTER 8

"Lucien!"

Chloe rushed back, catching him by the shoulder, bracing herself as he sagged against her, and helping lower him to the floor. Another few seconds and he would have fallen flat on his face. Blood rushed in her ears.

[Octarus, get Silya. Bring her to Lucien's room *now.*] She didn't listen for a response, instead knelt beside Lucien, trying to get him to move closer to the wall so he could lean against it. The illusion had vanished, leaving his far too pale real face.

She pressed a hand to his forehead. His skin was clammy. *Goddess damn it.* If they were still bonded, she would have a better idea what was wrong. Could it be poison? But no, they hadn't eaten or drunk anything at the theater.

"What's wrong?" she asked urgently, moving her fingers to his wrist. His pulse was fast but strong.

He shook his head slowly, squinting as though the lamplight hurt his eyes. "Just feel strange. Help me up."

"Is that a good idea?"

"Better than remaining on the floor."

"Maybe we should wait. You could faint."

"Chloe," he growled, "help me up."

Pale and clammy had turned to pale, clammy, and irritated. Hopefully that was a good sign.

"As long as you agree that it's your fault if you fall down again."

He didn't dignify that with a response.

Between the two of them, they managed to get him on his feet and over to the bed. Lucien flopped down on his back, breathing heavily, his eyes closed. Chloe went to pour a glass of water and was just carrying it back when someone rapped on the door. She pulled it open, and Silya pushed past her.

"What is wrong?"

Chloe waved at the bed, water sloshing out of the glass and over her skirt. She bit back a curse, more worried about Lucien than a damp dress, and put the glass down. "Lucien, he...collapsed when we returned from the theater. Can you help?"

Silya shot her a questioning look. "You are an earth witch, are you not?"

"Yes. But in Anglion I couldn't use my magic. I know plenty about the theory, but I'm out of practice."

She had no idea if seers were trained in healing, but Silya seemed to know about Andalyssian poisons, which suggested they probably were. After all, Andalyssians believed in balance in magic and taught the basics to anyone with talent. What they didn't do, unlike everywhere else in the empire, was let those with strong talents in one of the Four Arts to focus solely on that. At least, not women outside the church or men who had the earth sense so valuable to the miners.

What she really needed was an Illvyan healer. But she couldn't just snap her fingers and produce Valentin, or even turn back time to when she would have trusted her own abilities. Silya would have to do.

The seer shrugged. "It is not my strongest skill. I have had the training given to all who join the seers, and I learned herbcraft from my mother as a girl. It might be better to call for the healer who travels with the caravan."

The caravan was camped at the yards outside town. It would take a good half hour to send one of the guards there to fetch them. She wasn't willing to send Octarus on that errand when she might need him here, and there was no other sanctii in the caravan who he could communicate a message to.

"Let's try this first," she said. "Perhaps between us we can work out what the problem is. Maybe it's just the heat."

Silya looked doubtful, but she nodded and crossed to the bed. Lucien didn't look any better. Eyes closed, skin pale, lying still except for the too-rapid rise and fall of his chest. Chloe bit her lip as Silya closed her fingers around his wrist.

"What happened at the theater?" she asked.

Chloe joined her at the bedside and frowned, trying to think. "Nothing," she said, shaking her head. "We watched the performance, but there was nothing out of the ordinary about it. We talked to one of the performers and the theater owner briefly. And then we came back here."

"He didn't use his magic?"

"He did. He used illusions to disguise us. Does that matter?"

Silya muttered something in Andalyssian that Chloe couldn't quite catch but didn't sound complimentary. "Foolish man. He has worn himself out."

Chloe blinked. *Worn himself out?* It was true that Lucien's talent for truth seeking was so powerful that he was often not good at basic magics, particularly those that belonged to the other Arts. But the facial illusions fell firmly within the Arts of Air. Those came as naturally to him as breathing, even if his truth seeking meant he'd been encouraged into the judiciary as soon as he was old enough instead of being allowed to explore the more creative aspects of his powers. But he'd had no trouble using the magic Violette had taught them at any other time, and he'd worked the wards in the tent each night with no ill effects.

"What do you mean? We were only gone for two hours. That shouldn't bother him. He had no trouble with those illusions in Lumia."

Silya shot her a stern glance, placing Lucien's hand back on his chest. "Foolish child. When he used the magic in Lumia, you still shared your bond."

Chloe's heart skipped. She only just managed to avoid sitting down hard on the bed, her desire not to disturb Lucien keeping her upright somehow. "*What?*"

"There was a reason the healers didn't want you to dissolve that bond," Silya said. "From what I understand, there were...consequences after you broke it. Your husband...well, Domina Francis did not actually call it a relapse from the poison, but he was weakened. A 'setback in his healing' is the term the healers used. If he had not been so insistent in following you and the emperor had not agreed, I doubt Domina Francis would have been happy to let him leave the city."

"It hit him that hard?" Chloe's mouth dropped open, and she took a half step forward, halting when her knees hit the mattress. He was sick again? He'd shown no signs of being unwell in the last few days. Tired, yes, like the rest of them at the end of each day, but nothing like this. Then again, he hadn't been using his magic much. And clearly hadn't wanted to tell her what had happened back in Lumia.

Idiot man. She scowled down at him. He still had his eyes closed and, so far, hadn't reacted to Silya giving away his secret. Had he actually passed out, or was he merely pretending?

Idiot or not, if he was passed out, she wasn't going to shake him awake just yet. Better to leave him alone and focus on getting the truth out of Silya.

She turned back to the seer. "How sick was he?"

Silya shrugged. "I do not know the exact details. Your domina only asked me to keep an eye on him if he used his magic. Told me what to look for." She frowned. "If the two of you had told me he was planning to use the illusion magic, then I would have advised against it."

Chloe grimaced. That was probably exactly why Lucien hadn't told said anything. To either of them.

On the bed, Lucien muttered something under his breath.

"Do you have something to add, husband?" Chloe asked, frustration spiking the words.

"I'm fine," he said more audibly.

"That is obviously not true," she snapped back.

For a brief moment, his eyes opened, anger flashing before he closed them again.

"Perhaps you can argue later," Silya said. "For now, let us make sure he has not done any more damage."

Damage? What kind of damage? "From holding two illusions for a few hours? Is that possible?"

Silya just shrugged.

Chloe bit her lip. "All right. What do you need?"

"To start with, some time alone with him," Silya said. "And I think it would be a good idea if you sent for the healer. Perhaps you can go downstairs and ask the corporal to do so."

"If you think that's best."

"No," Lucien said in a far louder voice.

"What do you mean, 'no'?" Chloe asked. "You are unwell. You need the attention of a healer."

"If you send the corporal, then he'll inform the lieutenant, who will inform his commanding officer in his reports."

"Oh," she said, understanding. He didn't want this news getting back to the emperor. "You think Aristides would recall you?"

"Maybe." He blew out a breath as though speaking was an effort.

"Maybe he *should* recall you. If you're unwell, then this mission is madness."

"No." He shook his head. "I said I would find you, and now I'm going with you."

Idiot stubborn *man.* But arguing with him clearly wasn't going to help. They needed him to rest, not fight them.

She spread her hands and shrugged, looking at Silya. "Why

don't you examine him first and we'll see what you think? After that we can work out if we need more help."

Lucien made a protesting noise.

"I don't care," she said. "If you need a healer, you're getting a healer."

She bit her lip, considering. He would be furious if they ended up having to return to the city. Likely the innkeeper would know of a local healer they could call? But then she would have to explain what had happened. Besides which, any healer was likely to be a strong earth witch and possibly allied to the temple. They might report back through their own networks.

She didn't care. Deandra could wait.

She forced down the familiar sense of panic rising within her. She hadn't imagined breaking the bond would impact his health. He'd been using his magic easily in Lumia. Guilt twined with the panic, drying her mouth.

She swallowed. "You examine him, and I'll consider our options," she said to Silya. Maybe she could get word to the caravan's healer without using the guards? Only three of them had accompanied them into Fallea. They had a room farther down the hall, taking turns keeping watch outside. They hadn't insisted on going with them to the theater, so that hopefully meant whatever watch they were keeping was more relaxed than it would be in Lumia.

"Thirsty," Lucien muttered.

She looked at Silya. "Should he drink anything?"

Silya shrugged. "Do you feel as though you may throw up, Lord Castaigne?"

He shook his head. "No, just weak, hot."

Silya looked at Chloe. "I do not think it will hurt."

Chloe reached for the water she'd poured earlier, then hesitated before picking up her skirts so she could kneel on the bed beside him and lift his head. He didn't try to sit up, and panic surged again, memories of him ill in the temple in Lumia flooding through her.

"Water," she said. "Just take a few sips." She rested the glass against his lips, and he swallowed a mouthful or two.

"Mali," he said. "Send Octarus to her. She can send a healer discreetly. She won't panic. She's dealt with sanctii before."

Interesting. She had introduced Mali to Octarus just in case she had to summon the sanctii at some point.

Behind her, Silya coughed gently, and Chloe remembered that she was meant to be letting the seer examine Lucien. She climbed off the bed, managing not to spill the water, and let Silya do her work.

After a few minutes, the seer straightened and said, "I do not think he has done any damage, but he definitely feels drained. He needs to be more cautious in using his magic. Preferably not use it at all for a few days. And I would be happier if we were staying in town another day for him to rest." She glanced down at Lucien, who was now propped up against some pillows, his eyes open. "But I cannot imagine you are going to allow that, Lord Castaigne."

Lucien shook his head. "No."

Silya shrugged and turned back to Chloe. "Of course, the best thing that might help him would be if the two of you formed a new bond."

Chloe's eyes widened. Had she heard that correctly? Silya had been appalled by their bond when they'd first formed it in Andalyssia, yet now she was suggesting they should do it again? Exactly how bad was Lucien's health? "Do you truly think it would help?"

"Yes." Silya didn't look as though it was news she was happy to deliver.

Lucien's eyes went to the seer and then squeezed closed again as his jaw clenched.

Not an idea he liked either, then.

A shiver crawled down her spine. He didn't want to be bonded to her. What did that mean? That he wanted nothing more to do with her? But he'd followed her to Jinkara. Found her. Surely that meant he still cared in some fashion?

"If it would help—"

"That is also a no," Lucien said, his voice firm though his eyes remained shut.

Chloe flinched at his tone.

Silya made a humming sound of disapproval. "Regardless of what either of you feels about the idea, it is clear that your strength was supporting him, Lady Castaigne. Your domina had no objection to what you had done, so it must have been useful. You should not rule it out without considering carefully."

Chloe couldn't think of a response, mind whirling. Silya wouldn't have made the suggestion if she didn't genuinely think it would help. Andalyssians didn't use bonds in the same way as Illvyans. Chloe wasn't even sure they used them in any real fashion. Andalyssians believed magic should be balanced. In harmony with the goddess's intentions. Bonds could give a mage access to magic that they didn't usually have. She'd been able to use a little of Lucien's truth seeking, despite the fact that she lacked any real talent for illusion. And he'd been able to work earth magic he'd never managed before. They'd both been stronger.

But that, to Andalyssian eyes, meant they were out of balance. Reaching for things the goddess had never granted them in the first place. At least she thought that was the basis of Silya's objection.

Of course, there'd been the other part where she and Lucien, not married at the time, had spent the night together in a cave after a storm and had been discovered naked under a pile of clothes. They'd been trying to keep warm, not do anything scandalous, but Silya had taken advantage of the situation to throw a wrench in the Andalyssian mission and insist the two of them marry.

That part had been more politics than faith, most likely. And yes, maybe Silya was still playing some political angle. But she was also supposedly on their side for this mission. If she was suggesting it, perhaps it was truly what would be best for Lucien.

Not for the first time, she wished that she had never broken the bond. If only in that moment so she could tell whether Silya was sincere in her advice.

Clearly Lucien needed something. And Chloe owed him that much, didn't she? She had abandoned him on their wedding day. Exposed him to gossip and scandal. Possibly harmed him by taking away the healing access that her magic had been giving him.

And yet...what would it mean to be bonded to him again? It would give him power, yes, but they could feel each other's emotions through the bond if they didn't guard against it. And while the first time she'd only formed the bond to save their lives, she'd had no doubts that Lucien cared for her. And this time, well, if he didn't trust her...feeling that directly might be torture. Still, she needed him strong. Well. For that, she would endure his dislike if she had to.

"Maybe we should consider it. If it would help, then it might be the wisest course."

His eyes opened. "No," he repeated flatly.

"Why not?" she asked, indignation suddenly pushing past her hesitation.

"You made it clear you didn't want to be bonded to me. You broke the bond we had. You *left*."

"I didn't want you to be able to follow me," she said. "That was the only reason. It wasn't—"

She stopped before she could finish the sentence when Lucien's expression darkened, and she realized they were heading back into the same argument they'd had before. Not one she wanted to have in front of Silya.

"Fine. We will discuss this after you've rested."

He was glaring at her now, eyes as green as a cat's. She narrowed hers in return. Let him be angry. He was also as weak as a kitten, so it wasn't as though he could do much more than glare.

She turned her attention to Silya. "There is a method our healers use, where they share energy with a patient to boost their healing. Is that something you can do?" She knew the theory herself, and the healers had taught her a form of it when Lucien had been recuperating. But that had been utilizing the bond. She wasn't entirely sure she trusted herself to do without it. "I know the basics, so I can try if you don't."

Silya gestured apologetically. "I am afraid healing magic was never my preference. I know herbcraft, but that is different. If you know more than that, I think it would be wiser if you attempted it. I would not want to risk making things worse. He needs rest most of all. As much sleep as possible."

There was no clock on the wall in the small room, but in the distance, the bells began to chime the tenth hour. The caravan would be moving off early. They tended to travel with the sun. If Lucien was to get a decent night's sleep, they needed to stop talking and let him rest.

"Very well," Chloe said. "I'll try. Then we'll see if he improves. If he doesn't feel better, I'll call for you again, or we'll send for the healer."

"Good," Silya said. "I do have some remedies with me. One of them is...well, not a stimulant, but something he can try in the morning if he is still weakened."

A stimulant didn't sound like what was needed, rather something to put the stubborn man to sleep. But she could question Silya more about what exactly she had in mind in the morning before she agreed to Lucien taking it. As long as Silya's wasn't entirely made from plants native to Andalyssia, Chloe would be able to judge for herself what it might do. She had an extensive knowledge of herbs after years of owning her store in Kingswell. Well, at least the common herbs used by earth witches to the extent allowed in Anglion. It was more the magical side of healing that she was less versed in, having not been able to touch her power in that fashion in her exile. It had been a long time since her classes at the Academe. The healers had taught her a little about sharing power through the bond during Lucien's recovery, but that was very different to doing it without one.

But it seemed tonight, she was going to have to try, experience or not.

She drew a breath, pushing away the tremor of nerves in her stomach. "Thank you, Sejerin. I will call for you if I need you again."

Silya nodded and left, leaving Chloe staring down at Lucien, wondering if she was going to have to talk him into accepting any help from her at all.

"Very well, husband. It seems tonight you get me playing valet. Let's get you undressed and under the covers so you can sleep."

He opened one eye. "Why do I need to get undressed?"

"Well, for one thing, sleeping in your boots will be uncomfortable, and for another thing, it'll be hot."

One side of his mouth quirked. "You just want to get me out of my clothes."

"If I wanted to get you out of your clothes," she retorted, "I would tell you so. Not that it would do me much good. I don't mean to cast aspersions on your manliness, but at the moment, I doubt you would be able to do much even if I wanted you to."

He grunted softly. Hardly a denial.

She put her hands on her hips. "Truthfully now, how bad is it?"

His other eye opened. "You want the truth?"

"I wouldn't ask for it if I didn't."

Lucien pushed up on the pillows, and she had to stop herself from reaching out to help him, certain he wouldn't appreciate her trying to assist.

Sure enough, he waved her off with an annoyed flap of his hand. "Don't fuss. I'm all right."

"Clearly that isn't true. How long has this been happening?"

"Honestly, I'm not entirely sure. This is the first time I've tried to do a sustained amount of magic since you...."

"Since I broke the bond."

His mouth flattened. "Yes."

"But wait, surely you needed to use your truth seeking after the attack at the palace?" she asked, puzzled.

"I did," he said. "But truth seeking doesn't take effort for me. It's not like building and holding an illusion. It's just something I can do."

"But it's still magic." Certainly there were simpler magics that didn't take much effort. Lighting an earthlight, triggering a charm. Though talking to Octarus wasn't hard, and that was a form of water magic. So perhaps it made sense that Lucien's strongest ability was, to him, like breathing.

"Yes. But it's...just easy. I don't know why."

She didn't either. "So you weren't having any issues with your health in Lumia?"

He looked away.

"The truth, Lucien."

"There may have been a bad day or two when you first broke the bond. Imogene noticed. She told Domina Francis. The healers looked me over. They said I would be fine, that I just needed to watch my energy."

"And instead you came chasing halfway across the country after me?"

"I needed to know you were alive. When the bond broke—" He clamped his jaw shut, eyes closing again. Then he huffed a breath. "Well, let's just say, I didn't take it well when I thought you were dead. I won't bore you with the details. Imogene finally talked some sense into me. She pointed out that Octarus was nowhere to be found, and he hadn't gone on a rampage like he had after Rianne died, so you were most likely fine. She said I needed to focus on doing my job. Which I did. Until she noticed I wasn't myself and ratted me out to the healers. That's when I decided to come find you. I thought if I saw for myself, that might help matters." His eyes opened again, the green somehow chilled. "That and the emperor insisting that he wanted Deandra found. I figured that was probably where you'd gone when we couldn't find any word of you immediately. I thought you might have run back to Anglion."

Another thing she hadn't considered, that he might have thought she would flee the empire. Again. "There would be little point in doing that. Sophie would most likely just send me home again once she got wind of me being there. It's not as though it's impossible for the emperor to send people after me there now anyway. No, I left to follow Deandra."

"And what was your plan if the emperor *did* send people after you?"

She shrugged. "Try to get lost somewhere in the empire, I suppose, until I could find a way to prove my innocence."

"Running away has never enhanced anyone's reputation."

"An interesting perspective coming from the man who advised me to run in the first place."

"I advised you to leave town for a time," he said. "I never meant for you to flee the country." He laughed then, the sound slightly hollow. "It seems we need to work on our communication."

"Well, that would be easier if you let me reform the bond," she said, trying to entice him. Despite his denials, he was too pale, and she didn't like the way his voice sounded. Almost as though he was working too hard to sound normal.

He looked down. "I don't think it's a good idea."

"Why not?"

"Because I have to learn to live without it eventually. When you leave."

Her breath caught. "Is that what you want? A divorce?"

He groaned and flopped back on the bed. "Chloe, I don't want to talk about this just now. You heard Silya. I need to rest."

"And if I believed you *would* rest, I would leave this alone. But you have a simple solution, one that could help you. We did it once before, and we could do it again. You did it partially to save me back then, so why won't you let me help you now?"

"Because there's no need. I will be fine."

If he hadn't been flat on his back in the bed, she would have been tempted to throw something at him.

Idiot stubborn stupid *man.*

Then a thought struck her. "If Domina Francis was worried about you, she wouldn't have let you leave the city unprepared. She must have known you would have to use your magic at some point. Did she give you something? In case this happened?"

He grimaced.

"Truth," she said. "Did she send you with anything? Don't be an idiot. I can get Silya back here. I'm sure she has a bag full of strange Andalyssian remedies. Wouldn't you rather take something prepared by Domina Francis?"

He grimaced again. "If you put it that way, yes."

"I take it that she did give you something, then? Where is it?"

"In my trunk. The smaller one. There's a small bag with some pouches of pills. One with a blue cord. I was meant to take that if I had another spell like this."

CHAPTER 9

"*Another?*" Chloe said, trying not to sputter. "You said it wasn't bad in Lumia." She swept a hand at him in exasperation. "This is bad, Lucien."

"I told you the first day or so was bad," he retorted. "Do you want to do a blow-by-blow description, or do you want to get me my damn medicine?"

She backed away from the bed, shooting him a scowl. "What I really want to do right now is possibly throttle you for being an idiot."

"Well, that feeling might be mutual," he growled.

She stopped midstep. "I left to follow Deandra. I didn't have a choice."

His fingers strayed to the bridge of his nose and pressed hard. "There's always a choice, Chloe. You chose not to trust me to help you."

That stopped her in her tracks. There was an unmistakable tone of hurt underneath his words. One that required none of his power for her to recognize. Or to feel the answering sting of guilt and shame all over again.

"I was panicked. Not thinking straight. But I cannot change my choice now. I can only say, once again, that it wasn't you I was running from. And none of that changes the fact that you chose not to tell me that you'd been unwell. "

"I wasn't sure you'd care."

"What? I—"

He winced and waved her off. "Can we have this fight later, please? Just get the goddess-damned pills."

Reluctantly, she crossed the room. Sure enough, when she opened his trunk, a leather pouch stamped with the quartered circle of the goddess lay on the top of the neatly piled clothes. Almost as though he'd thought he might need it.

She gritted her teeth against a renewed flash of irritation as she unwound the braided ocher cord holding the pouch closed. There were four smaller pouches inside but only one tied with a blue cord. She opened it and peered at the contents. Pills. Just as he'd said.

She carried the pouch back to the bed, stopping only to retrieve the water glass. "Here."

He took the pills and gulped them down, then lay back down. He still looked dreadful, so hopefully whatever was in the pills would work fast.

"Will you at least let me try sharing some energy with you?"

One of his eyebrows lifted. "You can do that without the bond?"

She huffed in exasperation. "Why do you always forget that I'm an earth witch? I trained at the Academe just like you." The fact that she was more familiar with theory than practice was one she was going to ignore. And hope he wouldn't remember.

He grunted softly and waved a hand in a vaguely apologetic gesture. "Sorry. It's just with Octarus and everything else going on, your water magic has been more top of mind."

"That may be. But you're forgetting the part where I helped look after you while you were recovering."

"Yes, but we had a bond then."

"We could have a bond again if you weren't being stubborn," she pointed out.

He shook his head. "No."

She sighed. "It would help you."

"Not in the long run."

"But—"

"No. It's not up for discussion."

"All right. But don't cut off your nose to spite your face. We can do this without a bond."

"Good. Go on, then."

Right. How exactly was she supposed to do this without a bond?

She tried to remember her days in the Academe, listening to Madame Simsa and her other teachers talk about earth magic, skimming through the memories till she found the one she wanted. She could almost hear Venable Levoit's voice deep down in one of the still rooms talking about energy sharing. For a moment, the memory and the sense of being back there were so strong that it brought a wave of homesickness she hadn't expected. The Academe was more than just a school for her—it was part of what she thought of as home. She'd spent hours and days there with her father way before she was old enough to attend the school as a student.

"Are you all right?" Lucien asked.

She started, realizing she had been quiet too long. Green eyes caught hers, and she nodded. "Everything's fine. Just lie back and close your eyes."

"I'm not sure that's a good idea. A few days ago you threatened to stab me. "

"I was angry. Besides, I don't stab sick people."

He chuckled softly. "I guess I have to take your word for that."

"Yes you will." She felt as though she was balanced on a very thin thread. If he could trust her to do this much, then maybe it would be a first, tiny step to repairing what she'd broken between them. Rebuilding their friendship. She'd start with that before either of them had to grapple with the thornier issues of their future. "Close your eyes."

He shot her a last amused look, then obeyed, shifting slightly on the pillow. He was trying to look relaxed, but she could tell he wasn't.

She sat gingerly on the edge of the mattress, saw his jaw tighten a bit as he registered her weight beside him. Waiting for him to relax again, she then placed her right hand on his chest, the gesture instinctive. She'd made the same one countless times a day when he'd been sick in the temple, asleep and insensible to what was going on around him, unable to resist the urge to check that his heart was still beating.

It felt stronger now than it had back then, steady and reassuring, but she still waited, sinking into the rhythm of it, making sure it didn't falter, before she sent her magic down seeking a ley line. There wasn't one close by that she could find, just the vague echoes of something in the distance, but that was enough to latch on to and give her power a small boost.

She listened for the magic, hearing the familiar hum of hers around her. The chime of Lucien's power was so faint she could barely hear it, and she bit her lip. Some people showed no sign of magic unless they were using it, but his truth seeking was so strong that there was almost on echo of it around him, unless he consciously worked to hide it. Through the bond, it had been even more obvious, and the lack shook her more than she was expecting. At least he couldn't feel her reaction.

She drew in a calming breath and tried to focus simply on each heartbeat and the energy flowing through him, threading her own energy around his, bolstering it, to convince his body that everything was normal.

Lucien sighed softly, and something in his face relaxed. "That feels nice."

"Just rest," she replied softly. She sent another wave of energy through him and then withdrew her hand. "Just rest." Her hand trembled slightly, relief that she'd been able to help flooding her, and she curled it closed.

He opened his eyes. The green seemed brighter now, something lurking in their depths that made her skin tingle. "If you want me to rest, perhaps you shouldn't have just given me an energy boost."

"Not enough to keep you awake. Just enough to help you get back to where you were. We have to travel on in the morning." She started to slide toward the edge of the mattress.

"You need sleep, too."

"I'll go back to my room soon."

The green deepened slightly, sparking humor. "I thought you were worried about me. What if something happens in the middle of the night? You won't be here to know."

"So you don't want me to help you, but you want me to sleep with you?"

"Just sleep. I have been sleeping better these past few nights," he said almost resentfully.

She wasn't sure it was a good idea, but him admitting a vulnerability to her seemed like another tiny mend. "Very well. I'll stay." She hesitated. "I need to go back to my room and get my nightgown."

"Can't you sleep in your chemise?"

"I don't have that many sets of underthings with me. The nightgown will keep them fresher if we're back on the road tomorrow." She had sent some clothes down to be laundered by the inn, and they'd promised they would be ready first thing. She'd intended to rinse the ones she was wearing out before she went to sleep. Even with a cooling charm in her room, they would dry by morning.

"You could sleep without anything on."

"I don't think that's a good idea. Do you?"

"I'm sure you'd be perfectly safe. As you pointed out, I'm in no fit state to do anything."

"That, as *you* pointed out, was before you let me lend you

some energy."

He snorted. "I'm not sure it's enough for that." He patted the bed beside him, sliding over to the far side. "Just lie down. You'll be fine."

"I'll go get my nightgown, and then I'll come help you undress."

He blew out a dissatisfied breath. "Well, I guess if that's the best offer I'm going to get, I will take it."

"But you have to promise to sleep."

He touched his fingers briefly to his head and his heart. "I swear. I will try to sleep."

"Be sure that you do."

She pushed off the bed and padded across the room, slipping out the door, still not sure it was a good idea to agree to what he'd asked.

It was only a few steps down the corridor to her own door, but at the sound of her key in her lock, Silya's door opposite hers opened, and the seer poked her head out. "How is he?"

"Better," Chloe said. "He let me share some energy with him, and it seems to have helped a little. It's a start."

Silya raised an eyebrow. "And you are going to return to your own room?"

Chloe sighed. Why was everyone so terribly interested in her sleeping arrangements? "No, I'll watch over him," she said. "I'm just getting some things."

Silya nodded. "Good. A husband should be tended by his wife."

Chloe resisted the urge to roll her eyes. "I'm looking after him as best I can. You saw that I offered the bond, but he said no."

Silya snorted. "You hurt him when you left. He is wary."

"What does that mean?"

Silya tipped her head toward Lucien's door. "I think that is a question better asked of your husband," she said. "Good night, Lady Castaigne. Send your sanctii if there is any trouble during the night. Otherwise, I will see you at breakfast." She shut the door, firmly leaving Chloe staring, standing alone in the corridor, cursing softly under her breath.

Husbands were complicated, marriages were complicated, and dealing with Andalyssian seers was complicated as well. She wanted a good night's sleep but wasn't sure she would get it in Lucien's bed. No, she was more likely to lie awake, watching his chest rise and fall, as she'd done so many nights at Sanct de Sangre when he was recovering.

Oh well, at least that might give her more time to think of other things, like planning for Deandra or the troupe.

✧ ✧ ✧

She moved swiftly about her room, gathering her nightgown and other bits and pieces. She removed the pearls she'd worn to the theater and then the chain with Lucien's ring, too. For a moment she considered calling for a maid to help her change, but she didn't have a robe, and being caught in the hallway in just a nightgown would scandalize the locals. Instead, she carried the nightdress back to Lucien's room. As she entered, she caught him sitting up, bending forward and reaching for his booted foot.

She dumped her nightgown on the nearest chair. "You're supposed to be resting. Let me help you with that."

"I am not made of glass. I'll be fine removing my own footwear."

"Just let me help you."

He rolled his eyes. "I feel there is some irony in you insisting that you're allowed to help me when you are still resisting the fact that I came to help you."

"You resisted my help, too," she pointed out. "You refused the bond."

Something close to sadness flickered across his expression. "That's different."

"Why?" she asked.

"I've already said what I'm willing to say on that subject for tonight."

"You know, you think you're not like your mother, but you're just as stubborn as she is."

He scowled. "Let's add my mother to the things I don't want to talk about tonight." He stretched out a booted foot. "Here. The faster we do this, the faster we can both rest."

Had he even told his mother that he was unwell? Part of her selfishly hoped not. Jacquelin de Roche had enough reasons to be irritated with her without adding Lucien's health back to the list. She closed her hands around the ankle of the boot, the soft leather warm to her touch.

"Why is you refusing the bond different?" she asked as she worked his boot free. "It would help you."

Lucien flopped back on the bed, an arm covering his face. "The bond is too close. I don't want to share that again. Not when—"

She looked up from where she was working his second boot off his foot. "What?"

"Do you really want me to say it?"

For the second, or maybe even third, time that night, her heart felt as though it might stop. Did he want a divorce now?

"I—" she started to say, then snapped her teeth shut when she couldn't figure out what came after that.

Lucien was watching her, green eyes wary.

"Well?" he asked.

Her wits seemed to have evaporated. "I—" she said again. Her mind raced, thinking back to the night of their second wedding. Only a few days past two weeks ago. Back then, she thought she would still walk away from him eventually, but she'd been looking forward to enjoying him in the meantime. Now...after the panic she'd had when he'd collapsed, and the way the thought of his rejection stung, well, she didn't really know what her feelings were. Other than confused.

She rubbed her hand briefly on her collarbone. "It's been a long day," she said finally. "Perhaps we should just sleep."

His expression turned a little disappointed, but then he nodded briskly. "Very well." He gestured to his feet. "I'm sure I can take it from here. You can get changed." He nodded toward the far end of the room. "Don't worry, I won't watch."

Chloe retreated to the other end of the room, given there was really no other option but to either continue a conversation she wasn't ready for or get ready for bed.

Moving back to where she'd left the pile of nightclothes, she reached behind her to unfasten her dress. *Goddess damn it.* She needed help to unbutton the dress. She made a frustrated noise and turned back to find Lucien watching her.

"You said you wouldn't look," she said accusingly.

He smirked. "You made a sound. I looked up to see whether everything was all right."

He seemed a little too pleased with himself for her to believe him entirely.

She made an irritated gesture at the back of her dress. "I need help to get out of this thing. I should call for a maid."

"I may be a little under the weather, but I haven't forgotten how to unbutton a gown. Come over here and I can do it for you."

She stiffened. That seemed like a *terrible* idea.

At her hesitation, he said, "By the time you call for a maid, she arrives, and she undresses you, we'll have wasted another quarter of an hour or so. Time we could both be sleeping."

As if to emphasize his point, from outside the window came the chime of the local temple tower. It was growing late, and they needed to be back at the caravan just after dawn. That wasn't enough sleep for Lucien. It wasn't enough sleep for anyone, even if they were in full health. Back in Illvya, the aristos kept late hours, but most of them made up for it by also sleeping their mornings away. That wasn't an option if the caravan was to stay on schedule.

With a huff of breath, she crossed back over to the bed and turned, presenting her back.

He thumped the mattress a few times. "Sit. Unless you want me to stand."

He had her there. She couldn't risk him fainting.

Gritting her teeth, she sat and twisted so he could get to the buttons. "If you just do the first few, I'm sure I can manage the rest."

He snorted. "Be quiet."

His fingers moved down her spine, brushing the skin under the thin cotton chemise. The Miseneian gown required fewer layers than her Illvyan dresses. A shiver ran through her as the heat from his hand spread across her skin. Her nipples peaked, and she crossed her arms over her chest, pretending to catch the bodice of the gown to hide the reaction.

"There," Lucien said. "That's the last of them."

"Thank you," she muttered. "Now get into bed. You need to sleep."

"Go get changed. I'm not watching. My eyes are firmly closed."

A glance over her shoulder revealed that he had his eyes screwed up exaggeratedly tight, which made her smile reluctantly.

"Good," she said. "Keep them that way." At least until she managed to convince her body to stop reacting to the man. If he no longer wanted her, then it was going to have to just get used to doing without him.

"Well, I will," he said, "but that will slow down my own efforts at undressing."

"You can wait. Once I'm in my nightgown, I'll lie down in the bed and close my eyes and not watch you. Problem solved."

His chuckle floated in her ears as she scurried across the room to change.

CHAPTER 10

"Will you be wanting your horse, my lord?" Corporal Chartres asked, joining Lucien by the wagon early the next morning.

Lucien hesitated, fussing with the feedbag of the horse he'd been checking over. He didn't particularly want to travel in the wagon with Chloe and Silya fussing over him all morning, but riding was more taxing, and he wasn't sure that would be a good idea. Despite Domina Francis's pills and Chloe's assistance the night before, he still felt as though he could use about three more nights of sleep. He'd started checking over the horses more to give himself an activity that might help shake some of the lethargy from his limbs than any concern that Corporal Chartres wouldn't have had them harnessed in perfect fashion.

"Excuse me, Corporal." Chloe's voice came from behind him. "I just need a word with Lord Castaigne."

Corporal Chartres bobbed his head obediently. "I'll be back in a minute, my lord."

Lucien turned to face his wife. She wore a blue cotton frock she'd purchased the previous day, but her expression didn't match the airiness of the fabric. Instead, it suggested he was in some sort of trouble.

"Yes?" he said somewhat warily, checking behind him to

make sure Chartres was out of earshot. This seemed like it might turn into the kind of conversation that would be better for his men not to witness.

As he turned back, she leaned up on tiptoe and whispered, "You are not getting on a horse this morning. You need to rest. You will be joining us in the wagon." She finished this with a brief brush of her lips against his cheek, which he figured was more to convince any onlookers that they were merely having a friendly conversation between husband and wife and not the actual disagreement it was about to turn into.

"I am perfectly fine," he replied softly.

"You could barely keep your eyes open for the entire journey from the town back here to camp. It will hardly make a good impression if you fall from your horse."

"I'm not going to fall off my horse."

"You have no way of knowing that." Her eyes flashed with irritation, turning a darker shade of brown, like strong coffee. Which he could use.

"Can you not be sensible for once, after everything that happened last night?" she continued. "Or would that be too much of a blow to your male pride?"

She was right. But for some reason he was in the mood to argue, fatigue and frustration with the whole situation sharpening his temper. He'd slept better than the previous nights, mostly because he'd been too exhausted to do otherwise, but he still felt as though he hadn't. And despite his best intentions, he'd woken with her in his arms. Until her eyes had flown open, and she'd wriggled away from him as though she'd found a snake in her arms rather than her husband.

"It's my decision in the end." Beside him, the horse shook his head as though in agreement, snorting softly. Lucien patted his neck.

Chloe, however, did not agree. "No, it's not."

"What makes you so sure?"

"Because, as you pointed out last night, we did actually make vows, and I believe one of mine was something about tending to your well-being. I'm not going to let you faint, fall from your horse, and bang your stupid head on a rock in the desert. For one thing, I really don't want to have to explain to your mother why her favorite child and the head of the family is going to spend the rest of his years under the care of the goddess's healers with his brain addled."

Goddess *forbid*. Still, if he did fall from his horse and bang his head, this whole mess would be someone else's problem. Not entirely an unappealing concept.

"I can see you've thought this through thoroughly."

She stood on tiptoes and leaned into his ear again. "Yes, and if you refuse me, I will tell Lieutenant Envier exactly what happened last night."

He stiffened, and Chloe snorted. "At least that's made some impression on your stubbornness. Do you think the lieutenant will want you riding if he knows the current state of your health?"

Lucien grimaced. It would probably be all he could do to stop the lieutenant from suggesting they turn around and head straight back to Lumia if he admitted he was ill. "You win. I'll join you in the wagon."

The smile she gave him was triumphant. And pierced his heart. She was beautiful, his wife, and yet each day it felt like she was drifting further out of his reach. Before the attack at the palace, he thought that maybe he would be able to convince her that they could make it work together. But since she had so carelessly destroyed the bond, he wasn't so sure, or at least not so sure that he could bear to put in the effort and then lose her at the end of it anyway.

He gestured toward the wagon. "You go ahead. I need to finish talking to Corporal Chartres."

"Don't take too long," Chloe said, smiling smugly. "I believe Silya has a tea prepared for you."

Just what he needed. Some disgusting healer's tea.

The thought must have shown on his face, as Chloe lifted an eyebrow. "I would take the tea, my lord. I spoke to the caravan's healer just now, and the best they would be able to offer you would be something that would knock you flat for at least a day. Until we reach the next town and I can stock up on some things to make a tonic that I think might assist you, you'll do what Silya says and rest. If you're feeling better this afternoon, perhaps we'll ride for an hour. At most. Do we have an agreement?" She glanced meaningfully toward the front of the wagon, where he could now see the corporal and the lieutenant discussing something, their expressions businesslike.

In other words, conveniently close if she wanted to make good on her threat to inform on him.

He set his teeth, not sure if he was annoyed or impressed at how neatly she'd flanked him. Or perhaps just a little happy that she seemed to be genuinely worried about his health. "We do."

By the end of the day, Lucien was glad that Chloe had convinced him not to ride. It had been unusually hot, the sun boiling down, warming the inside of the wagon despite the cooling charms. Being on horseback under such heat would be an exercise in endurance, not an enjoyable experience.

Silya had dosed him with some sort of tea that he had to admit had helped his lingering fatigue. But even with that boost, he wasn't entirely sure quite how much of the day he had dozed on and off, lulled to sleep by the rocking rhythm of the wagon. Chloe and Silya had talked softly, or napped a few times themselves, and at one point, Chloe had produced a book from somewhere in her bags, tucked her feet up on the bench beside Silya, and read.

By the time they reached the campsite, even though he had

slept part of the day, he was more tired than he liked to admit, eager for their evening meal and then going to sleep as early as he could manage it. Which might depend on how much paper-work was waiting for him now that the caravan would have picked up mail in Fallea.

Chloe and Silya were both somewhat flushed and moving stiffly as they climbed down from the wagon. He resisted the urge to stretch. And made a mental note to talk to an ingenier when they got back to Lumia. Surely there was some way to make the wagons more comfortable. He hadn't noticed how bad the ride was when he'd traveled a few routes with his father. But then, he'd been eighteen and apparently made of rubber or something else equally impervious to the constant rattling ride.

Now he was all too clearly flesh and bone, neither of which appreciated being jolted around for hours on end. It wasn't outside the realm of possibility that he would travel with a caravan again. Besides which, it should be more comfortable for those who worked the caravans for him regularly.

The evening air was holding on to the heat, making him aware he was dusty and travel stained. The campsite only had rudimentary bathing facilities, so it didn't take long to wash up. He forced himself to eat despite having little appetite. He hoped that was because he'd slept part of the day away rather than his...hiccup from the previous night. When he'd been recovering from the firewort, it had taken several months for his appetite to return to normal. He didn't want a relapse and made himself finish off everything on his plate before he pushed it away.

"I need to get back to the tent. I'm sure there will be papers waiting for me. Chloe, are you ready to retire?"

She shook her head. "I'll just finish my conversation with Sejerin Silya and then I'll join you."

Meaning they probably wanted to discuss his treatment without him trying to convince them he didn't need it.

He nodded, resigned to the fact that he wouldn't be able to stop them, and left the two of them to talk, trying not to yawn as he located their tent. Private Blaise had drawn guard duty tonight, and Lucien nodded at him before he ducked inside. There was a pile of papers on the small folding table that served as his desk, and he bit back a groan. For a moment he envied Chloe, who could have Octarus transport an urgent message instantly if she chose, rendering paperwork unnecessary. But he was no water mage, and it was unlikely that he would bond a sanctii any time soon to help him avoid his responsibilities.

As though Lucien had summoned him with that thought, Octarus appeared in the middle of the tent. Lucien took an instinctive step back, only just managing to avoid knocking the table over. The sanctii looked around the tent curiously, and Lucien cleared his throat.

"Chloe is still talking to Silya," he offered.

Octarus gave him the sort of steady look that suggested he wasn't entirely sure if Lucien had a brain or not. Which was difficult with the craggy face of a sanctii, but Lucien had had enough experience with the sanctii in the forces to know how to interpret most of their expressions. "Sorry. I guess you know where she is."

Octarus nodded. "Always."

Something to remember.

Lucien felt a tremble in his hand, though not sure if it was just fatigue catching up with him or the rush of adrenaline from Octarus's sudden appearance having exacerbated his problems. Shaking hands had been another symptom of his poisoning.

He settled himself on the chair and folded his arms, tucking his hands against his sides, hoping that would help and the tremors would dissipate before Chloe arrived. "Did you have a question for me? Or are you just inspecting our tent?" The sanctii had kept a very low profile the last few days. Lucien hadn't seen him once.

"Worried," Octarus said, tilting his head.

What? "Who's worried? Chloe? Or you're worried about her? Is something wrong?"

Octarus shook his head. "No. But worried." But he made a curious gesture at Lucien and then toward the door flap in the direction where perhaps Chloe was. "Was better before."

Apparently Lucien's brain was working well enough to understand what he was referring to. *Perfect.* Now the sanctii was going to nag him about the bond, too.

"We're fine," he said, not wanting to discuss the current state of his marriage with a sanctii, of all people. "She's just eager to find Deandra and whoever else was behind the attack on the palace."

Octarus tilted his head again. "Not only," he said, but then Lucien heard footsteps outside and the sanctii blinked out of sight again, leaving Lucien staring at the spot where he'd been as Chloe swept through the tent flap.

"Good night, Private," she said firmly over her shoulder and lowered the piece of canvas into place, tying the knots to secure it and then putting her palm against the wards. Lucien saw a shimmer run around the tent as they flared briefly in response to her magic.

"Good evening," he said.

Her brows drew together as she scanned the tent. "I thought I heard you talking to someone."

He shrugged. There was no point in trying to lie. Octarus may well tell her that they had spoken. "Octarus was here."

Chloe looked startled. "Octarus wanted to talk to you?"

Her expression turned vague for a moment in a way that he associated with her talking to the sanctii.

"I am worried," she said. She looked at Lucien. "You look like you're about to fall over again." She walked over to the table and picked up the pile of papers, tucking them under her arm.

"I need to read those."

"I'm sure there's nothing so urgent that it can't wait until you've had a good night's sleep."

He put out his hand, catching her arm. "You don't know that. Anything could have happened."

"Well, if anything did happen, it's already been a day, so it can wait another night."

"I really don't think it can," he said. "I should have read some of them last night. Or in the wagon."

"You're hardly disproving my point. Last night you collapsed, and you napped for most of the day despite your insistence that you are perfectly well."

He stared down at his hand as another tremor ran through it, making it twitch against her sleeve. He pulled it back, but he knew it was too late and that she'd seen it.

"What was that?"

"I'm tired. My hand shook a little. Is that a crime?"

The expression on Chloe's face was a mixture of anger and, he thought, a little fear. "That hasn't happened since we were at Sanct de Sangre."

He made a dismissive gesture but flinched slightly when the movement made his wrist ache. "Another night's rest and I'll be fine," he said. "So let me have the papers so I can do my duty, and then we can go to bed."

He tried to sound sensible and reasonable and, above all, healthy, but apparently Chloe wasn't having any of it. She put the papers behind her back, out of his reach, frowning at him. "You need to let me reform the bond," she said through half-clenched teeth.

He pushed up from the chair. "I already said no to that."

"It's clear that a day's rest wasn't enough to restore your health. You need the bond."

"I said no," he gritted out, stomping over to the bed.

She followed. "You're being ridiculous."

"I just need sleep." He started to turn toward his trunks when her hand shot out, gripping his forearm.

"Stop treating me like I'm the enemy, Lucien."

He didn't know exactly what it was, but something about her tone snapped the last threads of control he'd been holding on his temper. "And why should I do that? You're hardly acting as an ally would."

"What's that supposed to mean?"

"Perhaps there's the fact that you fled our wedding night. That you broke the bond. That you didn't let me know where you were going. Didn't come to me. Didn't trust me to help you. If I'm an ally, you should turn to me. Instead, you ran. Just like you did the last time."

She threw up her hands in exasperation. "I don't see that there's any point going over why I ran again. If you want an ally, Lucien, perhaps you should learn to treat me as one. To offer me your trust."

"Why?" He snarled. "You clearly don't trust me."

"I'm trying to help you," she snapped back.

"I don't need your help."

"Oh really?" She stepped a little closer and put her hands on his chest. "I'm guessing if I shoved you hard enough, you would fall on your stubborn ass onto the bed."

"Try it," he suggested, "and we'll see what happens."

"You need to let me reform the bond," she repeated. "You need to be healthy for us to carry out this mission."

He shook his head, unable to contemplate sharing her magic again, to have that sense of her emotions, and worse, to let her feel the swelling mix of fear and love and desire and anger that she was still currently eliciting in him. She'd shown him once how to lock those emotions away from the bond, but right now, with the way he felt, he wasn't sure he would be able to.

He took her wrists and pushed her back gently. "You're the one who's overreacting," he said. "Silya doesn't think I'm about to drop dead, and she knows more about the effects of firewort than you do. So perhaps you should just have a little faith in me."

"Why should I trust you? You don't trust me." She sighed. "This is going around in circles." Her spine straightened, and her chin snapped up. "If you leave me no choice, then I'll be forced to take action."

"What, you're going to tie me to the chair and force me to take a bond? I don't think that's even possible."

He didn't know much about that kind of magic, but he did know that generally both parties to the bond had to be willing. That was true even with sanctii and petty fams. The history of the empire would have been a lot darker and bloodier if mages had been able to enslave people to their will.

"No, but I will send word back to the capital that you are ill."

"You wouldn't," he breathed.

She stepped back, folding her arms. "Just watch me."

Was she bluffing? "It's not safe for you in the capital."

"It's not safe out here for you if you won't take care of yourself," she retorted. "And you said Aristides didn't think I was guilty. I assume, therefore, that he could, should I request it, put me under suitable protection. Indeed, I imagine the judiciary would be willing to guard me as well, given that I'm one of the only witnesses to see any of the people actually involved in the attack in the palace."

Something flickered across her face that he couldn't quite interpret. He wondered if she was thinking about what it might be like to be interrogated by Truth Seekers. The thought of someone else doing that to her made him irrationally angry.

"I can simply tell Lieutenant Envier that they're not to take any messages from you."

Chloe let out a laugh more angry than amused. "One word from me and Octarus can be in touch with Ikarus or Martius or any of the sanctii who work in the Imperial mages. I can't imagine it would take long for them to send reinforcements to bring us home if the emperor was really concerned for your life. Plus, I could ask him to have someone inform your mother. At the very least, she'd send several squads of your personal guard. And if I tell them you're sick, I'm sure they would be happy enough to take my orders and rush you home."

"Why are you so concerned with my health? I would have thought you would be quite happy if I dropped dead and freed you from this marriage that you never wanted. In fact, that might neatly solve your problems. It would leave you as Lady Castaigne. You'd be rich, you'd be wealthy, and you'd be free to live out your life however you wanted."

At that point, she did shove him, furious. "Because, you idiot," she yelled, "you would be dead. And if you haven't noticed, I happen to care about you."

"You have a funny way of showing it."

"That's because you're an infuriating, stupid, stubborn man who always has to push things."

"I push things," he growled, "because I love you, Chloe."

"And I love you, too," she shouted back.

And then her hands flew to her mouth, her eyes widening in horror.

"You *what?*"

Her hands didn't move.

He closed the distance between them in one quick stride and peeled them away from her face. "Say that again."

She shook her head slowly, but there was something in her expression that made him think she wasn't so unwilling as she was pretending to be.

"Say it again, Chloe," he said, hand cupping her cheek.

Her gaze dipped. "I love you," she muttered.

Joy sang like victory through his veins even though he considered asking her to say it again. Just in case he was dreaming. But her cheek pressed into his hand, and then she lifted her face, eyes wide, and he put his other hand around her waist and pulled her close. Where he'd wanted her to be all along.

"Luc—"

He cut his name off with his lips. She wrapped her arms around his neck and kissed him back, hands curling against his back and shoulders as tightly as his were on her waist.

She hit his veins like a shot of kafiet. Hot and sweet and intoxicating. He wanted to drink her down, not sure he'd ever get enough.

She loved him. He didn't need the bond or his magic to believe it. Certainty filled him, spinning through every spike of want and longing jolting through his blood as they kissed, as she opened her mouth to him and he tasted her, hands trying to pull her closer still.

Never close enough.

He was just about to drag Chloe down to the mattress the way every instinct he had was screaming at him to when someone rapped on the tent frame, making the wards chime.

"What in the hell-cursed name of the goddess?" he muttered, pulling his mouth from hers reluctantly.

Chloe looked as dazed as he felt, eyes wide and dark. "Ignore it."

He shook his head, trying to ignore the effect of her breathy voice on his common sense. "They wouldn't interrupt if it wasn't important," he said, pushing her back gently. *Ice. Snow. Winter.* He tried desperately to think of cold things that might cool his aching cock as he crossed the tent and untied the flap. "What?"

Lieutenant Envier stood outside, his blue eyes looking somewhat apologetic. His uniform jacket was half unfastened and his brown hair messy, as though perhaps he'd been sleeping. He saluted quickly. "My apologies, my lord. I didn't mean to disturb you, but there's a messenger."

"A messenger?" *From where?* He tried to make his brain, still firmly focused on Chloe, work.

Lieutenant Envier stepped back, revealing a young blonde woman in the black uniform of the Imperial army standing a few feet behind him. The pins on her collar revealed her as both a lieutenant and a courier. Her braided hair was somewhat mussed, and there was dirt smudged on her face, but her spine was straight. She snapped a salute, her other hand gripping an Imperial courier's pouch.

Lucien beckoned her forward. "You have something for me, Lieutenant?"

She looked at him. "You are Lord Castaigne?"

"Yes," he said impatiently, "I am." He held up his hand to show her the signet ring that bore the tower and stars of Terre d'Etoi.

She looked at it, then nodded once and handed over the pouch. "A message from Lumia, my lord."

He regarded the pouch warily. The likelihood that it was going to be good news rather than bad seemed small. "Any idea what this is about?" he asked Lieutenant Envier.

The lieutenant shook his head. "She said she can only tell you, my lord. So perhaps we should go inside so you can read the message."

Lucien nodded. "Yes. No point putting it off." He nodded at the courier. "Come along, Lieutenant?"

"It's Lieutenant Arret, my lord."

Not an Illvyan name.

Before he could reply, she continued. "My instructions were to put the message in your hands only, my lord. I do not need to know what it says. I will wait here in case you have a response."

"You can find something to eat at the camp kitchens. I'll send someone to find you if there is a response. Envier, come with me."

Lieutenant Envier nodded as the courier saluted and turned on her heel. Lucien ducked back into the tent ahead of Lieutenant Envier. Chloe, he was glad to see, had straightened her dress, picked the scattered papers off the floor, and was standing by the bed sipping a glass of water. Her expression was relatively serene apart from two spots of pink in her cheeks.

Goddess. He desperately wanted to kiss her again. Make her repeat what she'd said so he knew that he hadn't imagined it. But that would have to wait despite the howling in his blood to close the flap, ignore everyone who wanted his time and attention, and drag her into bed.

From the way she bit her lip and looked down, then back up at him from under her lashes, he thought perhaps she felt the same.

"What is it?" she asked, voice still faintly breathless. Their eyes caught, and she looked away as the pink in her cheeks deepened.

Curse all messengers.

He forced his brain to focus on something other than her and the bed and held up the pouch. "Word from Lumia."

He sat at the desk and placed the courier pouch on its surface, trying to think. Hopefully Envier wouldn't notice that the pile of papers he was meant to be working on was nowhere in sight. He resisted the urge to look back at the bed to see where Chloe had put them.

He glanced back up at Chloe, but she was looking warily at the pouch.

"Go on," she said. "Open it. You need to know what it says."

The lieutenant might not have caught the nerves in her voice, but he did.

He opened the courier pouch by pressing his ring to the wax seal that held the strings together. Imperial couriers used charms keyed to individuals—in his case, usually to his signet ring. The strings unknotted themselves, and he pulled out an envelope. It wasn't from the emperor but rather from the judiciary. Responding to his information about the theater troupe, perhaps?

He pressed his ring to the second seal holding the envelope closed and extracted the letter. Satisfaction chased away some of his frustration as he started to read. "They think they've located the theater troupe."

"Where?" Chloe asked.

"Basali," he said. Halfway across the country, and not in the direction they were headed. He scanned the rest of the letter. "They suggest that we ride to Nysalla and portal across to Fierra. The garrison there is sizable. They'll send a navire to meet us there to take us to Basali."

"That's in Partha?" she asked.

"Technically it's Ancalla, I believe." He had investigated a case in the Ancallan capital once and vaguely remembered some of the geography. Basali was one of the larger towns on the trade route up to Partha from Illvya. "But close to the Parthan border. I'm sure we have a map somewhere if you need to see."

She waved the offer away. "Not just now. There are more important things to do, I'm sure."

She was right. He turned his attention to the lieutenant. "Tell the others to ready themselves."

"Very well, my lord," Lieutenant Envier said. "When do you want to leave?"

He frowned. Chloe had been wrong. They needed the map immediately. "Ask Mali for a map if you didn't bring one. We need to work out how many hours it'll take to ride to Nysalla."

The lieutenant nodded. "We were looking at the route earlier, my lord. Another day's travel with the wagons, so we might be able to make it in five or six hours if we ride."

"In that case, we may as well get some sleep. We don't want to risk the horses on these roads at night. It will only slow us down if one of them goes lame. We'll leave at first light."

CHAPTER 11

Chloe stared at Lucien as he closed the tent flap without really paying any attention to what he was doing. His expression suggested that getting a good night's sleep was the last thing on his mind, and she didn't know whether to back away or run to him, drag him down to the rugs, and beg him to take her.

Fortunately, the decision wasn't up to her.

He stalked across the tent, green eyes blazing, and had her back in his arms before she had a chance to come up with any reason to resist.

"Say it again," he muttered, lips pressed against her neck.

Her heart pounded, the sensations rushing through her equal parts elation and trepidation. "I love you," she whispered unsteadily, unable to deny it despite the whirl of emotion threatening to upend her.

Maybe he caught something of the fear underlying the words because he pulled back, eyes searching hers, the green searing through her. "You never said that before."

"You said you didn't trust me. Why would you believe me?" Even if she'd been ready to say it. To believe she could feel it and have it not end in flames and chaos.

"You're scared," he breathed, hand stealing around to rest on the back of her neck.

She bit her lip, then nodded, trying to find the breath to answer. "Yes."

"Because of Charl?"

"Do you blame me?"

"No." He shook his head and then leaned his forehead against hers. "But I am not Charl. I will not betray you. I won't hurt you. And if I ever leave you, it will be because my heart stopped beating."

She wanted to believe it. Knew she *should* believe it.

"If I could change one thing in my life," he continued, "I would go back to Imogene's betrothal ball. Make damned sure I crossed that ballroom and introduced myself to you as soon as I saw you. Make sure it was me who caught your eye so he never got the chance to hurt you."

Her heart ached, though she wasn't sure if it was with sorrow or joy. It was hard to imagine it, how her life might have been. But she had loved Charl—that much was true. And perhaps she and Lucien had needed to go through that to reach this place where they stood now.

"He hurt you, too," she said softly.

"Over and over again," he admitted. "Because he took you and he didn't cherish you, and then he threw us both away. I will never forgive him for that. I thought once that I could. But if he is what keeps you from me, then he will have broken us again. He will win. Do you want him to win?"

"No." She knew that for sure. Charl had broken her heart and demolished her life once. She couldn't give him the power to break the new life she had a chance to grasp now.

That truth was like light suddenly breaking over the horizon. She wanted a life of freedom. But she didn't want only that. She wanted someone beside her. Someone who saw who she was. Someone happy to let her fly but who would catch her when she fell. Who would be a safe place for her and she for him.

And the only man she trusted to do that was Lucien.

She should have known it when she'd chosen the marriage mark back in Deephilm. A tower. Brilliant starlight. A free flying raven. Strength and joy and discovery. Safety and delight and a life grown together.

"No," she repeated. "I don't want him to win. I want us to win. I want *you*." She laid her hands on his cheeks. The joy in his eyes nearly sent her to her knees. "Do you believe me?"

"Yes."

There was no magic behind the words, no song in the air to tell her he was using his power. But she only needed the certainty in his voice. It echoed through her, truth and trust, deep as the earth beneath their feet.

"I love you," she said again and then kissed him. The taste of him, the thrill of it, pushed any lingering doubts away. All that mattered was him.

Here. Now. *Forever*.

"I love you," she purred, tilting her head back to give him better access to continue doing whatever it was that was waking every nerve in her body with delight.

He laughed and moved his lips to her mouth, fingers working on the ties that held her dress together. "I love you."

She would have helped him, but she was busy with his coat, trying to push it off his ridiculously broad shoulders. Maybe she should make him buy some clothes that were more in the local style. Looser. Easier to remove.

Her dress fell from her shoulders before she'd made much progress.

He went still suddenly, and she froze, too. "Is something wrong?"

He touched the chain at her neck. "You're wearing your ring."

His tone was surprised but pleased. Had he thought she'd abandoned it when she'd abandoned him?

"Yes," she said. "I wanted to keep it safe. Keep it close."

He reached for the chain, then hesitated. "May I?"

She nodded, and he lifted the chain over her head. In mere seconds, he'd freed the ring and offered it to her.

"Will you?"

The hope and want in his voice made her shiver. "I will." She held out her hand, and he slid the ring back onto her finger, then lifted her hand to kiss it.

"This time it stays," he said.

"Yes."

He laughed then, the sound full of joy and satisfaction, and shrugged out of his jacket before pulling her close to kiss her.

After that, it was a whirl of rush and hurry that didn't register clearly until he was naked and lowering her to the bed, then covering her with his body. The shock of him against her, hard and hot in all the right places, stole her breath and she gasped, making him lift his head.

"Good noise or bad noise?"

She smiled up at the concerned face warring with the dark green heat in his eyes. "Definitely good. Come here." She tugged his mouth down to hers, starting the kiss again, letting the oh-so-right sensation of it flood her body.

He'd said "Mine" when he kissed her back in Jinkara. Now she knew it was true. And that he was hers in the same way.

Now all she could think of was proving it.

Lucien started to move his lips down her neck, clearly intent on having his way with her, of lighting every part of her on fire, his fingers slipping between her legs at the same time. But she was too impatient for that, and the way his fingers slid so easily told her she didn't need any more to rouse her. She reached down and closed her hand around his cock.

"Chloe?" He sounded half lustful, half startled.

"I want you," she said, lifting her hips.

She didn't have to ask a second time. He groaned as she pushed against him, and then he slid home with one deep thrust.

He curled his fingers with hers and lifted her hands above her head.

"Goddess," he breathed, turning desire to worship. He began to move within her, each thrust impatient. Fast and hard and hungry.

Exactly how she wanted it. Needed it. She needed to feel him inside her, as close as he could be.

She closed her eyes and moved with him, greedy for him, the rush of it making her all sensation and instinct. She lifted her legs higher around his hips, pulling him to her, once again caught in the storm of him, unraveled and reveling in it.

It was wild again. Fierce. Perhaps the last battle in the war between them. Breaking down all the hurt and the misunderstanding in the flood of pleasure and delight, in the bone-deep satisfaction and knowledge that this was how it was supposed to be.

She came suddenly, without expecting it, screaming as the orgasm hit her. Heard an answering roar as he followed, everything vanishing around them in a blur of pleasure.

He didn't let her rest for long, teasing her once more with lips and fingers until she was writhing. When she tried to pull him down to her, he laughed and said, "This time, you can do the work," and rolled so she was on top of him.

For a moment, time swept and shimmered, taking her back to that first night in Deephilm, when she'd tied his hands and ridden him, too angry to admit that what caught fire between them was anything but simple misguided lust. He felt the same beneath her now as she slid him home. The same and entirely different. She still hungered for him, but now she wanted more than just release from the fever burning between them.

She reached for something to anchor her, to keep her from dissolving entirely. Magic, Lucien, the ground—anything. "More. Please, Lucien, I need you."

"You have me." He thrust harder, his presence beneath her unmistakable but still not enough.

"More. Together." She kissed him wildly, nipping at his mouth, drinking the taste of him down. "I need you to be mine. All of you." She braced one hand on his chest, letting her magic sing around her as she rolled her hips in time with his.

"You want the bond?"

Oh. *Yes.* She hadn't realized it, but that was what she was seeking. The comfort of knowing him, of sharing so intimate. Something just for the two of them.

She nodded, seeking reassurance in his face.

"Why?"

"Because I don't want to lose you. Because I want to know you. Because it felt like my heart broke, too, when I broke it, and I've missed you every second since."

Was it a good idea to bring up what she'd done? Probably not. But there could be no lies between them now. "Because we're stronger together," she continued. "Better together."

She could drown in the green of his eyes, intent on hers.

"No taking it back this time," he managed, half breathless. "If you do this, it stays. You stay. We stay." His hands anchored her hips, stilling her. "So be sure."

"I'm sure."

"Then so am I." A laugh rumbled softly from his throat.

"Something funny?"

"Apparently you get to stab me after all."

She raised a brow. "Stab you?"

"Last time this involved a knife. And blood."

True. But there were other ways to form a bond. Sometimes all it took was will and magic and trust.

"No knives." She flung her senses out, seeking for a ley line. It was distant, but it answered her call willingly enough.

Lucien's eyes widened. "Goddess. You shine."

"And you sing," she said, bending forward to nip at his lip. Maybe a little blood couldn't hurt. "Sing with me. Let me in."

"Always."

He tilted his head back as she let her magic reach for his, pulling that deepest part of him toward hers, lighting up their power until it felt as though the tent was alight around them, sparks dancing through the air before her eyes like a thousand shooting stars.

Not stars, though. Magic. *His* magic. She laughed as she realized she could feel him again and let the magic run wilder through them. Something answered, sweeping them both up and throwing them together in a dizzying rush that felt like she was falling through every memory she had of him and maybe he had of her. A thousand glimpses of smiles and laughter and his face turning to hers and hers lighting up for him. The pleasure came, too, intensifying the feeling into something too strong to bear.

This time when she came, she felt him, too, even as he called her name and the magic flared again, carrying them both away.

✦ ✦ ✦

The next morning, Chloe woke early, stirred by the sound of footsteps crunching on the ground outside. Lucien's arm was around her waist, warm and reassuring, and a quiet sense of happiness hummed through the bond even though he was asleep. It made her smile. Which brought a flurry of images of her face smiling to her mind.

Not her memories. They couldn't be.

Her eyes widened.

Lucien's?

But how? Had they done something different with the bond?

It had been intense, yes. The magic crashing through them had been undeniable. As though all the barriers between them had fallen in that moment. But not *now*. She still felt like herself, knew the boundaries where she ended and he began. Knew what she felt through the bond was him, not her.

So why was she getting hints of his memories?

Surely it was only to be expected that it felt different. The first time had been desperation, and she'd still been mostly determined to keep him at arm's length. She hadn't known she loved him. Hadn't wanted their joining in the way she had last night. Hadn't *needed* it.

Of course it was stronger this time. But she didn't remember anything from her lessons at the Academe about bonded mages sharing memories. And until they returned to Lumia, she had no way to learn more.

But maybe that wouldn't be too long a wait, she realized as the next memory hit her. The fact that they had a possible lead on Deandra. That they could finally move fast with some hope of finding her. Which in turn would bring peace back to their lives.

Easy to feel certain of success now that her world felt anchored again.

She smiled again, resisting the urge to wriggle happily in the anticipation of success. Instead, she lay still and let the emotion fizz through her.

No light was filtering through the gaps around the tent flaps yet, but somehow she knew it was time to rise. She started to slide toward the edge of the bed, but Lucien's arm tightened around her waist.

"Where are you going?" he muttered sleepily.

"We have a long day ahead of us," she reminded him.

"What time is it?"

She turned in his arms, and they tightened around her even as he smiled. "I'm not sure. Early, but I'm guessing the lieutenant will come for us shortly."

He frowned as though slightly confused, but then the sleepy expression faded from his face, his gaze sharpening. "Right. Nysalla."

"Exactly," she agreed, wriggling gently against his hold. "We need to get underway."

Instead of letting her go, he pressed his lips to hers. "You know," he said softly, "another man might be insulted about a woman wanting to leave his bed so fast."

"That's not going to work," she said. "I admit I would prefer to stay right here, but at the moment, we have more important priorities. Like solving the problem of who tried to kill you and the emperor."

She twisted in his arms and planted a quick kiss on his mouth. "So as much as I would like to dally with you, my lord, I think we should get up."

He groaned, but his arm loosened. "Very well," he said, "but only because that part about keeping me alive seems important." He rolled himself over and on top of her too fast for her to stop him. "But only so I can do this."

He kissed her, and for a moment, the connection was a blinding rush of sensation, magic singing softly around her.

He pulled back, looking a little startled. "That seems different." His mouth curved, eyes heated. "I like it."

"I do, too. But this is not helping."

He pressed his hips into hers, and she bit her lip against the rush of need. "Are you sure?" Amusement and hunger echoed down the bond.

They were never going to make it out of bed at this rate. She summoned her willpower and tried to clamp down on the flow through the bond. It wasn't as easy as before, almost as though it resisted. But eventually the intensity of feeling subsided.

"I'm sure." She kissed his cheek and then pushed him away. "How are you feeling?"

"Besides sleepy and annoyed that my wife wants to get out of bed?" he asked.

"Yes," she said, laughing.

He paused as though considering the question. "Better."

She tilted her head. "Truly?"

He arched a brow. "Is that something you have to ask me now?"

"I thought you would prefer that we keep the truth seeking out of it, as before." She wasn't sure if that would be entirely possible, not if the bond was stronger, but she could try. But even as she waited for the answer, she knew he was strong again. She knew it in her bones. Not truth from his words but truth from her sense of him.

"I'm fine," he said.

"You don't feel anything strange?" She sat up, curious.

"Strange how?"

"Like what happened when we bonded?" Had he felt the same thing as her? That rush of connection?

"That was...intense," he said after another moment. "But no, I feel fine. Though I would prefer it if I could show you just how fine instead of letting you go." His voice had dipped lower, the rasp in it making her want him all over again.

"Something to look forward to at the end of the day," she said.

"Then may the goddess grant us swift travels," he said and kissed her again.

The goddess wasn't quite as cooperative as Lucien had hoped, but they still reached Fierra just before sunset. The long ride to Nysalla followed by a lengthy series of portal jumps, supplemented at times by time spent on horseback to reach the next portal they needed, had been nearly as tiring as a day in the wagon.

Chloe curled her fingers through Lucien's while they waited for the guards to sort themselves out as they exited the final portal and moved closer to him, appreciating his warmth. The night air in Fierra was cooler than Fallea, though still nothing approaching cold. He smiled at her, his thumb rubbing gently across her wedding band as though reassuring himself it was back where it belonged.

She smiled back. "You're still feeling well?" she asked, sending a questioning thread of power through him. His heartbeat, though perhaps a little fast, felt steadier than it had the day before, and she got no sense of anything wrong. The color was back in his face, the circles under his eyes gone. Clearly the bond was helping him. She'd still had flashes of his memories during the day, but if he was feeling anything different about the bond this time around, he hadn't mentioned it. And it seemed a small price to pay for him to be well again.

"Satisfied?" he asked, shaking his head, obviously sensing what she was doing. But the emotion that came through was amusement, not irritation.

"For now," she said, tossing her head. "But you'll tell me if you feel ill again, won't you?"

His expression softened. "Yes. Though I imagine you'll be the first to know anyway."

"Good," she said.

Silya, standing beside her, smiled approvingly. When the seer had seen them while they ate a hasty early breakfast before departing, she had looked pleased but asked no questions.

Lieutenant Envier looked around and beckoned to Lucien with a wave. Lucien squeezed Chloe's hand once and then joined the group of men on the far side of the portal. The lieutenant started talking again.

From their serious faces, Chloe could only guess that they were strategizing, and the thought made her somewhat annoyed to be excluded. She had no intention of sitting quietly and letting the men do all the work of catching Deandra.

"If you want to join them, Lady Castaigne, just go and join them," Silya said quietly.

Chloe blinked. "That doesn't sound like the polite Andalyssian female way of doing things."

Silya laughed. "Well, you may have noticed that I am not exactly a polite Andalyssian female. Besides which, *you* are not Andalyssian, and you clearly want to be part of their plans. So do not let them exclude you. Your husband does not strike me as the type who would be concerned by a wife who wants to be involved."

"No," Chloe said softly. "He's not."

Lucien wanted to keep her safe, yes, but he had never tried to make her smaller. Unlike Charl, who had distracted her from what had been her original plan for her life after the Academe, convincing her that there would be plenty of time to join the corps once they'd had a few years to settle into their marriage and the aristo life he enjoyed so much.

She winced slightly at the memory but then shook her head. She had no way to alter the choices she'd made, and she didn't want to waste any more time on regret. Not when she could spend it being happy.

Nodding at Silya, she straightened her shoulders and walked over to join the men.

The lieutenant noticed her first and sketched a quick bow. "Lady Castaigne."

"Perhaps you should call me Lieutenant de Roche, Lieutenant. At least when we're discussing strategy." It couldn't hurt to remind the man that she held the same rank as him in the army. "I assume that's what you've been doing."

Lucien nodded. "Just discussing the best approach to get to the barracks."

She frowned. "Is there any particular need for secrecy before we reach Basali?"

They were still hundreds of miles away. It would take two days at least once they were aboard the navire to get there. There was no reason to think Deandra was anywhere near Fierra.

"Just being cautious," Lucien said. "They have to know—or

worry, at least—that we're looking for them. We don't want anything unusual drawing attention. And we have to assume that whatever method they're using to communicate and plan, whatever network of support they've formed, is good."

"Hopefully not as good as the Imperial army," Chloe said, trying to ignore the fact that so far all the Imperial forces had been caught unprepared by the attacks to date. "And the sight of soldiers can't be uncommon here if they have a barracks large enough to land a navire at. Granted, the navires themselves may be of interest, still being new." It had only been less than a year since Imogene had finally made her idea of flying ships work. But the emperor was rapidly expanding his fleet of navires, as well as the crews of water mages and blood mages required to fly them.

Lieutenant Envier shrugged. "They still draw some attention. Which is why we don't necessarily want anyone to know this one has come to collect passengers."

That made sense. "Does that mean we stay in civilian clothes and move to the navire after dark?"

Lucien glanced at the horizon, where the sun had nearly set. "We're going to wait. We'll find an inn where we can eat dinner while we send a few of the men on ahead to touch base with the navire," he said. "Find out when the captain plans to get underway again. We may need to stay here for a night. If we do, then, as far as anyone else has to know, we will tell them we're planning to depart in the morning via the portals."

Chloe frowned. "Isn't that a waste of time?"

Lucien shrugged. "The captain sets the schedule for his vessel. I can't change that."

"You're a major," she pointed out.

"Who does not know how to fly a navire. I will not presume to overrule someone who does. We won't reach Basali faster if we fall from the sky because the mages grow too tired."

She grimaced. "It feels as though we're giving them time to get away."

"With all due respect," Lieutenant Envier said, "the troupe uses wagons. They weren't due to reach Basali for a few more days. We will be traveling at a pace much faster than a wagon's. Trust me, we'll be able to catch up."

"And in the meantime," Lucien said with a grin, "we can rest, as you have been so fond of telling me to do for the last few days."

✧ ✦ ✧

They rented a pair of rooms so they could wash, eat, and then drink too many cups of the local bitter coffee while they waited for the lieutenant to return. Despite the coffee, Chloe was yawning by the time he made it back, half an hour or so before midnight.

Envier looked as tired as she felt, stubble starting to shadow his jaw. She hoped he'd at least managed some time to eat at the barracks.

"Well?" Lucien asked quietly. "What is it to be?"

"We'll go to the barracks now," the lieutenant replied. "The captain says the mages are rested enough to fly tonight, though we'll probably have to land tomorrow night to let them rest again. There was a matter with a sail that needed some sort of repair, but apparently that has been taken care of, so they await your pleasure, my lord."

"Perhaps we should make that 'Major' now," Lucien said gently. "Once we're aboard the navire, we'll be under military protocol again."

Lieutenant Envier looked almost relieved about that. None of the guards had seemed particularly sad to leave the caravan, and no doubt most of them would be happy to be back in their uniforms.

Which left her only too aware that she hadn't brought any of hers with her. Perhaps just as well, when she still had no clear confirmation that the diplomatic corps wished her to remain amongst their number. But the nerves that tried to rise with that thought were quickly subsumed by the excitement of knowing they were on Deandra's trail once more. The anticipation bubbled through her veins, waking her up in a manner the coffee had failed to achieve.

It didn't take long to gather their things again before they were bundled into a carriage the lieutenant had waiting and driven across the now mostly silent and dark streets of Fierra to the outskirts of town. The barracks had sizable grounds, protected by a high fence and guards.

But they were waved through the gates quickly and driven around to the back of the cluster of low stone buildings, where the navire rested in a field behind the parade ground. As always, the sight of what was, for all intents and purposes, a large ship, resting on grass, was incongruous. An effect not lessened by the light glimmering around it from the lanterns both hanging from the deck rails and held by guards stationed at intervals around the vessel.

It looked like something out of a dream, as though it had lost its way trying to find an ocean and might rise up seeking its true home any second. Which it would once they were aboard.

Soldiers surrounded the carriage as soon as it halted, helping them alight and whisking luggage away.

"You can board whenever you're ready," Lieutenant Envier said before he hurried toward the navire.

"No time like the present," Lucien said, offering his arm.

"No," Chloe agreed, keen to be underway.

Still, when they reached the gangplank, she paused to stare up at the navire. The last time she'd been aboard one had been the frantic journey home from Andalyssia. Her memories of that trip were a blur of panic and exhaustion as she and Irina worked to keep Lucien alive and any spare moments she had were spent trying to spur the captain on to push the vessel as fast as possible, all the while doubting her ability to do the first and her authority to do the second.

[Strange,] Octarus said in her head.

[It's perfectly safe for you,] she replied. [Sanctii help fly the navires.] She hadn't thought to ask him before now if he had traveled on one, too caught up in wondering what was going to happen.

[Yes. Still strange] came the reply.

[Sorry. It's the faster way.]

[Yes.] He fell silent again.

"Everything will be fine," Lucien said reassuringly.

Was he catching the edges of her memory? Did he remember anything of that nightmare trip home? Perhaps not.

"After all," he continued, "the journey up to Andalyssia was quite comfortable."

Comfortable physically, perhaps. The navire hadn't been the problem with that part of their journey. No, that had been the awkwardness brought about by the fact that Chloe had had no idea that Lucien was to be part of the mission she was so excited to join. Back then, she had still hated him, still laying part of the blame for Charl's death unfairly at his feet.

To find out that he was part of her command on the assignment she'd hoped would be the start of her new life had been galling.

And of course, there had been the part where he had been the most experienced member of the crew when it came to speaking Andalyssian. Who, therefore, had taught the entire delegation for several hours a day, where Chloe could not escape speaking to him. She'd spent most of her time aboard either angry, mortified, or just doing her best to avoid him.

He grinned at her disgruntled expression. "And after all," he added, as though he could read the direction of her thoughts, "you like me now."

Behind them, Silya snorted. "If the two of you are done reminiscing, perhaps we could get aboard. I, for one, would appreciate some sleep."

She didn't seem fazed by the navire, though Chloe doubted the magic it used would be considered "balance." But Silya, and the rest of her countrymen who Aristides had summoned to the capital, had traveled down on a navire. So perhaps she'd had time to come to terms with whatever views she held of the vessels.

"After you, Sejerin," Chloe said, stepping back.

Silya snorted again and marched up the gangplank. Chloe grinned at Lucien and followed the seer.

A young woman in Imperial black, the arrow of a private at her collar, waited to greet them as they stepped off at the other end. "Major de Roche," she said, "Lieutenant de Roche, Sejerin Silya, welcome aboard. I will show you to your cabins."

"Oh, don't worry about that," a familiar voice said from behind the girl. "Or at least you take Sejerin Silya, and I'll deal with the major and the lieutenant."

"Imogene," Chloe shrieked and ran toward her friend.

CHAPTER 12

"What are you doing here?" Chloe asked, unable to decide whether she was delighted to see Imogene or annoyed that her friend had put herself in the middle of danger.

Imogene cast a look over her shoulder as she led them toward the lower decks. "I can't let you two have all the fun, can I?" Her bright blue eyes danced with amusement. As usual she looked immaculate, the black of her uniform free of any wrinkle or dust and her dark hair braided in perfect, neat circles at the back of her head. Though she did look slightly tired despite her unconcerned tone. But that was only to be expected. It was past midnight, and the navire must have pushed to get to Basali as fast as possible.

"You have an odd idea of fun," Chloe said.

Imogene grinned again and then turned back to watch where she was walking. "Better than waiting in Lumia while everyone runs around in circles trying to work out what exactly is going on."

"Has there been any progress?" Lucien asked.

Imogene didn't answer, just continued down the narrow passageway until she stopped at one of the cabin doors and opened it. "This one will be yours. Go on in."

When they were all safely inside, she closed the door and pressed her hand to the wall to activate the wards. It only took a quick glance around the small room for Chloe to confirm this cabin was much like the one she'd had on the navire that had taken her to Andalyssia. For all she knew, this was the same navire. Two bunks, a small round window, and a small table and armoire, both bolted to the floor.

Imogene finished checking the wards before she joined them in the center of the room. "No change," she said, shaking her head. "Alain is still protesting his innocence. So far, the emperor has taken no action against him, though he isn't allowed to leave the palace. Officially, that's because all the family are being closely guarded."

"And unofficially?" Chloe asked.

Imogene's mouth twisted. "Unofficially, no one is asking that question. The emperor has a very short fuse at the moment. Other than that, none of the investigations have yielded anything useful. The Andalyssians are supposedly investigating the poison on their end, but that hasn't led to any breakthroughs either. So your news of the theater troupe was welcome. Even if we can't find all the conspirators immediately, just knowing what the method is behind the memory spells would be a break-through at this point."

"And Aristides sent you to do what? Check up on us?" Lucien asked.

Imogene brushed a hand down the skirt of her uniform. "Not exactly. I told him it wasn't fair that I hadn't yet had a chance to go on a voyage on a navire. And this seemed as good a time as any." A half-wistful expression flitted across her face, then vanished.

"And he agreed?" Lucien said, surprise widening his eyes. "This isn't necessarily the safest of missions, and technically you're in the diplomatic corps."

"True. But you're in the judiciary and you're here," Imogene said pertly. "You're not a blood mage any more than Chloe or me. And unlike you, we both have sanctii to keep us safe."

"He's just grumpy because we've had a long and tiring journey," Chloe said, nudging Lucien with her elbow. "We haven't had much sleep the last few nights." She lifted an eyebrow at him, hoping he would take the hint that she would explain exactly why that was if he continued to make any kind of fuss about Imogene—or her, for that matter—taking part. "So perhaps we should all turn in."

Imogene nodded. "We'll be getting underway soon and then flying most of the day tomorrow. There isn't much you can do to help prepare the navire to depart, and there will be plenty of time to talk more on strategy once everyone has rested." She glanced toward the beds. "Well, as rested as one can be in these bunks. Also, there's a healer on board should you need one, Lucien." She raised a questioning brow at him.

"I'm fine," he said.

Imogene narrowed her eyes for a moment, her expression stilling. Then a smile spread across her face. "Oh, you're bonded again." Her gaze shifted to Chloe, blue eyes amused. "Isn't that *interesting*."

"Not particularly." Chloe made shooing gestures toward the door. "You need sleep, too." She wasn't sure she could even start to explain to Imogene everything that had happened since Lucien had found her, and she certainly wasn't going to provide the specific details about how they had reformed their bond. Though the look Imogene shot her before she left them alone made it clear that at least some explanations would have to be forthcoming if Chloe didn't want to be driven to distraction by Imogene trying to find out what had happened.

Chloe crossed to the bunks while Lucien locked the door, patting the mattress tentatively. Just as thin as she remembered. She suddenly wished she had gotten at least one night with Lucien on the softer pallets of their tent.

"Alone at last," Lucien said, coming up behind her and pressing a kiss to the back of her neck.

She put a hand on the edge of the upper bunk as her knees went weak. "Whatever you're thinking, I'm not sure these beds are up to it."

Lucien laughed and kissed her again, closer to her ear. "The army builds things sturdy."

She turned, and his hands gripped her hips. "I'm not sure *I'm* up to it." A yawn escaped to emphasize her point.

Lucien laughed but let her go. "All right. I'll be patient." He kissed her fast. "But you make it difficult." He gestured at the bunk. "Top or bottom?"

"You don't want to share?" It would be a squeeze to fit two people in one of the bunks but not impossible.

"You said you wanted to sleep. If we share, that's less likely."

"Top, then." She was shorter than Lucien. Less likely to brain herself on the ceiling climbing into the bunk or sitting up in the middle of the night.

"Good. But you're welcome to join me in the night if you get lonely."

Despite her best intentions, Chloe woke in the lower bunk with Lucien. She barely remembered leaving her own, or falling asleep after briefly checking in with Octarus after she'd clambered up into the top bunk. The sanctii had sounded distracted but otherwise content. She must have fallen asleep fast and been only half awake when she'd decided she missed Lucien and climbed down to join him.

"Good morning," he whispered and proceeded to demonstrate that the bunks were, indeed, sturdy, making love to her with a careful precision and stifling her cries with his mouth as she came. They both grinned foolishly as they washed and dressed, and it was an effort to school her expression to something more appropriate when they reached the wardroom for breakfast. Though the fact that she was out of uniform and everybody else was not dimmed her mood a little.

She distracted herself with the meal and tried to pay attention to Captain Bertrand as he introduced the other officers, then provided facts about how many others were on board and that they would meet before lunch to discuss the plans for Basali. Silya had apparently taken breakfast in her cabin, leaving the Illvyans to speak freely.

If she fooled the crew, she didn't fool Imogene, who grinned at her across the table throughout most of the meal and then caught her arm as they were leaving. "Come up on deck with me."

"Don't you have duties?" Chloe asked, glancing at Lucien, who had already peeled off to speak with Lieutenant Envier.

"Nothing urgent. And it will take everyone a while to get organized yet." Imogene nodded at the stairs leading up to the deck. "Come get some fresh air. I imagine we'll be cooped up for quite some time later."

Perhaps it would be better to leave Lucien alone to deal with whatever estate business had piled up over the last few days. Let him clear the decks before Basali. Through the bond, she could feel his focus was fixed firmly on the lieutenant. She nodded and followed Imogene back up on deck. The air was crisp—almost chilly—but the sunshine was brilliant as they walked past the teams of mages and sanctii flying the navire and up to the prow of the vessel, where the small observation platform was currently deserted. They used the stairs leading up to it as a seat, sitting close to ward off some of the bite in the air.

"I see you reformed the bond. Does that mean you have reconciled?" Imogene asked in her usual forthright fashion.

"Yes." There was no point denying it. Not when she could

hardly stop herself from grinning foolishly every time she thought of Lucien.

Imogene raised an eyebrow. "When you broke it, I thought you might take advantage of it, to push for a divorce, if he found you. It seemed to be what you might want."

"Once, perhaps." Chloe hugged her knees up to her, closer to her chest, wrapping her arms around her skirt.

"But not now?"

"No," she admitted, cheeks heating. "Not now."

Imogene slipped her arm through hers, leaning closer. "Is it so terrible to care for him?"

"I don't know if it's terrible, but it's certainly *terrifying*." Her happiness ebbed as a wave of fear washed through her.

"That's the part they don't tell you about love," Imogene agreed.

"Who said anything about love?"

"You don't need to. The two of you look completely besotted. Which, for Lucien, is nothing new. I had faith he would calm down once he found you. But you look at him like...well, I'm not sure I've ever seen you look that way."

Not even with Charl, being the implication. "I never expected to wind up a marquesse. All that responsibility," Chloe protested feebly.

Imogene made a small hum of sympathy. "No more than I expected to marry a duq," she said. "But we make the best of these things when the man is right."

"I thought I chose the right man the first time."

"Charl." Imogene hesitated. "Well, he did love you at first. I know that much. And how were you to know that he would do something so idiotic?" She nodded back down toward the ladder that led below deck. "At least you know Lucien will never betray you. He'd rather cut off both his hands than dishonor you."

"That's true," Chloe muttered. "But no, that's not what I'm afraid of."

"You lost Charl. It's natural to be afraid of losing another husband. But Lucien is healthy. And too smart to get himself killed in a stupid way. You have to learn to live with it. It's normal to be scared. If I think of Jean-Paul dying, I can't bear it either."

"So how do you?"

Imogene shrugged. "I don't think about it. There's no point. No one knows what the future brings. And I can either ruin what I have now by letting worry in, or I can live." She nudged Chloe again. "I think you should choose to live, dearest. You've wasted enough time."

As Chloe was about to reply, Imogene stood. "There's your Corporal Chartres. I expect he's been sent to fetch us." She gave Chloe a quick once-over as though considering her outfit. "Though you may have time to change. I brought some of your uniforms with me. I thought you might want them."

Chloe hesitated. "I'm not sure I still have the right to wear them."

Imogene shrugged. "No one said anything to me to indicate otherwise. I spoke to Colonel Ferritine several times before I left, and he just told me to tell you good luck." She raised an eyebrow, lifting her chin in challenge. "As I said, time to stop worrying and live."

It didn't take Chloe long to change her clothes and get back to the wardroom, but the seats around the long table were already nearly full when she returned. There was a spare beside Lucien, and she slipped into that as Imogene found a place lower down the table's length next to Silya.

At the head sat Captain Bertrand, who commanded the navire, and to his right was Captain Ilveut, who oversaw the squad of soldiers sent to assist in Deandra's capture. Her hair was as black as her uniform and braided off her face, which only emphasized her golden-brown eyes as they met Chloe's. Lieutenant Envier and the other guards who'd traveled with them from Miseneia sat farther down near Imogene. There were three men who hadn't been present at breakfast, but the introductions went quickly. Lieutenant James and Lieutenant Mirrea, both illusioners judging by their collar tabs. The third man was Corporal Gheligne, a young water mage who, somewhat unusually for his rank, had a sanctii.

Had he bonded a sanctii in unusual circumstances, too? She made a mental note to try to talk to him later.

Captain Bertrand looked across at Lucien and waved briskly at the table. "Major de Roche, I will hand this briefing over to you shortly. Everyone here—my crew and Captain Ilveut's squad —know the basics of the situation. So I was hoping you could tell us more about the illusion magic we might be facing."

"Yes," Captain Ilveut agreed. "We hope that Lieutenant James's and Lieutenant Mirrea's talents will be of assistance. Mamsille Bastiogne taught them a little of how she works the facial illusions for the opera before we departed, but they have not had time to fully master those skills. The rest of the squad have other magics, but it would be useful if they know what to look for if you can find a way to teach them."

Lucien nodded. "I'll do my best. Captain Bertrand, was there anything else you wanted to add?"

Bertrand shook his head.

Lucien started to speak, explaining the illusion magic, what exactly had happened in the parliament, and what else they had discovered.

"Do you think we'll be able to master the facial illusion?" Lieutenant James asked when Lucien finally wound down his speech.

Lucien spread his hands. "I hope so. It's not a simple magic. It took me some time to learn to use it reliably."

Lieutenant James looked a little daunted at that, but Chloe

wasn't sure he should be. Lucien was a powerful illusioner, but he had spent far more of his time using his truth seeking than perfecting the other aspects of his magic. The mages in the Imperial army practiced all sorts of illusions for all sorts of situations, along with other magics.

"The real skill, of course," Imogene said, "is spotting those who may be wearing the illusions in the first place. If Deandra Noirene or any of those who assisted her in the city are accompanying the troupe, I think it's safe to assume that they won't want to be recognized."

"No," Lucien agreed. "And how easy that will be depends on the skill of the illusioner casting them. We have to assume that whoever devised the illusions is very strong, so that may complicate matters if they're with the troupe."

"Then what's the plan?" Imogene asked.

Captain Ilveut said, "I have my orders to assist you, Major de Roche, and then, of course, to escort any prisoners back to Lumia." She lifted one eyebrow. "Our orders were clear on that. We are to try to take these people alive so they can be interrogated."

Lucien nodded. "Yes, but that is the other difficulty we face —the memory magics. Hiding their faces is one thing, but the memory magic is another kettle of fish altogether. That's why it's important we capture the illusioner behind this. We believe the facial illusions are of his doing, and if he's clever enough to do that, it's possible that he's behind the memory charms as well. Or he may be our best chance at finding out who created them. Keeping him alive is the main priority."

"Do you think there'll be sanctii?" Corporal Gheligne asked.

"Deandra is a water mage," Chloe said, "but when she left Lumia, she didn't have a sanctii. And if she had one with her at the parliament, none of the other sanctii have mentioned it."

Though she had no idea if anyone had thought to ask them directly.

She looked at Imogene. "We should check with Ikarus and Octarus."

Imogene nodded. "Yes, that's a good idea." She rapped the table once. "But Deandra was dismissed from the Academe before she could master the skills she would need to bond a sanctii safely. There aren't that many water mages about who would risk teaching someone like her the final steps to bonding. It would be too risky, and it would be unusual for a water mage with a sanctii to be traveling with a theater troupe. It's a waste of someone that skilled." She looked at Chloe. "What do you think?"

Chloe held out her hands. "You know more about that than me. But yes, it would be out of the ordinary. Unless the mage had other ties to the troupe. Perhaps if they had some sort of problem and needed to lie low." Or wanted a convenient excuse to move around the country to plot against the emperor.

Imogene frowned. "That may be possible. Though we do keep track of mages with sanctii. I don't remember any recent scandals."

"It may not have been recent. And we can't assume we know about all of them in the first place," Lucien said.

Imogene nodded again. "Yes, that's always possible. Some people will try the bond without the proper training."

"It might not be disgrace," Chloe said. "It could be something simpler, like marriage or some sort of family connection."

Imogene blinked. "Yes, I guess you're right. I hadn't thought of that."

"They could just like performing," Corporal Chartres chimed in from the end of the table. "I had a cousin who ran off with a theater troupe. He was a strong blood mage, and everyone expected him to join the army, but instead he auditioned for one of the opera companies in Elenia." He grinned. "The family doesn't exactly talk about him much at gatherings, but I hear from him occasionally, and he seems happy enough." He shrugged. "I guess it's a calling like anything else."

Chloe nodded. "Yes, you would have to love it, surely, to spend your life traveling around the empire for much of the time. Not being able to put down roots. That would take a certain devotion to the craft."

"Yes. And as Corporal Chartres said, it is impossible to rule out a water mage who wants to tread the boards," Lucien said. "We cannot entirely rule out a sanctii, though I think it's unlikely. And once we arrive, our own sanctii should be able to confirm the presence of anyone who they don't recognize. We should focus on how we're going to approach the theater company in the first place."

Imogene spoke first. "The easiest way would just be to swoop down and take them all into custody."

Captain Ilveut grimaced slightly. "That is one approach," she agreed. "It may raise something of a scandal if it turns out that the man you're seeking isn't part of the troupe."

"I'm not sure the emperor is overly concerned with scandal just now," Lucien said. "But I agree. Let's not win him any more enemies than he already seems to have. We need another plan."

CHAPTER 13

Chloe fanned herself with the playbill as she took her seat in the stalls of Basali's theater, the stiff paper swishing in rhythm with the jittery thump of her pulse in her ears. She may not have been as ardent a fan of the theater as Corporal Chartres's cousin, but she had always enjoyed attending. But hunting traitors turned the experience from enjoyable to nerve-racking.

The theater was larger and more elegant than the one in Fallea, as befitted a town that was probably four or five times as big. The Ancallan architecture leaned more to curves and flowing lines than Miseneian, all the visible wood stained a pale shade and inlaid with iridescent tiles that caught the light of the chandeliers and reflected it softly over the audience. The walls and seats were soft seashell colors, giving the overall impression of sitting inside one of the pearls that Ancalla's oceans were known for. The curtain hiding the stage was a bright sea blue, drawing the eye amidst all the gentler colors.

It was quietly beautiful and doing nothing at all to soothe her nerves. Even safely disguised by Lucien's illusions, the light-filled theater made her feel as though she was under a spotlight. Easy for Deandra to notice.

She shifted in her seat, trying to look calm. No reason to be so nervous. Lucien had done good work, and no hint of strain or distress had come through the bond. She hadn't wanted him to try the illusions on three of them, but in the two-day flight to Basali, the other illusioners hadn't yet mastered the spell. Lucien had insisted he could do it, and so far, it seemed he was right.

All that came through the bond was a solid confidence. Which eased her anxiety somewhat. Either he was sure they would prevail or he was damned good at hiding his true emotions. And with the bond so new and strong, she didn't think that was likely. Neither of them had yet succeeded in being able to completely control the flow of sensation the way they had previously. It would come with practice, she hoped, but until it did, it would be difficult to hide anything.

To prove her point, his hand squeezed hers reassuringly. She snuck a glance at him and was startled once more by the difference in his appearance. He had chosen the same unremarkable face he'd used in Fallea for his disguise. He'd varied hers a little, the hair a lighter honey shade that matched that of the locals. Imogene's was slightly darker but not by much. Chloe's eyes were brown, but Lucien had shifted Imogene's from their usual sparkling sapphire to a smoky gray and blurred the sharpness of her cheekbones and chin, shifting her from beautiful to merely pretty. The two of them resembled each other to suit the story they'd devised that Chloe and Lucien were a married couple, escorting her sister to the theater while she was in town.

Unlike Fallea, most of the conversations floating around them were being conducted in Illvyan, which only made her more aware of needing to play the part. Speaking Illvyan wouldn't afford any privacy here. Though she and Imogene could communicate via their sanctii if necessary.

She lowered the playbill to her lap and tried to study it so she wouldn't look around to see if she could locate the soldiers who were also seated throughout the crowd, dressed in civilian clothes. They'd been chosen to blend in with the locals. Corporal

Chartres, with his pale skin and red hair, had remained at the barracks, much to his chagrin.

He'd tried to hide it, but his disappointment dulled his usual eager demeanor. It made her feel old. Once upon a time, she would have been the eager young corporal if her life had played out as it had first been planned. Now she was older and more cynical and perfectly happy to avoid any danger where she could. Tonight, unfortunately, was not going to be a situation where that was possible.

The hum of the crowd around them was pleasantly anticipatory, and reading the bill, she understood why. The program was to be two short plays and a series of songs and other acts. Ambitious for a traveling troupe. She knew one of the plays, had seen it many years ago in Lumia, and she remembered the staging then as relying on realistic scenery. The few times she'd seen traveling troupes perform, they had used props that were mostly suggestive of the setting. Staging the performance as it had been done in Lumia would require some degree of illusion. Hopefully that meant they had indeed found the correct troupe. But that remained to be seen. After all, most sizable troupes could afford to pay an illusioner if they chose to do so.

There was no easy way to send someone to scout out the troupe in advance. The performers had been inside the building all day, rehearsing, and the theater had doormen at all the entrances, not letting anyone inside. Captain Ilveut had vetoed using a sanctii in case there was one traveling with them. Once the theater was open, there would be legitimate reasons for a sanctii to be in the building—after all, there were water mages with sanctii at the barracks—but not before.

Chloe shifted again and craned her neck toward the stage.

"Stop squirming," Imogene whispered. She held out a bag of sugared nuts. "Here, eat something. It will calm your nerves."

Chloe's stomach suggested that this was possibly not true, but she selected one, nibbling on it while she passed the bag on to Lucien, who looked down at it and then placed it in his lap without taking anything for himself.

The sugar was a little bit of a distraction, but Chloe still felt as though every nerve was straining as she waited for the lanterns to dim and the curtain to rise.

[Octarus?] she asked silently.

[Yes.] The response came almost immediately.

[Any sign of Deandra?]

[No.] He sounded almost disappointed.

[Any other sanctii?]

[No. Could be hiding.]

[If they were, could they sense you?]

[Maybe.]

[Well, let me know if you sense anything.]

She settled back, trying to subtly scan the crowd. Lieutenant James was a few rows in front of them and off to the left, watching the stage carefully. The illusioners hadn't mastered the facial illusions yet, but they could sense when they were in use. The strain she'd seen in their faces as they worked to perfect the magic had only reinforced both her admiration of Lucien's power and her concern that he might overreach again. But even as she thought it, he moved his leg so his knee tapped her thigh and smiled at her reassuringly, sending a wave of calm down the bond.

He held out the bag of nuts and said, "Here, have another, darling."

She managed to smile as she accepted the sweet. At least the local version of evening wear didn't include gloves. Satin and kid and sticky sugar were not a good combination. The Ancallan dresses were soft and flowing with embroidered linen over robes.

Finally, just when she thought she might scream if it took another minute longer, the lights in the theater dimmed and the crowd fell mostly silent.

A small band of musicians still hidden from view behind the curtain began to play, and gradually the curtains drew back to reveal the set for the first play. As each of the actors arrived onstage, she searched for signs of magic. It would be difficult to hear any magic beneath the music, but now she had Lucien's ability to see it as well.

But for the first play, it seemed no illusions were required, nor were any of the actors using any form of magic. The scenery was deftly implied by different layers of painted fabrics and cunning use of lights. There was a short interval before the second play started, and she turned to Imogene and Lucien, raising an eyebrow questioningly. They shook their heads as though to say they hadn't noticed anything.

They filed back out to the foyer, where vendors were selling other forms of local sweets and snacks, plus cold tea and ale in cups made of some sort of waxed paper that were quite clever in their way. She spotted a couple of the soldiers at a distance, but none of them approached, which meant they hadn't spotted anything either. They returned to their seats, and Chloe's stomach twisted, doubting that they had the right troupe. Which would put them firmly back where they'd started, with no real idea how to find Deandra. Lucien's hand settled back over hers, and she curled her fingers into his, trying to relax.

When the curtain rose again, the stage had been transformed into the semblance of a flower garden that was startling in its authenticity.

Lucien straightened, his attention narrowing with an almost audible snap. It wasn't hard to see that the flowers were an illusion. There were no musicians onstage, and the sound of the power used to build the effect hummed through the theater.

The illusions were just as good as Violette's, the flowers moving gently in a nonexistent breeze. The performance began, and after ten minutes or so, she realized that there seemed to be more actors than during the first play. More than one troupe could reasonably be expected to employ, suggesting that facial illusions were being used.

It was tempting to reach down to the ley line that ran

through Basali to help her determine which actors were disguised, but that risked drawing attention if the illusioner was also using the ley line to fuel their efforts.

Unlike the illusions Violette cast in the opera house, the troupe's illusioner could not have been relying on preset illusions set around the stage to be triggered by the performers. The troupe was only in town for three days of performances, and setting the illusions would be too much work for little reward if they had to be deconstructed every few days and rebuilt to fit each new theater. Lucien had told her at one point that Violette could spend a week setting illusions for an opera. If the illusioner was casting his illusions fresh, then he had to be nearby. In the theater, in fact, unless he was extraordinarily strong.

Unlikely. Those with truly spectacular magic rarely went undetected by the empire. One of the Academes or the temple or the Imperial services found them eventually.

[Can you find the illusioner?] she asked Octarus.

An image of a handsome man dressed all in black came in response. From the glimpse she could see of his surroundings, it looked as though he was standing somewhere backstage. Chloe tried to fix him in her mind. His short hair was dark rather than the blond of many of his actors, and a pearl dangled from one ear. Gold rings winked on several of his fingers. His eyes in his tanned face were maybe blue, maybe green, and he was concentrating hard on something—as you would expect from an illusioner in the middle of a performance.

[Thank you. Can you tell the others?]

[Yes] came the reply. A few seconds later, Imogene's head turned toward Chloe. Clearly the message had reached Ikarus and therefore her.

Imogene didn't speak, merely widened her eyes slightly and tilted her head at Lucien. Chloe nodded and then leaned toward Lucien, pulling his head down as though to press a kiss on his cheek.

"Octarus thinks he found the illusioner," she said softly in his ear. "What do you want to do?"

Lucien had charge of this operation, and he needed to make the call as to when they would swing into action. There was no reason for the illusioner to run in the middle of a performance, and the others in the troupe were currently mostly on the stage in full view. Difficult for them to flee even if they wanted to.

Lucien glanced around. "Let's wait until the end. Then at least people will have gotten their money's worth." He glanced at the stage. "I've seen this play before. There's not much left of it. Can you ask Octarus to pass the word along to the other sanctii that we'll wait? We'll come up with a plan and send word to the captain."

Captain Ilveut and those of her squad who weren't in the audience were waiting in buildings nearby. Lieutenant Envier was closer still, in an inn near the theater.

Octarus would most likely already be doing just that. But she nodded and gave him the message.

It took an eternity for the play to finish. The audience applauded for a long time, hindering them even more. She knew the appreciation was deserved, though. She hadn't paid full attention to the play after Octarus had found the illusioner, but clearly the troupe was good at their job. If Deandra was connected to them, hopefully she hadn't drawn them into her plots.

But if she had, then that wasn't Chloe's problem. And she needed to focus on the job at hand. Find Deandra and then worry about consequences later.

Eventually the applause died away and the crowd began to disperse. She was impatient to get out of the theater, checking in with Octarus every few minutes to see if the illusioner had moved.

He'd shown her a reassuring image of the man each time. He hadn't moved much, his focus still on whatever he was doing.

Probably safe to assume that he had no idea his life was about to be turned upside down.

Imogene slipped her arm through Chloe's as the crowd finally began to leave the auditorium. "Just breathe, darling," she said softly. "Everything will be fine."

She sounded calm, and the words rang true. But Chloe's life had been altered in the blink of an eye a few too many times for her to have as much faith that everything would go their way.

The theater cleared slowly, the audience taking their time to move out to the lobby. She didn't often miss the trappings of the aristo lifestyle, but she had to admit that it would have been much faster if they'd been seated in a box.

When they walked through the doors, Chloe spotted Corporal Gheligne loitering near the noticeboard that advertised coming attractions. She caught Lucien's eye and tipped her head in the corporal's direction. The three of them moved to join him, making a show of greeting him like an old friend. Imogene made a loud comment about the crowd and the heat, which gave them all the excuse to move out of the theater and a little farther down the street to the spot where the lieutenant should be able to see them from the room he'd taken in the nearest inn.

"Did Octarus see Deandra?" Lucien asked softly as they walked.

Chloe shook her head. "No. But he's been watching the illusioner."

His mouth flattened. "We need both of them."

The illusioner was clearly powerful, but it was Deandra who cast the memory charm on Chloe during the attack at parliament, fogging her senses. She was the only one who they could clearly link to that attack. The one who was definitely involved. If anything, it was more important to catch her than the illusioner.

"I could go look," she said.

Lucien stopped walking. "No. Too risky. She might notice the illusion."

"Octarus can hide me,"

That drew her a trio of startled looks.

"Excuse me? Octarus can do *what*?" Imogene said.

"He can cast an illusion that makes it difficult to see me,"
Chloe replied. "It's how I got out of the palace after the attack."

Imogene's brows flew upward, and Corporal Gheligne looked
as though Chloe had just grown an extra head.

Lucien looked annoyed rather than surprised. Which was her
fault. She hadn't told him exactly how she'd fled the palace.

"I've never heard of a sanctii doing—" Imogene started to
say, but Lucien cut her off with a jerk of his hand.

"Let's worry about whether we think it should be possible
later," he said.

Corporal Gheligne nodded. "I agree, sir. If Lieutenant de
Roche thinks she can, it is worth the attempt." He glanced over
his shoulder toward the window as though he wished the lieutenant would join them. "Take advantage of all means at our
disposal and so on."

"If it's some kind of illusion, it will be difficult in a crowded
space," Imogene cautioned. "The illusion may hide you, but it
can't turn you into a sanctii and make you incorporeal. It seems
risky. Someone might bump into you, and then the game will
be up."

Chloe hadn't thought of that. But she couldn't waste the
chance, even though Imogene was right. She had to trust
Octarus. "If we can wait until everyone goes back inside for the
last part of the performance, I won't have to worry about that. I
can dodge one or two people easily enough. The illusion doesn't
stop me from seeing others."

Lucien's mouth turned down.

"Why don't we just ask Octarus if he thinks it's safe?"
Imogene said. "He'll be able to tell you."

Chloe had already started to do that. Octarus confirmed that
the illusion should hold as long as she didn't have a direct colli-
sion with someone.

She turned back to the others. "He says so." She looked up at Lucien, willing him to trust her. His reluctance was flooding through the bond. She tried again to dampen the flow, succeeding a little, but no doubt he knew what she was feeling. "It's worth a try. I can just circle through the lobby, check the retiring rooms, and go backstage. Simple."

"It's too risky," Lucien said.

"Everything about this is risky. But Octarus can protect me."

"A sanctii appearing in the middle of the theater is hardly going to keep the situation calm," Lucien retorted.

"If he has to intervene," Chloe retorted, "then it won't be calm anyway. Besides, Ikarus is here and several other sanctii. If we get into trouble, Octarus can also let all of you know within a second. The theater isn't very big, after all. There'll be help in no time at all."

She felt his desire to say no, protectiveness and fear flashing through the bond. But other than "You're my wife and I don't want you in danger," there was no rational reason not to send her. He needed to be Truth Seeker, not husband, and make decisions with his head, not his heart.

Eventually he swallowed and nodded. "All right. Ten minutes, no more. If you're not back within that time, someone else will come after you."

"Good," she said, stepping back from the others and glancing around. The theatergoers had mostly returned to the building. There was an alley a few feet behind her. She drifted in that direction until she was happy she was out of sight, though Imogene, Lucien, and the corporal were all watching her. Hopefully no one could see through them.

[Octarus, shield me please?]

[Done.]

A collective indrawn breath from the three watching her made her smile. She walked back over to Lucien and touched his shoulder, making him flinch. "Ten minutes," she promised, then picked up her skirts and half ran back to the theater.

She slipped through the outer doors thanks to a couple of stragglers leaving. There were still a few people in the lobby, who had apparently decided that drinking ale and laughing loudly was more interesting than the performance, but it was easy enough to avoid them as she crossed the foyer and made for the hallway that led to the retiring rooms, hoping there might be another door leading to the working parts of the theater.

They had only been able to obtain basic information about the theater's layout, but in the opera house in Lumia and the theater in Fallea, the stairs that led down behind the stage to the levels below had been at the rear of the building. She hesitated a moment but then remembered she had someone who could give her directions.

[Which way?]

[Straight ahead.]

She followed his directions until she reached a door marked Private. She opened it after checking there was no one around to see the door seemingly open by itself and peeked through. Beyond was a corridor, the decoration far more basic. No shimmering tiles or pretty colors, just whitewashed walls and well-worn floorboards. Clearly not intended to be seen by the public.

She slipped through and moved a little way down the corridor, waiting for Octarus to tell her the next steps. Just in time, as a woman in a green gown so heavily covered in sequins and beads that she could only be one of the performers came rushing past her in the opposite direction, muttering something under her breath before crashing through the door that Chloe had just vacated.

Chloe shrank back against the wall until she was certain the woman wasn't rushing back, then began to move again. A babble of voices was audible from somewhere ahead, but she couldn't hear the lobby or any sound from the theater itself, so clearly there were aural wards in place. Useful to allow the performers and stage crew to work freely behind the scenes without worrying about being heard by those watching, but it also meant she might not hear anyone approaching her until it was too late, so she moved slowly, though she was all too aware of time ticking away.

The first door she reached was open, and a glance inside revealed a group of women in what must be their dressing room. They were busy changing costumes and touching up their makeup. No betraying hum of magic came from any of them, so she moved on after asking Octarus to remember their faces.

The next few rooms were also dressing rooms, but the fourth door was closed. She contemplated it for a moment, then decided it was too risky to try opening it with others close by. She was about to move on when she heard a familiar voice.

[Octarus. Who's in this room?] she asked urgently.

The sanctii's response came almost immediately. An image of Deandra. Her face hadn't been altered by an illusion, but she had made an effort to disguise herself. Her hair was an odd red-blonde shade, though Chloe couldn't tell if it was dye or a wig. Smoked-glass spectacles hid her eyes, and her skin was a deeper gold, which could be stage makeup or too much sun.

Chloe wouldn't have necessarily glanced at her twice on the street, but combined with her voice, it was unmistakably her.

They had her. Had them *both*. The excitement made her hands shake as she asked Octarus to tell the others. Now she just had to make it out of the theater safely before the soldiers and sanctii—who would be immune to any magic Deandra might try —moved in to take control.

She glanced down the hallway to the final door. Safer to go forward rather than back. It had been simple good fortune that so far no one had bumped into her.

[Octarus, is that an exit?] she asked, not wanting to wind up trapped in the dead end of a storage closet or worse.

Deandra's voice came again, laughing. Hopefully that was a good sign that no one had noticed Chloe or her illusion.

[Yes. Yards. And a gate,] he confirmed, and Chloe blew out a breath of relief before she could help herself. The noise sounded loud in the empty corridor, but she doubted anyone else could hear. Still, she headed for the door as fast as she dared, pushing through just as she heard Deandra's voice again, growing louder, and the click of a door down the hall.

She rushed through the exit and shut it behind her to find herself in some sort of yard behind the theater. She didn't wait to see whether anyone had noticed this time, just picked up her skirts and ran to find the others.

CHAPTER 14

When Chloe had first left Lumia, pursuing Deandra more on instinct than a well-thought-out plan, she hadn't really considered what she would do if she found her. Far easier to let the soldiers do what they were trained to do.

They were so well organized that it seemed to take no time at all. As soon as the performance ended and most of the audience had left the building, the squad of mages and sanctii moved in while Chloe, Lucien, and Imogene stayed in the inn, getting updates from Octarus and Ikarus. The theater's owner put up some initial resistance but gave in quickly enough. It took just about an hour to transfer the whole troupe back to the barracks. While the prisoners were being organized, the three of them changed into their uniforms, updated Silya, and then waited in the mess.

Half an hour later, Captain Ilveut reported that the members of the troupe had been secured in separate rooms around the barracks, watched over by sanctii. Deandra and the man Octarus had identified as the illusioner were locked in two of the three cells of the barracks' small brig, where they could be watched more closely. So far only three of the others had been identified as having magic: a blood mage who seemed to be the troupe's equivalent of a guard but who had offered no fight when faced with a squad of Imperial soldiers, an earth witch who claimed to be a cook and healer, and another illusioner, a younger woman, who could only be a year or two out of whatever Academe she had studied at. Their names had already been sent back to Lumia for confirmation of their talents. If they had studied at an Academe anywhere in the empire, they would be known.

"Which leaves us, sir, with how you want to proceed?" the captain asked when she'd finished relaying all the information.

Lucien waved her to a seat. "Pour yourself some tea, if you want it, and we can discuss what happens next."

Captain Ilveut looked grateful for the chance to rest a minute. Lucien let her drink, scribbling rapidly in a small notebook. Whatever he was writing, his attention was fully focused on the notes, the bond revealing only determination and focus, no hints of concern. His Truth Seeker mode, perhaps. He showed no ill effects from having maintained their disguises for hours, thank the goddess.

Eventually he put down his pen. "I think we should start with the nonmagical members of the troupe. We can't be sure that what they tell us will be true with the memory magic, of course, but they seem the most likely to choose to tell us something if they know."

"I agree," Captain Ilveut said.

"You can't interrogate them all tonight," Chloe protested. "There's what, nearly thirty of them?"

"They won't take too long. I just need to talk with them briefly. Show them a Truth Seeker is involved. If anyone knows something and wants to talk, there's always a chance they'll crack fast. But if not, then it won't hurt to let them consider the prospect of more Truth Seekers back in the capital until we've dealt with the others."

His voice was cool, almost detached, and the bond felt almost...distant. As though he was deliberately trying to keep her separate from this. She'd rarely seen him in full Truth Seeker mode. Out of his loyalty to his judicial oath of confidentiality, he'd never talked about the details of his work with her and Charl. She'd been able to tell when he was dealing with something difficult—he became distant and preoccupied—but that was different to seeing him in action. It would have been strange even without the complications of the bond.

But he was there to do a job that he did better than almost anyone else in the empire. Even if his magic could be foiled, he had years of experience in interrogating criminals. She had to stop thinking like a worried wife and trust him. Not least because he outranked her, and there was nothing she could do to stop him anyway.

"Is there anything I can do to help?" she offered.

For a moment, she caught a flicker of images of her, standing somewhere in a dark corridor, face pale, eyes huge, but they dissolved again before she could identify where she was.

"No, not for this part," he said. "You and Imogene may as well get some rest."

Chloe was expecting Imogene to protest, but she just nodded. "That's sensible. We have long days ahead of us."

"You won't try Deandra without me?" Chloe asked.

"No. You were the one who saw her in Lumia. You know her better than me. It will be helpful to have your assistance. But there is no need for you to...."

He hesitated, and suddenly she understood what she'd seen. His memory of her outside Charl's cell. He was trying to spare her, not put her back in an environment that might trigger all that old pain again. She didn't know whether to be simply pleased at his concern or annoyed that he thought her fragile. Simpler to just accept, perhaps, that in this case, he was probably right. She would be most useful speaking to Deandra, and to do that, she needed her wits about her. She should rest.

"Then I'll wish you good hunting, Major," she said, pushing her chair back. "Come find me when you need me."

✦ ✦ ✦

Chloe startled awake just after dawn as the barracks began to stir. The heavy treads of booted feet thudding outside the room she and Lucien had been assigned echoed the thump of her own heart as it took her a minute to remember where she was.

Lucien lay beside her, though she didn't remember him coming to bed. How much sleep had he had?

"I forgot the damned wards," he grumbled, screwing his eyes shut tighter as though trying to deny he was awake.

"Do you want me to set them now?" An aural ward would dull the sound enough for him to go back to sleep.

"No." He rolled over on his back, grimacing. "If the barracks is waking, then I'll be needed again."

"You need rest."

"I'll be fine. If Deandra and her friend prove uncooperative, then we'll be on our way back to Lumia by this evening anyway. Come to think of it, even if they do cooperate, we'll be taking them back to the capital." He slitted one eye open. "Maybe we should take advantage of this bed before we're back in those damn bunks for a few nights." A curl of inviting heat stole through the bond.

Tempting. Even sleep deprived and rumpled, he looked delicious.

Another set of boots stomped past their door.

"No wards, remember?" she said regretfully.

"We could be quiet."

Somehow she doubted that. Not with the bond so fresh, amplifying everything between them. "Not that quiet. Besides, if you don't show up for breakfast, they'll just send someone to look for you."

He sighed but rolled again, dropping a kiss on her mouth before sitting up. "You know, perhaps the Andalyssians are sensible about their marriage rites after all. They give newly wedded couples a month mostly to themselves."

"We're not exactly newly wed," she pointed out.

"It was only a few weeks ago," he growled.

"For the second time."

"A second time where we once again failed to manage a wedding night."

She winced slightly. No wedding night because she had run. Though the attack on the palace would likely have disrupted it anyway. "I'm sure your mother would be happy to have a third ceremony of some kind."

He scowled. "Don't even joke about that possibility."

She winced again. "It might be nice to say the vows without being forced to do it."

Neither of their weddings had been at their own instigation. And even though the second ceremony had been less fraught, neither of them had known if they would stay married. She'd promised him a year. Now things were different. Now he could have a lifetime and it wouldn't be enough.

"We can do that without an audience," he said. "But I'm more interested in the part where we get uninterrupted time together. Once all of this is settled, I'm taking you to Terre d'Etoi for a while and making sure everyone leaves us alone."

"You're the marq. Do you really think they'll leave you be the first time you come home in months?"

"They will if I tell them to. Besides, there are several hunting lodges on the estate. We can hide away. Use Octarus as our seneschal. No one will get past him."

She smiled at the thought. "I like that idea."

"Good," he said. "Then let's get to work."

✦ ✦ ✦

Getting to work began with breakfast with Imogene and Silya.

Imogene yawned over coffee. "Any progress?"

Lucien shook his head. "None of the regular troupe seemed to know anything. Most of them, I believe, probably knew nothing about what was happening. They were terrified enough at the thought of being interrogated by a Truth Seeker that I think they would have tried to confess if they had any idea what was going on."

"They are actors," Imogene retorted.

"If it's an act, it's a very good one, and they're wasting their talents with a wandering troupe." Lucien reached for another piece of toast from the platter in the center of the table. "We'll take them all back to Lumia regardless. They can wait until we reach the capital and have a better idea how to untangle the memory charms. Today I'll try Deandra and her illusioner."

"Captain Ilveut told me his name is Istvan. Istvan Vargas." Chloe frowned at Silya. "Is that a Parthan name?"

Silya shrugged. "Partha is something of a mishmash when it comes to such things. He could be Parthan or from one of the smaller countries in that part of the empire. Could have a Parthan mother and a father from elsewhere. The name is not Elenian or Andalyssian. But that does not rule out him having connections to those countries, or others, of course."

"Well, we'll see if he wants to be forthcoming about his family history." Lucien stirred sugar into his coffee. "Thank you, Sejerin. We should be on our way back to Lumia tonight, so I hope you won't be too bored today."

"I will not. Captain Ilveut asked if I would help the soldiers searching the troupe's belongings. Just in case there are any Andalyssian poisons lying around, I assume."

"I see," Lucien said. "Well, thank you for the assistance."

"I will be with the navire's mages," Imogene said. "We'll be ready to leave when needed, but send for me if you think I can help in the interrogations in any way." She yawned again as she stood, then mouthed an apology and departed.

Silya followed her shortly afterward, leaving Chloe alone with Lucien.

"Who are you going to talk to first?" she asked.

"Istvan. We know more about Deandra. She's likely to be a tough nut to crack, particularly if she's used that damned memory magic. But the illusioner, well, perhaps he may see reason and want to talk rather than having his whole world brought down around his ears. He might be easier. At worst, I'll figure out if he's a lever to use against her."

"You think he didn't know what she was doing?"

He shrugged. "It's unlikely he's innocent. Someone had to have helped her. Deandra's no illusioner, so she was using scriptii if she was disguising her face. There aren't that many legitimate uses for such illusions outside the theater, so he had to know she was up to something, at least, if he taught her."

"What about the memory magic?"

"Well, we don't know what that involves yet. But if he was helping her with illusions, he may know that magic, too. Or who invented it. The question is whether he'll try to save his own skin and cooperate. It's always hard to judge. Some men are willing to die for their cause. Some, when you get right down to it, merely think they are until faced with the true consequences. Let's hope he's one of those."

"And you think he'll just tell you?"

"It might shake him a little if I show him that I can do one of those, but that's not the part we're interested in. The part we need to understand is the memory magic and whether that was his idea or Deandra's. Or someone else entirely."

"Deandra certainly seems to be able to cast it," Chloe agreed. "But I don't know if she could have worked out how to do it on her own. She never had that level of brilliance at school. She was good enough but not unusually powerful. And her strongest talent was water. The memory magic may involve that. Water mages work with sanctii, who can, at least, add things to our memories. That's what the reveilé is, after all. Or maybe earth.

Valentin said the healers can ease memories. It could be a combination of both. There's no way to know."

Lucien nodded. "No. But if you have an illusioner clever enough to come up with ideas like the facial illusions, he may have the inclination to experiment."

True. It wasn't uncommon. After all, she'd grown up surrounded by the Academe's venables, who were always developing new magics even if they didn't let their students experiment unsupervised.

"And if he does have a bent for experimentation," Lucien continued, "he might come up with things for mages of all kinds to try. Or he may be a strong illusioner and be skilled enough in the other Arts that he can figure things out himself. Not everyone's like me."

Another truth. Most mages had one or two talents that they had the most affinity for. But some were more...balanced. Not in the Andalyssian sense of the word but able to use all of the Four Arts to some degree. And it wouldn't be unusual for a Parthan to know something of Andalyssian beliefs about balance. Perhaps that might encourage a person to see if they could use all the Arts if they tried.

"Maybe Silya can tell us more about Parthan beliefs," she suggested.

"Time enough for that while we travel back to Lumia."

"I guess," she said. Then another thought struck her. "Has anyone thought to check them for a bond? That would explain them being able to do more than they should be able to. Like us."

"They're nothing like us," he said firmly. "But we can check. And today, don't forget to use my magic if you need to. We don't need to tell them. They'll know they're talking to one Truth Seeker. Two will make no difference. Maybe you'll notice something I don't."

"Do you think that's likely?"

"Who knows? You're a clever woman. Your father's daughter. Perhaps you should have become a venable, not a diplomat."

"Perhaps I will once I tire of traveling."

One brow lifted. "You'd consider it?"

"I have no idea," she said. "I always loved the Academe, but it was Papa's territory, not mine. Besides, I'm sure being your marquesse will give me plenty to do even if I retire from the corps one day."

He looked pleased at that. "No doubt it will. But if you wanted to pursue other things, we would make that work. No cages, remember?"

"I do," she said. "But today, let's focus on the actual cages and the people in them rather than my old age."

He laughed, which made her grin back. "Very well. To business. I'm not expecting much, but today we'll see if we can at least rattle them a little, even if they won't talk. Make them doubt each other. Deandra doesn't strike me as the type to take a perceived betrayal well. Maybe we can lure her into a mistake."

"Perhaps. But don't let your guard down. Don't forget she was expelled for cheating. She was always ruthless when she wanted to be. She'll try to get the upper hand."

His mouth twisted as he considered this. "How well did you know her?"

"Not that well. She was older. And I always thought she had...well, an unpleasant streak. One of those girls who is sweet on the surface but nasty if you cross them. Imogene and I avoided her where we could."

"I'm familiar with the type," he said. "It's not that uncommon in people who commit crimes. They seem to lack...I don't know, the part of you that lets you see other people as real and not just pieces to be moved around the game board to suit your own purposes."

She nodded. "Yes, something like that. She seemed to feel that things should always turn out precisely how she wanted them, and it made her angry when they didn't. As though she was more important than other people. You see it in aristos, too. It's not just mages."

Lucien nodded. "I can't argue with that. But we're not all that way."

"No." She reached out and laid her hand over his. "You're not. So don't take any silly risks?"

"I won't." His head tilted a moment. "Are you ready?"

The nerves fluttering in her stomach suggested not, but she nodded anyway. It wouldn't get any easier if she delayed. Besides, her desire to get to the bottom of the plots that had upended her life was stronger than her hesitance.

"Absolutely."

✦ ✦ ✦

The barracks' brig was nothing like the dauntingly grim stone building that housed Lumia's main prison, but Chloe's palms started to sweat at the sight of the soldier guarding the barred outer door.

She tightened her hold on the bond. Lucien was focused, and she didn't think she'd given herself away yet. He would have stopped if he was catching any hint of distress.

Not Charl. Her fingers curled into her palms, and she fought to relax them.

Not Charl. No one was about to be executed. At least not tonight. What happened once they returned to Lumia and the judiciary made a verdict about any of the prisoner's involvement was out of her hands. And most importantly of all, perhaps, Lucien didn't think she had anything to do with this.

Was that what she was really worried about? That Deandra might somehow convince him that Chloe was part of the conspiracy?

Foolish. Lucien loved her. He'd reformed their bond.

That didn't mean Deandra couldn't toy with him, of course. Accuse Chloe in the hopes of saving her own skin, knowing Lucien's strongest magic was somewhat handicapped by the memory charms.

Setting her teeth as the guard saluted them and unlocked the door, she then followed Lucien inside.

As jails went, it wasn't as bad as she had feared. It was sparse, the wooden floors and white walls matching the rest of the barracks. There were no windows, the only light coming from lanterns hanging from the ceiling, both over the desk and in front of each of the three small cells that lined the back third of the room. They had solid sides, but the front walls were bars rather than the iron doors set in stone of Lumia's prison.

Wards shimmered over nearly every surface. She distracted herself trying to identify them. Locks, of course, and aural wards, as well as others she didn't entirely recognize but guessed might be some kind of ward against magic itself.

Deandra occupied the left-hand cell and the illusioner the right, with the middle one kept empty.

Both prisoners were watching Chloe and Lucien. Their hands were shackled in front of them, but otherwise they looked normal, still in the clothes Octarus had seen them in. Istvan seemed nervous, though not particularly so. In contrast, Deandra's brow creased, her mouth twisting angrily as she recognized Chloe. Chloe just stared back steadily. Deandra's eyes dropped first.

Yes. I found you. Now let's see who's so clever.

To the right of the door was a large desk where a lieutenant sat, filling out a stack of forms. He climbed to his feet, one hand smoothing his sandy hair before he saluted. "Major de Roche," he said politely. "Lieutenant de Roche. Have you come to speak with the prisoners?"

"Yes," Lucien said.

"Very well, sir." The lieutenant nodded toward Deandra's cell. There was a door leading out of the room in the left-hand wall. "I'm Lieutenant Usiel. We have a...well, it's not a proper interrogation room by judiciary standards, but it's private and secure. Your choice, sir—you can talk to them in the cells or in there."

Lucien contemplated the door. "Is there any way to observe the room from outside?"

The lieutenant shook his head. "Sorry, sir. It's not an official interrogation room as I said. There's no mirrored glass."

Chloe didn't know exactly what he meant. She'd never been inside one of the judiciary's interrogation rooms. When Lucien had spoken to her after Charl was arrested, he had at least shown her the courtesy of doing so at home with her father and Martius as witnesses.

"And there are aural wards on the cells?" Lucien asked.

"Yes, sir. The prisoners can't hear anything that happens outside their own cells. And they have no way of seeing into the others. We usually only have people in here for short periods of time, and it's often useful to keep them isolated."

Lucien nodded as though he understood that tactic. Chloe understood it, too. The temple in Kingswell had kept her alone in those first few weeks after she'd fled to Anglion, when they were deciding whether she was to be allowed to live. The cell she'd stayed in hadn't been barred, but she'd been locked in with no contact with anyone other than a few dominas and priors. It had been exceedingly unpleasant, and she had no doubt a more thorough isolation might well encourage people to confess faster. Particularly if the cells also blocked off any sound.

"All right," Lucien said after a moment. "I'll start with Mestier Vargas. In his cell. I don't think we need a room."

"Very well, sir," the lieutenant said. "I'll call a sanctii to fasten his shackles down. We've been careful not to let them touch anyone."

"I will do," Octarus said, blinking into view.

To his credit, Lieutenant Usiel didn't react, but across the room, Deandra flinched and then frowned, looking from Chloe to Octarus. Of course, she had no way of knowing that Octarus was Chloe's.

Lucien lifted an eyebrow at the sanctii. "They are not to be harmed."

"Understand," Octarus said. "But help."

Chloe looked at Lucien. "He deserves the chance to help get justice for Rianne. Let him help."

[Be careful,] she said to Octarus.

He grunted at her mentally and then turned to the lieutenant. "Key."

Usiel handed over a key and walked to Istvan's cell. "I'll drop the wards and unlock the door. You go in, hook his shackles into the bolt on the rear wall, and lock it again, nothing more."

Octarus nodded, eyes fixed on Istvan.

The illusioner looked nervous. But not as nervous as Chloe would have expected if he wasn't used to sanctii. Interesting. He'd either trained at an Academe or knew water mages with sanctii.

It didn't take long for Octarus to carry out the task. He scowled at Istvan for a long moment but then left the cell, taking up a position near the door.

"All yours, Major," the lieutenant said. "As long as you stay a few feet away, there's no way he can touch you."

Lucien nodded. "Put the wards up after we're in the cell. It's vital Mamsille Noirene can't hear any of this."

"Is that wise, sir? Her cell is warded. And I can't help you once you're inside."

"As you can see, the lieutenant has a sanctii. He can get around the wards faster than you can act. We'll be fine." He took a step forward.

"Wait," Chloe said, putting a hand on his arm. "What if he tries something he doesn't need to touch you for?"

Lucien shrugged. "Well then, I guess I'll find out who the more powerful illusioner is, won't I? Don't worry, I have done this before. Just stay behind me."

She had no intention of going nearer to Istvan than she had to. Deandra had gotten to her once, and she was determined not to let that happen again.

She followed Lucien into the cell, pausing only to smile at Deandra before stepping out of her view. Let her worry about what was happening. Wasn't that what Lucien wanted?

"Mestier Vargas," Lucien said. "Good morning."

The illusioner scowled, his honey-brown eyes sharpening. "Who are you?" he said in faintly accented Illvyan.

"I am Major de Roche." Lucien tapped his collar insignia: the emperor's sun topped by a stylized eye, done in black, unlike the gold of other ranks. "Do you know what this means?"

The illusioner nodded equally coolly. "Yes, I'm not an idiot. I know what a Truth Seeker is."

"Good. Then perhaps this will go easier."

"I still don't know why I'm here."

"Then let me clarify that for you," Lucien said. "We'll start with aiding and abetting an attack on His Imperial Majesty Aristides Delmar de Lucien."

The man bristled. "An attack? Don't be ridiculous. I haven't been near Lumia in months."

Lucien shrugged. "That remains to be proven. Easy enough to find out, of course, where your travels have taken you. Your troupe has quite the reputation, and I'm sure we can trace it through the networks of theaters. It shouldn't be that hard to establish. No doubt the theater's owners will be all too eager to cooperate when we mention we're investigating treason."

Which would thoroughly ruin the troupe's chances of ever finding work again. A fact that didn't escape Istvan. His mouth flattened. "You'd ruin me for no reason."

"My loyalty is to the emperor. Protecting him is reason enough. I'm sure if you are proven innocent, he would offer an apology. Maybe some recompense. All in all, this will go easier on everyone if you simply tell me the truth. We could start with your name."

"You seem to know that already."

"Humor me," Lucien said in an entirely humorless voice.

"Istvan Vargas."

"Very well."

Lucien turned for a moment, glancing back at the lieutenant, who was already scribbling notes.

"And where are you from?"

Istvan named a town Chloe didn't recognize.

"And that's in Partha?" Lucien prompted.

Istvan nodded.

"Thank you," Lucien said. "So, since you say you haven't been to Lumia, let us start with something that may be more familiar to you."

He straightened his shoulders a moment and then waved his hand over his face in a familiar gesture, casting the illusion spell once more.

Istvan bumped back into the wall he was shackled to, his face twisting in genuine shock. "Who taught you how to do that?"

"Recognize the spell, do you?"

"I invented it," Istvan said, "for my troupe. I've only taught it to a few people."

"Yes, well, one of them taught it to a friend of mine who works at the opera in Lumia. Which would have been of no interest at all to the Imperial Truth Seekers until people using the same magic attacked the parliament. Mestier Vargas, how about we start with the names of everyone you think you've taught the spell to?"

CHAPTER 15

It was difficult to keep track of time during an interrogation. But it didn't take Lucien long to realize that Istvan wasn't going to break easily. The Parthan kept his answers short and to the point, not offering any additional information. Almost as though he'd been questioned before and knew how best to get through it.

According to Lucien's magic, Istvan believed what he was saying. The only useful thing he'd really gotten out of the man was a confirmation that he and Deandra were lovers.

Even when Lucien transitioned from simple queries about his background to more specific questions about the troupe's movements for the last year, there wasn't even the faintest suggestion of a lie.

Which meant they might have a bigger problem than first anticipated.

He glanced back to Chloe, who had observed the whole process silently. If she was uncomfortable standing in a cell, she showed no hint. For a moment, his memory of her face just before she'd stepped inside Charl's cell to say her final goodbye hit him, his gut twisting with remembered guilt.

She blinked suddenly, as though she'd felt something of that, though they were both keeping as tight a grip on the bond as they could.

"I think that's enough," he said, nodding toward the cell door. "Get the lieutenant's attention and have him open the door."

She nodded, and he saw Octarus blink back into view beside Lieutenant Usiel. The sanctii said something they couldn't hear, and the lieutenant reached for the key he'd laid on his desk.

Lucien turned his attention back to Istvan. "Anything else you want to tell me before we transport you to Lumia for further questioning?"

"No," Istvan said.

Clearly the man was smart enough to know there was no point in objecting to the news that he would be taken to Lumia if he had nothing to offer that might help his case.

"Then we're done here. Once we're out of the cell, the sanctii will undo your shackles. I'd advise you not to try anything with him."

"Are the shackles really necessary?" Istvan asked.

"I can have a healer examine your wrists if they're causing any injury," Lucien said. "Other than that, they will remain for now." He wasn't satisfied that it was safe to make it easier for Istvan or Deandra to touch someone by leaving their hands free.

He paused, in case the question might be a delay tactic, buying time while Istvan gathered his nerve to offer some information, as sometimes happened. But no, the man merely shook his head and leaned back against the wall, closing his eyes as the cell door opened.

✦ ✦ ✦

Chloe stood silently outside the cell as the lieutenant locked it and Octarus freed Istvan from the wall.

Lucien ushered her and Usiel back toward the desk, turning his back on the cells, not wanting to give Deandra or Istvan a chance to read their lips. "I think we'll give Mamsille Noirene time to contemplate things before we talk to her. Let her worry that we're not talking to her immediately because we got what we needed from Istvan. Perhaps she'll decide she needs to save herself. Lieutenant, under no circumstances are those wards to be dropped. The prisoners must not communicate."

The lieutenant saluted. "Understood, my lord."

"Thank you."

He didn't need to tell Chloe they were leaving. She moved to the door quickly, clearly keen to be gone. Her pace didn't slow as they walked away from the brig.

They had hardly stepped back into the main section of the barracks when Imogen and the barracks commander, Colonel Hislock, descended on them.

"Well?" they demanded, almost in unison.

Lucien held up his hand. "Our illusioner isn't going to give us what we want willingly." He looked at Imogene. "Will the navire be ready to leave tonight?

"Yes. Captain Bertrand is keen to get underway before sunset if we can. Is that likely?"

"I think so. I'm not expecting Deandra to be cooperative. Colonel, has anyone else from the troupe decided to talk since last night?"

"No, they're all remarkably tongue-tied. And nervous," the colonel answered, a frown marring his tanned face. He had iron-gray hair and eyes, the very image of a serious Imperial officer.

"I imagine being held by the Imperial army would do that to anyone," Chloe said with a half smile.

Colonel Hislock acknowledged her point with a brief nod. "Yes, there is that. The truth is yet to be determined, I suppose, Major?"

"Yes. This magic we're dealing with, well, it makes things difficult. Actually, I have some thoughts on that, but first, I think my wife and I will take a quick break and discuss what we just heard before we decide on how to tackle Mamsille Noirene." He yawned, his jaw cracking, and saw Chloe frown.

Imogene agreed. "That sounds sensible. You need to pack your things anyway, and then one of the privates can transfer them to the navire. I can have food or tea brought to your room if you're hungry."

Lucien shook his head. "No, I just need a short break. An hour or so, and then we'll try Deandra."

✦ ✦ ✦

When Lucien had locked their door behind them and activated the wards, Chloe asked, "Do you want to sleep?"

He closed the gap between them and held her close, tucking her head under his chin. "I just need to breathe a moment."

Frustration pulsed through the bond, spiking through her like pins jabbing. Either he was more tired than he was admitting or he had deliberately loosened the iron-tight grip on the bond he'd held during the interrogation.

She let his emotions run through her, hoping that sharing them with her would lessen their hold on him. For a moment, she breathed with him, telling herself everything was fine, that it was Lucien she was feeling.

Frustration was natural. He was used to being good at his job without having to work at it too much. But now with the memory charms, he was working with his magic shackled as firmly as Istvan's hands.

She tipped her head back so she could talk. "Did you notice him lying at any point?"

"No. Not so far." He let her go, stepping away so she wasn't craning her neck so far. "Did you?"

"No," she said. "No sign of a bond either. Though bonds can be dissolved and reformed as needed."

He smiled at that. "Yes they can. I think with Deandra, I need a different approach."

"Such as?"

His mouth flattened. "I'm not sure. But I think I should dig into the details. Cover more time. There has to be a limit to how many of a person's memories you can remove and not affect them in other ways."

She screwed up her nose, thinking. "I heard about cases in Anglion where people hit their heads or had accidents and lost their memories. It changed them."

Lucien nodded. "That happened to one of our grooms in Terre d'Etoi. Kicked in the head by a stallion. He was lucky to survive, but he became much more difficult after that. Quick to anger when he'd always been gentle. His wife divorced him in the end, I believe. What we really need is someone like Valentin. He knows more about mind magic than we do."

"Yes," Chloe agreed. "So maybe you can just leave Deandra until we return to Lumia."

"No. I have to at least try."

Chloe paused. "Well, Truth Seekers can do other things, can't you? You can...encourage people to cooperate."

"Yes, though we tend to prefer not to have to resort to that so soon. And if she's used those damn charms, I'd be terrifying her for no good reason if she can't remember what she's done." He paused, mouth twisting. "Actually, that brings me back to my point."

"Your point?"

"That you can only erase so much of a person's memory before it would become obvious. This conspiracy is not a 'cobbled together at the last minute' proposition. There must have been planning and communication. Not being able to answer questions about things that happened six months or a year ago because 'you don't remember' is going to be a tell at some point.

It's not like Deandra fogging your memory of seeing her at the parliament, where it was a one-off encounter. Maybe I simply didn't go far enough back with Istvan. But he thought he was telling the truth. And he gave details. Which means he remembers details."

"What if they don't just erase the memories?" Chloe asked. "What if they replace them? Like an illusion for the mind. You go off and plot for two weeks, and then when you come back, you lose those memories and remember being with the troupe for two weeks."

Lucien had gone still. "Is that even possible?"

"I have no idea. But it's not inconceivable. A sanctii can implant a language in someone's brain. And Octarus shows me images of things he remembers."

"You think this is some sort of sanctii magic?"

She shrugged helplessly. "I don't know. It's just a thought."

"A good thought. We should talk to Imogene and some of the others. Even Silya."

"Andalyssians don't bond sanctii."

"No, but I don't want to rule anything out." He rubbed a hand over his chin and yawned again, then frowned. "They don't have Truth Seekers in Anglion, do they?"

"Not that I've ever heard about. I mean, I guess it is a talent that some may have, but I can't imagine that the temple would have looked very favorably on it. Especially not since they started twisting the goddess's beliefs, anyway. Someone who could know lie from truth would be dangerous. Maybe they killed anyone who showed a sign."

He frowned. "How do they go about solving crimes?"

"The same as everyone else does," she said, waving a hand around the barracks. "I mean, it's not as though every barracks in the country has a Truth Seeker. Talk to people, gather evidence, hold a trial."

"Not that helpful when our most likely evidence in this case is a confession from one of the conspirators. Though I should check whether anything has been found in the troupe's belongings. They should have gotten through most of them by now."

"Silya might know. She was helping them."

"We can find her after this. Though I suspect somebody would already have told us if they'd found anything that might incline Deandra or Istvan to confess."

Chloe shook her head. "It's sad, really. If they are in love. I wonder how she met him."

"Don't go getting sentimental about Deandra Noirene on me now. You already told me that she was never a nice person to begin with."

"True. But love doesn't always distinguish the truth about nice or not, does it?"

He looked mock indignant. "Are you saying I'm not nice?"

"No," she said. "I know you're nice. Terrifying though that truth may be."

He smiled. "Well, at least that's something." He cast a glance at the bed. "You know, they won't be expecting us to reemerge for some time."

She rolled her eyes. "You need to reserve your energy."

"Maybe it would give me energy."

She pushed him away, laughing. "Lie down, Truth Seeker. Think about how you're going to get Deandra to talk."

✦ ✦ ✦

Chloe's stomach didn't feel any easier upon returning to the brig. But she wasn't going to let Lucien talk to Deandra alone.

The lieutenant who'd assisted them before must have gone off duty, because the man seated behind the desk watching the prisoners was Lieutenant James. Istvan was slumped on the small bench in his cell that served as a bed and didn't look up as Lieutenant James stood to greet them.

Deandra, however, was once again standing by the front of her cell, and the look she gave Chloe was no friendlier than it had been previously.

"Major. Lieutenant. Have you come to speak to Mamsille Noirene?" Lieutenant James asked.

"Yes. But I think we'll use the interrogation room. Can you unlock it so I can look inside, please?" Lucien asked.

Lieutenant James nodded and crossed to the door, ignoring Deandra, who turned her head to watch him as he passed. Light shimmered over the door as he placed his hand above the lock. "After you, sir."

Chloe followed Lucien past the lieutenant. The interrogation room was windowless like the rest of the brig, but earth lights on the walls lit it well enough. A rectangular table was bolted to the floor in the center of the room. On the side farthest from the door was a single chair, also bolted to the floor. On the nearer side were two identical chairs that weren't. The table had a large metal ring protruding from its surface on the side of the bolted chair. For the shackles to be hooked to, she realized. Like the ring in the wall of the cell.

She shivered briefly. When she'd visited Charl in prison for the final time, they had done her the favor of letting him forgo the shackles. Not that it had made much difference. They had embraced briefly, and after that, their meeting had gone downhill. Charl sobbing and desperate, and Chloe moving between heartbreak and disbelief, futilely trying to offer her husband some comfort. He'd asked for her forgiveness, and she had pretended to give it. She'd sent the servants away on her return home and spent the night alone, curled on the sofa near the fire in the living room, unable to get warm, racked by nausea and terror. The next morning, Lucien had arrived to tell her he thought she should leave, and her life had changed forever.

"This will do nicely," Lucien said, glancing around. "All right, Lieutenant, move the prisoner. Lieutenant de Roche can call her sanctii to assist."

The lieutenant shot her a half-wary glance. Had he not realized she had a sanctii? But he just said, "Yes, sir. Lieutenant, could you come with me?"

They all trooped back out of the room to stand by his desk while Chloe called Octarus and explained where they wanted him to take Deandra.

She didn't put up any resistance when he entered her cell, though she cast one frantic glance back toward Istvan's cell when Octarus first led her out of hers and into the interrogation room.

But Istvan was still on the bench, and from the way Deandra's face fell, Chloe had to assume she couldn't see him from where she stood. And she couldn't bring herself to feel any sympathy for Deandra as they followed Octarus into the interrogation room.

The sanctii moved quickly, fastening Deandra's shackles to the ring in the table as they watched him.

[Thank you,] Chloe said to him as she and Lucien took their places.

[Stay?] he asked in return.

[Yes. But out of sight. We don't want her focused on you. Lucien needs to work.]

Octarus nodded, then vanished. As soon as he did, Deandra's gaze focused back on Chloe like a snake watching prey.

Lucien straightened beside her, easing his chair forward slightly so he was closer to her.

Deandra laughed. "Don't worry, my lord Truth Seeker," she said, lifting her hands the scant inch the bolt allowed. "It's not as if I can do much like this, is it? I won't hurt your wife."

The last part had the ring of truth, but Chloe didn't relax, just kept her focus on Deandra, waiting for Lucien to begin.

"I think you're in quite enough trouble as it is, Mamsille Noirene, without adding assault of a marquesse to your crimes. Though I guess in some ways we can probably already add that one."

"Oh?" Deandra said, head tilting. "I don't believe I've crossed paths with your wife, my lord. At least not in many years. I believe the last time was in an inn, when she was still a student. We had some fun."

Chloe wouldn't have described that encounter as fun. The night before her Ascension, Deandra had insisted on telling her fortune, and the whole thing had been...unsettling. But Deandra's words felt true. Which meant if it had been her at the parliament, she had erased the memory.

"Very well," Lucien said. "We'll set that matter aside for now."

Deandra eased back, at least as much as her hands would allow. The table was wide enough that she'd have no chance of accidentally touching them, which was clever. A blood mage might be able to harm someone at a distance, but unless Deandra had a sanctii, there wasn't much she could do to hurt them. And there'd been no sign of a sanctii. The others would have noticed a stranger by now.

Lucien also leaned back, looking calm. "You know, this will be faster—and easier—if you tell us what we want to know."

She lifted an eyebrow. "That would be easier if I knew exactly what I've been accused of."

"Well, as I told your companion, at the moment you're being held for your suspected participation in an attack on the empire."

"An attack?" She lifted an eyebrow. "Do you mean what happened in Lumia a few weeks ago? We read about it, of course, but we've been traveling up here."

"Well, we're checking on that," Lucien said. "I'm sure your life with the troupe lets you stay out of sight when you want. But you're a handsome enough woman. I'm sure people will remember if you were present wherever the troupe was at the time of the attack."

Deandra's eyes shifted slightly, and she didn't respond.

"My wife tells me that you were a brunette when you

attended the Academe." He gestured to her hair. "Any particular reason for this?"

She tossed her head. "Perhaps a woman just feels like a change now and then." Her eyes flicked to Chloe. "After all, we don't all have multiple magics to make our hair interesting, do we?"

No, but she was a water mage, whose hair should be dark from her magic.

If she was dyeing her hair, there was a reason. Possibly that reason was to blend in more with the mostly blonde Parthan women in the troupe. Easier for her to not be noticed amongst them. Or noticed if she *wasn't* amongst them, perhaps.

After all, who would pay attention to one more blonde woman in a group of them? It was a clever strategy. Presumably she might use the facial illusions when she was away from the troupe, but she wasn't an illusioner, and casting them on scriptii would be a lengthy process for Istvan, so better to use more ordinary means to make herself less conspicuous where she could.

She was too clever, by half really. Lucien was right. They weren't going to get a confession out of her easily.

But Lucien kept up a steady stream of questions, pressing for more details than he had with Istvan, finding different ways to phrase the questions about whether she'd been in Lumia and whether she was plotting against the emperor.

But Chloe's gut tightened with each answer given. They all felt true. Deandra believed them.

Eventually Lucien fell silent. Deandra stared at him, a small smile playing on her lips.

Lucien pushed back his chair. "That will do for this evening."

"Am I free to go?" Deandra asked.

"No. We will be continuing this conversation in Lumia."

Her eyes went wide for a second. "On what grounds?"

"I'm an Imperial Truth Seeker. I'm not yet satisfied with the outcome of my investigation. That's all the grounds I need."

She looked startled at that. Interesting. Was she confused

that he hadn't believed her despite whatever magic she'd used on her memories?

"But if you are unclear on the powers I hold under the law," Lucien continued, "then let me remind you. The word of a Truth Seeker is taken to be fact. I can give my word and seal your fate. Or not, depending on what I find." He rose then, pushing back his chair. "I look forward to hearing more of your words once we're back in Illvya."

Deandra's jaw had gone tight, but she still managed to glare at Chloe as she stood. "You have done well for yourself, Chloe. Your husband is quite formidable. Something of an improvement, I would imagine, going from a mere minor lordling to a marq. Lumia must have been all talk about it."

The barb was supposed to sting. Once, it might have. But not with Lucien standing solid by her side and her certainty of how he felt about her.

She just raised her chin. "Perhaps, Deandra, rather than trying to needle me, you should think more about the reason that I was able to acquire a second husband. Because my first was foolish. Catastrophically so. He thought he could plot against the emperor successfully. He was wrong. He died because he was wrong." She returned a smile just as poisonously sweet as the one she'd been offered. "Something you might do well to think on."

CHAPTER 16

Lucien lost some of his calm demeanor once they left the brig. Irritation spiked through the bond, making Chloe's temper flare in response. The rational part of her knew it wouldn't be wise to go back to the brig and shake Deandra until she confessed, but the temptation was strong.

Even as she had the thought, Octarus made a humming noise of approval in her head, and she had to warn him to stay calm. Easier said than done, perhaps.

They made their way directly to the colonel's office and informed him that they wanted to question each of the troupe members again.

"You have only three hours before the navire will be departing, and it will take at least an hour to transfer them all on board," Colonel Hislock objected, his bushy gray eyebrows drawing down.

"That will be enough time. I only need to ask them one thing, really," Lucien said.

The colonel looked doubtful, but he nodded. "Very well, Major. Then I suggest you get underway. Do you want me to send a message to the navire, tell them to plan for a delay?"

"No. But I'll want to speak to Major du Laq and Captain

Ilveut once I'm done. Perhaps you could ask them to return to the barracks if they're already on board."

"I saw Captain Ilveut a few minutes ago, but I'll send for the major."

"Thank you. Chloe, come with me."

"Are you going to tell me what's going on?" she asked as they waited for the first of the prisoners to be brought to the conference room he'd commandeered.

"Deandra said she hadn't left the troupe. I need to see what the troupe has to say about that." That was all the explanation he offered.

She simply watched as he asked the same few questions over and over again: Had Deandra been with the troupe a month ago? Where had the troupe been in the last two months? Did she ever leave the troupe?

The answers to the first were an unequivocal "Yes." No one remembered Deandra having left the troupe during the time of the attack. Though the costumier had offered that Deandra kept to herself doing the books and other paperwork rather than mingling with the troupe at times. From the tone, Chloe gathered the two weren't friends.

The information about the troupe's route was consistent with what they'd already established. Whether or not Deandra left the troupe sometimes drew more mixed results. Most people said she did but, when pressed for details of when, drew a blank.

Lucien worked his way through the troupe steadily and they were back in the wardroom in less than two hours to find Imogene pacing restlessly. Captain Ilveut sat at the long table, calmly sipping tea.

"We couldn't have done this on board?" Imogene asked. "We need to be gone in less than an hour."

"Now that the prisoners are all on their way to the navire, it's better to talk here," Lucien said. "No chance of anything being overheard."

"There was little chance of that anyway," Colonel Hillock said dryly. "Our wards are solid. I imagine the navire's are, too."

"I know, but the navire is small, and it will be crowded with so many prisoners."

"Did you find what you wanted?" Imogene asked.

Lucien rubbed the back of his neck. "Mamsille Noirene was, as anticipated, not helpful. But the troupe was more...interesting."

"How so?"

"None of them remember Deandra leaving the troupe in the last month or so."

"That seems more unhelpful than interesting," Imogene said, looking confused.

"Perhaps. But they all remember that time period. They could all tell me about it."

"What does that matter?" The colonel cocked his head in confusion.

"It means that if their memories have been affected in any way, then they've been altered, not erased," Lucien said.

That brought a moment of startled silence to the room.

Captain Ilveut recovered first. "Can that be done?"

"A few days ago, I wouldn't have thought so. But now, I'm not so sure," Lucien replied. "But there was something...not quite right about the way they answered my questions. They all believe what they're saying is true, but they all sounded...too similar."

They did? Why hadn't she noticed that? "In what way?" Chloe asked.

"Thirty people, all with different jobs in the troupe. Different lives. Different experiences. But I asked about the performances that they'd told us about previously, particularly the one in Kilvarnon the day of the attack on the parliament, when Chloe saw Deandra. And so did Octarus. I'd expect an actor to say something like 'Oh yes, that was a good perfor- mance' or maybe that they'd made some small mistake—actors will always tell you about those. And perhaps the costumier might remember damage to a costume, or the stagehands an issue with the set, but no, they all talked about one thing." He turned to Chloe. "Do you remember?"

She frowned, sorting through her memories. "The fire?"

He nodded. "There was apparently a small fire backstage," he explained to the others before focusing on Chloe again. "Do you remember what they said?"

"That someone had knocked over a candle. But Deandra helped put it out and got...Pierre, was it? Got him to safety."

"Yes."

"A fire *would* make an impression," Imogene said.

"It would, but they all explained it nearly identically. Not what they'd been doing when the fire started, but that someone knocked over a candle, and Deandra helped put it out and got Pierre to safety. They all said that. Almost to the word."

"They shouldn't all have such a similar memory," Chloe breathed, realizing what he was getting at.

"No," Lucien agreed. "They shouldn't. I think we've found a thread to tug on. I think someone must be planting memories to cover up when something is erased. Especially where there are gaps of a longer period."

Imogene shuddered. "That's awful. And I'm not sure how you would do it."

"A sanctii," Chloe said. "They can do things that impact our minds. Like the reveilé. Even if no sanctii is actively helping now, one of them must have helped a mage learn how to do this."

"That's no better," Imogene said, looking horrified. "Are we sure they couldn't have used a decoy? Someone made to look like Deandra?"

"I can't rule that out. Istvan is clearly powerful. I'm sure he could do it, particularly if the decoy was able to keep to herself," Lucien admitted. "But it doesn't explain the story about the candle. We need to talk to people who know more about this. Valentin and the healers. And the venables. Perhaps the archives at the Academe might yield something. Find out if anyone has ever tried anything like this before. I imagine it would be kept quiet if it had."

"Yes it would," Chloe agreed. "Neither the emperor nor the Academes would want it to be widely known if a mage tried to tamper with someone's memory to that extent. Not if a sanctii was involved. That would make people scared of sanctii. We'd end up like Anglion. Or worse."

"Henri didn't mention anything back in Lumia," Imogene said.

"He was only thinking about charms that might erase a memory, not replace them. That's something more to go on. And he doesn't know everything that's in the archives. Not even the chief archivist knows that. But they will know how to look," Chloe offered.

"All right. So, we wait until we return to Lumia," Imogene said. "Which means we all need to get back to the navire."

Chloe had hoped she would be able to sleep better once they were heading back to Lumia. But apparently not even Lucien proving again that the bunk beds could indeed withstand uses the army probably hadn't intended after dinner was enough to soothe her to sleep. He was sleeping. She was wide awake, mind whirling from thought to thought but not coming to rest on any one useful idea. Which was exhausting in itself.

Somewhere above her the navire's hour bell chimed the tenth hour. Perhaps Imogene would still be awake.

She slipped out of the bunk gingerly, but Lucien didn't stir. It didn't take long to dress, but when she knocked on Imogene's cabin door, there was no answer. A quick peek into the mess room also yielded no sign of her friend.

She made her way back up on the deck. Given the hour, it was mostly empty, just the mage pairs flying the navire and a few other crew moving around, doing the kinds of things crews did.

She glanced toward the prow and spied a familiar figure wrapped in a cloak standing on the observation deck, looking out at the star-strewn sky. The boards of the deck were slick from the cold, and she picked her way across carefully.

"You're up late," she said, climbing the stairs.

Imogene turned her head and smiled tiredly. "I could say the same for you." Both her hands were wrapped around a mug of something that steamed gently in the night air.

"True." Chloe gestured at the sky surrounding them and the faint glimpses of moonlit land below. "Couldn't resist enjoying the view from your creation?"

Imogene grimaced, one shoulder hitching, and sipped the tea. Chloe caught a waft of mint and something sharper that she thought might be axelberry, which gave her pause. That combination was generally used for settling an upset stomach, and Imogene famously had a cast-iron constitution.

She nodded at the mug. "Don't tell me the woman who invented the navires gets queasy flying in them?" she said.

This time Imogene's grimace was more of a wince. "Not exactly," she muttered.

Chloe studied her friend. Imogene looked, she thought, paler than usual, though it was difficult to judge properly in the moonlight. She cast her mind back over the past few hectic days. Imogene had seemed tired, but then they all were. "Are you sick?" she asked, worry shading her words.

"Not exactly," Imogene said again, and then she placed her hand over her stomach.

Understanding dawned. "Oh. You're *pregnant*," Chloe breathed.

Imogene flashed a quick smile. "I think that is likely, yes."

She couldn't help smiling back. "You think? You're not sure?

Were you and Jean-Paul...trying?" she finished, for lack of a better word.

Imogene took another sip of tea. "We discussed it. We've discussed it many times. He is, after all, a duq. There is the line to consider."

"Yes, that's true." She hesitated, not wanting to push if it was a sensitive subject. She'd been a little surprised when she'd first seen Imogene again in Anglion to learn that she and Jean-Paul hadn't had children. Granted, it was perfectly possible that Imogene had tried while Chloe had been exiled, though she hadn't felt it was her place to ask. But Imogene had access to the best healers in the empire. Surely if she and Jean-Paul wanted children urgently, they would have had them by now. Some women were unable to carry a child, of course, but there would have been rumors around court about that. And, she imagined, Imogene might have told her sometime during the months she and Lucien had spent at Sanct de Sangre. "But now discussions have turned to action?"

"Yes. It was never quite the right time before. I had things I wanted to do, and he was willing to wait. But now I feel ready." She glanced down at her stomach. "I went to see the healers when we decided. They told me it might take some time, after all, I'm hardly young and I have been drinking the teas for many years. Apparently your body needs to adjust when you stop."

Chloe considered. "And how long ago was that?"

Imogene grinned again. "Not quite three months."

Chloe counted back. "That was when we were still staying with you in Sanct de Sangre."

Imogene nodded.

"You never told me that you were thinking about having a baby."

Imogene glanced back toward where the mages flying the navire were seated with their sanctii. "Shh. I don't want the whole ship to know."

"Sorry." Chloe lowered her voice to a whisper. "But that still doesn't change the fact that you never told me."

Imogene shrugged. "You had enough going on without listening to me debating the pros and cons of having children. Not when Lucien was so ill."

Chloe nodded slowly. "I suppose. But we've missed out on too many years of girl talk. I want you to tell me these things." She nudged Imogene gently. "I will always have time for my best friend."

That brought Imogene's smile back. "I promise to bore you with endless discussions of pregnancy and child rearing in the future."

Chloe laughed. "You have a deal. Can I at least squeal silently for a moment? My best friend is having a baby." A thought suddenly occurred to her. "Does Jean-Paul know?"

Imogene shook her head. "Not yet. I was feeling perfectly well when we left. It's only been the last day or so that I've felt nauseous."

"What about your...?" Chloe paused delicately. "Have those been late?"

Imogene nodded. "They've always been somewhat unpredictable. You know that. I really hadn't been paying much attention. After all, there has been quite a lot happening to distract me."

Chloe wriggled in delight. "This is so exciting."

Imogene's smile this time was rueful. "It is," she said, "but I will be a little more delighted when my stomach decides to behave again."

Chloe nodded sympathetically. "You could ask the healer for something stronger to help with that."

"I know well enough about the remedies they'll suggest," Imogene said. "After all, I may not have had a baby before myself, but there have been plenty among the estate workers and mine and Jean-Paul's families. Besides, I have a best friend who's an earth witch and used to run a store that specialized in these kinds of remedies, I believe."

"You're an earth witch, too," Chloe pointed out.

"Yes, but I haven't spent my time learning the healing arts."

True. She had focused more on being a water mage and a mage ingenier when she wasn't working for the diplomatic corps.

"Though I may have to brush up," Imogene continued. "I can't imagine a child of Jean-Paul's won't find exciting ways to get into trouble."

Chloe laughed. "I'm not sure the blame will be solely Jean-Paul's. You are hardly shy and retiring."

"I feel remarkably retiring right now," Imogene said, sipping the tea again. "But apparently sleeplessness comes with the nausea."

"Sounds delightful," Chloe said. "Sadly, most of the herbal aids for sleep are not recommended for pregnancy. You really should speak to a healer to find out what's safe. There are charms and exercises of the mind, I believe. I could probably help with the nausea, but I don't have most of what I'd need with me. We could ask Silya, but she would know what they were for."

Imogene shook her head. "No, I don't want her to know." She lifted the tea. "This helps. It's only another day and a half. A little nausea isn't going to kill me."

"No," Chloe agreed. "But if you feel worse, please tell me straight away. You don't want to take any chances. Are you going to tell Jean-Paul when we get back to Lumia?"

"I will. Or at least that there's a possibility." Imogene smiled and then grimaced. "He's going to be unbearable. He'll probably try to confine me to my room and pad me with feather cushions for the entire time."

Chloe giggled, picturing Jean-Paul. It was easy to imagine him in overprotective father mode, all his considerable attention focused firmly on Imogene, growling at anyone who so much as glanced in her direction. "He does seem like he might lean that way."

"I have too much to do to be locked away, so first I need to be sure." Imogene gestured at her stomach. "I don't suppose you know enough healing magic to tell, do you?"

"I'm not sure," Chloe said. Then she remembered something. "You should ask Ikarus."

Imogene's brows rose. "Ikarus?"

"Papa told me once that Martius always knew when my mother was pregnant. It makes sense—they know more about us than we understand, I suspect. And Ikarus is bonded to you, so he would surely notice such a change in your body."

"I hadn't thought of it," Imogene said. "He has been keeping close on the journey, but he hasn't said anything."

"Perhaps he didn't want to spoil the surprise for you. Ask him."

Imogene blinked, then closed her eyes, clearly talking to her sanctii. The smile that crept across her face almost immediately was all the answer Chloe needed.

✦ ✦ ✦

Chloe laid a hand on Lucien's chest, feeling his heartbeat steadily. The bunk was cramped, but she didn't mind. This was the last night of their journey, as they would be landing in Lumia sometime tomorrow. Who knew when they would simply be able to spend time together again? The investigation would demand all of Lucien's attention for quite some time unless Deandra or Istvan came to their senses.

Lucien made a sleepy questioning noise.

"Sorry, did I wake you?" she asked.

"No, I was awake." He laid his hand over hers, tightening his arm around her. "Not ready to sleep yet."

"You should rest."

"I will. Let me enjoy the moment."

Something tugged at her through the bond, a thread of affection twined with...fear, perhaps.

"Are you worried about what happens when we get home?"

"No. Or not only that." He pressed a kiss against the top of her head.

"Then what?"

"You'll think it's strange."

"Try me."

He sighed. "Sometimes I think you're a dream. That you might vanish again if I fall asleep."

"I'm not going anywhere," she said gently. "Though I would have thought that you would consider me more a nightmare with all the trouble I've brought to your life."

"Never," he said as he stroked her wedding ring. "As long as we're together, I will be perfectly happy." Then he shifted restlessly. "I was thinking maybe I should try again with the troupe members. Maybe I missed something else. Maybe it would be easier if I spoke Parthan and could question some of them in their native tongue."

"One of the sanctii aboard might know it. You could do a reveilé."

He shook his head. "By the time I got over the goddess-damned headache, we'd be back in Lumia anyway. Those things always hurt like a son of a bitch. And they interfere with magic."

"They do?" she asked. "I don't remember that when I learned Andalyssian. The headache, yes, but not the magic."

"Maybe it's me. My head always feels too crowded afterward, like it's not only mine. I wouldn't attempt to use my truth seeking while that was going on."

She laughed. "You think too much."

"Perhaps, but you can't tell me you enjoy a reveilé any more than I do."

She grimaced. "No, having someone force a whole language

into your head is not pleasant." Then she paused, taken by a thought. "You know, we haven't actually asked the sanctii about the memory magic. Not directly." She frowned, trying to wriggle free to move into a sitting position. Difficult given the size of the bunk. "And it's odd that they haven't volunteered anything. Octarus is very focused on finding Rianne's murderers, and he hasn't said anything."

"Do they know?"

"I don't think we can assume they don't. They listen in on what we say. We should ask them."

"You want to talk to Octarus now?"

"No. I think we should talk to Ikarus and Octarus together. Imogene's been bonded a lot longer than I have. She knows more about the rules."

"There are rules?"

"Yes. Well, protocols, I guess. About asking about the sanctii realm. Or the kinds of magic they can do."

Lucien threw back the covers and swung out of the bank. "All right. Let's go find Imogene."

✦ ✦ ✦

Imogene wasn't in her cabin.

"I know where she might be," Chloe said and led Lucien up onto the deck. Sure enough, Imogene was on the observation deck again, her back to the navire, staring out at the night sky. Lucien overtook Chloe, his long legs giving him an advantage. She didn't catch up until he was nearly halfway across the deck. "Slow down," she said. "You don't want to scare her." She lifted her voice. "Imogene. There you are."

Imogene turned, her face creasing in surprise. "I thought you two were sleeping."

"It's a restless night, it seems," Lucien said.

"Yes. Perhaps we should form a club for the sleepless." She cast a wary glance at Chloe, who gave a discreet headshake to reassure her that Lucien knew nothing of the baby. "Are the two of you merely taking in some night air, or did you want to talk to me?"

"We've been talking about the memory magic," Chloe said.

"Of course you have." Imogene rolled her eyes a little. "Lucien, I thought you might take the opportunity to rest while we travel back to Lumia. I should have known better."

"Yes," Chloe agreed, "relaxing might be something we need to work on. But, regardless, we realized that we haven't actually asked the sanctii about the memory charms."

"We don't usually ask the sanctii about their magic," Imogene said warily.

"No, but this is important."

Imogene didn't look convinced. "I know you think a sanctii may have assisted, but we have no proof of that. I'm not sure they would tell us without at least a hint of proof about sanctii involvement."

"What sort of evidence would they need to help us?" Lucien asked.

"I don't know." Imogene shrugged. "What happens in the sanctii realm is closely guarded. And what happens here, well, the mage is in control. It's not the sanctii's will."

"That's not strictly true, though, is it?" Lucien said. "You and Chloe don't control everything Ikarus and Octarus do."

"They wouldn't commit crimes of their own free will," Imogene said. "Bonds have been severed for that, and the sanctii's name gets added to the list of those who cannot be bonded, which leaves them stuck back in their realm. I suppose they might help their mage if they were ordered to do so."

"Elarus helped Sophie and Cameron when they were attacked at the emperor's ball," Lucien said. "There was another sanctii there, helping the attackers. The one Elarus subdued."

Imogene frowned. "Yes. But Elarus is something of a law unto herself, it seems."

Chloe couldn't argue with that. It was just as well that Elarus was bonded to a queen as unconventional as she was.

"Do we know who the other sanctii was?" Lucien asked.

"I'm not sure anyone ever asked. The man who attacked Cameron was killed, which snapped their bond and sent the sanctii back to their realm. What happens there is not our business."

"But if this is all one larger plot, perhaps there is reason to want to talk to that sanctii. Or at least find out who they were bonded to." Lucien frowned. "I'm trying to remember if the dead man was ever identified. I'll have to check the notes from the investigation. But regardless, isn't the fact that a sanctii helped in that attack enough of a connection to at least ask?"

Imogene hesitated. "I don't know."

"Then what harm is it to ask?" Chloe said. "At worst, they refuse us."

"Very well. But not here." Imogene jerked her chin back at the mages flying the navire. "Somewhere private. And well warded. Ikarus and Octarus may understand us asking, but I don't want every sanctii on board suddenly annoyed with us."

No. That wouldn't be good. "The wardroom? We can enhance the wards if we need to."

"That seems as good an option as any," Lucien agreed.

✦ ✦ ✦

It took a few minutes to reach the wardroom, tell the private on duty he wasn't to let anyone else in, and then reinforce the wards to Imogene's satisfaction.

The hum of the magic was loud by the time they had

finished. Chloe tried to block it out and turned to Imogene. "Do you want to ask Ikarus first, or should I ask Octarus?"

"Best we do them together." Imogene's expression went blank, and Chloe followed her example and called Octarus.

He appeared a few seconds before Ikarus. The two sanctii exchanged an inscrutable look before they turned their attention to the humans. In the lamplight, they looked more like pieces of night come to life than usual, the flickers of light over their gray-and-black skins blending them with the shadows in the room.

Were they conversing silently? No way to know. Ikarus, she noticed, placed himself between Octarus and Imogene. Extra protective due to the baby, perhaps?

She widened her eyes at Imogene, making a little "go on" gesture at her. Imogene had been bonded to Ikarus a lot longer than Chloe had with Octarus, and it seemed safer to approach this subject over the lens of the more stable relationship.

"We have a request," Imogene said.

"Yes," Ikarus said in his graveled voice.

"We need to know about memory magic. We thought maybe a sanctii might be involved. It's possible that memories are being added, not just taken away. That seems like the reveilé. Is it something a sanctii could do?"

This time the two sanctii exchanged a look that was too long to be anything other than them discussing it. Chloe waited quietly, watching Octarus.

"Should," Octarus said eventually, dipping his head toward Ikarus.

"No," Ikarus grunted.

Octarus grunted back, the sound a rasp of displeasure. [He will say no,] he said in Chloe's head.

Just as Ikarus said, "We cannot ask. This is forbidden."

"Is the magic forbidden, or talking about it with humans?" Imogene asked.

Ikarus folded his arms. "Forbidden." He clamped his mouth shut, brow wrinkling, clearly not willing to say anything else.

[Stubborn,] Octarus said.

[If he won't, can you ask Elarus?] Chloe said. [She seems to do things other sanctii don't.]

For a start, Elarus was female. The only female sanctii currently bonded in the empire. They rarely came to the human realm, but Elarus had sought Sophie out. For what reason, Chloe had no idea. But she'd seen the male sanctii defer to Elarus on numerous occasions, and, if she had to guess, she would say Elarus outranked them in some fashion. If the sanctii had such things as rank.

[No,] Octarus said.

[So Ikarus isn't just being stubborn. There is some sort of, what, protocol?]

There was silence before he replied. [Elarus could tell. We cannot.]

Chloe looked at Imogene, who was clearly having a similar conversation with Ikarus.

Lucien cleared his throat. "If someone could speak out loud, that would be helpful," he said in a calm tone.

Both the sanctii shot him a look, and he held up his hands. "I'm not saying the two of you should do anything forbidden, but I would like to know what's going on, if that's possible, please."

Imogene huffed out a breath. "They don't want to tell us, and they don't want to ask Elarus. I'm not entirely sure why." She looked at Ikarus.

He waved a hand at the walls. "Cannot speak to her here anyway."

Goddess damn it. They hadn't thought of that.

"We're traveling over land, not ocean," Imogene objected. "Can't you return to your realm? The sanctii help fly the navire, after all."

"Fly. Not talk," Octarus insisted.

"Very well," Imogene said after another silent exchange with Ikarus. "Thank you, anyway."

The sanctii disappeared again. Though Octarus said, [Talk,] in Chloe's head before he vanished. She didn't know whether he meant he wanted to talk to her or that she should continue talking to Imogene. But if it was the former, it was going to have to wait.

Lucien folded his arms. "It seems we need a different plan."

"Yes, there's clearly something more at play," Chloe said, crossing to the wardroom's long table to sit, suddenly feeling exhausted. Imogene followed suit. "Though they didn't say *we* couldn't ask Elarus. Only that they wouldn't."

"Their reluctance suggests that perhaps we're on the right path. If this is something the sanctii are nervous about discussing, then it's clearly something they don't tell us about. Which, admittedly, could be almost anything about them." He huffed in frustration but joined them at the table.

"The reveilé was discovered by a water mage," Chloe said. "That's what they taught us at the Academe."

"Yes. It makes you wonder whether it was the other way around. His sanctii taught him."

"We need to talk to my father. And the other venables. Maybe even some of the army's water mages. Though they tend to stick to the rules more," Chloe said. Then grinned and looked at Imogene. "Present company excepted, of course."

"Which is something else we can't do while we're on this ship." Imogene gestured vaguely at the walls. "We need to wait until we're back in Lumia."

"Then there's the small matter of Elarus being in Anglion with Sophie. The sanctii don't communicate over the sea, do they?" Chloe asked.

"No," Imogene said. "But the emperor has more than a few navires. Some travel to Anglion. Perhaps Sophie and Elarus would be willing to come talk to us."

"Cameron won't like that. Bringing Sophie back here, where people tried to harm her," Lucien replied.

He probably had a point. Chloe leaned back in her seat,

considering. "People were plotting against her in Anglion, too. I think she would be as happy to get to the bottom of this as Aristides."

"Organizing a royal visit isn't something that just happens overnight," Imogene objected.

"It doesn't have to be an *official* royal visit. Their Majesties can just come and talk to us, stay on the damn ship if they need to, though I can't imagine Elarus would appreciate that. And then they can go home again. Without anyone being the wiser," Chloe said.

Imogene looked skeptical. "I don't know about that, but if that's what you want to suggest, my vote is that you're the one who gets to tell Aristides."

Lucien barked a laugh. "I second that."

Chloe put her hands on her hips and stared at them. "Cowards."

"Think of it this way," Imogene said. "If Elarus comes and she can help us with the answer, it will go a long way to improving your reputation at court again."

Chloe narrowed her eyes. "You both keep telling me I have nothing to worry about in that respect."

"You don't," Imogene said airily. "But it still can't hurt that you're seen to be helpful. Is it helpful to propose something that's going to be difficult for the emperor?"

Lucien shrugged. "It won't be difficult for him. If he agrees with us, it will be done. As Imogene has said, I'm sure Queen Sophia will be willing to help us if she can. Someone might just have to tie her husband to a chair for the entire voyage so he doesn't lose his mind."

He glanced at Chloe, smiling lopsidedly. "Perhaps he and I and Jean-Paul can form a club for the hard done by husbands of willful women."

Imogene snorted. "I suggest you try, my lord. And see how far you get."

CHAPTER 17

When they finally descended the gangplank in Lumia and worked their way around the squads of soldiers waiting on the docks to transfer the prisoners, Chloe spied a familiar carriage waiting for them. She turned to Lucien, who had stretched his arms wide as though happy to be back on solid ground, with more room to move than the navire. "You sent word ahead?"

"Naturally. The staff needed to know what date we would be returning so they could reopen the townhouse."

His tone was matter-of-fact, and Chloe sighed. The need to do that hadn't even crossed her mind. "One day I might learn to think like a proper aristo lady." She wasn't sure she truly believed she was back in Lumia, let alone facing the prospect of being a marquesse for the rest of her life.

Lucien chuckled. "You've had other things on your mind. You will grow accustomed." He nodded toward the carriage. "Shall we, my lady?"

"Yes. I, for one, will be glad of a bath." And to sleep in a proper bed again. Not that there would be much time for sleep in the days ahead.

"Plenty of time for that. The prisoner transfer will take a

while. Aristides will be expecting a report, but I'm sure he'll grant us a few hours' grace."

The emperor wasn't exactly famed for his patience. But Lucien knew him better than she did.

Chloe glanced back toward the navire and saw Imogene descending, her head turning as she searched the crowd. When her face broke into a brilliant smile, Chloe assumed she'd spotted Jean-Paul somewhere in the throng. Apparently, Lucien wasn't the only one who'd sent ahead. She smiled, imagining Imogene getting to tell Jean-Paul her news. "Even if there's a message waiting for us when we get home, we'll just have to pretend we didn't see it immediately. I'm not going straight to see the emperor after three days of washing in a basin." Facing Aristides would be hard enough with feeling grimy and wrinkled.

She slipped her hand through Lucien's arm, but they only managed to get another fifty feet or so toward the carriage when a familiar figure stepped into their path.

"Captain Brodier," Chloe said, jerking to a halt, stomach swooping.

"Lieutenant," the captain said. "Welcome back to Lumia." Her tone was professional, her expression neutral.

With her white-blonde hair and ice-blue eyes, Honoré had a daunting presence at the best of times. Running into one of her superior officers for the first time since technically abandoning her post wasn't the best of times. "Thank you. I'm glad to be back," Chloe said, trying to sound calm.

Honoré turned to Lucien. "Major de Roche. Would it be possible to have a few moments with the lieutenant?"

Lucien looked at Chloe, and she wanted to ask him to stay, but she realized that in this situation, she needed to follow protocol. Honoré was her immediate commanding officer. Lucien, though he outranked her, was in another branch of the services altogether. If he tried to overstep and interfere in what-ever Honoré wanted to say, that would be only more trouble. She sent him a little pulse of reassurance through the bond, and he nodded once. "I'll be in the carriage," he said and strode off.

Chloe turned back to Honoré. "Captain. What can I do for you?"

Honoré straightened her shoulders. "I'm glad to see that you have returned, Lieutenant."

Chloe opened her mouth to start to explain, but Honoré held up a hand. "I'll make this short because I'm sure you've had a long journey, and I understand that you're involved in ongoing business for the emperor." She lifted an eyebrow. "For that reason, Lieutenant, we have been ordered to overlook the fact that you left the city without informing us."

Chloe winced. "I'm sorry. I know it was...not protocol. But the circumstances were unconventional."

Honoré straightened. "Unconventional," she said slowly. "That seems to be becoming your default mode of operation."

"I didn't intend to leave. But...." She didn't know how to explain. *She* knew why she had left, but the army would interpret her actions however they chose, regardless.

Honoré nodded. "I understand, Lieutenant, but you also need to understand that in the diplomatic corps, you are just a lieutenant. A very newly minted one. You are not a marquesse, and there are rules to be followed. This time, there are to be no repercussions, but you cannot keep relying on that being the case in the future. After all, a diplomat who cannot follow protocol is of no use to the corps."

Chloe nodded, swallowing against her suddenly dry mouth. The warning was clear enough: Next time, they wouldn't be so lenient. "I understand. And I am grateful for another chance. It won't happen again."

Honoré sighed and then smiled ruefully. "Well, it seems you have a knack for finding trouble, or sniffing out trouble, at least. That can also be a useful talent. You just need to learn to resolve it in a more collegiate fashion, perhaps." She glanced over her shoulder at the carriage. "But go on, Lieutenant. I'm sure you have business to attend to. Once this investigation has concluded, you'll be reassigned back to the corps, and we will take things from there."

"Thank you," Chloe said with a brief salute. "I'll try not to let you down."

She managed to keep the smile off her face until she had moved past Honoré and was heading to the carriage.

Well, that was one question settled. She hadn't been thrown out of the corps, at least. And she still had a chance of making a career.

Of course, that was the least of her problems faced with the more immediate issues of the investigation.

✧ ✧ ✧

She reached the carriage, and Oscar, their driver, opened the door for her. She stepped up and swung herself into her normal place opposite Lucien, only to realize that he wasn't alone.

"Good morning, Chloe," Jacqueline de Roche said.

Seated next to her son, she was as immaculate as ever, dressed in a green and bronze day dress that made Chloe all too aware that her uniform was rumpled and travel stained. She managed to clamp down on her immediate instinct to get straight back out of the carriage, instead casting a startled glance at Lucien, who was looking studiously polite. She made herself smile and turned to face her mother-in-law. "Good morning, Jacqueline. How kind of you to come to meet us."

She saw Lucien's eyes widen fractionally, but he just thumped on the carriage roof to let Oscar know they were ready to leave.

Almost immediately the carriage lurched into motion. *Perfect.* Trapped with her no doubt disapproving mother-in-law for the duration of their journey home.

Jacqueline smiled tightly. "I had to see for myself that you had indeed returned to the city after all the drama of your wedding ball."

"Mother," Lucien said warningly, "what happened at the ball was not Chloe's fault. It was an attack on the emperor. If not for her, many people could have died."

Jacqueline pressed her lips together, straightening on the seat. "Be that as it may, it does not change the fact that your ball turned into exactly the kind of scandal that we were trying to avoid."

Lucien stiffened, and annoyance pulsed through the bond. "I don't care about that. I don't think many people consider an assassination attempt a mere scandal. The attack on the emperor would have happened at some point, regardless of whether or not Chloe and I were having a wedding ball."

His tone was sharp. Chloe wished she could turn invisible. Of course, she could ask Octarus to shield her, but she could only imagine what Jacqueline's reaction would be to that.

But at least the woman's attention was temporarily focused on her son—who was getting the full force of the famous de Roche glare. "There are those who say she was involved."

"And I say she was not. The only narrative we will be accepting is the one where Chloe averted the attack on the palace. She then bravely followed one of the perpetrators and helped the Imperial mages track her down, enabling us to bring her and some of her fellow conspirators back to the city to be interrogated so we can get to the bottom of this whole damn mess. A narrative which, may I add, has the benefit of being true. Do you understand?" Lucien glared back, green eyes turning cold. Of the two, Chloe rather thought he was the more intimidating.

"I—" Jacqueline started.

"No," Lucien said firmly. "*Do you understand?* I accept that you were not thrilled about the manner in which Chloe and I were married, but we held our second wedding as you requested to address that. The fact that someone chose to use our ball as a target is not something Chloe or I could have controlled. And her reputation as my *wife*," he growled, "is one that you, as a senior member of this family, will do nothing but support. Do I make myself clear?"

Jacqueline blinked at him, not answering.

Chloe didn't say anything either. Lucien was daunting in his Truth Seeker mode. Apparently, he was equally impressive when he chose to play the marq in earnest and put his foot down.

"Well?" he asked, staring at Jacqueline.

Jacqueline's mouth flattened, but then she nodded. "I understand." She looked at Chloe. "As long as you understand the position of this household."

Chloe nodded. "I'm well aware of the importance of the Castaigne estate and the family. That's one of the reasons why I want nothing more than to see the empire returned to peace. It's safer for all of us, including the future of this family. And I hope you understand that I honor the vows I make, including those to the emperor and to the Imperial mages. That may make me different from other people who have been the marquesse before me, but that does not mean I cannot be a good one or that I do not understand the importance of the undertaking. And I think it would be easier for all of us if we could work together rather than apart."

Lucien leaned forward slightly. "And working together, Mother, does not mean that we will simply accept everything that you want us to do. The responsibility for the house is ours now. And while we will appreciate your guidance and counsel, final decisions will also be ours."

Jacqueline settled back in the seat. Her expression was stern at first, but then reluctant approval stole over her face. "Good," she said finally. "I am glad that you are both aware of your responsibilities."

"Mother, there has not been one minute of my life that I

have not been aware of my responsibilities to the family. You and Father raised me well, so now you have to trust me to do what I consider is right."

"But your magic," she said. "You cannot—"

He held up a hand.

"I have rarely employed my ability as a Truth Seeker in matters of the house," he said. "And, after all, neither you nor Father had that ability, and you did well enough, as have many generations of our ancestors. The current limitations to my magic impact my role as Truth Seeker, not as the marq. And, if I have my way, they will be temporary."

"Does that mean you have found the people who carried out the attack?" Jacqueline asked.

"You know I can't talk to you about my work," Lucien said. "So, now that we've cleared the air, perhaps you can tell us what's been happening here whilst we've been away."

That much she was happy to do. Chloe and Lucien only had to murmur the odd word of encouragement for the entire length of the journey back into town. They delivered Jacqueline to Maison Castaigne, and Chloe blew out a breath of relief as the carriage set off again.

"That was...interesting," she muttered, glancing out the window to see Jacqueline marching up to the front steps without looking back. They could, of course, have gone to the townhouse first and then let Jacqueline return with the carriage—the de Roche stables were at Maison Castaigne, not at the townhouse—but she rather thought Lucien was making a point that he got to choose what happened, not his mother.

Lucien huffed out a breath. "Just what we didn't need. But maybe it's just as well. We needed to have the discussion sooner or later. And I think she understands our position now."

"I hope so. I would rather be friends with your mother than enemies."

He laughed. "You and me both. And don't worry. She can be fierce when she thinks she's protecting the family. I understand that. But as long as she's satisfied that you are also going to be equally fierce in that cause, then I think she'll leave us be."

"Apart from always keeping an eye on us to make sure I'm not dancing in front of the palace in an inappropriate frock or something equally scandalous?"

Lucien's eyes gleamed. "I would like to see you in a scandalous frock. But perhaps we can keep those for more private situations."

Chloe snorted. "Yes, that might be best. I would be perfectly happy if we lived a very boring life from now on."

Lucien laughed again. "If you're going to be a diplomat, it seems unlikely." His head tilted in curiosity. "What did Captain Brodier have to say?"

Chloe spread her hands. "Only that I've been assigned to the investigation for the immediate future, and then I'm to report back to the corps once it's done for my next assignment."

A pleased grin spread over his face. "See, I told you I had nothing to worry about."

Chloe shrugged. "I'm not entirely sure that's true. I got the distinct feeling that they had been ordered to let the fact that I effectively deserted slide. But I will have some fences to mend."

"Well, it is a corps full of diplomats. View it as good practice."

✦ ✦ ✦

As Lucien had predicted, a request from the emperor to attend him arrived three hours after they arrived home. When they reached the palace, they were met by Imogene, who had received her own summons. Louis, Aristides's seneschal, whisked them through the palace to the family wing and into one of Aristides's private offices.

The emperor was already seated behind the desk, and Lucien

hid his surprise and bowed. He wore a white linen shirt and black trousers. The shirt sleeve on the right side had been short-ened to accommodate the bandage wrapped around his forearm. The only sign of his normal finery were the rings covering his fingers, though several of them had black stones rather than his usual diamonds.

Lucien was relieved to see Aristides looking somewhat recov-ered, the cut on his face mostly healed, but the fury in the emperor's eyes was banked, not extinguished. He cast a warning glance at Chloe and stepped forward when Aristides demanded their report in clipped tones, determined to take the brunt of any displeasure himself.

When he finished his retelling, supplemented by Chloe and Imogene interjecting occasionally, Aristides regarded them with an expression that suggested that he thought perhaps the three of them had spent far too much time in the hot sun during their travels. "You think someone is using a sanctii to create false memories? Is that even possible?"

"We are looking into that, Your Imperial Majesty," he said carefully. "But we cannot dismiss it entirely. Not when things such as a reveilé are possible."

Aristides looked stern. "And how long before we know?"

"That is the complicated part, Your Imperial Majesty," Chloe said before Lucien could answer. "We asked our sanctii, but there are protocols around speaking of their magics. They couldn't answer."

Aristides lifted an eyebrow. "Do your sanctii not have to do as you say?"

"That is not exactly how it works," Imogene said.

"They did tell us that Elarus would be able to speak to us," Chloe added hastily.

"Elarus? What is different about her?" Aristides asked.

"We don't know much about the differences between females and males in sanctii society, but based on what we've seen, well, my guess is Elarus is...higher ranked? However that works in their world," Chloe said.

The emperor's eyebrows lifted higher. "You think she is an aristocrat of some kind?"

Chloe spread her hands. "It's only speculation, Your Imperial Majesty. But that would explain why she's allowed to speak to us about things that they cannot. I'm sure Queen Sophia would ask her on our behalf."

"Queen Sophia is not here," Aristides pointed out. "Which means her sanctii is not here either, unless you are also about to inform me that sanctii have learned how to cross an ocean freely."

Chloe shook her head. "No, Your Imperial Majesty, but we could send a navire for Sophie. It would take, what, four days at the most, three if the winds are favorable?"

Aristides looked somewhat exasperated. "What makes you think Sophia would be willing to come here? At this point, Illvya seems more dangerous than Anglion."

His expression darkened again.

Lucien cleared his throat. "We believe Queen Sophia will be as eager as you are to uncover the details of this plot. Her palace was attacked as well. She only holds her throne because King Stefan and then Queen Eloisa were both murdered. I think it would be foolish, at this point, to assume that there are no connections between the attempts here and in Anglion. After all, Illvyan magic was used in Anglion in the attack on the palace. Someone had to provide the scriptii. And if the memories of those who were involved were amended with this magic, then that could explain why we've never gotten to the bottom of it."

"That and the fact that the temple was likely actively working to hide it," Aristides said slowly.

"Yes," Chloe agreed. "Domina Skey was ruthless enough to do whatever she thought was necessary in her execution of her attempt to control Eloisa. Including using forbidden magic."

"She wasn't a water mage, though," Aristides said.

"No. But you don't have to be to use a scriptii. You just have to be able to work the trigger and then destroy the object if it's not set to destroy itself."

The emperor pursed his lips, twisting the heavy Imperial signet on his left hand restlessly. "It seems we may have been overly hasty in allowing them to execute Domina Skey."

Lucien couldn't argue with that. "Perhaps. But this plot is not the work of one person alone. There will be others." His hand curled into a fist. "This is important, Your Imperial Majesty. If Elarus is willing to help, it may be our best hope."

Aristides sighed, looking suddenly exhausted. He probably hadn't had a good night's sleep since the attack. Given the suspicions over Alain, in his place, Lucien wouldn't sleep either. But it was Lucien's job to ensure that the emperor acted as the emperor, not the dismayed father.

"All three of you agree on this?" Aristides asked.

"Yes, Your Imperial Majesty. I understand that you may be reluctant to believe me, and I cannot prove to you that I'm telling the truth, but I think this is the best course of action," Chloe said with a ring of authority that made Lucien think of his mother.

Perhaps Chloe was becoming the marquesse after all.

Aristides scrubbed a hand over his face, the rings on his hands glinting. "So be it. I will send a message to Queen Sophia and request her assistance. Perhaps I should send Lady Margaretta to carry it. That would take care of one set of problems, at least. It has been somewhat difficult to prove to the Anglions that our society is a safe and peaceful one when they have been subject to nothing but chaos and mayhem since they arrived."

Lucien cleared his throat. "That may well be an argument for keeping them here rather than sending them away. If we can show them that we have gotten to the bottom of the crime, give them a chance to see us, how we work together and keep order, then that may leave a better impression than sending them home in the wake of an attack."

Aristides considered for a moment. "You may be right. Though I cannot stop them if they choose to leave. Or if Queen Sophia requests their return."

"Has Lady Margaretta given any indication that she wants to leave?" Chloe asked. "She stayed after what happened at the parliament. I don't think she scares easily."

"No, she has not asked," Aristides admitted. "I do not suppose you would care to go, Lieutenant de Roche? It would fall within the remit of the diplomatic corps."

Did he want her out of the city? Or was he offering her a way to get away from danger? Lucien tried to keep his face neutral but sent reassurance over the bond to Chloe. If she wanted to go, he would let her. She might well be safer in Anglion. Though the thought of being separated made his jaw tighten.

"No, Your Imperial Majesty. I believe it's better that I stay here with Lucien. The healers...well, they are still keen for us not to strain our bond."

Aristides quirked an eyebrow. "I understood that you had broken that bond?"

"We had. But we have formed another."

"Does this mean you have come to the end of your mutual idiocy?"

"Your Imperial Majesty?" she squeaked.

"I mean you have given up whatever nonsense it is that had you seemingly determined to deny that you are in love with each other."

"*What?*" Lucien choked.

"I am not an idiot, Lucien," Aristides said, looking amused for the first time in the entire conversation. "You married her in Andalyssia because there was no other choice. But you made no effort to get out of it once you returned."

"I was unconscious for quite some time."

Aristides snorted. "And then wide awake for even longer. You could have divorced her. You did not. Chloe could have even asked me to let her out of the marriage, given the circumstances, but she did not. You two care about each other. You just need to stop pretending otherwise and get on with it." He waved a hand. "Yes, there are complications from your past, but what is done is done. Do not turn away from happiness. You never know when things can change for the worse." His eyes narrowed. "Though I trust you will not be asking if there can be celebration of your nuptials. I am not sure the empire can stand the excitement of whatever might happen at a third de Roche wedding ball."

Imogene giggled at that. Easy for her to be amused.

Lucien recovered first. "No, Eleivé, that won't be necessary."

Aristides actually smiled at that. "I am glad to hear it."

He turned his attention to Imogene. "And you, Major? Sophia knows you."

Imogene's amusement shifted to a polite aristo mask. "If you insist, Your Imperial Majesty, but I would prefer to remain with my husband *at this time*."

The emperor frowned, looking as though he was about to tell Imogene that it was his preferences, not hers, that were important.

Lucien felt an odd combination of amusement and concern from Chloe. Did she know why Imogene was refusing?

"There are matters of our estate that are...pressing," Imogene added in a gentler voice.

Aristides's eyes narrowed as he looked at her for a moment, and then the side of his mouth lifted, apparent understanding lightening his expression. "Well, far be it from me to stand between you and the duties of the du Laq house."

The amusement flowing through the bond increased as Imogene's expression turned to relief.

She rested one hand on her stomach briefly before clasping her hands behind her back, and suddenly it hit him. She was pregnant. That would explain the late-night chats with Chloe aboard the navire and the endless cups of herbal tea she had drunk on the return journey.

He fought to keep a smile off his face. Protocol required that everyone pretend that a pregnancy didn't exist until the couple announced it. Though Imogene couldn't be very far along—the lines of her uniform were as sleekly tailored as ever. Which was another reason she may not wish to travel. Or say why.

"Very well," Aristides said. "I am sure Colonel Ferritine can find someone to send. We have had several delegations back and forth already. Anything else?"

"No, Your Imperial Majesty," Lucien said.

"What will you do while we wait for Queen Sophia to arrive?" Aristides asked, clearly entertaining no notion that Sophie would refuse to come.

"Research," Chloe said. "We need to hunt through all the archives and see if we can find anything similar to this that has happened before."

"You think someone else has learned this magic in the past?"

"Or something similar. Given what it allows people to do, I can only think that if it has, no one would have wanted it known." She tilted her head at Aristides. "Do emperors share knowledge of such things, Your Imperial Majesty?"

Her tone was cautious. Aristides's father had died young. The emperor had ascended to the throne at eighteen. And while he'd been raised as the heir from birth, there may well be things his father had never had time to share.

"I have archives of my own," Aristides admitted. "I have never heard of such a thing, but many of my forebears kept diaries and records of one kind or another. I used to have to study parts of them when I was younger."

"That must have been enlightening," Lucien said.

"Some of it," Aristides agreed. "Though much of it was long entries about negotiations of tariffs and tax quotas, which, while enlightening, is not what anyone would describe as exciting. I preferred the anecdotes about military history. I suspect I was too young to be shown anything too scandalous during my education. And I have never needed to turn my attention to magical misdeeds in the past. But there are full copies held in the palace archives. I shall consult my record keepers."

CHAPTER 18

Two days later, Chloe had a distinct urge to set fire to the entire archives. After far too many hours of trawling through ancient texts unearthed by the archivists, including Venable Orleane, the Academe's Chief Archivist herself, she was wondering if mages were deliberately oblique in writing about their magical discoveries. She put down the latest dusty tome, which seemed to focus far more on the author's obsession with irrigation in the town he'd settled in than actual water magic, and groaned.

Lucien and Imogene, seated across the table from her, looked up hopefully.

"Don't get excited. That was frustration, not discovery." She pushed back her chair and stood, stretching her arms wide to ease the ache in her back from too many hours spent hunched over books.

From above her came a squawk. She looked up at Mai, perched in what had become her usual position on the top of the nearest bookshelf. Ever since Chloe had set foot back in the Academe two days ago, the raven had been her constant shadow. She shouldn't have been able to get into the archives, which were off-limits to students, let alone birds, but her antics had been something of a welcome counter to their unsuccessful search for any clues about memory magic. They had found plenty of references to such things being forbidden and too dangerous to try, but not so much on why.

They had more luck learning about how the healers eased a memory, but that, as Valentin had already explained, wasn't the same as erasing it completely. There were a few herbal concoctions that could have the same effect, but they were also temporary.

Even the record of the incident that had earned Deandra her expulsion was lacking in any useful detail about how she'd been planning to erase the memory of the student who'd been manning the library the night Deandra tried to steal old exams.

Henri had admitted that he'd been more focused on simply dealing with the expulsion, given the magic had clearly been unsuccessful. Nothing similar had happened since, maybe precisely because of how strongly the story of Deandra and her fellow conspirator had been impressed upon new generations of students.

Cheat and lose any hope of graduating from any of the empire's Academes.

Mai squawked again. Chloe held out her arm in invitation, knowing the raven would just keep interrupting if she didn't. Mai swooped down, landing gracefully on Chloe's forearm.

"I should take Mai back to the tower before Mestier Allyn comes looking. It's getting late." They had been in the library since midday, only taking short breaks for meals because not even Henri could convince Venable Orleane to allow food or drink in the library.

Lucien rubbed the bridge of his nose, nodding agreement, "I think we have done as much as we can for today. I need to check in with the judiciary, and we're not going to find anything if we're all falling asleep." So far, Lucien had not been called to interrogate any of the prisoners again. Instead, the Advocate General had insisted some of the other Truth Seekers try.

So far none of them had had any more success than Lucien.

They, too, had noticed odd similarities in the testimony provided by the members of the troupe, though nothing that was proof enough to condemn Deandra or Istvan. Who had, so far, remained staunchly insistent on their original stories. Istvan had offered a little more information on who he'd taught his facial illusions to, mostly other illusioners working in theaters and opera houses like Violette. They were being brought to the capital, too, but so far no one had admitted to using the magic for anything other than entertainment.

"Imogene, can I call your carriage?" Lucien asked when no one disagreed.

"Yes, thank you." She flashed a smile that failed to hide her relief. She'd insisted on accompanying them to do the research but had looked distinctly pale and queasy at several points over the last few days, despite her protests that she felt fine. Rising, she began to gather her things, clearly keen to leave. "Shall we meet again in the morning? Perhaps the palace will have found something useful today."

Lucien stood, too. "I'm not sure there is anything to find. Aristides has an entire team of archivists combing the records, and they haven't uncovered anything yet." He sighed and rolled his shoulders before coming around the table to join Chloe.

Mai turned her head and squawked at him, the sound annoyed.

"I agree with that sentiment, young raven," he said, smiling as Mai bobbed her head. "But sadly, yelling at things does not magically fix them." He turned and headed back toward the row of desks near the front of the archives, clearly intending to ask one of the mages on duty to call for Imogene's carriage.

Chloe tilted her arm up, trying to encourage Mai to move to her shoulder where her weight was more comfortable. "I don't think any of the librarians will approve if we all start cawing like ravens," she said to Imogene. Then she squawked as Mai leapt to her shoulder and started tugging at a piece of her hair, teasing it free from its braid. "Ow."

Octarus appeared beside her, looking down at the bird. "Gentle, small friend," he rumbled.

Mai let go of the hair and fluttered over to his shoulder instead.

The two of them seemed to be becoming fast friends, which made Chloe nervous. Whatever the reason for their connection, she wasn't entirely sure she was ready to accept what that might mean for her. Mai shadowing her every move within the Academe likely meant that the bird was trying to claim her, much as Tok had done with Sophie.

But with a newly acquired sanctii and a newly acquired husband she still wasn't entirely used to, adding a petty fam to the list hadn't been in her plans.

She would have to make up her mind soon, or likely Mestier Allyn would want to send Mai to another Academe, where there might be a mage who appreciated her attention.

Lucien came back to them. "Your carriage will be ready shortly, Imogene."

"Thank you," she said. "I'll go wait for it. I'm sure between the three of you, you can escort one small raven back to the tower."

Chloe nodded and started stacking the books in front of her into two piles: those she'd already read through and the ones she'd start again with in the morning. "Good night. We'll see you in the morning. Octarus, we need to take Mai back to the tower."

It didn't take long to hand Mai over to Mestier Allyn, who distracted the raven with her dinner while Chloe and Lucien made their escape, returning home to eat the meal Madame Garot had waiting for them.

Afterward, Lucien retired to his study to deal with estate issues, and Chloe curled up on his sofa with a book on water magic that Henri had loaned her. When the clock on his mantelpiece chimed nine, she was starting to yawn. Time to convince Lucien to stop working and retire for the evening. Their days weren't likely to get shorter any time soon. Indeed, once Sophie and Elarus arrived in another day or so, they were likely to get longer still.

But she had only just closed the book when there was a knock on the study door, and Madame Garot came in, bearing an envelope.

"My lord, a message. They said it was urgent," she said, handing the letter to Lucien before leaving them alone.

Urgent? That was either good news or bad. Chloe's heart started to race as Lucien broke the seal and pulled out the letter.

She held her breath while he read.

"It's from Maxim," he said, glancing up from the note. "They need me. They think Istvan is starting to crack. They want to bring me back in to apply some pressure."

"So late?" The thought of him returning to the judiciary now didn't sit easy. Especially without her. But it seemed the request was for him alone or he would have said "they need us," not "they need me." The judiciary wasn't aware that the bond let her share some of his talent, and she'd prefer it stayed that way.

"Better not to give him a chance to rest and change his mind," Lucien said. He turned the page over and made a humming noise of surprise.

"What?"

"They want to try offering him the chance to see Deandra. It seems they've decided she's his weak point."

"Is that usual?"

"It's not unheard of. Sometimes the smallest things turn out to be the key in these situations. If he truly cares for her, he may cooperate if he thinks it will help her."

She winced, and he cocked his head. "You don't approve?"

She pushed up from the sofa, suddenly feeling the need to move. "I think he's foolish if he believes she cares. And he's going to pay a price for that foolishness."

Lucien crossed to her, enfolding her in a hug. "This must bring back old memories."

"Doesn't it for you?" She swallowed, trying to push away the regret and guilt and anger that always followed in the wake of her memories of Charl.

"Some. But I've been doing this for a long time. I can separate the past from the present when it comes to the work. It's something we all have to learn." He released her. "You should go to bed. I'll be back as soon as I can."

He was out the door a few minutes later, leaving her alone in the townhouse, which suddenly felt too empty. She lingered in the front hall, uncertain what to do next.

She heard Madame Garot coming up behind her, the rattle of the keys she wore at her waist as good as a bell around a cat's neck. "Can I get you anything, my lady?"

"No, thank you. You should go. I'll be fine."

Though that much might not be true. She felt restless, unsettled now that Lucien was gone. She had been in the townhouse without him before, of course, but the weeks before the wedding had been a whirlwind, and she'd been glad for any chance to catch her breath. Now she felt...adrift. And not a little resentful that she'd been excluded, if she were honest.

Sleep didn't appeal, so she retreated to Lucien's study, taking up her book again. But she couldn't settle to reading and found herself pacing around the room, unsure of the source of the tension. Was it a trace of nerves from Lucien reaching her through the bond or just worry because she hadn't gone with him? She'd never really focused on how far from her he could be before she couldn't feel him. It was different from a bond with a sanctii. Octarus's own magic meant he could always find her, and she could always talk to him. But she didn't feel Octarus like she did Lucien.

She closed her eyes for a moment to see if she could feel him now. Maybe. A faint sense of him to the north of the townhouse, which was in the general direction of the palace.

Maybe she would be less on edge if they were closer. Perhaps she could go visit Imogene in the palace. It wasn't that late by aristo standards. The social season would normally be in full force, and even though some of the balls and entertainments had been reined in or delayed since the attack on the palace, no doubt some were still being held. The alliances of marriage formed during these events each year were too important to how the whole system of the noble families operated to cancel entirely.

Imogene hadn't mentioned that she had an engagement this evening, but that didn't rule it out. But even if Chloe arrived at their suite at the palace or their house in Coteau-Arge to find them not at home, doing something felt better than just sitting and waiting.

Mind made up, she rang for Madame Garot and asked her to send for a carriage. It rolled up in front of the townhouse nearly twenty minutes later, and one of the guards assigned to the house emerged out of the darkness as she descended the front stairs. "Lady Castaigne? Are you going out? Lord Castaigne didn't mention it."

"Lord Castaigne didn't know," she said tightly. "And yes, I intend to visit the Duquesse of Saint Pierre."

She thought he might argue with her, but he just nodded. "Very well, my lady. If you can wait a moment, I'll assign someone to go with you."

"I thought you all would have accompanied Lord Castaigne?" she said.

"Two of us did, my lady. Which leaves five of us here at the house."

"Five? Has the detail been increased?"

"Temporarily, yes."

Polite but brisk, which she interpreted as not wanting to tell her the specifics. Well enough. She didn't need anyone to spell out why they currently had more guards.

He walked to the carriage and opened the door for her. "Wait here and someone will be with you shortly."

Once, she might have thought it fun to ignore his request and tell Oscar to go on without waiting. But it would be foolish to put herself at risk on a whim.

The lieutenant worked quickly, and soon enough she felt the carriage settle a little under the weight of a guard joining Oscar in the driver's seat before Oscar's deep voice said, "Ready when you are, my lady."

"Thank you. The palace, please."

She settled back into the velvet and leather seat. It was far more comfortable than a caravan wagon. Oddly, the thought brought a small pang of regret that they weren't still with the caravan.

Perhaps she should ask Lucien if they could join one again at some point. Without the worry of having to find Deandra, she suspected it would be fun despite the discomforts. Time alone with Lucien without the full weight of his responsibilities was something she was going to have to pay attention to carving out for them. Though she suspected that to do so, she would have to take up some of the responsibilities related to Terre d'Etoi and the estate herself.

Maybe that would win Jacqueline's approval.

Lumia was quiet as they progressed through the darkened streets. They passed a few grand aristo houses lit up in ways that suggested they were hosting some form of entertainment, but it was still slightly early for the crush of carriages lining up to deliver the aristos who would be attending that might have slowed them down.

Regardless of the seeming calm, she could almost hear Lucien telling her to sit back from the window. But she couldn't resist drinking in the streets of Lumia. She'd been back half a year or so now and had spent a good portion of that time away from the city that she'd missed so desperately while in exile. She wasn't ready to take its sights for granted just yet.

The carriage swung around the corner, and she saw the temple complex with the silhouette of the palace behind it. The dome of the temple gleamed in the moonlight, and the rows of lanterns lining the path to the main temple flickered and glowed.

Acting on a whim, she tapped the wall behind her.

"Yes, my lady?"

"I'd like to stop here, please."

It wasn't until she'd crossed the threshold into the temple that she started to question the impulse. She had attended the rites every week in Anglion, but knowing she was under constant scrutiny and that the Anglion dominas would kill her for her water magic should she give them the excuse, had suppressed any sense of real devotion to the goddess. Getting to know Domina Francis a little on her return had begun to make her feel more comfortable, but it would be a lie to claim she felt any real urge to offer devotion to the goddess.

Perhaps, though, it would be enough to regain some of the comfort the rites had brought before her life had been upended. Any connection to let her pay respect to the power that expressed itself through her magic.

And, Goddess knew, a moment of comfort and calm would be welcome.

Oscar and Lieutenant Evanne, the guard, had looked at her strangely when she'd ordered them to wait outside, but they hadn't tried to stop her.

She passed several dominas and priors as she made her way to the main temple, but they did nothing more than smile and murmur greetings. Some of the smaller temples throughout the city would lock their doors at night—though there was always a domina available should they be needed—but the main temple was never locked.

The massive doors were ajar rather than wide open as they would have been in daylight hours. She picked up a bundle of oil-anointed salt grass from one of the baskets sitting on either side of the doors and slipped through them. She would make her offering and be on her way again. That should satisfy whatever urge had led her here.

Inside, the lamps burned low, and without the sunlight coming through the windows that circled the edges of the dome and broke the expanse of inlaid marble walls, the temple was darker than usual. But the central altar fire burned bright. So bright it was difficult to see if anyone else was inside at first. She moved slowly, trying to keep her footsteps quiet. It was impossible to entirely deaden the sound of her boot heels on the marble floor, and two women, sitting on the benches closest to the altar fire, turned as she approached.

It took her a moment to recognize them. Not just any two dominas tasked with keeping watch during the night. Rather the two women who she probably least needed to know she had come here.

Silya and Domina Francis.

Silya's eyebrows rose as Domina Francis's face broke into a smile. "Lady Castaigne. Welcome." She rose from the bench, touching the quartered circle pendant hanging from her neck briefly, a smile lighting her eyes, her red hair gleaming in the light of the flames.

"Domina Francis, my apologies. I didn't mean to disturb you."

"No one who comes seeking the goddess is a disturbance to me, my dear." The domina gestured at the bundle in her hand. "You wished to make an offering?"

"I...yes." There was no point explaining her conflicting feelings. Easier to make the offering, make her excuses, and leave.

The domina, perhaps sensing her confusion, merely gestured toward the altar fire. Chloe moved past her and picked up one of the knives waiting on the tiled edges of the hearth. The metal was warm from the flames, the light catching the edge of the steel. She pricked her finger, the movement long ingrained, and rubbed a dot of blood on the salt grass before tossing the bundle into the flames.

It caught with a quick flare of blue flame, a dancing lick of fire that looked almost joyful as the embers sparked up toward the dome above. The sweet salt smell of the smoke wafted over Chloe, carrying in its wake a sense of...welcome? Or perhaps that, too, was just the familiarity of it.

"There," Domina Francis said from behind her. "That's the formalities out of the way. Why don't you come and sit with Silya for a while? As much as I enjoy my hours in the temple, I have other duties to see to tonight."

It was couched in a friendly tone, but it was more request than suggestion. Domina Francis outranked Chloe by any measure of calculation, so it was impossible to refuse. Nor did the part of her still bound by her duty to the corps think it would be politic to leave a foreign seer unsupervised in the temple if asked to accompany her.

She turned away from the flames, bobbing a curtsy to Domina Francis, who merely smiled and brushed a hand along her cheek.

"Go well, child," Domina Francis said. "All is as it should be."

It would be nice to believe that. But that would require more faith than she could currently muster. She took her place beside Silya as Domina Francis glided away. No clicking boot heels for her.

The temple grew silent around them, the crackle of the altar flames the only real noise.

"I did not expect to find you here, Lady Castaigne," Silya said eventually.

"Nor I you," Chloe replied before she thought. She winced,

hoping Silya wouldn't take it the wrong way. But the seer looked more amused than upset, her icy eyes almost reflecting the firelight to turn a warmer shade.

"You are surprised to find a seer in a temple?" Silya asked.

"It's not an Andalyssian temple," Chloe countered.

"No, it is not. And I will confess I miss the scent of proper incense, but given the goddess had not seen fit to object to how you Illvyans do it, it is hardly my place."

"You must miss home."

"I will see it again," Silya said, sounding confident. "It has not been so long. And the goddess has not told me to leave."

Sparks drifted up from the fire, catching Chloe's attention. "You saw ravens flying north," she said slowly. "But we didn't make it all the way north."

"No, but that was the direction our quarry lay." Silya made a soft noise Chloe couldn't interpret. "A vision is a guide, not a map."

"I will take your word for it."

Silya tilted her head. "You have never had a message from the goddess? I thought water mages had the skill."

"Some," Chloe said. "Some have foretelling. But not me." She shivered briefly. It wasn't entirely true. She'd had moments of knowing. Of seeing something in the glint of water or glass. But she had never pursued that part of her magic. She would never claim to know the future. She wasn't sure she wanted to. That was more for people like Deandra.

"Are you sure?" Silya asked. "There is something—" She broke off, shaking her head suddenly.

"Have you seen something? Anything that might help?"

"No. The goddess is quiet. Perhaps she is waiting for the Anglion queen to arrive before she shows us the way. Or perhaps we will find it without her. Where is your husband tonight?"

"He was called back to the palace."

"To see the prisoners?"

"I think so."

"Without you?" Silya looked surprised.

"I'm not a Truth Seeker."

"You are bonded to one. And clearly you are bound up in this matter. It has shaped your life, has it not? Whatever these plotters want?"

"I suppose," Chloe said. "Though not by my choice."

"Though you could choose now," Silya said softly. "Ask the goddess to show you a path. Perhaps she will answer."

Chloe shivered. "Why would she talk to me when she won't speak to her own seer?"

"That is not for me to know. But one thing I have learned in my time in her service is that she finds it easier to speak if you are listening."

"Perhaps," Chloe said. She stared at the flames. "Illvyans use liquid for scrying."

"Do you truly think that matters to the goddess?" Silya asked. "Just quiet your mind and see what happens."

There was no graceful way to get out of at least making an attempt. Or the semblance of an attempt.

She closed her eyes. The glimpses she'd been granted before, so fleeting she'd never been sure they weren't imagined, had required water, yes, but maybe she should trust Silya.

Help me, she thought for want of anything more eloquent. *Help me bring peace to your lands.*

There was no immediate answer. No voice tolling like a bell through her mind to offer her wisdom. But still she held for a moment, knowing if she gave up too quickly it was likely that Silya would just tell her to try again.

Her thoughts wandered, thinking of everything that had happened. Lucien and Charl and Deandra. Magic and mayhem and love lost and found. Death and beginnings. Lucien. Always back to him.

He was still too far away for her to truly feel the bond, but in her mind, she could almost see it. A river of sparks, stretching from her heart, twining through the air. Like part of the ley line had floated above the earth, perhaps. Or at least part of it seen through Lucien's eyes. There was no sound, just light, light that flickered and danced at first and then solidified into an arc so bright that she felt dazzled even though it wasn't real.

Lucien.

She smiled as she let him anchor her. As she watched the light. Until it suddenly flickered again, the sensation of it tugging at her.

Then it vanished completely.

Her eyes flew open, and she bolted to her feet.

"Chloe?" Silya said, her voice concerned.

"I have to go."

CHAPTER 19

To Chloe's relief, once the carriage got closer to the palace, her sense of the bond returned. She had practically sprinted out of the temple, only holding back panic by the thinnest of margins and urging Oscar to hurry. He was pushing the horses, the carriage jolting beneath her, but there were limits to how swiftly it could travel in the city.

Her pulse pounded faster than the sound of the horse's hooves hitting the cobblestones. She rubbed a hand over her heart, eyes closed, concentrating fully on the bond.

Not gone. Not broken.

Whole.

Which meant Lucien was, too.

Despite the reassurance, her stomach swooped restlessly, the sudden sense of urgency that had punched through her in the temple not easing despite knowing the bond was fine. Surely it must have been her mind playing tricks on her.

Silya had planted the idea of a vision, and Chloe's mind had woven something born of all her worries. Not real. But still devastating.

What had Lucien felt when she'd broken the bond? Memory flashed through her: knees hitting the carpet, fear ricocheting through his body, finding all the empty spaces where the bond should be and filling them with wrenching loss. She braced one hand on the carriage wall, the force of it making her gasp. So real that it took her a minute to make her brain accept it was Lucien's memory, not hers.

Goddess, is that what he felt?

She owed him more of an apology. Hers had lasted minutes, and it had still been too much.

Find him first, feel guilty later.

The carriage swung into the palace grounds, the sound of the wheels changing from the clatter of cobblestones to the steadier hum of moving over gravel. She squeezed her eyes more tightly, trying to work out where Lucien was. Most of the theater troupe had been taken to the main prison, but the palace had an actual...well, they no longer called it a dungeon, rather a suite of cells used for prisoners who needed additional containment and care. Warded so heavily that apparently it was difficult to find them if you didn't know where to look.

She had a general idea, and she directed Oscar to take the carriage behind the palace itself and into the warren of other buildings that made up the complex. Her sense of Lucien grew stronger, and she smiled with relief.

"Lady Castaigne?" Lieutenant Evanne opened the door moments after the carriage came to a halt. "I thought you wanted to visit Their Graces." He jerked his head back toward the palace.

"Change of plans," she said, climbing out. "I need to go to the Imperial cells."

His brows flew up. "My lady?"

She had no time to soothe his surprise. "You heard me. Can you take me there?"

"They are—"

"You can tell me they're off-limits, but I'm part of this investigation," she said, hoping he wasn't going to be stubborn. "And while we share a rank in the army, when it comes to all of this"—

she waved her arm back to the palace in a gesture meant to indicate the royal family, the aristocracy, and the whole damned empire—"I outrank you. And I may be needed, so just take me. I assure you I will deal with anyone who objects." If there were any repercussions, well, she would deal with that. Lucien would understand once she explained.

Fortunately, some combination of her doing her best impression of Imogene and Jaqueline at their most imposing, the fact that the men guarding the cells knew she was part of the investigation, and her twisting the truth slightly to say she had something to tell Lucien about the case got her through the door. Lieutenant Evanne handed her over to one of the judiciary guards, who escorted her down a level and then into a wide corridor separating two sections of the cells to where Lucien, several guards, and Rene and Lucette, two of his fellow Truth Seekers, were conferring.

As though he could sense her, Lucien turned, and their eyes met. She couldn't entirely hide the sigh of relief that escaped her. Nor could she miss his surprise and alarm as he strode to meet her.

"Is something wrong?" he demanded, his eyes rapidly scanning her from head to toe.

She shook her head. "I just—" Goddess, how could she explain without sounding mad? *Distraction might be the better tactic.* "What are you all doing out here?"

"Waiting to try an experiment. Istvan seems sincere in his desire to protect Deandra. He wants to see her, and we're probably going to allow it. But first we want to see if we can nudge him a little further in the direction we want."

Nudge? She wasn't sure she liked the sound of that. Truth Seekers could manipulate people if they had to, though she knew Lucien preferred not to unless it was a last resort. "How, exactly?"

"We've told him we're shifting him to another cell. We'll walk him along here"—he gestured at the length of the corridor

—"and, at the same time, move Deandra. Let him see her but not talk to her. Close but not what he wants. But maybe enough to push him closer to confessing to get to her. It depends. He claims they're in love. He seems to believe it, and whatever else they might have been doing to their memories, I doubt they can fake an emotion to the point that he's willing to confess to protect her. They're not bonded, so there's no way she can be manipulating him that way. Whether or not she's playing with his emotions remains to be seen."

"That sounds risky."

"Plenty of guards, plenty of sanctii. We have it under control. We're just going to walk them past each other and then straight back to the cells." He straightened and turned back to the others as a door at the far end of the corridor opened. "Here they come." He hustled her back to the group of guards and Truth Seekers. "Keep behind the others."

Alarm turned her stomach upside down, nearly as badly as it had at the temple. She planted her feet, sticking right by his side. [Octarus, be ready.] The thought was instinctive, every inch of her braced for trouble.

Though what kind of trouble, she had no idea.

A group of guards came through the door escorting Istvan, a sanctii walking closest to him. The man looked paler than the last time she'd seen him, and he was unshaven but otherwise seemed healthy enough despite his hands still being bound. His eyes widened when he saw Lucien. "My lord Truth Seeker," he called as he came nearer. "You owe me an answer to my request."

"I don't believe I owe you anything," Lucien replied sternly.

Chloe wanted to watch Istvan but couldn't help turning when she heard the door she'd come through opening behind them. Another group of guards walked through, Deandra in their midst, her mouth set in an angry line.

"Deandra!" Istvan yelled. He struggled briefly, then subsided when two of the guards grabbed his shoulders.

Deandra's eyes narrowed at the sight of him. She, too, was

pale, and she wore a plain gray dress, her hair bound in one long braid. She flashed Chloe a poisonous glance, then lifted her chin and kept walking.

"*Deandra*," Istvan called desperately as the two groups grew close.

Lucien moved to keep pace with Deandra's escorts, and Chloe, despite the sensation that she should be running in the opposite direction, stuck close to him.

"Do not worry, my love. You will be free. I'll make sure of it," Istvan continued.

Deandra's head twisted toward him, her expression alarmed. "Do not do anything stupid."

"You will be fine. They will know it was me."

Deandra's expression, instead of turning relieved, suddenly looked enraged. "You idiot," she shrieked and lunged toward him, the suddenness of the move taking the guards by surprise. She almost made it to Istvan, her bound hands reaching, fingers bent like claws, mouth snarling as though she wanted to kill him, not help him.

Chloe barely registered the thought before Lucien somehow inserted himself between them. Istvan stumbled back, expression horrified, and Lucien reached for Deandra, clearly intent on stopping her.

"You!" Deandra's face was pure hatred now. She thrust her shackled hands toward Lucien, closing her fingers around his wrist.

There was a sudden clashing chord of music in the air that speared through Chloe's head like a knife, and light flared around Lucien, the bond vibrating with the same painful noise before she felt the connection begin to fade, her sense of him dissolving as it had in the temple.

"No!" Instinctively she reached her magic back toward him, trying to strengthen the bond and push Deandra's magic out. But her sense of Lucien continued to fade.

[Octarus. *Help me!*] she shrieked silently.

[*Hold.*] The sanctii's voice boomed through her head like thunder.

Something pulsed through her, chasing away the clashing sensation of Deandra's magic, replacing it with something almost as overwhelming, memories and emotions storming through her like it had when they'd bonded, the magic loud as a thunderclap. Her knees started to buckle, and she braced herself, trying to pull Lucien free.

The storm of sensation lightened somewhat as Octarus appeared beside her, wrenching Deandra away from Lucien.

The magic began to calm, but as she reached for the bond, she knew something had gone wrong. It felt like fog, barely there, and she clutched Lucien's hand desperately, hoping the contact might keep them grounded. Keep them together. *Save* them.

Deandra's gaze didn't shift from them, like a wolf's on its prey, not even struggling against Octarus, who had his arms wrapped around her, holding her still.

Chloe ignored her and focused on Lucien. He blinked before his eyes met hers. "Chloe. What are *you* doing here?" Something flashed over his face that was half surprise, half pleasure before his expression went dazed again.

Her grip tightened in shock. "I came to meet you. Don't you remember?"

He frowned, his head shaking a slow no. "When did you return from Anglion?"

Anglion? He doesn't remember that I came home? Bile rose in her throat as, from behind her, she heard Deandra laugh triumphantly.

"Get her back to her cell. Use sanctii. She can't hurt them," Chloe hissed at the nearest soldier. "Lock her down. Lock them both down. No one is to go near them."

She focused back on Lucien, who still stared at her as though he couldn't believe she was real.

Like he hadn't seen her for ten years.

Goddess. She swallowed hard, not sure she wasn't going to be sick.

Had Deandra just ripped the months since her return from his mind? The bond felt so distant, and her own head throbbed as though someone was driving nails into her skull. "And someone fetch the Duq of Arbronet. Quickly."

Deandra laughed again, and Chloe whirled to face her. "I wouldn't laugh if I were you. Assaulting a Truth Seeker is a capital offense. Think about that when you're back in your cell."

Lucette and Rene stepped up beside Chloe as sanctii appeared to surround Deandra and Istvan, bundling them both away. "Lieutenant de Roche, what's wrong?" Lucette asked.

"I think Mamsille Noirene just stole my husband's memories."

As she spoke, a wave of dizziness washed over her as the reality of the words hit home. He didn't remember her. Didn't remember *them*.

Sweet goddess, no.

She couldn't breathe and bent forward, trying to force air into her lungs while still keeping an eye on Lucien.

Octarus appeared beside her again, rumbling a warning at Lucette as she stepped closer. Chloe leaned against the sanctii, hoping he would keep her upright.

The next few minutes passed in a blur as she tried to breathe while Lucien said nothing.

Lucette touched her arm, face creased with worry. "We should get Lucien to the infirmary."

Chloe nodded in agreement and straightened. Lucien still looked stunned, his expression half wary, half joyful. "When did you get back?" he repeated.

She ignored the question. "Can you tell me what day it is?"

He frowned for a moment, rubbing his forehead, and then named a date that made terror run down her spine. It was the day she'd set sail from Kingswell to return to Lumia.

He really didn't remember.

"We can fix this," she said, more to convince herself than anybody else. "We will fix this." Panic drummed through her already aching head.

He frowned. "Is something wrong?"

She fought down the fear to summon a reassuring smile. "You've been hit by a charm. It's affecting your memory. I think it's best if you go to the infirmary, and we'll get the healers and Valentin."

He frowned at her. "You call the Duq of Arbronet by his first name now?"

She shook her head at him. "Just come along," she said, hiding the urge to either panic or return to the cells and tear Deandra's heart out.

She slipped her arm through Lucien's, ignoring the spear of pain when he looked startled at the gesture. But he relaxed soon enough. When Deandra had fogged her memory, she'd felt...almost drunk. Lucien just seemed confused yet calm. Of course, Deandra had only taken a few moments from her. Not *months*.

Inside her head, she asked Octarus, [Can you fix this? Can *we* fix this?]

[No, not yet.]

Not yet? What does that mean? She fought back the panic and tried to think. Not *yet*? So they had to wait? For what?

Oh. [Can Elarus fix this?]

Goddess, she had to.

Octarus made a noise in her head that was the verbal equivalent of a shrug. [Perhaps. How long?] She got a brief image of a navire.

[How long until she arrives?] She struggled to remember. [A day or two, I think.]

She looked at Rene, who had taken Lucien's other arm. Lucien hadn't protested, which only made Chloe more worried. "When we get to the infirmary, I want an update on Queen Sophia's progress, if that's possible."

✦ ✦ ✦

It took some time to get Lucien into a room in the palace infirmary against his protests that there was nothing wrong with him. They'd only just managed to get him to sit down and remove his boots when Valentin came hustling into the room, Irina on his heels. The duq's light gray eyes sought Chloe immediately and he crossed to her, one hand tugging at the pearl dangling from his ear. Irina followed, concern clear on her face. Both of them were dressed for the palace, not their work as healers. Though not full-blown evening wear, which explained how they had arrived so fast.

"Thank you for coming," Chloe said, relief ringing through her voice. Her head throbbed again, and she set her teeth. She needed Valentin to focus on Lucien, not her.

Valentin smiled crookedly. "Well, we were in our apartments at the palace, so it's not so far away." He drew Chloe back toward the door, lowering his voice. "What happened?"

Chloe glanced at Lucien, who was still arguing with the healer helping him with his boots. She turned back to Valentin. "Deandra," she said softly. "She used magic on him. He seems to have lost his memory of the last few months."

Valentin's gaze snapped to hers. "How long?"

"He doesn't remember that I came home," she admitted, her voice cracking. She clenched her jaw, willing herself not to cry, and rubbed her temple. The pain was getting worse. Her skull felt as though it had been stuffed full of rocks, her thoughts, when she let her focus slip, filled with a strange fog of...well, she wasn't entirely sure what.

Valentin winced. "I see."

He turned to Irina. "Perhaps you should get Chloe something hot to drink. I'll need to examine Lucien before we can decide anything further."

After sending Chloe a sympathetic look, Irina nodded and left.

Valentin turned to the bed, stepping up to Lucien. "All right, then, Lord Castaigne. I'm going to take a look at you."

Lucien frowned. "Your Grace, I think they're causing an unnecessary fuss. I feel perfectly well."

Valentin shook his head. "Sorry, but in this case, they're right to fuss. What do you remember about today?"

Lucien's frown deepened. "I'm not sure. I was at home, writing a report on a case. And now I'm here at the judiciary." For the first time, his expression grew concerned. "What's going on?"

Everyone turned to Chloe, expecting her to explain. But when she tried to speak, all she could manage was a muffled squeak of distress as her head throbbed harder, her mouth and throat suddenly dry. She waved at Valentin, who began to explain to Lucien what the memory magic could do, carefully skirting around the issue of just how much time he might have lost.

Chloe had only the faintest sense of his confusion and panic, which didn't help contain hers. She tried to tamp hers down but didn't dare try to lock down the bond when the connection felt so alarmingly fragile.

"You look like you're about to fall over," Irina said softly, reappearing at Chloe's side, holding a cup of tea in one hand. With her free hand, she guided Chloe toward the lone chair in the room. When Chloe tried to protest, she said, "You can still see him from the chair. You're not doing him any good if you collapse," in a tone so stern that Chloe obeyed automatically.

She sank into the chair, accepting the teacup, which rattled in its saucer before she managed to control the tremor in her hands. She sipped it when Irina prompted her, the hot sweet tea steadying her a little. Enough to concentrate on Valentin and Lucien's conversation. It was largely one-sided, Valentin repeating information patiently while Lucien looked incredulous.

Only after Lucette had sworn to him that Valentin was telling the truth did his expression change from disbelieving to appalled.

"How long until I remember?" he demanded.

Valentin spread his hands helplessly. "We don't know. But Elarus and Queen Sophia are on their way."

"The queen? Is it wise for her to leave Anglion so soon? She was just crowned," Lucien asked, confusion creasing his brow.

He remembered Sophia was queen? Relief flooded through Chloe. That gave a limit to how far back in time he'd been thrown.

When no one answered him immediately, his frown deepened. "There's something you're not telling me, Your Grace." His gaze turned to Chloe. "Or maybe more than one thing. I still don't understand why Chlo—Madame de Montesse is here."

"She was helping with your investigation," Valentin said slowly.

"Did they send her from Anglion? Do the Anglions know something about this magic? Is that why Queen Sophia is coming?"

Valentin raised his eyebrows at Chloe as though asking how she wanted to handle the questions.

Short of sedating Lucien, she couldn't see how they were going to avoid explaining to him that he'd lost months of his memories.

And if anyone was going to tell him, it had to be her. After all, she'd made vows to the man. She was his wife—even if he didn't remember her.

She passed the tea back to Irina and stood, taking a moment to smooth her dress while she reassured herself that her legs would hold her up. Taking the three steps across to Lucien felt like stepping over a gaping abyss. As though it would be far too easy to tumble back into it and be smashed if he didn't react well to the information.

What if he never remembered what they'd shared? Would he still want her?

She chewed her lip, staring into the green eyes that she knew as well as her own. He gazed back, his expression unreadable for a moment.

"Just tell me," he said softly. "You never were one to beat around the bush."

"No, I wasn't," she agreed, managing a small smile. He remembered they had been friends. That might be a place to start again if they needed to. He'd said he'd been in love with her since he'd met her. Could what Deandra did touch that? Ruin it? Or did they have a chance? She wanted to reach for his hand, but perhaps he wouldn't understand.

She took a breath. "I came home close to six months ago."

His eyes widened. "Six months? How did I not know that? Have you been hiding away?"

"You did know. You saw me the day I got home. We ran into each other on the docks."

What little color had been left in his face drained away. "I don't remember that." He swore suddenly, head turning to Valentin. "You're saying I've lost six *months*?"

"About that, it seems," Valentin said calmly. "We can work out exactly how long if we need to. If you can remember that Queen Sophia took her throne, then that gives us a boundary of a sort."

"*If* we need to?" Lucien asked incredulously. "Of course we need to." He turned back to Chloe. "Months? You've been home for *months*? Perhaps you should catch me up on the salient details of what's happened. And of this case we're investigating."

She pressed her hand to her stomach, feeling queasy all over again at the thought of trying to explain.

His gaze dropped to her hand, and his eyes widened. "You're wearing a wedding band." He looked closer. "And my old signet ring. Chloe, why are you wearing my signet ring?"

"Because we're married," she blurted.

THE REBEL'S PRIZE   275

His jaw dropped open. "*Married?* What? How?"

"That's a rather more complicated tale than I think we should deal with right now," Valentin said. "You need to rest."

"You need to fix me," Lucien snapped. "Goddess damn it, if I'm married, I want to remember. So do whatever earth magic healer nonsense you need to, but I need you to fix this, Valentin. *Now*."

"Ah, for that, you are going to have to be patient, I'm afraid. We don't know how to undo the magic yet. We—"

He didn't get any further. Or if he did, Chloe didn't hear it. Because the panic trickling through the bond suddenly became a torrent that drowned out anything else, shutting off her senses and sweeping her into a maelstrom of fear and confused images.

She felt her grip on the bond dissolving under the over-whelming flood of power and shrieked for Octarus in her mind just before everything went black.

CHAPTER 20

Chloe drifted awake to the sound of voices.

"Should it be taking this long?"

"She has to wake up eventually. We gave her a sleeping draught, nothing more."

"Well, we can't wait much longer." A hand touched her shoulder, bringing a familiar scent. "Chloe, open your eyes for me."

"Papa?" She struggled to do as Henri asked. Her lids felt heavy. Her whole *head* felt heavy. Her thoughts moved slowly, seeming to spiral downward from the top of her head to the base of her skull, weighing her down against the pillow beneath her head.

"Yes, it's me," Henri said. "Open your eyes."

She cracked one eye open with an effort, squinting against the light. Henri's face swam into view, leaning over the bed, somewhat fuzzy. She forced the other eye open, trying to focus.

"There you are," Henri said, straightening. "How do you feel?"

"Like I've been run over by a charguerre. And thirsty."

"That part we can address," Imogene said, stepping into view. She held out a glass of water. "Valentin said you would most likely be thirsty when you woke."

"What happened?" Her memory was blurry. "Did someone use the memory charm on me again?" Goddess, she hoped not. She sipped water, telling herself not to overreact. The water soothed her throat and seemed to clear her mind.

"Not you—Lucien. Do you remember?" Imogene asked.

Now it was coming back to her. The moment when she'd thought she'd lost the bond again. The confusion of panic of trying to pull Lucien free of Deandra's magic and the storm of magic she still didn't understand. And then how frail the bond had been.

"Is Lucien all right?" Heart thumping, she focused on the bond. It took a moment. Still weak. Still strange. But there.

"Yes. He's sleeping now, too. He wouldn't calm down when you fainted. Valentin decided it would be best to let the two of you sleep, see if that lets things stabilize," Henri said.

Chloe glanced around the room. Not the infirmary where Lucien had been. Or the temple. The room was too finely furnished for that. Obviously a bedroom. "Where are we?"

"One of my guest rooms in our suite at the palace," Imogene said. "Valentin wanted the two of you apart, in case it was some sort of complication of your bond that made you faint."

Chloe sat up at that. "I should go to Lucien. He'll need me."

Henri put a hand on her arm. "He's under Valentin's supervision. Even Domina Francis has seen him. He will sleep for some time."

"All the more reason for me to be there when he wakes up." She would wait for as long as needed. She had kept vigil at his bedside before, lending him her strength. She would do it again.

"Perhaps," Imogene agreed. "But it might be a better use of your time to find a way to help him."

"How?" Chloe asked.

"By talking to Sophie and Elarus," Imogene said with a grin.

"They're here?" Chloe pushed the covers away and then froze. "How long was I asleep?"

"Most of the day. Queen Sophia arrived this morning. The

winds were favorable, and the navire made good time," Henri said.

"Does she think she can help? Has she seen Deandra?"

"Given what happened, we thought it would be better if Elarus spoke with you first," Imogene said. "But now that you're awake, I can send a message to let them know and ask if they're free in an hour or so."

"Why not now?" If Elarus had a way to heal Lucien, they needed to know.

"Well, for one thing, you need to eat and bathe. And for another, the queen and her retinue have only been in the palace a few hours. They will still be settling in and, I would imagine, speaking with Lady Margaretta and whoever the emperor had assigned from the diplomatic corps. I believe they are to dine with the emperor later this evening."

"They?"

Imogene grinned again. "The King Consort came with her."

"Cameron's here? Is that wise?" Given how recently Sophie had come to the throne in Anglion, both of them leaving the country seemed foolhardy. Though she doubted anyone would have been able to persuade him to let Sophie travel back to Illvya without him, Elarus or no Elarus.

"I think that is something for them to decide," Henri said. "And you have more pressing issues to concern yourself with. So, if you're feeling well enough, I suggest you do as Imogene said and eat something and bathe. Then we can have a healer examine you." He bent and pressed a kiss to her forehead. "And now that you're awake, I shall go home and let your mother know."

Her mother. Who didn't deserve the anxiety having a daughter like Chloe brought.

"Tell Mama I will see her soon," she said apologetically. "And that I'm sorry."

✦ ✦ ✦

It was closer to an hour and a half by the time Valentin arrived.
He was dressed as a duq, not a healer, for once, the heavily
embroidered and beaded deep red satin of his evening jacket
somewhat out of place in the mostly white-and-yellow furnish-
ings of Imogene's sitting room. The sunlight through the
windows was beginning to turn deep gold as the afternoon drew
to a close. Perhaps he had plans for the evening, because he
wasted no time in beginning his examination.

Chloe, feeling steadier, at least, after eating and changing
into the clothes Imogene had obtained from Madame G, tried to
submit to his questions patiently.

Eventually he stepped away. "As far as I can tell, you haven't
been harmed. But you might want to be careful with your magic
for the next few days." He took a seat beside her on the sofa.
"Your bond still seems...odd."

She tensed. "What do you mean?"

"It wasn't exactly conventional before," he said. "But now it's
—" He squinted at her, head cocked. "—wider but less substantial, if I had to guess. It's the latter part that worries me."

"It changed when Deandra attacked Lucien," Chloe admitted. "I'm not sure exactly what happened. It's still there, but
you're right, it feels...distant." She squeezed her hands together,
trying to stay calm.

Valentin, however, wasn't fooled. He patted her clenched
hands gently. "Well, it may just be the effects of the memory
charms. I suggest we focus on seeing if there's anything that can
be done about that. If not, well, I would recommend you talk to
the Academe. I'm sure your father will be eager to help. The
venables have probably forgotten more about bonding than I'll
ever know."

She hadn't thought to ask Henri. "Don't healers deal with

them here?" In Anglion, the only bonds were the marriage rituals. Firmly the business of the temple. As were most things to do
with magic. The habit of thinking about them that way was hard
to shift, apparently.

He sat back, the hand that bore his signet tugging at his ear.
"They're not that common. Bonds that go wrong even less so.
But I'm sure the Academe can help. There must be things you
could do to strengthen it again."

"Lucien doesn't even remember he's married," Chloe pointed
out. "He might not want to."

To lose him now.... Fear spiked the back of her throat at the
thought. She just *couldn't*.

"I doubt that," Imogene snorted. "I was watching when you
told him you were married. He seemed very eager to regain his
memory. Which I think means he's very much in favor of the
idea of being married to *you*."

"Or outraged and wants to divorce me," Chloe muttered.

Valentin smiled. "I don't think that's likely. I was at your
wedding ball, remember? Lucien plays his cards close to his chest
much of the time—a consequence of what he does, I suspect—
but he looked at you like his whole world revolved around you.
And you've known each other a long time. Even if he's lost the
memory of what's happened since you returned, that won't
change whatever there was between you before. You were
friends before you...left, weren't you?"

"Yes," she admitted. She smiled at him, her nerves easing. He
was right. Lucien loved her before. Even without the memories,
maybe there was a chance for them. But she wanted him to
remember. The thought of him being harmed in any way made
her angry.

"What about your memory of the night of the parliament
attack?" Valentin asked. "Have you remembered anything more?"

She shook her head. "No. It's still foggy." Whatever the
magic was, time wasn't the answer to reversing its effect. "Has
anyone spoken to Istvan? Or Deandra?" She remembered giving

orders that no one was to talk to them, but whether those orders had been followed was another question.

"Deandra has sealed her fate, attacking Lucien," Valentin pointed out.

She didn't want to think about that. "We still need to see if she—either of them, really—will talk." She turned to Imogene. "Do you know if anyone has tried?"

"No. Not that I've been told. Lucette came to check on you. The Advocate General is apparently furious but is not a man to act hastily. Istvan and Deandra are both cooling their heels back in the cells, and no one has gone near them other than to feed them. Everyone agreed it was best to wait for Elarus."

"Good," Chloe said. The clock on the marble mantlepiece chimed the half hour, and she stood, too aware of the minutes ticking away. "We need to talk to Sophie. Thank you, Valentin." She looked him up and down. "Are you supposed to be attending a ball?"

He pulled a dismayed face, looking down at his jacket. "Hosting dinner for the Andalyssians. Irina insisted."

"Difficult in-laws. I understand." She gave him a sympathetic grin.

"Sejerin Silya is more terrifying than even *your* mother-in-law."

"She's not so bad," Chloe said. "Silya, that is. She might surprise you."

"I'll settle for just getting through the evening. So far, I get the distinct impression that I am not their ideal addition to the family," Valentin said. "Please feel free to interrupt and send for me for any reason at all."

She snorted and shook her head. "You can't leave Irina alone to deal with all of them."

An odd expression crossed his face. "No. They seem to have resigned themselves to the fact of our marriage, but who knows what they might try on their own?"

She laughed. "Well, then. We both have our work cut out for us tonight. I'm going to talk to Sophie and Elarus."

"Good. Lucien should wake in a few hours. I gave him a stronger dose than you. The rest will be good for him, and having some answers when he wakes up would be even better. We can give him another dose if you need more time. Just let me know."

Imogene set a quick pace through the palace, and it took Chloe a minute or two to get her bearings, the route they were taking unfamiliar. But she eventually realized where they were headed. "Why are we going to the East Wing?"

"That's where Sophie and Cameron are," Imogene said, not breaking her stride.

"Doesn't visiting royalty usually stay in other parts of the palace?"

"Yes, but between Lady Margaretta's delegation and the Andalyssians, there is enough going on in the guest wings. Besides, the East Wing is the most heavily guarded part of the palace, particularly now."

True. Though if someone was still minded to make another attempt on the emperor, perhaps housing his allies farther away might be wise. Then again, Sophie was also a target.

As though to prove Imogene's point, as they turned a corner, a stern-faced, dark-haired Imperial guard stepped into their path, coming to full attention and neatly blocking their access to the door behind him.

"The Duquesse of Saint Pierre and the Marquesse of Castaigne to see Her Royal Majesty Queen Sophia," Imogene said, seemingly unfazed by the fact that the man was bristling with weapons.

Far too many weapons. The guards protecting the royal family were always armed, though generally in a less obvious manner. Chloe donned her best demur and unthreatening expression.

The guard bowed his head. "Yes, Your Grace. We were told to expect you. Please proceed through the door and wait. Someone will come to escort you beyond that point. There are additional security protocols in place at the moment."

"Thank you. We are aware," Imogene said dryly.

The guard just nodded, not even attempting a full bow before opening the door. Imogene waltzed through and Chloe followed, thanking the guard just before he shut the door firmly behind them, wards humming to life as he did so.

Imogene came to a halt, impatience darkening her face. But apparently, she wasn't going to disobey the guard's orders because she stayed where she was, tapping the fingers of her right hand against her skirts.

There was no sign of their escort. Chloe, as impatient as Imogene appeared, tried to distract herself with the art on the walls. Most of the paintings she'd seen in other parts of the East Wing were landscapes and still lifes, possibly to compensate for the fact that the public parts of the palace had an abundance of portraits of the emperor, the empress, and their children. Not to mention a whole gallery devoted to the various generations who had formed the de Lucien dynasty.

But to break the pattern, on the nearest wall, flanked by two smaller pictures of the palace, hung a large portrait of the family. They were clothed more informally than some of their portraits but still wearing Imperial gold and silver. The emperor shone like the sun in the center of the portrait, Empress Liane in gold and silver to his right, and Alain, dressed entirely in silver, to his left, with the four younger children—Madeleine, Alyce, Cecilie, and Tomas—standing on either side of their mother or brother. They wore mostly white with touches of gold or silver, clearly delineating them from their brother, the heir. Around their feet lay three long-haired white hunting hounds, and Princess Alyce held a white cat with golden eyes.

Chloe grimaced a little, looking at Alain's haughty expression. Imogene came to join her.

"Alain always was full of himself, even at that age," she said.

"How old do you think he is here?" The crown prince looked young, his face rounder.

"I think he was twenty-two or three. The emperor had this commissioned for one of Liane's birthdays, but she never liked the picture, apparently. Too formal to be a cozy family portrait but too relaxed for the gallery."

"Hardly relaxed," Chloe said. "Just think of the poor servants who had to fetch all those crowns from the vaults and polish them." The crowns in the portrait weren't the heavy formal ones worn at official functions but were still elaborate. Aristides's was gold, studded with yellow diamonds and sun motifs. Alain's was a smaller version in silver with white diamonds, matching rings on the hand he held at his waist. The younger children wore simpler circlets.

"Not to mention the artist. I wonder if they posed together. That would be a nightmare."

"I'd rather have them all there than deal with Alain alone," Chloe muttered, glancing around to make sure they weren't overheard.

"True," Imogene agreed. "I can't imagine him being patient or pleasant. Sitting for a portrait is dull at times, but there's no reason to take it out on the artist."

Before Chloe could answer, a dark-haired woman in Imperial livery came bustling out of a side passage. Chloe turned and, for a moment, had a strange sensation that Alain was watching her from the portrait. She shook off the fancy as the servant curtsied and spoke. "My apologies for the delay, Your Grace, Lady Castaigne. I will take you to see Queen Sophia."

✧ ✦ ✦

Sophie waited until the servants had left them alone before she threw her arms around Chloe and hugged her hard. The familiar scent of gillyflowers, popular with the Anglion court ladies, wafted around her, and Chloe was taken straight back to Kingswell and her store.

"It's so good to see you!" Sophie said when she finally released Chloe and turned to hug Imogene in turn. "Both of you."

Behind her, Cameron, tall and dark-haired, stood smiling, blue eyes watching his wife, as usual.

Chloe nodded, trying to catch her breath. "And you, Your Majesty. You made good time."

Sophie's expression turned more serious, her tea-colored eyes intent on Chloe. "Let's not bother with 'Your Majesty.' Sophie is faster. I want to get to the bottom of this as much as anyone. If this magic was used in the attack on my palace, then Anglion deserves to know. King Stefan and all the others deserve justice. Eloisa deserves justice." She glanced over her shoulder at Cameron, who nodded.

"No argument here, love," he said gravely. "But I'm sure Madame de Montesse is keen to begin the work rather than talking about it."

The King Consort was a man of few words in her experience and one who preferred to take action. She suspected that, in this case, he was more interested in making sure everything was dealt with and Sophie safely returned to Anglion as fast as possible more than he was worried about helping Chloe. But she had no argument with that. She felt the same about Lucien. And after all, their goals were aligned no matter what their individual motivations.

"It's Madame de Roche now, or Lady Castaigne, really,"

Imogene pointed out with a smile. "But you are correct. We should get to work."

Sophie rolled her shoulders and sat back on one of the three sofas in the small room. She tucked her feet up under her pale blue silk gown in an un-queenly fashion and gestured for the others to sit, too. Her hair was braided simply around her head, and if not for the glorious dark blue sapphires dancing at her ears and circling her throat, the shade a near perfect match to her betrothal ring, she could have been a student at the Academe rather than a queen.

But Chloe knew better than to underestimate her. Sophie was young, but she had outwitted her enemies and survived, against all odds, to end up on the throne. Her hair was red and black like Chloe's own rather than the deep brown it had been when they'd first met, testament to the strength of her magic. The strongest earth witch in Anglion's royal line for decades, not to mention the first water mage accepted in that country for far longer. Her reign had the potential to change her country for the better, and it would only help secure her hold on power if she avenged the king and queen assassinated before her.

She sat on the sofa opposite Sophie, and Imogene joined her. Cameron took his place beside his wife. His clothing was more sedate, though the shades of blue and gray matched hers, his only jewelry his wedding ring.

"Thank you for coming. I know it's not the best time for you to leave Anglion, but we need to ask Elarus some questions. Is she willing to talk to us?" Chloe asked.

Sophie shrugged one shoulder. "Talk, yes. Whether she will answer all of them is up to her. Particularly when your message suggested the topics might be...delicate in nature."

"Octarus and Ikarus refused to answer them," Chloe admitted. "But they thought Elarus might."

"Then I guess we will have to see. Elarus, would you join us, please?" Sophie said.

Elarus appeared behind the queen. She was taller than the

other sanctii, her skin darker, more black shaded with gray rather than the reverse like most of the others. She wore a long black tunic, and her dark eyes found Chloe's before nodding a greeting.

"Hello, Elarus," Chloe said. "Thank you for agreeing to talk to us."

Elarus nodded again, gesturing toward Sophie. "I will help. If can."

In other words, she reserved the right to not answer.

Well, there was little to be done about that. Chloe glanced at Imogene, who just nodded slightly, as though happy for Chloe to take the lead.

Chloe took a deep breath. "All right. Let's start at the beginning." She began to explain what had happened at the parliament first. Elarus's expression remained calm throughout the retelling, but before Chloe could move on to the night at the palace, the sanctii held up her hand.

"Memory taken?" she asked, nodding at Chloe.

"A short one, yes," Chloe agreed. "At least, that's what we think happened. A friend saw me talking to a woman in a green. I don't remember doing that. Octarus saw her, too. He showed me the memory, and I recognized her. I knew her at school a long time ago, but I don't remember speaking to her at the parliament."

Elarus frowned and stepped around the sofa to move closer to Chloe. She stared at her a moment, then said something short and sharp in the sanctii tongue. Chloe thought it might be "Come," but her memory of the language was hazy at best. She knew some basic common words that Henri and Martius had used during her childhood but hadn't had time since bonding Octarus to try to learn more.

But she must have been right about the meaning because Octarus appeared in front of Elarus. He shot one quick glance at Chloe, his eyes wide before he focused firmly on Elarus, inclining his head respectfully.

Elarus continued speaking sanctii to him. Chloe tried to watch Imogene and Sophie, seeing if she could judge by their reactions what was going on, but the discussion between the sanctii didn't last long. Elarus barked out one last sentence, then turned to Chloe. "You will show me this memory?"

"The parliament? Yes, I can do that."

Elarus beckoned her closer and stretched out a hand toward her temple when Chloe reached her. The sanctii's touch was rough but warm.

"Show me," she said.

Chloe closed her eyes and tried to recall the reception at the parliament. The parts she could, anyway. As the images began to flow, she started to hear something like the echo of a bass voice chanting in the distance. Sanctii magic? She'd never heard it before, but perhaps it was different with Elarus.

The images began to move faster, becoming more real, almost as though she was experiencing the moment all over again. When they jumped suddenly from her entering the retiring room to Violette speaking to her afterward, Elarus pulled away with a grunt.

"What is it?" Sophie asked as Chloe opened her eyes.

"Bad," Elarus said, her voice harsher than usual. "Bad magic."

CHAPTER 21

"Yes," Chloe agreed. "And I only lost a few minutes. There are others who have lost more. And some who we suspect may have had memories taken and false ones put in their place."

Beside her, Imogene stiffened, but Chloe didn't see any point in beating around the bush. If Elarus was going to refuse to talk, better to know sooner rather than later.

Sophie frowned at her. "False memories? How is that possible? When I received my reveilé from Martius, I distinctly remember your father telling me that a sanctii couldn't implant new information in my mind, that Martius was merely going to make it easier for me to use the Illvyan I had learned."

Chloe fought to keep the surprise off her face. Henri had lied?

As the initial shock faded, she realized she understood why. It wasn't as though Sophie had been queen at that point, merely an Anglion refugee, albeit one with both magical powers and potential political power. "I think my father was being...judicious with his words, perhaps not wanting to scare you," she said in her best soothing diplomatic tone. "That was when you were still newly arrived, was it not? If you already knew Illvyan, then what he said was true, as I understand it. The reveilé, in those circumstances, merely makes what we know more accessible. But it's also possible for a sanctii to teach a language that a mage has very little or even no knowledge of. It hurts more, and you still have to work to gain the fluency, but the Imperial army uses the technique regularly."

Sophie looked briefly disgruntled at this explanation before she waved a hand as though dismissing the issue. "I see" was all she said.

"There are very strict rules about the reveilé," Imogene added in a conciliatory tone. "Languages are one of the few things it's used for. Most of the time, it's considered better to learn things the normal way. Some knowledge, gained too quickly without experience and time to assimilate, is just too dangerous." She tipped her head at Sophie. "You were lucky when Elarus taught you water magic."

Sophie looked briefly guilty. "It certainly wasn't pleasant," she agreed. "Though at least it also taught me sanctii. But Elarus is unusual, and I agree it would be best to discourage such experiments."

"Yes," Imogene said. "We're told that people made mistakes in the past."

"But not what those mistakes are, exactly," Chloe said slowly, shifting in her seat. "At least, I don't remember our lessons covering much detail."

"I learned a little more when the army trained me to bond Ikarus," Imogene said. "But those were mostly tales of people trying to get a sanctii to teach them the bonding rituals and them failing their attempts. A cautionary tale. But we had long lists of regulations regarding the kinds of things that we do not ask sanctii to do hammered into our heads. But they never really explained why. Other than it was forbidden."

Octarus opened his mouth as though he was going to add something, but Elarus rumbled at him, and he closed it again.

"So, a sanctii can put information in someone's mind. And clearly a sanctii can take information in the first place. That's how they learn languages from a human, isn't it? Which means they must be able to find the memory of that language that we hold," Cameron added.

"Yes. But they don't remove the knowledge of the language from the person they learn from," Imogene said.

"Just because they don't doesn't mean they can't," Cameron said. "Are you sure it's never happened?"

Chloe shrugged. "We can't answer that. But I suspect Elarus can."

All four of them stared at Elarus.

"*Forbidden*," she said.

"Forbidden to talk about or forbidden to do?" Sophie asked. She touched the sanctii's arm gently, and Elarus blinked at her.

"Both," Elarus said. "To change...someone...this way is not our way. We should not. Even if can. Even if asked. It is wrong. It is *forbidden*." Her voice rasped the last word, and it seemed to echo around the room.

"Even if a mage asked? If a sanctii was bonded?" Chloe asked.

"Mage force, bad for mage," Elarus growled. "Sanctii would tell...others."

Others? More powerful sanctii? Or free sanctii? Free sanctii who, like Elarus, could get to the human realm without a bond. Chloe hadn't known that was possible until she'd heard about Elarus. Perhaps no one had. Did that explain the bonded mages who had disappeared over the years? It had always been assumed that their sanctii had somehow broken the bond and killed them after being pushed to a limit. But was it instead other sanctii meting out justice on their behalf? She chewed her lip, not wanting to ask.

"And no sanctii would break this rule?" Imogene asked tentatively. "Ever?"

There was a long moment of silence, and Chloe held her breath.

"Sometimes sanctii are foolish," Elarus said with a gravelly sigh.

"There was a sanctii who attacked Cameron," Chloe said. "You intervened that night. What happened to them?"

Elarus's black gaze caught hers. "Realm," she said firmly. "He will not leave again."

That could mean banished or dead. Chloe wasn't going to ask. Better to keep her focus on convincing Elarus to help. "It is likely that the plots in Anglion, the ones that killed Queen Eloisa and her father, the people who tried to kill Sophie, might use this same magic. That it's all part of one big plan," Chloe said. "He might know something." She hesitated. "Or have taught a mage to do this magic. Is it possible? Deandra used it on me, but she had to learn it somewhere. Can you tell if it's human magic or sanctii magic?"

Elarus didn't respond immediately, and Chloe rushed on. "There are others who have been affected. The people who were working in the same place as Deandra. We think she may have altered their memories somehow. Could you tell if you looked at their memories as you did mine?"

"Maybe," Elarus said. But then she twisted her hand in Chloe's direction. "Yours is...confused by that."

"That?" Chloe asked blankly.

[Mate,] Octarus offered. [Bond feels wrong.]

Oh. "My bond stops you from knowing?"

Elarus glanced back at Sophie, and Sophie's face went still for a moment.

"She just asked if your bond has always been like this." Sophie stared at Chloe, eyes narrowing. "Yours looks different to ours."

"Ours is unusual, love," Cameron said gently.

"So is that," Sophie countered, waving at Chloe. "It's...foggy, yet somehow too bright. And uneven." She tilted her head, squinting more. "Where is your husband?"

"In the infirmary," Chloe said. "Deandra used a memory charm on him. He's lost quite a bit of time."

Sophie's mouth made a small *o* of sympathy. "How long?"

"He doesn't remember anything since just before I returned home," Chloe admitted. "Including our marriage."

Cameron winced and reached for Sophie's hand.

"And did your bond look like that before?" Sophie asked.

"No," Imogene said, also turning to study Chloe. "It was stronger when they reformed it than the first time—"

"Reformed?" Sophie asked, then shook her head. "Sorry, that is a tale for another time. Go on, Imogene."

"It was stronger," Imogene said, squinting sideways at Chloe, "but like a normal bond. You're right, it looks strange now."

Elarus said something in sanctii.

"Were you there when this happened?" Sophie asked Chloe.

"Yes. I felt the bond...dissolving. I tried to hold on. Octarus helped me."

"How?" Elarus asked, the question directed at Octarus.

He replied in sanctii, making a complicated twisting gesture with his hands.

"Mate does not remember?" Elarus asked.

"No," Chloe said. "Nothing."

"Fix first," Elarus said, then paused and held out a hand palm up. "Maybe."

✦ ✦ ✦

"It will be all right," Imogene whispered to Chloe as they stood outside Lucien's room at the infirmary, waiting for Valentin. They'd sent a message to him as soon as Elarus had announced that she would try to heal Lucien, but despite that, the six of them and the two sanctii had reached the infirmary first. The guard at the door likely would have let her in, given she was Lucien's wife, but it was probably wiser to wait for Valentin.

"You don't know that," Chloe whispered back.

Imogene said, "Elarus wouldn't offer if she didn't think there was a chance that she could do this. That would be cruel." She tucked her arm through Chloe's. "Just don't faint again. Concentrate on Lucien."

As if she needed to be reminded of that. Every nerve strained toward the door, wanting to be inside. With him. Even though she dreaded seeing him look at her and knowing he didn't remember anything about the time they'd shared. None of their smiles. Or kisses. No memory of making stars dance in the air for her or setting her alight with his touch.

Unbearable. Her throat burned with the loss.

Please, let this work. She didn't know quite who she was pleading with. Elarus. The goddess. Fate. Whoever was willing to grant her wish and give Lucien back his memories.

"Sorry to keep you all waiting," Valentin said from behind.

Chloe whirled to face him. His expression was almost relieved. "Sorry to interrupt your evening, Your Grace."

He flashed a grin at her. "Irina will cope with her compatriots alone for a time. But she'll be displeased if I'm gone too long." He gestured at Sophie and Cameron. "Care to introduce me, Lady Castaigne?"

Of course. Protocol first. Sophie was, after all, a queen. "Your Grace, this is Queen Sophia of Anglion and her King Consort, Cameron. Your Majesties, this is Valentin du Leon, the Duq of Arbronet. Also one of our best healers."

Valentin bowed elegantly. Still wearing his red satin jacket and black trousers, he looked as though he stood in a ballroom, not a sick room. "Your Majesties, I have heard much about you both. I hope we can perhaps get to know one another during your stay. Though, I gather from your note, Chloe, that there are more pressing matters to deal with first." He offered Sophie one of his dazzling smiles. Her mouth quirked in appreciation.

"Elarus, Her Majesty's sanctii"—Chloe nodded in her direction—"thinks she might be able to help Lucien."

"Then it is sanctii magic?" Valentin asked, grin replaced by a far more intent expression.

"We didn't get as far as the specifics," Chloe confessed. "Elarus looked at the gap in my memories, and she says there is something strange about our bond. She wanted to see Lucien."

Valentin glanced at Elarus and then Sophie. "Well, far be it from me to stand in her way. It's not as though we've made much progress on our own. As long as you are happy for her to try, Chloe." He tugged at the golden hoop in his left ear, expression neutral, as though he was giving her a chance to change her mind.

"I trust Elarus," Chloe said firmly. "She might be his best chance."

"Then let's not waste time," Valentin said, crossing to Lucien's door and waving the guard aside.

It took a minute for them to arrange themselves inside Lucien's room and for another round of introductions to be made. Lucien's expression turned from puzzled to wary to eager as Valentin explained that Elarus wanted to examine him.

To Chloe's relief, he didn't object, though his apprehension and a jumble of other emotions that were difficult to untangle drifted through the bond. His eyes sought hers. "Is this what you want?" he asked slowly.

"Of course. I want you whole, Lucien. I need you." She moved up beside the bed. She hadn't touched him since Deandra had attacked him. It didn't feel right to take his hand as she would have if he remembered. But it felt wrong not to show him she supported him. And standing with him while a sanctii rummaged through his mind was the least she could do.

He stared up at her for a moment, as though still not quite sure she was real. "Goddess," he muttered softly enough that she was the only one close enough to hear. "I want to remember *you*."

"You will." She held out a hand, and he took it. She twined her fingers with his. "I will do whatever it takes, I promise you."

He smiled then, the expression lighting his face, making him handsome enough to steal her breath as a whisper of heated longing stole over her senses. Not hers. *His*. She had known that he'd been in love with her for a long time. Even through the years she'd been in exile, despite having no hope of ever seeing her again. Now she could feel it, knowing it to be true. She didn't want to give that up.

She tightened her grip, willing herself not to cry. "Whatever it takes," she vowed.

"I believe you," Lucien said. He turned back to Elarus, not letting go of Chloe's hand. "Very well, Elarus. What do you need?"

Elarus moved to stand on the opposite side of the bed. Octarus joined Chloe.

[Mate. Soon,] he said cryptically, his black eyes watching Elarus. Something about his posture suggested he was nervous, but Chloe didn't have time to worry about that.

[Good.]

"Touch?" Elarus asked Lucien, and he nodded. She looked across to Sophie.

The queen joined her at the bedside, offering a smile of reassurance before she spoke. "She'll need to put her hands on your temples, Lord Castaigne. Just relax. Try to think of the last thing you remember before there's a gap in your memory." Her gaze shifted to Chloe. "You focus on the bond. You might feel Elarus, too. I'm not sure exactly how this works. Just stay calm."

"Can Cameron feel her through you?"

"Our bond doesn't look like that," Sophie said, gesturing at the space between Lucien and Chloe.

Hopefully her and Lucien's bond wouldn't look strange after Elarus did whatever she did. "Let's just see what happens."

✧ ✧ ✧

Lucien tried to relax as Elarus put her fingers against his temples. His heart was beating too fast, and he hoped the sanctii wouldn't think he was scared of her. Though he was, a little. Not of her, precisely, but of what she was about to do. Chloe's face—subtly different to the last memory he had of her but no less beautiful, if not more, despite the changes—was tense, her fingers tangled in his.

Which was difficult to believe in itself. They were married? How was that possible? What had happened to bring that about? Valentina and Irina had told him something of the tale after he'd woken, that he and Chloe had worked on an assignment in Andalyssia together. Irina—clearly Andalyssian—seemed proof enough that it was possible if he ignored the fact that the notorious Duq of Arbronet had apparently married her. That seemed fantastical in itself. But knowing Chloe was home and was apparently *his?* It still seemed as though he might be dreaming. As though he'd finally conjured her from his dreams after ten long years.

But if she was a dream, then that didn't explain the bond that was clearly real. He didn't need to see her face to know she was worried and doing her best not to show it. Or to feel the anger underlying that worry. Anger, he hoped, directed at the woman who had supposedly done this to him. He had no recollection of that really either, just a jumbled impression of being taken to the infirmary after the attack. There was a foggy memory of a blonde woman laughing but nothing more.

"Remember," Elarus said. "Think back."

Right. He closed his eyes. He was supposed to be thinking of his latest memory before the confusion of the last day. He'd been working on a case. An embezzler in one of the merchant guilds who had been clever but not quite clever enough...and then...nothing. Until yesterday when Valentin had explained what happened and he'd seen Chloe.

His *wife.*

"There," Elarus said.

A dazzle of light seemed to pass through him, dancing behind his closed eyelids, beautiful but also vastly powerful. Elarus. It didn't feel like a reveilé. It didn't hurt for a start, but it was still unsettling despite the wonder.

Then Elarus lifted her hands and it vanished.

His eyes snapped open. "Is something wrong?"

The sanctii growled something in her own language.

"Slowly," Sophie said. "Tell me slowly."

"What is it?" Chloe asked.

Sophie shook her head, her braided hair flashing red and black. "She is...upset."

"*Bad* magic," Elarus snapped.

Definitely upset.

Chloe's face paled. "None of us disagree with that. But can you reverse it?"

Elarus looked at her and then at Octarus, rasping out another rapid series of sentences. He answered, his tone as close to apologetic as she'd ever heard from a sanctii.

"Are they arguing?" he asked.

Sophie frowned. "They are saying something about Lucien's memories. Elarus thinks that...Chloe has them. Can that be right?"

What? "Chloe?"

She squeezed his hand, shaking her head as though she had no idea what Elarus was referring to. "The bond was stronger the second time. It felt like there was less...distance between us. Is that what she means?"

"Elarus?" Sophie asked.

The sanctii shook her head and gestured at Octarus. "He pulled memories. Put in her."

CHAPTER 22

"I—" Chloe froze, remembering her frantic plea to Octarus when Deandra attacked Lucien. "I asked Octarus to help me. I thought the bond was breaking, and I was trying to hold on to it. It felt very strange, but I—" She stopped again. "If I—or we—did something, then I have no idea what."

"Help," Octarus said stubbornly. "Otherwise lose."

Was what he had done forbidden? If so, she wasn't letting him take the blame. "He was doing as I asked," she said, narrowing her eyes at Elarus. "He's bonded to me. Anything he did was because of me."

Elarus tilted her head slowly. "Mate. Bond. Scared. I understand." She looked past Chloe to Octarus. "But we must fix. And not do again."

Octarus nodded, stepping back a little.

"I have no problem with that," Chloe said. "If we can prove Deandra and Istvan and whoever they were working with did this, if we can stop them, there's no reason for anyone to ever need to do what I did again."

Elarus nodded. "Good." She held out one large hand across the bed.

Octarus took her hand and stretched his other to Chloe.

Sophie, watching intently, gave Chloe a small smile of encouragement.

"Ready?" Elarus asked.

From near the door, Chloe heard Valentin clear his throat. But if he was about to interrupt, then she wasn't going to let him. There was only one person who could make the decision to try this or not. If she held Lucien's memories, then she wanted more than anything for him to have them back. Every messy second of them. But only if that was what he wanted, too.

"Lucien?" Chloe said. "This is up to you."

He smiled at her, the grin half bravado, half determination. "It's not even a choice. Elarus, do your worst."

The sanctii snorted. Chloe had a moment to brace herself before magic roared through her in a rush of sound and light that left her uncertain of where or who she was.

[Stay.] Octarus's voice came sure and strong in the middle of the storming magic. [Hold.]

How could she hold against the strength of this magic? Goddess forfend, if this was what a sanctii's true power was, then perhaps the Anglions were right to be scared of them.

But she was no Anglion to quake in the face of magic. She was the daughter of a master mage, trained by master mages. Latest in a long line of Illvyan magic, of those who'd built the empire and the magic that protected and sustained it. A daughter of men and women cloaked in raven black and wielding power. She would hold.

And she would give the man she loved whatever he needed.

She gave herself up to the magic, laying down any defenses she could think of, seeking only the security of the link of the bond, which somehow sang to her even in the storm of Elarus's power. She held tight to that and let the rest rush through her, let Elarus take whatever she needed.

At the edge of awareness, she heard Lucien cry out and the storm vanished. She sucked in a breath, trying to ground herself back in her body.

"Well," Sophie said, her voice shaky, "that was certainly something."

Chloe opened her eyes slowly, not sure she trusted herself to respond. The first thing she saw was Lucien, green eyes blazing up at her.

"Something indeed," he agreed, smiling. "Chloe, love, let's not do that again. Two bonds and whatever that was seems like enough for one lifetime." He glanced sideways at Elarus. "Just as well that Silya wasn't here. I'm fairly certain she wouldn't consider this balance."

Chloe stared at him a moment, then began to smile. "You remember Silya," she said, not quite daring to hope it had worked.

This time his smile was wicked. "I remember everything." He tugged at her hand, and she bent down and kissed him. Hard. Light sparking through her again, joy echoed and returned through the bond that now felt clear and strong and sure. Lucien's hands twined in her hair, pulling her closer.

After a minute or so, someone cleared their throat.

"I think," Imogene said, amusement clear in her tone, "perhaps we should give them a minute or two alone before we decide what happens next."

It took longer than a minute, both of them too lost to find the willpower to stop kissing. Eventually Lucien wrenched himself away, lust fogging his senses, aware that they couldn't go any further. Part of him roared in frustration. Chloe's eyes were wide and dark, her face flushed, her breath coming fast, and he wanted nothing more than to pull her fully into bed with him. But he was all too aware of the audience just outside the door. Not to mention the small matter of Deandra and Istvan.

Fuck. Duty won. By the thinnest of margins.

"No one's done anything to Deandra, have they?" he asked. Assaulting a Truth Seeker was a capital offense. With the emperor in his current state of mind, Lucien wouldn't have been shocked if Aristides ordered her immediate execution upon learning what she'd done.

"No. She's still in the cells. Istvan, too. As far as I know, no one has talked to them since Deandra—" She broke off, biting her lip.

He pulled her close again, and she took a shuddering breath, her face pressed into his neck. "I'm fine," he murmured soothingly. "Elarus fixed me."

She nodded and sat up. "I know, it's just—"

"I know. But right now, we have to focus on the case. We have all the time in the world for each other." He felt his smile go lopsided. "Not that that's enough."

She laughed, still sounding slightly shaky, and slid off the bed. "No. But case first. Then we can hide away at Terre d'Etoi and ignore the world."

"I like that idea. So, find me some clothes."

While he dressed, his mind raced. His head ached, though not as badly as after a reveilé. He could live with it. But he needed to get back to work.

His fingers worked buttons and tugged clothes into place while he tried to sort through his memories of the last day or two. The time around the attack seemed the haziest, but he ran through it several times until something gave him pause just as he was pulling on his left boot.

"Istvan. Istvan said he would tell us it was him. That's a confession. Or near enough to one." He stood, turning his attention to Chloe. "And no one has spoken to him since?"

"After what happened to you, apparently everybody thought it might be safer to wait for Elarus."

Lucien swore. He understood the caution, but it was difficult to predict whether time would cause a suspect to crack or give them time to regain their composure. "He might have changed his mind."

"I don't know about that," Chloe said. "Deandra showed her true colors. Perhaps he'll be eager to save his own neck now that she's already—" She bit the word off, face paling slightly.

"She condemned herself," he reminded her gently. "You didn't cause any of this. She chose her path a long time ago."

"I know."

He wasn't sure she accepted it, though. Or perhaps it was just memories of Charl biting at her that made her feel guilty about Deandra's likely fate.

"The best thing we can do now, love, is make sure everyone else who helped her is also brought to justice. If you want to be able to hide away with me, then the empire needs peace. Which means, I think, that we should get back to Elarus."

✦ ✦ ✦

A group of amused faces greeted Chloe as they emerged.

Sophie recovered first, though hints of laughter danced in her eyes. "Lord Castaigne," she said. "How are you feeling?"

"Much better, thanks to you and Elarus, Your Majesty." Lucien swept a deep bow. "I am in your debt."

Sophie's smile was fierce. "I think if we can bring these conspirators to justice once and for all, then there will be no debts, my lord. A safe and peaceful kingdom for my people is all I want. I'm sure the emperor would say the same."

Chloe glanced at Imogene, but before she could ask the question, Imogene said, "Yes, His Imperial Majesty is aware that Lucien has recovered. He's waiting somewhat impatiently for an update."

"He can wait a little longer," Lucien said. "I think we should be able to bring this to a conclusion now." His attention shifted to Elarus. "If Elarus can confirm whether there is sanctii magic involved."

When she didn't immediately answer, he added, "I assure you, Elarus, that the emperor will let you decide if there is to be any punishment in your realm for any sanctii who may have assisted in this. Our laws state that a sanctii's actions are laid at the feet of their mage. There will be no repercussions for your people. The mages may need to consider their rules around bonds, but that is a matter for them. And, given the nature of this plot, I doubt the trial, or any evidence given, will be made public. Other than the executions, perhaps."

Elarus considered him, then nodded. "Some sanctii. Some human," she said. "But sanctii teach, I think."

"And you can tell if this magic has been used on someone?" he asked. "Now that you've seen the...impact on me?"

She nodded again. "Yes."

"Can it be reversed?" Valentin asked, interrupting.

Was he thinking of the prince? Chloe sucked in a breath, waiting for Elarus to answer. Would she recover her memory of Deandra at the parliament?

"No. Not unless like them," Elarus said, sweeping a hand between her and Lucien. "Bond. And sanctii."

That answered that. Octarus had been the key to saving Lucien. And he had been bonded to Rianne when Deandra had taken Chloe's memory. So they were gone for good. But instead of anger at the news, all she felt was grateful, her hand curling into Lucien's.

Goddess.

They had been so fortunate. Without the bond, Lucien would have lost all those months, all those moments where they had come together. He loved her, but there was no guarantee it would have been the same. She could have lost him.

Lucien looked as though he'd expected that answer. "That rules out most people."

"And rules out recovering the memories the conspirators

have erased. Memories of their crimes," Chloe said. Which meant it wouldn't be as simple as restoring those and then the Truth Seekers being able to use their magic without doubt.

"No," Lucien agreed. "But we just need to find one thread to pull on. One confession we can be certain is true. Then we will be able to bring them to justice."

He hesitated, considering his next question. "We have a theory that there is another magic at work. Replacing memories, not just removing them. Could you do that?"

"Perhaps," Elarus said. "Though should not. It is not like the words. That is gift. Not...deceit." She looked at Sophie and muttered something.

"She said it's wrong to change someone that way," Sophie said.

"Could you tell if it had been done?" Lucien pressed. "And when the false memories start?"

"Maybe. Can show?" Elarus asked.

"Yes," Lucien said. "If I'm right, we can show you more examples than you will need."

✦ ✦ ✦

It turned out he had been right about that. It didn't take Elarus more than a minute with the first member of the theater troupe, the costumier who had seemed to dislike Deandra, before she pulled her hand away from the woman's temple and said, "Yes. False."

"Can you see where the false memories begin?" Lucien asked.

Elarus turned back to the costumier. The woman's eyes were wide, her face pale, but she didn't flinch when Elarus reached out to touch her again. The sanctii was silent for much longer, her eyes half closed, clearly concentrating. "Yes," she said eventually.

Sophie, who had been standing with her, one hand on the

woman's shoulder to reassure her, asked, "Can you show me...what it feels like?"

"And me?" Chloe asked before she could think. She wanted to know. *Needed* to know what to look for.

Elarus hitched a shoulder but then extended her hand. "Can show how to see false. When...maybe not. Might hurt," she warned.

"That's all right." Chloe closed her eyes, not sure what was about to happen. Would Elarus somehow show them what she'd seen in the costumier's mind? Or—

Pain sheeted through her skull. Like a reveilé but not quite as bad. It was gone almost as quickly as it had arrived, leaving in its place a sense of the costumier in her head, like she remembered from her classes in healing at the Academe. A picture of a person and their body formed by earth magic. But it didn't feel whole...almost as though there were two of her, one a blurred reflection.

"Oh," she said, opening her eyes. "I see." She tried again. The reflection was easier to separate, though she saw no way to tell how long it had been in place. She sighed and let the image go, turning to Sophie. "I see...a reflection of her. The doubled memory, I guess. I'm not sure I could tell when the false memories start, though," she admitted. "How about you?"

Sophie frowned. "No. I can see the reflection—that's a good description—but there's no end to it. Perhaps we need more practice."

"Time is rather of the essence," Lucien said.

"I agree," Sophie twisted her wedding band, eyes narrowed in concentration. "Elarus, can you teach other sanctii to see what you see? Our magic is different, after all."

Elarus nodded. "Some. Not all."

"Some would be enough." Sophie shivered suddenly, and Cameron huffed out a breath.

"Are you all right?" Chloe asked, stepping closer. The last thing they needed was Sophie collapsing as well.

Sophie waved her off. "I'm fine. Sanctii magic always feels cold to me. Don't worry." She glanced around the group. "All right, we have a plan. Chloe and I can help find the members of the troupe who have been tampered with." She paused, frowning. "Would it look any different if the person has magic?"

"Stronger, not different," Elarus said. "Can show."

It took some time to work through more members of the troupe and confirm that they both were able to tell who had been impacted by a memory charm. They decided to leave the time frames until later, use them as confirmation if Istvan or Deandra talked.

After the first four, Valentin asked Elarus to teach him, too. After that, it didn't take long.

Everyone in the troupe showed the same signs of the memory magic. And most of them were shocked and unhappy to learn of it. The few who seemed less surprised, the apprentice illusioner and several of the actors who lacked any magic, were placed under stricter watch. The illusioner had already been in a separate cell, but the actors were isolated, too.

But it was less than an hour before the task was complete, and they all gathered in one of the palace's many meeting rooms. Its walls were pearly gray, and the upholstery of the chairs surrounding the long table were close to charcoal, as were the curtains. Paintings of long-dead emperors lined one wall.

A serious room for serious business.

"What happens now?" Valentin asked, expression somber. "Do we tell the emperor?"

Lucien shook his head. "I'll talk to Alain last. I want the emperor to have the truth of whether or not he was—is —involved."

"So we start with Deandra and Istvan?" Chloe asked.

"Istvan, I think. Deandra knows she's most likely going to be executed. She has no incentive to help us. In fact, I suspect she will take some pleasure in thwarting us however she can until she takes her final breath."

She couldn't fault his instincts. That sounded like Deandra. "You think Istvan will talk now?"

"I hope that seeing what Deandra did to me—and knowing she was most likely trying to do it to him—may have disabused him of the notion that she cares for him. He may hold out some hope of gaining some leniency if he talks. Lucette and Rene have been laying that groundwork, as I understand it."

"And will he get it?"

"That depends. The best he can hope for is life in prison, I think. But some people will take that over death."

"And if he doesn't talk?" Sophie asked.

"Can look," Elarus said. "Find old memories. Can't hide all. Can't lose all."

Well, that answered that. Chloe hoped she was right. Even if Istvan talked, he might not know everyone involved.

Lucien's eyes had widened slightly. "We will be grateful, should it come to that, Elarus. But we'll start with Istvan. This is a matter for our human world. I want to hear from those who are trying to destroy it."

CHAPTER 23

Chloe followed Lucien into the interrogation room, trying to control her nerves. In contrast, all she felt from him was a rock-solid level of certainty. The Truth Seeker who had his man. Or was about to.

Unlike the room in Basali, this one was built for the judiciary, which meant there were smaller observation rooms to each side of it, illusions concealing the windows that allowed the watchers to see in. There were enough wards on the walls that she assumed it must be difficult even for most mages to tell where they were. But with the bond linking her to Lucien, she could spot them easily.

Which probably meant Istvan could, too, given his talent for illusion. But if he did, he gave no sign of it.

He sat on the far side of a table much the same as the one in Basali, shoulders low, hands shackled. His head lifted as they came in, and his eyes widened in surprise.

"Mestier Vargas," Lucien said smoothly, pulling out a chair for Chloe and then sitting beside her. "I trust you've had time to think on your lover's actions since yesterday."

"You remember?" Istvan blurted. "But how is that—" His jaw snapped shut.

"Lieutenant de Roche is going to touch your hand," Lucien said. "Do not move or try anything or her sanctii will take it badly. And I will let him show you just how much."

Istvan nodded, teeth clenched. His skin was cold under Chloe's fingers, but she didn't have to look long to see the doubled reflection. She drew back, nodding at Lucien. Elarus could confirm the period of time later, once they knew how the magic might impact his confession, should they get it.

Istvan was staring at her, brow creased as though he was trying to work out what she could have done with a touch.

Lucien leaned forward, snapping his fingers. "Mestier Vargas, I suggest you focus on me."

Istvan jerked his eyes back.

"Good. We will continue. And you are correct. I remember yesterday perfectly well. Which means I can tell you that you had a very lucky escape. My memories were protected because Lieutenant de Roche and her sanctii were able to intervene on my behalf. If Deandra had reached you, you would not have been so fortunate. Who knows what she would have ripped from your mind?" He shrugged, the gesture all studied nonchalance that suggested he didn't much care. "I'm not sure she feels the same way about you as you profess to do for her, Istvan. Why protect her? She was ready to destroy you."

Chloe tensed, willing Istvan to give in. Lucien had carefully avoided mentioning that Deandra was likely going to be executed either way. If Istvan hadn't worked that part out for himself, better to keep him focused on her betrayal, not his grief. Anger might drive him to confess. Or self-preservation. Grief might not.

For a moment, Istvan's chin lifted, his eyes defiant, and Chloe thought he was going to be stupid. But then he shook his head, just once, and sighed. "If I confess, will I live?"

"I will recommend leniency," Lucien said. "I cannot control the emperor's final decision. He is, as you can possibly imagine, not in a mood to be merciful just now. I can guarantee that you will die if we have to have a sanctii rip confirmation of your guilt from your mind rather than you confessing."

Istvan digested that silently. Chloe made sure she looked only at him, not to either side where she knew Sophie, Imogene, Valentin, and Elarus, not to mention every Truth Seeker and various other palace officials Lucien had been able to muster on short notice, sat watching.

"Very well," Istvan said at last. "I will tell you what I can."

"How much is that?" Chloe interrupted, earning herself a quick disgruntled look from Lucien. "I can tell that your memories have been altered. I assume Deandra did that to you?"

He nodded. "She did. Though I was willing." He smiled then, the expression lopsided with regret before he shook himself, the smile sharpening. "But not quite as much under her spell as she thought I was. She showed me the memory magic. She learned it from a water mage in Elenia. Or that's what she told me. Sanctii magic originally. I helped her refine it, learn how to cover up the memories lost when needed. That part requires some illusion magic to build the memories. It's complicated." His expression was self-satisfied for a moment. "I doubt many illusioners could do it, frankly. She needed me. And she trusted me to use the scriptii on myself when she told me to. But I didn't. Not always. Not in the beginning."

"You still remember some of it," Chloe breathed. *Thank the goddess.*

"Yes," Istvan said. "I do. I met Deandra in Partha. Nearly seven years ago. She was beautiful and funny, and I allowed myself to be charmed. I invited her to watch us perform, and after that night, we became lovers."

Had Deandra seen his skill with illusion and thought she could use him? Chloe bit back the question, not wanting to distract Istvan.

"She started to travel with us, and I...well, I fell in love." He shook his head, mouth twisting. "And slowly, she began to sound me out on my politics. She knew I was Parthan and that I had family a few generations back who were from Andalyssia. Knew the north does not always love the emperor and the empire. I have never had particularly strong feelings about that. Or I hadn't back then. But she knew what she was doing. She painted a picture of an empire where there was more freedom returned to each country. Of an emperor more willing to give countries most of their autonomy."

Alain? Willing to give up power? That seemed unlikely.

"She meant the crown prince?" Lucien prompted.

Istvan nodded. "Yes. The silver crown, she—or they—call him. We even changed the name of the troupe. She thought it amusing, but really, it just made it easy for those who might share her sympathies to find us."

The painting. Aristides in gold, Alain in silver, an emperor in waiting. Who had decided he'd waited long enough, perhaps. Chloe couldn't stop the shiver that crawled down her spine. How long had Alain's resentment been festering, twisting him into a man willing to attempt to murder his own father?

"She drew me in," Istvan said. "Turned me to her cause. There had been attempts on the emperor that had failed—the Andalyssians, for one—but she said they had learned. That they were expanding their forces. And for years that was how we worked. We traveled around, met with people, passed on messages, built a network of support. That was the plan. Work slow, gather resources, plant the seeds of rebellion. Until Alain was free to act and claim the crown. I thought it would take longer."

"What changed?" Lucien asked.

"Anglion," Istvan said. "The temple there, they were part of it. They wanted to free the land from the crown, they said. But it went wrong. The king died, and Eloisa took the throne. That was the plan. They thought they could control her. But they hadn't counted on Sophia. Who could have predicted that? A virtual nobody being such a strong witch? And avoiding the temple's control simply by fucking the wrong man at the wrong time? It was a disaster."

Chloe flinched. Istvan was probably lucky Cameron didn't burst through the door and strangle him for that comment.

"Still, the Anglions showed that a change of ruler could be brought about seemingly by accident. Apparently, at that point, Alain decided it was the right moment to try again. It seemed...hasty to me. Possibly he was worried the Anglions would find some of the trails leading to him. They didn't. So it began."

"And you know for sure it was Alain?" Lucien asked.

"Deandra met with him once, when we performed in Lumia. She thought she was cunning about it, but I followed her. I've seen enough portraits of the man to recognize him. And I heard them talking. She called him 'Your Imperial Highness.' It was either him or someone wearing a damned good illusion. And I would have known if that were the case."

He paused, stretching his fingers for a moment. "After that, she was more insistent about the scriptii. She watched me use them, so I can't provide details. But I will give you the names of everyone I know who was involved. And I hope you choke her with them."

✦ ✦ ✦

"We need to talk to the prince."

Valentin was the first to speak when Chloe and Lucien finally stepped out of the interrogation room. Nearly two hours had passed since Istvan had started his confession. Lucien hadn't taken any notes as the man had talked, just continuing to draw him out and probe for details. Hopefully the other Truth Seekers had written everything down. Their word was evidence, but the

names Istvan had given them suggested a wide network of traitors, and the details would be needed.

She could sense Lucien's fatigue through the bond but knew
he wouldn't rest yet.

"Yes," Lucien agreed. "I'd rather hear it from him. Not that
we need to, after that. Once Elarus confirms the boundaries of
the damage to his memory, I will know what parts of that we can
trust. But for Aristides's sake, confirmation from Alain will make
it cleaner."

If the prince confessed, his father wouldn't have to condemn
him. Alain would have condemned himself.

"Treason against his own damned father," Valentin snarled. "I
never liked the little snake, but I didn't think he was twisted
enough to try something like this."

His outrage was echoed on everyone's faces. Sophie's wore a
strange mix of grief and resolute anger. She knew better than
most of them what the murder of a ruler did to a country.

"Neither did I," Lucien said, voice harsh.

"Power does strange things to some people," Sophie
murmured. "It's a sickness, almost." She reached for Cameron's
hand, and he took it, drawing her in to stand tucked into his
side.

"And sicknesses must be cured," Valentin said. "Or where
they can't be cured, cut out." He straightened, looking sterner
than Chloe had ever seen him. "The prince has spread his poison
too long."

"Yes. But not for much longer," Lucien stated. He turned to
Sophie. "Your Majesty, thank you for your assistance. I think I
may need Elarus if the prince proves stubborn. I'm sorry to ask
it of you, but will you come with us?"

"Of course," Sophie agreed without hesitation.

✧ ✧ ✧

There was silence as they moved through the palace, heading for the prince's apartments. Lucien had sent for Colonel Perrine, the head of Aristides's Imperial Guard. He was waiting for them at the entrance to the East Wing, expression grim.

"My lord Truth Seeker," he said, bowing formally as Lucien reached him. "Do you need my assistance?"

"I need to see the crown prince," Lucien said. "And then His Imperial Majesty."

Sorrow softened the colonel's expression before he controlled it, so fast that Chloe wasn't sure she'd actually seen the flash of pain. Almost as though he'd been expecting this news. As the head of Aristides's guard, a man who had devoted his life to protecting the emperor and his family, he may have already drawn his own conclusions. But suspecting them was different to having them confirmed.

And knowing he'd missed the traitor in their midst all these years.

Perrine nodded at the guards barring the door and led them through the apartment where the prince was currently residing. Away from his wife and children, thankfully.

No. Best not to think about Nathalie. She knew too well what kind of pain the crown princess was about to experience.

But there was nothing she could do to spare the princess, and she needed to see this through before she could let any emotion into the process.

Istvan's confirmation that the prince was at the heart of the conspiracy had been bad enough. One man's ambition and impatience and so many lives lost or ruined. The echoes of Octarus's rage that had been pulsing through her since Istvan had confessed wasn't the only fury she was working to contain. Lucien's was banked but clear to her, as hers must be to him.

They couldn't afford to let that lead them to a mistake that might mean the prince avoided facing his crimes. Bringing him to account was the real prize now.

A bitter prize, perhaps, but that didn't change anything.

Alain had played at rebellion, trying to gain power before it was rightfully his. He had lost.

Whatever his motivations, that much was clear. The game was done. And she had survived. Her prize would be happiness, she hoped. A future. One that couldn't entirely make up for what she'd lost, but one she would relish and fill with joy and love.

With Lucien by her side.

Her eyes stung, and she pulled her thoughts back, summoning the self-control the long years of exile had taught her to banish the tears and school her face to blankness as the colonel produced a key.

"Your Imperial Highness?" he said, pushing the door open. "Lord Castaigne is here to see you."

He waved them forward, and the six of them filed inside. No sign of the prince. The colonel locked the door behind them, then crossed to another door, which Chloe thought most likely lead to some sort of sitting room if this suite was similar to others in the palace.

The colonel knocked, but there was no answer, and his brows drew down.

He pulled the door open, took a half step forward, and then froze. Just for a second or two before he turned and said in a voice like stone, "Your Grace, I think perhaps your services are required."

Valentin turned pale. "Goddess, don't tell me—"

He strode forward into the room, and Colonel Perrine held up a hand when Lucien tried to follow. "Wait, please, my lord Truth Seeker."

Oh goddess. Chloe swayed, her mind conjuring images of what Alain may have done.

[Come?] Octarus demanded. He must have sensed her distress.

[No. Not yet.] The last thing they needed was an angry sanctii.

"He's alive," Valentin called back. "But, Sophia—sorry, Your Majesty, I think we may need Elarus."

At that, Lucien stepped forward, shoulders set. "Perrine, I need to be in there. I have to stand witness."

The colonel's mouth flattened, but he stepped back. Chloe followed Lucien inside, bracing herself. Sophie, Cameron, and Elarus were hard on her heels, but they all pulled up sharp at the sight of Valentin kneeling beside a sofa, one hand on Alain's wrist.

The prince was awake, or at least his eyes were open. His expression was vacant, and he didn't so much as blink to indicate he knew they were there. Strewn around his feet were a dozen or more pieces of blackened stone.

"Scriptii," Sophie said in a stricken voice, her face twisting.

Valentin nodded once, his mouth twisting in anger. Or distress, perhaps. "Memory charms would be my guess," he said. "He's used them on himself." He waved a hand in front of the prince's face, but there was still not so much as a flicker of reaction from Alain. "Elarus? Can you tell what he's done?"

Nothing good, it seemed.

Elarus left Sophie's side to join Valentin. She studied the prince briefly, then touched his forehead. She jerked her hand back, hissing something in sanctii. A word Chloe knew from her childhood when Martius used to supervise the games she played with her sisters.

Broken.

In her head, Octarus roared something she wasn't sure was rage or satisfaction, and she only just managed to stop herself from clamping her hands to her ears. Lucien shot her a startled look, but she smiled shakily, trying to reassure him as Octarus appeared beside her as though he wanted to see for himself.

"Gone," Elarus said. "Too many memories gone."

Lucien scrubbed a hand over his chin, looking grim. "A confession of a kind, I suppose," he said. "Perhaps he thought he would be able to just erase the memories of his treachery."

Or he knew exactly what would happen and had chosen that versus facing his crimes. The thought sickened her. As did the knowledge of what this would do to his family. She breathed in, fighting for composure. "How did he know that we had Istvan's confession? Did someone warn him?"

"We can investigate, but we may never know," Lucien said. "Valentin, what do you think? Is he likely to recover?"

"I doubt it. He feels...empty to me. We see it sometimes after an apoplexy or a severe injury to the head. The brain can only take so much harm."

"Will he live?" Lucien asked.

"I don't know. Some of the patients I've seen with this kind of damage do linger for years. Under the care of the healers, of course. One thing is certain, though."

"What?" Chloe asked blankly.

"The emperor needs a new heir."

EPILOGUE

"Where are you taking me?" Chloe demanded, half laughing as Lucien hurried her through the back halls of the palace.

He grinned smugly. "Hush. We're trying to stay out of sight, remember?"

"If you wanted to stay out of sight, we should have stayed home," Chloe protested. "Or asked Octarus to hide us."

Home. Where they had a nice big bed that had been used for little but sleeping lately. But no, he'd been adamant that they needed to come to the palace. And that he would tell her why only once they got there.

"I don't think using a sanctii to sneak into the palace would be wise even for us," Lucien said, his smile fading.

"No," she agreed with a sigh.

The palace was still at a high level of alert. Nearly a month had passed since Istvan's confession and Alain's...well, destruction was the closest word. He lived, but nothing really remained of the man he had been. While she wasn't overly sad about what the prince had done to himself, she hated the grief he'd caused his family. She hadn't seen Aristides smile once since they brought him the news of his son.

The official word was that the prince had fallen from his

horse and suffered an injury to the head that he was not expected to recover from. The royal family were in seclusion out of respect, and the emperor would name a new heir in due course.

Most likely Madeleine. She was the next oldest of Aristides's children and had a sensible head on her shoulders. She would be the empire's very first empress when she succeeded her father, hopefully many years from now.

"Stop thinking about Alain," Lucien ordered, though his eyes were briefly serious. "No work today, remember? The whole day is ours." He lifted her hand to kiss the back of it. "Let's not waste it."

The first day off they'd had in weeks, in fact. The prince's misuse of the memory charms meant he couldn't provide any information, though it seemed a clear admission of guilt. But, in the end, they hadn't needed Alain. Between Istvan's contributions and the names Elarus had extracted from Deandra when Aristides, his eyes black with fury and grief after learning about Alain, had asked her to, the list of the conspirators was substantial. There had been little time for anything but work as the Imperial forces swung into action across the empire and in Anglion, rounding up conspirators. Fortunately, Deandra hadn't taught her memory magic to others, nor had she been able to produce enough scriptii to protect all those involved. The Truth Seekers were able to extract confessions without issue in most of the cases. Where the memory charms had been used, the sanctii stepped in to assist.

Istvan had received a life sentence. Most of the others had not been shown any mercy. The executions had already begun, Deandra's being the first. Lucien had attended. So had Octarus. Chloe had stayed away. Henri had told her that Octarus had gone to the Raven Tower afterward, standing with Mai at the top of the turret for nearly an hour.

Apparently, he did it regularly. Henri was already making not-so-gentle suggestions that she needed to bond with Mai. She didn't disagree, but she just needed the time.

Soon, she hoped.

"Do I have to drag you into one of these rooms and rumple you a bit to get your attention?" Lucien said, interrupting her thoughts. Heated desire suddenly pulsed through the bond, and she blushed.

"No. Sorry. Free day. No wasting it."

It was their motto now. No more wasted time. Cherish what they had.

"Good," Lucien said. "Because we have arrived."

She wasn't sure where "here" was, other than a guest suite.

Lucien knocked on the door, and, to Chloe's surprise, Silya opened it. The seer's hair was loose over her shoulders, and she wore an Andalyssian-style dress in green, the edges of the skirt and sleeves embroidered with stylized trees. For the goddess, perhaps. She looked, for once, nearly relaxed.

"Sejerin." Chloe bobbed a curtsy, pleased to see her. "I thought you might have returned to Andalyssia. Didn't some of you go home last week?"

"Some," Silya said. "Not all. I will return when the goddess tells me it is time. I want to make sure I understand this memory magic first so we can guard against it in the future. Domina Francis and I are agreed on that." She stepped back from the door. "Please come in."

Somewhat confused as to why Lucien wanted to spend time with Silya, Chloe nodded and followed him inside. Silya led them to a small sitting room. No fire burned in the grate, but a familiar smoky scent filled Chloe's nostrils.

Andalyssian incense. A smell that had filled the air in Deephilm. Once upon a time, it would have made her nervous, but the Andalyssian members of the conspiracy had already been identified and tried. Unsurprisingly, they had mostly been from the disgraced House Elannon, though happily not Andrej, the current head of that house. He had passed judgment on his relatives without flinching, apparently, determined to remove the stain from his line once and for all, no matter the cost. Perhaps Mikvel would forgive them in time.

There had been enough pain.

Sitting in the chair closest to the empty grate was an Andalyssian woman, silvery blonde hair braided back from her face. Her dress was similar to Silya's, though a sunny shade of yellow with the embroidery calling to mind flowers, not trees. Her pale blue eyes were alight with curiosity, mouth curved in a welcoming smile. Chloe didn't recognize her. She hadn't had time to meet all of the Andalyssians who'd traveled to Lumia at the emperor's command, though she and Lucien had spent time with Valentin and Irina's relatives at a lunch hastily squeezed in between commitments.

"Lord and Lady Castaigne, this is Allia Datskyef," Silya said, drawing Chloe back to the present. "She is married to one of Ashmeister Datskyef's nephews."

Chloe tried to remember if she'd met any Datskyefs in Deephilm. Possibly, but Allia's face wasn't familiar. Which left her still none the wiser as to why Lucien wanted them to meet.

Allia rose and bobbed a curtsy. "My lord, my lady, a pleasure."

"Lord Castaigne, I will leave you to explain the rest," Silya said. "Allia, I will be in the study if you need me."

"Lucien?" Chloe queried as Silya slipped out the door.

He smiled at her and took her hand, his fingers caressing her wedding band. "I know we said we wouldn't have another wedding—"

"Goddess, no," Chloe agreed fervently. "Two is enough."

Allia giggled at that, the sound as silvery as her hair.

"Still," Lucien said, tugging her hand to pull her closer, "I would like us to have something to mark our marriage that's ours alone. And Allia here happens to be—"

"Let me guess, you're a tintzmach?" Chloe said, understanding dawning.

Allia laughed again. "Indeed, my lady. I have that honor. And I always carry my tools with me."

Chloe turned to Lucien. "You want to make the marriage marks?" The ceremonial tattoos, inscribed by a tintzmach, were an Andalyssian tradition, not an Illvyan one. They'd had the temporary marks made for their forced ceremony in Deephilm. But that wasn't what he was suggesting.

Real marriage marks, inked above the hearts of the couple, lasted forever.

He nodded. "I do." He tapped his chest. "Our vows are forever. I know that. But I want you close, even when we're apart." He bent and kissed her swiftly. "And I never got to see yours. Maybe this time we can manage a wedding night just for us." Another pulse of desire fogged her senses. Her cheeks grew hot as Lucien straightened. "Allia has the designs we chose before. She sent for them when I asked Silya about this. Though we can change them, if you prefer. What do you say?"

When he'd had time to do that, or anything else other than snatch meals and sleep, she had no idea. But the fact that he had spoke volumes. He loved her. And he wanted to wear a symbol of their love on his skin for the rest of his life. And so would she.

She didn't need the proof—his love sang through the bond at her, a constant testament of his devotion. Right now, it was fiercer than ever. She let it flood through her. They had rebuilt some control over it, but she still caught echoes of his memories at odd moments. Like now, when a thousand different views of her face shimmered over her, all of them beautiful to him. She sent back one of her own. The marriage mark she'd seen inked on his chest in Deephilm. And her own that he'd never gotten to see.

In return came more love and a certain eagerness that, this time, he would.

She laughed as he grinned at her, eyes very green. He was right. This would be something just for them. A vow no one could take away.

She took both his hands, twining their fingers. "Yes," she said, joy bubbling through her. "The answer to you, Lucien de Roche, is always yes."

THE END

Join my VIP reader's list and get an EXCLUSIVE short story
featuring Chloe and Imogene
CLICK HERE (or scan the QR code below)

A NOTE FROM M.J.

I hope you loved THE REBEL'S PRIZE.

This is the end of the Daughter of Ravens trilogy. Have you read Courting The Witch, a prequel novella featuring Imogene and Jean-Paul? I'll be starting a new romantasy series, the Dragon Forged series next year.

As an indie author, it really helps me when readers get the word out about my books, so if you enjoyed the book, please consider leaving a review at the store where you purchased it and tell your friends! If you want to stay up to date with all my news, find out about new releases and sales, then please sign up to my newsletter using the QR code below and get an exclusive short story!

ABOUT THE AUTHOR

M.J. Scott is an unrepentant bookworm. Luckily she grew up in a family that fed her a properly varied diet of books and these days is surrounded by people who are understanding of her story addiction. When not wrestling one of her own stories to the ground, she can generally be found reading someone else's. Her other distractions include yarn, cat butlering, dark chocolate and watercolor. To keep in touch, find out about new releases and other news (and receive an exclusive freebie) sign up to her newsletter at www.mjscott.net. She also writes contemporary romance as Melanie Scott and Emma Douglas.

You can keep in touch with M.J. on:

Instagram @melwrites
Facebook AuthorMJScott
Pinterest @mel_writes
TikTok @mjscottwrites

Or email her at mel@mjscott.net

ALSO BY M.J. SCOTT

Romantic fantasy

The Four Arts series

The Shattered Court

The Forbidden Heir

The Unbound Queen

Courting The Witch (Prequel novella)

The Daughter of Ravens series

The Exile's Curse

The Traitor's Game

The Half-Light City series

Shadow Kin

Blood Kin

Iron Kin

Fire Kin

Urban fantasy

The TechWitch series

Wicked Games Wicked Words

Wicked Nights Wicked Dreams Wicked Ways

The Wild Side series

The Wolf Within

The Dark Side

Bring On The Night

The Day You Went Away (free prequel short story)

ACKNOWLEDGMENTS

There were times when I wasn't sure how to get these two to their HEA but here we are! Thanks to everyone who kept asking for more Chloe and Lucien, I hope you've enjoyed the ride.

Thank you to Deranged Doctor for the wonderful cover art!

Huge thanks as always to my Mum, the Lulus, Sarah, the Diva Kitty, and everyone else who's been giving writerly inspiration and real world fun. Smooches.

Made in United States
Orlando, FL
01 November 2023

38485829R00202